THE DOGS OF RIGA

Other Kurt Wallander mysteries by Henning Mankell

FACELESS KILLERS

THE WHITE LIONESS

SIDETRACKED

THE FIFTH WOMAN

ONE STEP BEHIND

FIREWALL

THE DOGS OF RIGA

A Kurt Wallander Mystery

Henning Mankell

Translated by Laurie Thompson

THE NEW PRESS
NEW YORK

© 1992 by Henning Mankell
English translation © 2001 by Laurie Thompson

Originally published as *Hundarna i Riga* by
Ordfront Förlag, Stockholm, 1992
English translation first published in Great Britain by
The Harvill Press, London, 2001
Published in the United States by
The New Press, New York, 2003
Distributed by W. W. Norton & Company, Inc., New York

ISBN 1-56584-787-3 (hc.)
CIP data available

The New Press was established in 1990 as a not-for-profit
alternative to the large, commercial publishing houses
currently dominating the book publishing industry.
The New Press operates in the public interest rather than for
private gain, and is committed to publishing, in innovative
ways, works of educational, cultural, and community value
that are often deemed insufficiently profitable.

The New Press, 450 West 41st Street, 6th floor,
New York, NY 10036
www.thenewpress.com

Printed in the United States of America

2   4   6   8   10   9   7   5   3   1

THE DOGS OF RIGA

CHAPTER 1

It started snowing shortly after 10 a.m.

The man in the wheelhouse of the fishing boat cursed. He'd heard the forecast, but hoped they might make the Swedish coast before the storm hit. If he hadn't been held up at Hiddensee the night before, he'd have been within sight of Ystad by now and could have changed course a few degrees eastwards. As it was, there were still seven nautical miles to go, and if the snow started coming down heavily, he'd be forced to heave to and wait until visibility improved.

He cursed again. It doesn't pay to be stingy, he thought. I should have done what I'd meant to do last autumn and bought a new radar. My old Decca can't be relied on any more. I should have gotten one of those new American models, but I was too stingy. I didn't trust the East Germans, either. Didn't trust them not to cheat me.

He found it hard to grasp that there was no longer a country called East Germany, that a whole nation-state had ceased to exist. History had tidied up its old borders overnight. Now there was just Germany, and nobody really knew what was going to happen when the two formerly separate peoples tried to work together. At first, when the Berlin wall came down, he had felt uneasy. Would the enormous changes mean the carpet would be pulled from under his feet? His East German partners had reassured him. Nothing would change in the foreseeable future. Indeed, this upheaval might even create new opportunities.

The snow was falling more heavily, and the wind was veering towards the southwest. He lit a cigarette and poured coffee into the mug in the special holder next to the compass. The heat in the wheelhouse was making him sweat, and the smell of diesel oil was getting up his nose. He glanced towards the engine room. He could see one of Jakobson's feet on the narrow bunk down there, his big toe sticking out through a hole in his sock. Might as well let him sleep on, he thought. If we have to heave to, he can take over the watch while I get a few hours' rest. He took a sip of the lukewarm coffee and thought again of what had happened the night before.

He'd been forced to wait in the dilapidated little harbor to the west of Hiddensee for over five hours before the truck appeared, rattling through the darkness to collect the goods. Weber had insisted that the delay was due to his truck breaking down, and that could well have been true. The truck was an ancient, rebuilt Russian military vehicle, and the man had often been astonished that it was still running. There again, he didn't trust Weber. Weber had never cheated him, but he'd made up his mind once and for all that he was not be trusted. It was a precautionary measure. After all, the stuff he took to the East Germans was worth a lot. Each time, he took 20 or 30 computers, about 100 mobile phones and just as many car stereos—goods worth millions of kronor. If he got caught, he wouldn't be able to talk his way out of a long prison sentence. Nor would he be able to count on an ounce of help from Weber. In the world he lived in, everybody thought only about number one.

He checked the course on the compass and adjusted it by two degrees to the north. The log indicated that he was holding to a steady eight knots. There were six and a half nautical miles to go before he would see the coast and turn towards Brantevik. The grayish-blue waves were still visible ahead, but the snow seemed to be getting heavier.

Five more trips, he thought, and that's it. I'll have made all the money I need, and I'll be able to make my move. He lit another cigarette, smiling at the prospect. He would put all this behind him and set off on the journey to Porto Santos, where he'd open a bar. Soon, he'd no longer need to stand on watch in the leaky, drafty wheelhouse while Jakobson snored on his bunk down in the engine room. He couldn't be sure what his new life would hold, but he longed for it even so.

Abruptly as it had started, it stopped snowing. At first he didn't dare to believe his luck, but then it became clear that snowflakes were no longer swirling past his eyes. I might be able to make it after all, he thought. Maybe the storm is passing and heading towards Denmark?

Whistling, he poured himself some more coffee. The bag containing the money was hanging on the wall. Another 30,000 kronor closer to Porto Santos, the little island just off Madeira. Paradise was waiting.

He was just about to take another sip of coffee when he caught sight of the dinghy. If the weather hadn't lifted, he'd never have noticed it. There it was, though, bobbing up and down on the waves, just 50 meters to port. A red rubber life raft. He wiped the condensation off the glass and peered out at the dinghy. It's empty, he thought. It's fallen off a ship. He turned the wheel and slowed right down. Jakobson, woken by the change in speed, stuck his unshaven face up into the wheelhouse.

"Are we there?" he asked.

"There's a life raft to port," said the man at the wheel, whose name was Holmgren. "We'll get it. It's worth a thousand or two. Take the wheel and I'll get the boat hook."

Jakobson moved over to the wheel while Holmgren pulled the flaps of his cap down over his ears and left the wheelhouse. The wind bit into his face and he clung to the rail. The dinghy came slowly nearer. He started to unfasten the boat hook that was attached to the side of the wheelhouse. His fingers froze as he struggled with the catches, but eventually he released it and turned back to the water.

He gave a start. The dinghy was only a few meters away from the boat's hull, and he realized his mistake. There were two people inside. Dead people. Jakobson shouted something unintelligible from the wheelhouse: he too had seen what was in the life raft.

It wasn't the first time Holmgren had seen dead bodies. As a young man doing his military service, a gun had exploded on a maneuver, and four of his friends had been blown to bits. Later, during his many years as a professional fisherman, he had seen bodies washed up on beaches or floating in the water.

It struck Holmgren immediately that they were oddly dressed. The two men weren't fishermen or sailors—they were wearing suits. And they were hugging, as if they'd been trying to protect each other from the inevitable. He tried to imagine what had happened. Who could they be?

Jakobson emerged from the wheelhouse and stood by his side.

"Oh, shit!" he said. "Oh, shit! What are we going to do?"

Holmgren thought for a moment.

"Nothing," he said. "If we take them on board we'll only end up with difficult questions to answer. We haven't seen them, simple as that. It is snowing, after all."

"Shall we just let 'em drift?" Jakobson asked.

"Yes," Holmgren answered. "They're dead after all. There's nothing we can do. Besides, I don't want to have to explain where this boat has come from. Do you?"

Jakobson shook his head doubtfully. They stared at the two dead men in silence. Holmgren thought they looked young, hardly more than 30. Their faces were stiff and white. Holmgren shivered.

"Odd that there's no name on the life raft," Jakobson said. "What ship can it have come from?"

Holmgren took the boat hook and moved the dinghy around, looking at its sides. Jakobson was right: there was no name.

"What the hell can have happened?" he muttered. "Who are they? How long have they been adrift, wearing suits and ties?"

"How far is it to Ystad?" asked Jakobson.

"Just over six nautical miles."

"We could tow them a bit nearer the coast," said Jakobson, "so that they can drift ashore where they'll be found."

Holmgren thought again, weighing the pros and cons. The idea of leaving them there was repugnant, he couldn't deny that. At the same time, towing the dinghy would be risky—they might be seen by a ferry or some other vessel.

He made up his mind quickly. He unfastened a painter, leaned over the rail and tied it to the life raft. Jakobson changed course for Ystad, and Holmgren secured the line when the dinghy was about ten meters behind the boat and free of its wake.

When the Swedish coast came into sight, Holmgren cut the rope, and the life raft with the two dead men inside disappeared far behind. Jakobson changed course to the east, and a few hours later they chugged into the harbor at Brantevik. Jakobson collected his pay, got into his Volvo and drove off towards Svarte.

The harbor was deserted. Holmgren locked the wheelhouse and spread a tarpaulin over the cargo hatch. He checked the hawsers slowly and methodically. Then he picked up the bag containing the money, walked over to his old Ford, and coaxed the reluctant engine to life.

Ordinarily he would have allowed himself to dream of Porto Santos, but today all he could picture in his mind's eye was the red life raft. He tried to work out where it would eventually be washed up. The currents in that area were erratic, the wind gusted and shifted direction constantly. The dinghy could wash up anywhere along the coast. Even so, he guessed that it would be somewhere not far from Ystad, if it hadn't already been spotted by someone on one of the ferries to or from Poland.

It was already starting to get dark as he drove into Ystad. Two men wearing suits, he thought, as he stopped at a red light. In a life raft. There was something that didn't add up. Something he'd seen without quite registering it. Just as the lights changed to green, he realized what it was. The two men weren't in the dinghy as a result of a ship going down. He couldn't prove it, but he was certain. The two men were already dead when they'd been placed in the dinghy.

On the spur of the moment, he turned right and stopped at one of the phone booths opposite the bookshop in the square. He carefully rehearsed what he was going to say. Then he dialed 999 and asked for the police. As he waited for them to answer, he watched the snow begin to fall again through the dirty glass of the phone booth.

It was February 12, 1991.

CHAPTER 2

Inspector Kurt Wallander sat in his office at the police station in Ystad and yawned. It was such a huge yawn that one of the muscles under his chin locked. The pain was excruciating. Wallander punched at the underside of his jaw with his right hand to free the muscle. Just as he was doing so, Martinsson, one of the younger officers, walked in. He paused in the doorway, puzzled. Wallander continued to massage his jaw until the pain subsided. Martinsson turned to leave.

"Come on in," Wallander said. "Haven't you ever yawned so wide that your jaw muscles locked?"

Martinsson shook his head.

"No," he said. "I must admit I wondered what you were doing."

"Now you know," Wallander said. "What do you want?"

Martinsson made a face and sat down. He had a notebook in his hand.

"We received a strange phone call a few minutes ago," he said. "I thought I'd better check it with you."

"We get strange phone calls every day," Wallander said, wondering why he was being consulted.

"I don't know what to think," Martinsson said. "Some man called from a phone booth. He claimed that a rubber life raft containing two dead bodies would be washed up near here. He hung up without giving his name, or saying who'd been killed or why."

Wallander looked at him in surprise.

"Is that all?" he asked. "Who took the call?"

"I did," Martinsson said. "He said exactly what I've just told you. Somehow or other, he sounded convincing."

"Convincing?"

"You get to know after a while," Martinsson replied hesitantly. "Sometimes you can hear right away that it's a hoax. This time whoever called seemed very definite."

"Two dead men in a rubber life raft that's going to be washed up on the coast near here?"

Martinsson nodded.

Wallander stifled another yawn and leaned back in his chair.

"Have we had any reports about a boat sinking or anything like that?" he asked.

"None at all," Martinsson replied.

"Inform all the other police districts along the coast," Wallander said. "Talk to the coastguards. But we can't start a search based on nothing more than an anonymous telephone call. We'll just have to wait and see what happens."

Martinsson nodded and stood up.

"I agree," he said. "We'll have to wait and see."

"It could get pretty hellish tonight," Wallander said, nodding towards the window. "Snow."

"I'm going home now anyway," Martinsson said, looking at his watch. "Snow or no snow."

Martinsson left, and Wallander stretched out in his chair. He could feel how tired he was. He'd been forced to answer emergency calls two nights in a row. The first night he'd led the hunt for a suspected rapist who'd barricaded himself in an empty summer cottage at Sandskogen. The man was drugged to the eyeballs and there was reason to think he could be armed, so they'd surrounded the place until 5 a.m., when he'd given himself up. The following night Wallander had been called out to a murder in the town center. A birthday party had gotten out of hand, and the man whose birthday it was had been stabbed in the temple with a carving knife.

He got up from his chair and put on his fleece jacket. I've got to get some sleep, he thought. Somebody else can look after the snowstorm. When he left the station, the gusts of wind forced him to bend double. He unlocked his Peugeot and scrambled in. The snow that had settled on the windows gave him the feeling of being in a warm, cozy room. He started the engine, inserted a tape, and closed his eyes.

Immediately his thoughts turned to Rydberg. It was less than a month since his old friend and colleague had died of cancer. Wallander had known about the illness the year before, when they were struggling together to solve the murder of an old couple at Lenarp. During the last months of his life, when it was obvious to everybody and not least to Rydberg himself that the end was nigh, Wallander had tried to imagine going to the station knowing that Rydberg wouldn't be there. How would he manage without the advice and judgment of old Rydberg, who had so much experience? It was still too soon to answer that question. He hadn't had any difficult cases since Rydberg had gone on sick leave for the last time and then passed away. But the sense of pain and loss was still very real.

He switched on the windscreen wipers and drove slowly home. The town was deserted, as if people were preparing to be besieged by the approaching snowstorm. He stopped at a gas station off Österleden and bought an evening paper. Then he parked outside his flat in Mariagatan and went upstairs. He would take a bath and make something to eat. Before going to bed, he'd phone his father, who lived in a little house near Löderup. Ever since his father had become confused and gone wandering through the night in his pajamas the year before, Wallander had made a habit of calling him every day. He knew it was as much for his own sake as for his father's—he always felt guilty about not visiting him more often. Still, after that incident the year before, his father had a home helper who visited him regularly. This had improved the old man's moods, which were sometimes unbearable. Even so, Wallander's conscience pricked him: he felt he didn't devote enough time to his father.

Wallander had his bath, made an omelette, phoned his father and then went to bed. Before pulling down the roller blinds at his bedroom window, he looked out into the street. A solitary street-light was swaying in the gusty wind. Snowflakes danced before his eyes. The thermometer read –3°C. Maybe the storm had blown over? He lowered the blinds with a clatter and crept into bed, falling asleep almost immediately.

The next morning he was at the station by 7:15 a.m. Apart from a few minor road accidents, the night had been surprisingly quiet. The snowstorm had faded away before it had really got going. He went over to the canteen, greeted a few colleagues on traffic duty who were dozing over their coffee, then took a plastic cup for himself. The moment he'd woken, he'd decided to devote his day to writing up reports from the paperwork piling up on his desk—above all on the assault case involving a gang of Poles. Needless to say, everybody accused everybody else. There were no reliable witnesses to provide an objective version of what had happened, but even so, a report had to be written, although he had no illusions about someone being found guilty of breaking someone else's jaw.

At 10:30 a.m. he disposed of the last of the reports and went for another cup of coffee. On the way back to his office, he heard his telephone ringing. It was Martinsson.

"Remember that life raft?" he asked.

Wallander had to think for a moment before it came to him.

"The man who called knew what he was talking about. A rubber life raft with two bodies in it has washed up on the beach at Mossby Strand. It was discovered by a woman walking her dog; she called the station, as hysterical as they come."

"When did she phone?"

"Just now," Martinsson said.

Two minutes later Wallander was on his way along the coast road. Peters and Norén were ahead of him in a patrol car, sirens blaring. Wallander shuddered as he saw the freezing breakers slamming onto the beach. He could see an ambulance in his rearview mirror, and Martinsson in a second police car.

Mossby Strand was deserted. As he clambered out of his car, the icy wind met him head-on. The beach shop was boarded up, and the shutters were creaking and groaning in the wind. High up on the path that sloped down to the beach was a woman waving her arms about agitatedly, the dog beside her tugging at its lead. Wallander strode out, fearful as usual about what was in store for him—he would never be able to reconcile himself to the sight of dead bodies. Dead people were just like the living. Always different.

"Over there," screeched the woman hysterically. Wallander looked in the direction she was pointing. A red life raft was bobbing up and down at the water's edge, where it had become stuck among some rocks by the bathing jetty.

"Wait here," Wallander told the woman.

He scrambled down the slope and ran over the sand, then walked out along the jetty and looked down into the rubber boat. There were two men, lying with their arms wrapped around each other, their faces ashen. He tried to capture what he saw in a mental photograph. His many years as a police officer had taught him that the first impression was always important. A dead body was generally the end of a long and complicated chain of events, and sometimes it was possible to get an idea of that chain right from the start.

Martinsson waded out into the water to pull the life raft ashore, wearing gum boots. Wallander squatted down to examine the bodies. He could see Peters trying to calm the woman. It struck him how fortunate they were that the boat hadn't come ashore in the summer, when there would have been hundreds of children playing and swimming on the beach. What he was looking at was not a pretty sight, and there was the unmistakable stench of rotting flesh despite the fierce wind.

He took a pair of rubber gloves from his jacket and searched the men's pockets carefully. He found nothing at all. When he opened the jacket of one of the men he could see a liver-colored stain on the chest of the white shirt. He looked at Martinsson.

"This is no accident," he said. "It's murder. This man has been shot straight through the heart."

He stood up and moved to one side so that Norén could photograph the life raft.

"What do you think?" he asked Martinsson.

Martinsson shook his head.

"I don't know."

Wallander walked slowly around the boat without taking his eyes off the two dead men. Both were fair-haired, probably in their early 30s. Judging by their hands and clothes, they were not manual laborers. Who were they? Why was there nothing in their pockets? He continued walking around and around the boat, occasionally exchanging a few words with Martinsson. After half an hour he decided that there was nothing more for him to discover. By then the forensic team had begun their methodical examination. A plastic tent had been put up over the rubber boat. Norén had finished taking photographs; everybody was bitterly cold and couldn't wait to get away. Wallander wondered what Rydberg would have said. What would Rydberg have seen that he'd missed? He sat in his car with the engine running to keep warm. The sea was gray and his head felt empty. Who were these men?

It was several hours before Wallander was able to give the ambulance men the okay, and they moved forward with their stretchers. By then, Wallander was so cold that he couldn't stop shivering. They had no choice but to break a few bones to release the men from their embrace. When the bodies had been removed, Wallander gave the boat another thorough investigation, but found nothing, not even a paddle. He gazed out to sea, as if the solution was to be found somewhere on the horizon.

"You'd better have a talk with the woman who discovered the life raft," he said to Martinsson.

"I've done that already," Martinsson said, surprised.

"A serious talk," Wallander said. "You can't talk seriously in this wind. Take her down to the station. Norén must make sure this boat arrives there in the same state it's in now. Tell him that."

Then he returned to his car.

This is when I could have used Rydberg, he said to himself. What is it that I can't see? What would he have been thinking now?

When he got back to the station in Ystad, he went straight to see Björk, the chief of police, and reported briefly on what he'd seen out at Mossby Strand. Björk listened anxiously. He often seemed to Wallander to consider himself to have been attacked personally whenever a violent crime was committed in his district. At the

same time, Wallander respected his boss. He never interfered
in the investigations being carried out by his officers, and he
was generous with his encouragement when a case seemed to be
running out of steam. Sometimes he could be a bit tempera-
mental, but Wallander was used to that.

"I want you to take charge," Björk said when Wallander had
finished. "Martinsson and Hansson can give you some help. I
think we can assign several men to this case."

"Hansson's busy with that rapist we arrested the other night,"
Wallander pointed out. "Wouldn't it be better to use Svedberg?"

Björk agreed. Wallander got his way, as usual.

As he left Björk's office, Wallander realized he was hungry. He
was prone to put on weight, so he did without lunch, but the dead
men in the boat worried him. He drove into town and parked as
usual in Stickgatan, then made his way down the narrow, winding
streets to Fridolf's Café. He ordered some sandwiches and drank
a glass of milk, going over what had happened in his mind.
The previous evening, shortly before 6 p.m., a man had made an
anonymous call to the police and warned them of what was to
happen. Now they knew he'd been telling the truth. A red rubber
life raft is washed ashore, containing two dead men. At least one
of them has been murdered, shot through the heart. There is
nothing at all in their pockets to indicate who they are.

That was it.

Wallander took out a pen and scribbled some notes on a
paper napkin. He already had a long list of questions that needed
answering. All the while, he was conducting a silent conversation
with Rydberg. Am I on the right track, have I overlooked anything?
He tried to imagine Rydberg's answers and reactions. Sometimes
he succeeded, but often all he could see was Rydberg's drawn,
haggard face as he lay on his deathbed.

By 3:30 p.m. he was on his way back to the station. He called Martinsson and Svedberg into his office, closed the door and instructed the switchboard to hold his calls.

"This isn't going to be easy," he began. "We can only hope the postmortems and the forensic team's examination of the life raft and the clothes come up with something. All the same, there are a few questions I'd like answered right away."

Svedberg was leaning against the wall, notebook in hand. He was in his 40s and balding, born in Ystad, and rumor had it that he started feeling homesick the minute he left the town. He often gave the impression of being slow and lacking in interest, but he was thorough, and that was something Wallander appreciated. In many ways Martinsson was the opposite of Svedberg: he was coming up on 30, born in Trollhättan, and had set his sights early on a police career. He was also involved in Liberal Party politics, and according to what Wallander had heard, had a good chance of being elected to the local council in the autumn elections. As a police officer, Martinsson was impulsive and sometimes careless, but he often had good ideas, and his ambition meant that he worked tirelessly when he thought he could see a solution to a problem.

"I want to know where this life raft came from," Wallander said. "When we know how long the two men have been dead, we'll have to try and work out which direction the boat came from and how far it's drifted."

Svedberg stared at him in surprise.

"Will that be possible?" he asked.

"We must talk to the meteorological office," Wallander said. "They know all there is to know about the weather and the wind. We ought to be able to get a rough idea of where the boat has come from. And I want to know everything we can find out about the life raft itself. Where it was made, what type of vessels might carry such rafts. Everything."

He nodded towards Martinsson.

"That's your job."

"Shouldn't we begin by running a computer search to see if the men are listed anywhere as missing?" Martinsson asked.

"You can start by doing that," Wallander said. "Get in touch with the coast guard, contact all their stations along the south coast. And see what Björk has to say about bringing in Interpol right away. It's obvious that if we're going to trace who they are, we'll have to cast our nets wide from the very beginning."

Martinsson nodded and made a note on a sheet of paper. Svedberg chewed thoughtfully on his pencil.

"The forensic team will go over the men's clothes thoroughly," Wallander continued. "They must find some clues."

There was a knock on the door and Norén came in, carrying a rolled-up nautical chart.

"I thought you might need this," he said.

They spread it out over his desk and pored over it, as if planning a naval battle.

"How fast does a life raft drift?" Svedberg asked. "Currents and winds can slow it down as well as speed it up."

They contemplated the chart in silence. Then Wallander rolled it up again and stood it in the corner behind his chair. Nobody had anything to say.

"Let's get going, then," he said. "We can meet here again at 6 p.m. and see how far we've gotten."

As Svedberg and Norén left the room, Wallander asked Martinsson to stay behind.

"What did the woman have to say?" he asked.

Martinsson shrugged.

"Mrs. Forsell," he said. "A widow. Lives in Mossby. She's a retired teacher from the grammar school in Ängelholm. Lives here all the year round with her dog, Tegnér. Fancy naming a dog after a poet! Every day they go out for some fresh air on the beach. When she walked along the cliffs last night, there was no sign of a life raft; but it was there this morning. She saw it at about 10:15 a.m. and called us right away."

"Ten fifteen a.m.," Wallander said thoughtfully. "Isn't that a bit late to be walking a dog?"

Martinsson nodded.

"That occurred to me as well, but it turned out she'd been out at seven o'clock too, but they walked along the beach in the other direction."

Wallander changed the subject.

"The man who rang yesterday," he asked, "what did he sound like?"

"Like I said. Convincing."

"Did he have an accent? Could you tell how old he was?"

"He had a local accent. Like Svedberg's. His voice was hoarse; I wouldn't be surprised to find he's a smoker. In his 40s or 50s, I'd say. He spoke simply and clearly. He could be anything from a bank clerk to a farmer."

Wallander had one more question.

"Why did he call?"

"I've been wondering that," Martinsson answered. "He might have known the boat would drift ashore because he'd been mixed up in it himself. He might have been the one who did the shooting. He might have seen something, or heard something. There are several possibilities."

"What's the logical explanation?"

"The last one," Martinsson answered without hesitation. "He

saw or heard something. This doesn't seem to be the type of murder where the killer would choose to set the police on his trail."

Wallander had come to the same conclusion.

"Let's go a step further," he said. "Seen or heard something? Two men dead in a life raft? If he isn't involved, he can hardly have seen the murder or murders. That means he must have seen the raft."

"A life raft drifting at sea," Martinsson said. "How do you see something like that? Only by being in a boat yourself."

"Exactly," Wallander said. "Precisely. But if he didn't do it, why does he want to remain anonymous?"

"Some people prefer not to get involved in things," Martinsson said. "You know how it is."

"Could be. But there might be another explanation. He might have quite a different reason for not wanting to get mixed up with the police."

"Isn't that a bit far-fetched?"

"I'm only thinking aloud," Wallander said. "Somehow or other we have to trace that man."

"Shall we send out an appeal for him to get in touch with us again?"

"Yes," Wallander said. "Not today, though. I want to find out more about the dead men first."

Wallander drove to the hospital. He'd been there many times, but he still had trouble finding the newly built complex. He paused in the cafeteria on the ground floor and bought a banana, then went upstairs to the pathology department. The pathologist, whose name was Mörth, hadn't yet started the detailed examination of the corpses. Even so, he was able to answer Wallander's first question.

"Both men were shot," he stated. "At close range, through the heart. I assume that is the cause of death."

"I'd like to see your report as soon as possible," Wallander said. "Is there anything you can say now about the time of death?"

Mörth shook his head.

"No," he said. "But that's an answer in a way."

"Meaning what?"

"That they've probably been dead for quite a long time. That makes it more difficult to pin down the precise time of death."

"Two days? Three? A week?"

"I can't answer that," Mörth said, "and I don't want to guess."

He disappeared into the lab. Wallander took off his jacket, put on a pair of rubber gloves, and started to go through the men's clothes, which were laid out on what looked like an old-fashioned kitchen sink.

One of the suits was made in England, the other in Belgium. The shoes were Italian, and it seemed to Wallander that they were expensive. Shirts, ties and underwear told the same story: they were good quality, certainly not cheap. When Wallander had finished examining the clothes twice, he realized he was unlikely to get any further. All he knew was that in all probability, the two men were not short of money. But where were the wallets? Wedding rings? Watches? Even more bewildering was the fact that the men had not been wearing their jackets when they were shot. There were no holes or powder burns on them.

Wallander tried to conjure up the scene. Somebody shoots two men straight through the heart. When they're dead, whoever did it then puts their jackets on them before dumping the bodies into a life raft. Why?

He went through the clothes one more time. There's something I'm not seeing, he thought. Rydberg, help me.

But Rydberg had nothing to say.

Wallander went back to the police station. He knew the post-mortems would take several hours, and that he wouldn't get a preliminary report until the next day at the earliest. Back in his office, he found a note on his desk from Björk, saying they should wait another day or so before calling in Interpol. Wallander felt himself getting annoyed: he often found it hard to sympathize with Björk's cautious approach.

The meeting at 6 p.m. was brief. Martinsson reported that there was no record of any missing persons who could possibly be the men in the life raft. Svedberg had had a long discussion with someone at the meteorological office in Norrköping who had promised to help the moment he received a formal request from the Ystad police.

Wallander told them that, as expected, the pathologist had confirmed that both men had been murdered. He asked Svedberg and Martinsson to consider why someone would have shot two men and then put their jackets back on the bodies.

"Let's keep going for a few more hours," Wallander said. "If you're involved in other cases, either put them on ice for the time being or pass them on to somebody else. This is going to be a tough nut to crack. I'll see to it that we get some more men first thing tomorrow."

When Wallander was alone in his office, he unrolled the chart on his desk again. With his finger, he traced the coastline as far as Mossby Strand. The raft could have drifted a long way, he thought. Or no distance at all. It might have been drifting backwards and forwards on the tide.

The phone rang. For a moment he tried to decide whether to answer it: it was late, and he wanted to go home and think about what had happened in peace and quiet. But he lifted the receiver.

It was Mörth.

"Have you finished already?" Wallander asked, surprised.

"No," Mörth said. "But there's something I think is important. Something I can let you know now."

Wallander held his breath.

"The men are not Swedes," Mörth said. "At least, they weren't born in Sweden."

"How can you tell?"

"I've looked at their teeth," Mörth said. "Their dental work wasn't done by a Swedish dentist. Could have been by Russian ones, though."

"Russian?"

"Yes. Russian dentists. Or dentists from one of the Eastern bloc countries. They use quite different methods from us."

"Are you absolutely sure?"

"I wouldn't have called otherwise," Mörth said, and Wallander could tell he was annoyed.

"I believe you," he said quickly.

"There's another thing," Mörth continued. "Something that might be at least as important. These two men were no doubt very relieved when they were shot, if you'll pardon my cynicism. They'd been tortured pretty comprehensively before they died. Burns, peeled skin, thumbscrews, the whole damned lot."

Wallander sat in silence.

"Are you still there?" Mörth asked.

"Yes," Wallander said. "I'm still here. I'm just letting what you said sink in."

"I'm quite sure about it."

"I don't doubt that for a moment. This is a bit out of the ordinary, though."

"That's precisely why I thought it was important to phone you."

"You did the right thing," Wallander said.

"You'll get my full report tomorrow," Mörth said. "Apart from the results of laboratory tests that will take a bit longer."

He hung up. Wallander went out to the canteen. The room was deserted. He poured out the last drops from the coffee machine and sat down at one of the tables.

Russians? Men from the Eastern bloc, tortured? Even Rydberg would have thought that this looked like a difficult and lengthy investigation. It was 7:30 p.m. when he went to his car and drove home. The wind had died down, and it had suddenly become colder.

CHAPTER 3

Shortly after 2 a.m. Wallander woke with terrible chest pains. He was convinced that he was about to die. The constant stress and strain of police work was having its effect. He was paying the price. He was motionless in the dark, filled with despair and shame. He had left things too late; he was never going to make anything of his life. His anxiety and pain seemed to grow more and more intense. Afterwards he wasn't sure how long he'd lain there, unable to control his mounting fear, but slowly he had managed to reassert his self-control.

He got carefully out of bed, pulled on some clothes, and went down to his car. The pain seemed less intense now; it came and went in waves, moving out into his arms, losing something of its initial force. He got into his car, tried to make himself breathe calmly and then drove through the deserted streets to the hospital's emergency entrance. He encountered a nurse with friendly eyes, who listened to him, and didn't seem to regard him as a hysterical, rather overweight hypochondriac. Wallander lay on a stretcher, listening to a drunk ranting in one of the treatment rooms, the pain coming and going, until suddenly he found a young doctor standing beside him. He described his chest pains once again. His stretcher was wheeled into a treatment room and he was wired up to an EKG machine. They took his blood pressure, felt his pulse, and answered various questions: no he didn't smoke, he hadn't experienced chest pains before, as far as he knew there was no history of heart disease in his family. The doctor scrutinized the EKG reading.

"Nothing special here," he said. "Everything seems to be normal. What do you think might have caused this?"

"I have no idea."

The doctor studied Wallander's records.

"You're a police officer, I see," he said. "I imagine things can get a bit hectic at work now and then."

"It's like that more or less all the time."

"What about your alcohol intake?"

"I like to think it's normal."

The doctor sat down on the edge of a table and put down the record cards. Wallander could see that he was very tired.

"I don't think you've had a heart attack," he said. "It might be your body sounding the alarm, announcing that everything isn't as it should be. You're the only one who can know about this."

"That's probably it," Wallander said. "I ask myself every day what my life is doing to me. And I realize I don't have anybody I can talk to."

"You should," said the doctor. "Everybody should."

He stood up when his pager started peeping like a fledgling in his pocket.

"I'm going to keep you overnight," he said. "Try to get some rest."

Wallander lay there quite peacefully, listening to the hum of an invisible air-conditioning fan. He could hear voices in the corridor.

All pain has a cause, he thought. If it isn't my heart, what is it? The guilt I have at failing to devote enough time and energy to my father? Worry because I suspect the letters my daughter sends me from her college in Stockholm don't tell the full story?

That things are not at all as she describes them, when she says she likes it there, and is working, and feels that at last she's doing something she wants to be doing? Could it be that although I'm not conscious of it, I'm constantly afraid she's going to try to take her own life again, as she did when she was 15? Or is the pain due to the jealousy I still feel at Mona leaving me, even though that was a year ago now?

The light in the room seemed very bright. He felt that his whole life was characterized by a sense of desolation that he simply couldn't shake off. How could the kind of pain he'd just been feeling be caused by loneliness? He couldn't come up with any solution that didn't immediately fill him with doubt.

"I can't go on living like this," he said out loud. "I've got to get my life sorted out. Soon. Now."

He woke up with a start at 6 a.m. The doctor was standing by his bed, watching him.

"No more pain?" he asked.

"Everything feels okay," Wallander said. "What can it have been?"

"Tension," the doctor said. "Stress. You know best yourself."

"Yes," Wallander said. "I suppose I do."

"I think you should have a thorough examination," the doctor said. "If nothing else, we need to be sure there's nothing physically wrong with you. It will make it easier for you to look inside your own head and see what kind of shadows are lurking there."

Wallander drove home, took a shower, and had a cup of coffee. The thermometer read −3ºC. The sky had cleared, and the wind had dropped. He sat there for a long time, thinking about the previous night. The pains and his stay in the hospital had taken on an air of unreality. But he knew he couldn't just ignore what had happened. His life was his own responsibility.

*

It was 8:15 a.m. before he felt he could face work.

As soon as he got to the station, he became embroiled in an argument with Björk, who was insisting that the forensic squad in Stockholm should have been brought in at once to make a thorough investigation at the scene of the crime.

"There was no scene of the crime," Wallander said. "If there's one thing we can be sure about, it's that the men were not murdered in that life raft."

"Now that we don't have Rydberg to rely on, we need outside help," Björk said. "We don't have the expertise. Why didn't you close off the beach where the life raft was found?"

"The beach wasn't where the crime was committed. The raft had been drifting at sea. Are you suggesting that we should have fixed a plastic ribbon around the waves?"

Wallander was getting angry. True, neither he nor any other of the officers in Ystad had Rydberg's experience, but that didn't mean he was incapable of deciding when to call in assistance from Stockholm.

"Either you let me make the decisions," he said, "or you run the case yourself."

"There's no question of that," Björk said, "but I still think it was an error of judgment not to consult Stockholm."

"Well, I don't."

That was as far as they could go.

"I'll come and see you shortly," said Wallander. "I've got some stuff I'd like your opinion on."

Björk looked surprised.

"Have we got something to go on?" he asked. "I thought we were up against a brick wall."

"Not quite. I'll be with you in ten minutes."

He went back to his office, called the hospital, and was astonished to get straight through to Mörth.

"Anything new?" he asked the pathologist.

"I'm just writing my report," Mörth answered. "Can't you wait another couple of hours?"

"I have to update Björk. Can you at least say how long they've been dead?"

"No. We have to wait for the results of the lab tests. Stomach content, extent of cell tissue decay. I can only guess."

"Do it."

"I don't like guessing, you know that. What good will it do you?"

"You're experienced. You know what you're doing. The test results will only confirm what you suspect already, they won't contradict them. I only want you to whisper in my ear. I won't pass it on."

Wallander waited.

"A week," Mörth said finally. "At least a week. But don't tell anybody I said that."

"I've forgotten it already. You're still certain they're Russian or East European?"

"Yes."

"Did you find anything you didn't expect?"

"I don't know anything about ammunition, of course, but I've never come across this type of bullet before."

"Anything else?"

"Yes. One of the men has a tattoo on his upper arm. It's a sort of saber. Some kind of Turkish scimitar, or whatever they're called."

"A what?"

"It's a sword. You can't expect a pathologist to be an expert on obsolete weaponry."

"Does it say anything?"

"What do you mean?"

"Tattoos usually have some inscription. A woman's name, or a place."

"There's no inscription."

"Nothing else?"

"Not at the moment."

"Okay, thanks for all this anyway."

"It wasn't very much."

Wallander hung up, fetched himself a cup of coffee and went to see Björk. The doors of Martinsson's and Svedberg's offices were open, but neither of them was there. He sat down and drank his coffee, listening absentmindedly as Björk finished a phone conversation, which seemed to be getting rather heated. He jumped as Björk slammed down the phone.

"That was damnedest thing I've ever heard," Björk said. "What's the point of continuing?"

"A good question," Wallander said, "but I'm not sure what you're referring to."

Björk was shaking with anger. Wallander couldn't remember ever having seen him like this.

"What's the matter?" he asked.

Björk looked at him. "I don't know if I'm supposed to say anything about it," he said, "but I really have to. One of those bastards who murdered the old couple in Lenarp, the one we called Lucia, was let out on leave the other day. Needless to say, he never went back. Presumably he's fled the country. We'll never catch him again."

Wallander couldn't believe his ears.

"Leave? He hasn't even been inside for a year yet, and that was one of the most brutal killings we've seen in this country. How the hell could they let him out on leave?"

"He was going to his mother's funeral."

Wallander's jaw dropped.

"But his mother's been dead for ten years! I remember that from the report the Czech police sent us."

"A woman claiming to be his sister turned up at Hall Prison, pleading for him to be let out to attend the funeral. Nobody seems to have checked anything. She had a printed card saying there was going to be a funeral in a church at Ängelholm—obviously a forgery. There still seems to be some souls in this country naïve enough to believe that no one would forge a funeral invitation. They let him go with a warden. That was the day before yesterday. There was no funeral, nor was there a dead mother, no sister. They overpowered the guard, tied him up and dumped him in some woods near Jönköping. They even drove the prison commissioner's car to Kastrup Airport via Limhamn. It's still there, but they aren't."

"This just isn't true," Wallander said. "Who in hell's name could give a criminal like that leave?"

"Like the ads say: Sweden is fantastic," Björk said. "It makes me sick."

"Whose responsibility is it? Whoever gave him leave should be locked up in the cell he's left empty. How is a thing like that possible?"

"I'll look into it," Björk said. "But that's the way it is. The bird has flown."

Wallander's mind went back to the unimaginably savage murder of the old couple in Lenarp. He looked up at Björk in resignation.

"What's the point?" he wondered. "Why do we bust ourselves to catch criminals if all the prison service does is let them go again?"

Björk didn't answer. Wallander stood up and went over to the window.

"How much longer can we keep going?" he asked.

"We have to," said Björk. "Are you going to tell me now what you know about those two men in the rubber boat?"

Wallander told him what he knew. He felt depressed, tired and disappointed. Björk made a few notes as he was speaking.

"Russians," he said when Wallander had finished.

"Or from an Eastern bloc country. Mörth was certain of that."

"I'd better contact the foreign ministry," said Björk. "It's their job to get in touch with the Russian police. Or Polish. The Eastern bloc."

"They could be Russians living in Sweden," Wallander said. "Or Germany. Or why not Denmark?"

"Even so, most Russians are still in the Soviet Union," Björk said. "I'll contact the foreign ministry right away. They know what to do in a situation like this."

"We could put the bodies back into the life raft and ask the coastguards to have it towed out into international waters," Wallander answered. "Then we could wash our hands of the case."

Björk seemed not to hear.

"We'll have to get some help in identifying them," he said. "Photographs, fingerprints, clothes."

"And a tattoo. A scimitar."

"A scimitar?"

"Yes, a scimitar."

Björk shook his head and reached for the phone.

"Just a minute," Wallander said.

Björk withdrew his hand.

"I'm thinking about the man who telephoned," Wallander said. "According to Martinsson, he had a local accent. We should try to trace him."

"Have we any clues?"

"None. That's precisely why I suggest we put out an appeal. We can keep it general. We can appeal to anybody who's seen a red rubber boat drifting around, and ask them to get in touch with the police."

Björk nodded. "I'll have to speak to the press in any case. Reporters started calling ages ago. How they can find out so quickly about what happens on a deserted stretch of beach is beyond me. It took them precisely half an hour yesterday."

"You know we have leaks," Wallander said, reminded once again of the double murder at Lenarp.

"What do you mean, we?"

"The police. The Ystad police."

"Who does the leaking?"

"How am I supposed to know that? It ought to be your job to remind all staff to be discreet and observe professional secrecy."

Björk slammed his fist down on his desk, as if administering a box on the ears. But he didn't answer Wallander directly.

"We'll make an appeal," was all he said. "At midday, before the news on the radio. I want you to be at the press conference. Right now I must call Stockholm and get some instructions."

Wallander got to his feet. "It would be great if we didn't have to," he said.

"Didn't have to do what?"

"Find whoever shot the men in the life raft."

"I'll find out what Stockholm has to say," Björk said, shaking his head.

Wallander left the room. Martinsson's and Svedberg's offices were still empty. He glanced at his watch: nearly 9:30 a.m. He went down to the basement of the police station where the life raft had been placed on wooden trestles. He used a strong flashlight to examine it thoroughly, looking for the name of a firm or country of manufacture, but he found nothing, which surprised him. He couldn't come up with a satisfactory explanation for why that should be. He went around the rubber boat once more, and this time noticed a short piece of rope. It was different from the rope holding the wooden floor in place. It had been cut off with a knife. He tried to imagine what conclusions Rydberg would have drawn, but his mind was a complete blank.

He was back in his office by 10 a.m. Neither Martinsson nor Svedberg answered when he phoned their offices. He pulled out a notebook and started to write out a summary of the little they knew about the two dead men. People from the Eastern bloc, shot through the heart at close range, then dressed in their jackets and dumped in a life raft that still hadn't been identified. Plus, the men had been tortured. He pushed the notebook away: a thought had suddenly struck him. Men who've been tortured and murdered, he thought: you hide the bodies away, dig graves for them, or send them to the bottom of the sea with iron weights attached to their legs. If you load them into a life raft, the likelihood is that they will be found.

Can that have been the intention? That they would be found? Doesn't the life raft suggest the murder took place onboard a ship? He crumpled up the top page of the notebook and threw it into the wastebasket. I don't know enough, he thought. Rydberg would have told me not to be impatient.

The phone rang. It was 10:45 a.m. The moment he heard his father's voice, he remembered that he was supposed to go and see him. He should have been in Löderup by 10 a.m. so they could drive to a shop in Malmö to buy canvases and paints.

"Why haven't you come?" his father asked angrily.

Wallander decided to be perfectly straight with him.

"I'm sorry," he said. "I'd forgotten all about it."

There was a long pause.

"At least that's an honest answer," his father said finally.

"I can come tomorrow," Wallander said.

"Make it tomorrow, then," his father said, and hung up.

Wallander wrote a note on a piece of paper and fastened it to the telephone. He'd better not forget tomorrow.

He rang Svedberg: still no reply. Martinsson answered, though—he'd just come back to his office. Wallander went out into the corridor to meet him.

"Do you know what I've discovered today?" Martinsson asked. "That it's more or less impossible to describe what a life raft looks like. All different models made by different manufacturers look the same. Only experts can tell them apart. So I went to Malmö, and I've been visiting the various importers."

They had gone to the canteen to fetch some coffee. Martinsson got some biscuits, and they went to Wallander's office.

"So, now you know all about life rafts," Wallander said.

"Quite a bit, but I don't know where this one comes from."

"It's odd that there isn't any logo or a notice of country of manufacture," Wallander said. "Life-saving equipment is generally covered in all kinds of notes and instructions."

"I agree. So did the importers in Malmö. But there is the possibility of a solution: the coastguard. Captain Österdahl, a retired officer who has devoted his whole life to working on the Customs boats—15 years in Arkösund, ten years in the Gryt archipelago. After that he moved to Simrishamn, and was based there until he retired. Over the years he drew up his own register of different types of vessels, including rubber boats and life rafts."

"Who told you this?"

"I got lucky when I called the coastguard. The man who

answered had worked on one of the Customs boats that Österdahl skippered."

"Good," said Wallander. "Maybe he can help us."

"If he can't, then nobody can," Martinsson said philosophically. "He lives out at Sandhammaren. I thought I'd drive out and fetch him so that he can take a look at the boat. Have there been any developments?"

Wallander told him Mörth's conclusions while he listened attentively.

"So we may have to cooperate with the Russian police," he said when Wallander had finished. "Can you speak Russian?"

"Not a word. You know, it might mean that we can drop the whole business."

"No harm in hoping."

Martinsson suddenly became thoughtful.

"That's the way I feel sometimes, in fact," he said after a while. "That I wish we could just drop certain criminal cases. Because they're so awful. Too bloody and unreal. When I was at the police academy, we didn't learn how to cope with tortured corpses abandoned in life rafts. It's as if developments in crime have left me behind. And I'm only 30."

In recent years Kurt Wallander had often felt the same way as Martinsson. It had become more difficult to be a police officer. They were living at a time characterized by a sort of criminality that nobody had experienced before. It was a myth that a lot of police officers left the force in order to become security guards or work for private firms for financial reasons. The truth was that most police officers that left the force did so on grounds of insecurity.

"Maybe we ought to go and see Björk and request advanced training in how to deal with tortured humans," Martinsson said.

Wallander knew that there was nothing cynical in what Martinsson was saying, just the insecurity he himself often felt.

"Every generation of police officers seems to say the same thing," he said. "We're no exception."

"I can't remember Rydberg ever complaining, can you?"

"Rydberg was an exception. But I'd like to ask you something before you go. The man who phoned. There was nothing to suggest he might be a foreigner, was there?"

Martinsson had no doubt.

"Nothing at all. He came from around here. Full stop."

"Has anything else struck you about that conversation?"

"No."

Martinsson stood up.

"I'll go to Sandhammaren now, to look for Captain Österdahl," he said.

"The raft's in the basement," Wallander said. "Good luck. By the way, do you have any idea where Svedberg is?"

"I haven't a clue. I don't know what he's up to. Contacting the meteorological office, perhaps."

Wallander drove to the town center for lunch. He thought of the unreal incident of the night before, and ordered a salad.

He was back at the station shortly before the press conference was due to begin. He had made a few notes on a piece of paper, and checked in with Björk.

"I hate press conferences," Björk said. "That's why I'll never become national police commissioner. Not that I would anyway."

They walked together to the room where the reporters were waiting. Wallander recalled the mass of journalists who came when they were dealing with the double murder at Lenarp. Now there were only three people sitting there. He recognized two of them: one was a lady on the *Ystad Recorder* who wrote precise and lucid reports; the other was a man from the local office of *Labor News*, whom he'd only met once or twice before. The third person was a man with a crew cut and glasses. Wallander had never seen him before.

"Where's the *South Sweden Daily News*?" Björk whispered in his ear. "And the *Skåne Daily News*? Not to mention local radio?"

"No idea," Wallander said. "Let's get started."

Björk stepped up onto the dais in one corner of the room. His speaking style was rather hesitant and distant, and Wallander hoped he wouldn't go on any longer than necessary.

Then it was his turn.

"Two dead men have been washed ashore at Mossby Strand in a life raft," he said. "We haven't been able to identify the bodies. As far as we know there has been no accident that could be linked with the life raft, nor do we have any reports of anybody being lost at sea. That means we need assistance from the public. And from you."

He didn't mention the anonymous phone call.

"We'd like to ask anybody who might have relevant information to contact the police. That's all."

Björk returned to the platform.

"We'll try to answer any questions you might have," he said.

The friendly lady from the *Ystad Recorder* asked whether there wasn't an unusually high number of incidents of violence in Skåne, where everything used to be so peaceful.

Wallander snorted to himself at the question. Peaceful, he thought. It's never been especially peaceful around here.

Björk said that there really hadn't been a significant increase in violent crimes reported, and the lady from the *Ystad Recorder* seemed satisfied with his answer. The local correspondent from

Labor News had no questions, and Björk was just about to close the conference when the young man in glasses raised his hand.

"I've got a question," he said. "Why haven't you said that the men in the raft had been murdered?"

Wallander looked quickly at Björk.

"At this stage we cannot be certain how the two men died," Björk said.

"Come on, that's not true. Everybody knows they were shot through the heart."

"Next question," Björk said, and Wallander could see he had broken into a sweat.

"Next question?" the reporter said angrily. "Why should I ask another question when you haven't answered my first one?"

"You've had the only answer I can give you at present," Björk said.

"This is absurd," said the reporter. "But I will ask another question. Why don't you say you suspect that the two murdered men are Russian citizens? Why do you call a press conference when you either don't answer questions or don't reveal the facts?"

How the hell did he find out about all that? Wallander thought to himself. On the other hand, he didn't understand why Björk wasn't coming clean. The journalist was quite right. Why should they conceal facts that were patently obvious?

"As Inspector Wallander just pointed out, we haven't yet been able to identify the two men," Björk said. "That's precisely why we are appealing to the general public. We hope the press will make a splash of this so that people know we are looking for information."

The young reporter stuffed his notebook demonstratively into his jacket pocket.

"Thank you for coming," Björk said.

At the exit Wallander cornered the lady from the *Ystad Recorder*.

"Who was that reporter?" he asked.

"I've no idea. I've never seen him before. Was what he said true?"

Wallander didn't answer, and the lady from the *Ystad Recorder* was sufficiently polite not to press him.

"Why didn't you come clean?" Wallander asked when he had caught up with Björk in the corridor.

"These damned reporters," Björk growled. "How did he find all that out? Who's responsible for the leaks?"

"It could be anybody," said Wallander said. "It could even be me."

Björk stopped dead in his tracks and stared at him, but didn't comment.

"The foreign ministry have asked us to lie low," he said instead.

"Why?" Wallander asked.

"You'll have to ask them that," Björk said. "I'm hoping to get some more instructions this afternoon."

Wallander returned to his office. He was starting to get fed up with the whole business. He sat down and unlocked one of his desk drawers. It contained a photocopy of an advertisement for a job. The Trelleborg Rubber Company was looking for a new head of security. With the ad was the application letter Wallander had written the week before. He was trying to decide whether to send it in. If police work had become a sort of game, with information being either leaked or held back for no good reason, he no longer wanted to be involved. Police work was more than this as far as he was concerned. He couldn't operate in an environment in which his job wasn't constantly underpinned by rational and moral principles that would never be questioned.

His train of thought was interrupted by Svedberg, who nudged the door open with his foot and marched in.

"Where the hell have you been?" Wallander asked.

Svedberg stared at him in astonishment.

"I left a note on your desk," he said. "Haven't you seen it?"

The note had fallen on the floor. Wallander picked it up. Svedberg had told him he could be contacted at the meteorological office at Sturup.

"I thought we could take a shortcut," Svedberg said. "I know one of the men at Sturup Airport. We go bird-watching together at Falsterbo. He helped me to try and work out where the raft might have come from."

"I thought the meteorological office in Norrköping was doing that."

"I thought this way would be quicker."

He took some rolls of paper out of his pocket and spread them on the table. Wallander could see diagrams and columns of numbers.

"We calculated on the assumption that the raft had been drifting for five days," Svedberg said. "The wind directions have been pretty constant in recent weeks, so we were able to be quite accurate. Of course, it won't help us much."

"Meaning?"

"That the life raft probably drifted quite a long way."

"Meaning?"

"It could have come from countries as far apart as Denmark and Estonia."

Wallander stared at Svedberg in disbelief.

"Is that really possible?"

"Yes. You can ask Johnny yourself."

"Good work," Wallander said. "Go and tell Björk. He can pass the information on to the foreign ministry. Then maybe we can get rid of the whole affair."

"Get rid of?"

Wallander told him what had happened earlier in the day. He could see that Svedberg was disappointed.

"I don't like dropping something I've started," Svedberg said.

"Nothing is certain. I'm just letting you know."

Svedberg went off to see Björk, and Wallander went back to his job application. All the time, the raft with the murdered men was bobbing up and down in his mind.

Mörth's postmortem report was delivered at 4 p.m. He was still awaiting the results from the laboratory tests, but he estimated that the men had been dead for approximately seven days. They had probably been exposed to salt water for about the same length of time. One of the men was about 28, the other slightly older. Both had been in good health. They had been subjected to extreme torture. East European dentists had treated their teeth. Wallander put the report aside and looked out the window. It was dark already, and he was hungry.

Björk called to say that the foreign ministry would get back to him in the morning with further instructions.

"In that case, I'm going home," Wallander said.

"Do that," Björk said. "I wonder who that journalist was?"

They found out the next day. Placards for the *Express* were full of the sensational discovery of dead bodies on the Scanian coast. The front-page story revealed that the murdered men were almost certainly Soviet citizens, and that the foreign ministry had been brought in. The Ystad police had been ordered to hush up the whole affair, and the newspaper wanted to know why.

But it was 3 p.m. the following afternoon before Wallander saw the placards. By that time, a lot more water had flowed under the bridge.

CHAPTER 4

When Wallander arrived at the police station shortly after 8 a.m., everything seemed to happen at once.

The temperature had risen above freezing again, and the town was enveloped in a steady drizzle. Wallander had slept well, without experiencing a recurrence of the previous night's problems. He felt rested. The only thing that he was worried about was the mood his father might be in when they drove to Malmö later that day.

Martinsson met him in the corridor, and Wallander could see at once that he had something important to tell him. Everyone knew that when Martinsson was too restless to stay in his own office, something had happened.

"Captain Österdahl has solved the mystery of the life raft!" he bellowed. "Have you got a minute?"

"I've always got a minute," Wallander said. "Come into my office. See if Svedberg's here yet."

A few minutes later they were gathered in Wallander's room.

"People like Captain Österdahl ought to be put on a register, you know," Martinsson said. "The police should set up a department on a national basis whose only job is to work with people who have unusual expertise."

Wallander nodded. He'd often thought the same thing himself. There were people with comprehensive expertise in many esoteric fields dotted around the country. Everybody knew about the old lumberjack in Härjedalen who had identified the top to a bottle of Asian beer that had defeated not only the police, but also the experts at the Wine & Spirits monopoly. The lumberjack's evidence had helped to convict a murderer who would otherwise have gotten away with it.

"Give me somebody like Captain Österdahl any day, rather than these consultants who run around stating the obvious for huge fees," Martinsson continued. "And he was only too glad to help."

"And was he of help?"

Martinsson took his notebook out of his pocket and slammed it down on the desk. It was as if he'd pulled a rabbit out of an invisible hat. Wallander could feel himself getting irritated. Martinsson's dramatic gestures could be trying—but perhaps that was the way provincial Liberal Party politicians behaved.

"We're all agog," Wallander said, after a brief silence.

"When the rest of you had gone home last night, Captain Österdahl and I spent a few hours examining the life raft in the basement," Martinsson said. "It couldn't be earlier, as he plays bridge every afternoon, and he refused to break that habit. Captain Österdahl is an old gentleman with very firm views. I hope I'm like him when I get to that age."

"Get on with it," Wallander said. He knew all about opinionated old gentlemen—his father was constantly in the back of his mind.

"He crawled around the life raft like a dog," Martinsson went on. "He even smelled it. Finally he announced that it was at least 20 years old and had been made in Yugoslavia."

"How could he know that?"

"The way it was made—the mixture of materials. Once he'd considered all the evidence, he didn't hesitate for a second. All his reasons are here in this notebook. I really admire people who know what they're talking about."

"Why wasn't there a label stating that the boat was made in Yugoslavia?"

"Not boat," said Martinsson. "That was the first thing Captain Österdahl taught me. It's a raft, and nothing else. And he had an excellent explanation for why there was nothing to indicate its country of origin. They often send their life rafts to Greece and Italy, and firms there fit them with false labels. It's no more unusual than watches made in Asia having European trademarks."

"What else did he have to say?"

"Lots more. I think I now know the history of life rafts by heart. There were various types of life raft, even in prehistoric times. The earliest seem to have been made of reeds. This particular type is most commonly used on smaller East European or Russian freighters. You never find them on Scandinavian vessels. They're not approved by the shipping authorities."

"Why not?"

Martinsson shrugged.

"Poor quality. They can collapse. The rubber used is often sub-standard."

Wallander thought for a moment.

"If Captain Österdahl's analysis is correct, this is a raft that comes direct from Yugoslavia, without having been via Italy or wherever and given a manufacturer's label. So we're talking about a Yugoslavian vessel."

"Not necessarily," Martinsson said. "A certain proportion of these rafts go to Russia. I imagine it's part of the compulsory exchange of goods between Moscow and the dependent states. He said he'd seen an identical raft on a Russian fishing boat that was seized off Häradskär."

"But it's definite that we can concentrate on an East European ship, is it?"

"That's Captain Österdahl's opinion."

"Good," Wallander said. "At least we know that."

"But that's just about all we do know," Svedberg said.

"If the man who telephoned doesn't get in touch again, we won't know nearly enough," Wallander said. "All the same, it looks as if these men have drifted over here from the other side of the Baltic."

He was interrupted by a knock on the door. A clerk handed him an envelope containing the final details of the postmortem examination. Wallander asked Martinsson and Svedberg to stay while he glanced through the papers. He reacted almost at once.

"Now here's something," he said. "Mörth has found some interesting traces in their blood."

"AIDS?" Svedberg asked.

"No, drugs. Large doses of amphetamines."

"Russian junkies," Martinsson said. "The Russians tortured and murdered a couple of junkies. Wearing suits and ties. Adrift in a Yugoslav life raft. At least it's different. Makes a change from shifty bootleggers and minor assaults."

"We don't know that they are Russian," Wallander said. "The bottom line is we don't know anything at all."

He dialed Björk's number.

"Björk."

"Wallander here. I'm with Martinsson and Svedberg. We wonder if you've had any more instructions from the foreign ministry."

"Not yet. I expect they'll be in touch soon."

"I'm going to Malmö later this morning."

"Go. I'll let you know when the call comes. Have you been pestered by any journalists, by the way?"

"No, why?"

"I was woken up at 5 a.m. by the *Express*. The telephone hasn't stopped ringing since then. I have to admit I'm a bit worried."

"It's not worth getting upset about. They'll write whatever they want, no matter what happens."

"That's precisely why I'm worried. It will make a mess of the investigation if all kinds of rumors start appearing in the press."

"If we're lucky, that will encourage someone who has useful information or has seen something to get in touch with us."

"I very much doubt that. And I don't like being woken up at 5 a.m. Who knows what one might say when one's half asleep?"

Wallander hung up.

"Let's keep calm," he said. "Continue with your own investigation for the moment. There's something I have to sort out in Malmö. Let's meet again in my office after lunch."

Svedberg and Martinsson left. Wallander felt vaguely uneasy at having given them the impression that he was going to Malmö on work business. He knew that police officers, just like everyone else, spent some of their working time on private matters when they had the opportunity, but he still felt uncomfortable about it. I'm old-fashioned, he thought. Even though I'm just over 40.

He told reception that he was going out and could be contacted after lunch. Then he drove down out through Sandskogen and turned off towards Kåseberga. The drizzle had stopped, but a stiff wind was starting up.

He stopped in Kåseberga to fill up his gas tank. As he was early, he drove down to the harbor, where he parked the car and got out to brave the wind. There wasn't a soul in sight. The kiosk and smokehouses were all boarded up. We live in strange times, he thought. Parts of this country are open only in the summer. Whole villages hang up "closed" signs for most of the year.

He walked out to the stone jetty, in spite of the cold. There wasn't a ship in sight. His mind turned to the men in the life raft. Who were they? Why had they been tortured and murdered? Who had put their jackets back on?

He checked his watch, then returned to the car and drove straight out to his father's house, which looked as though it had been flung down in a field just south of Löderup. As usual, his father was painting out in the shed. Wallander was hit by the pungent smell of turpentine and oil paint. It was like returning to his childhood. One of Wallander's earliest memories was the remarkable smell that surrounded his father as he stood at his easel. Nothing had changed over the years. His father always painted the same picture, a melancholy sunset. Now and then, if whoever commissioned the painting wanted one, he would add a grouse in the foreground.

Wallander's father was a drawing-room artist. He'd honed his skill to such a level of perfection that he needed never to change his motif. It was only when he'd reached adulthood that Wallander realized that this had nothing to do with laziness or a lack of ability, but that this continuity gave his father the sense of security he needed in order to live his life.

The old man put down his brush and wiped his hands on a dirty rag. He was dressed as he always was, in overalls and cut-off gum boots.

"I'm ready," he said.

"Aren't you going to get changed?" Wallander asked.

His father looked at him in bewilderment.

"Why should I get changed? Do you have to wear a suit in order to go shopping nowadays?"

Wallander could see that there was no point arguing. His father's obstinacy was inexhaustible. And the old man might get angry, making the trip to Malmö intolerable.

"Do as you like," he shrugged.

"Yes," his father answered. "I'll do as I like."

They drove to Malmö. His father gazed out at the scenery.

"It's ugly," he said suddenly.

"What is?"

"Skåne is ugly in the winter. Gray mud, gray trees, gray sky. Grayest of all are the people."

"You might be right."

"Of course I'm right. No question. Skåne is ugly in the winter."

The art shop was in the center of town, and Wallander was lucky enough to find a parking space right outside. His father knew exactly what he wanted: canvases, paint, brushes, some palette knives. When it came to paying, he produced a crumpled wad of bills from one of his pockets. Wallander kept in the background and wasn't even allowed to help his father carry his purchases out to the car.

"That's that," his father said. "We can go home now."

It occurred to Wallander that they might stop somewhere and have a meal. To his astonishment, his father found that a splendid idea. They stopped at the Svedala motel and went into the cafeteria.

"Tell the head waiter we want a good table," his father told him.

"This is a self-service cafeteria," Wallander said. "I rather doubt if there's a head waiter here."

"In that case we'll go somewhere else," his father said abruptly. "If we're going to eat out, I want my meal served to me."

Wallander eyed his father's filthy overalls uneasily, but then remembered a rather seedy pizzeria in Skurup, and they drove there and ordered the lunch of the day, poached cod. Wallander watched the old man as they ate, and it occurred to him that he would probably never get to know his father before it was too late. In the past he'd thought of them as quite different people, but now he wasn't so sure. His wife, Mona, who'd left him the previous year, had often accused him of the same obstinacy, the same pedantic self-absorption. Perhaps I just don't want to recognize the similarities, he thought. Maybe I'm frightened of getting like him. Pig-headed, incapable of seeing anything he doesn't want to see.

At the same time he could see that being pig-headed was an advantage for a police officer. If he hadn't been what some outsiders would no doubt have categorized as overly stubborn, a great many cases that he'd been responsible for wouldn't have been solved. Obstinacy wasn't so much an occupational disease; rather it was an essential requirement.

"Have you been struck dumb?" His father interrupted his train of thought crossly.

"Sorry. I was thinking."

"I don't want to go out for a meal with you if you haven't got anything to say."

"What do you want me to say?"

"You can tell me how you're doing. How your daughter's doing. You can even tell me if you've found yourself a new woman."

"A new woman?"

"Are you still sulking about Mona?"

"No, I'm not sulking, but no, I haven't found a new woman, as you put it."

"Why not?"

"It's not all that easy."

"What do you do?"

"What do you mean?"

"Is that really such a difficult question? I'm simply asking how you go about finding yourself a new woman."

"I don't go dancing, if that's what you think."

"I don't think anything. I just wonder. You get odder and odder as the years go by."

"Odder?"

"You should have done like I said. You should never have gone in for the police."

So, we're back where we started are we? Wallander thought. *Plus ça change.* . . . The smell of turpentine. A freezing cold spring day in 1967. They were still living in the converted smithy outside Limhalm, but soon he would escape. He's been expecting the letter; he runs out to the mailbox as soon as he sees the mailman's van; tears open the envelope and reads what he's been waiting for. He has been accepted by the police academy and will enroll in the autumn. He races back, throws open the door to the cramped studio where his father is painting.

"I've been accepted by the police academy!" he cries. But his father doesn't congratulate him. He doesn't even put down his brush, just carries on painting. Wallander can still remember that he was busy tinting the clouds red from the setting sun, and how it dawned on him that he was a disappointment as a son. He was going to become a police officer.

The waiter came with their coffee.

"I've never understood why you didn't want me to become a police officer," Wallander said.

"You did what you wanted to do."

"That's no answer."

"I never thought a son of mine would sit down at the dinner table with maggots from dead bodies crawling out of his shirtsleeves."

Wallander was stunned by the reply. Maggots from dead bodies crawling out of his shirtsleeves?

"What do you mean?" he asked.

But his father didn't respond. He just drank up the last drop of the tepid coffee.

"I've finished," he said. "We can go now."

Wallander asked for the bill, and paid. I'll never get an answer, he thought. I'll never know why he was so against my joining the police.

They drove back to Löderup. The wind was kicking up. His father took the canvases and paints into his studio.

"When are we going to have a game of cards?" he asked.

"I'll come by in a few days," Wallander replied.

He drove back to Ystad. He couldn't make up his mind whether he was angry or shocked. Maggots from dead bodies crawling out of his shirtsleeves? What on earth did he mean?

It was 12:45 p.m. when he returned to his office. By then he had decided to demand a proper answer from his father the next time he saw him. He resolved to put the conversation out of his mind in the meantime, forcing himself to be a police officer again. The first thing he had to do was to contact Björk, but before he got around to dialling his number, the phone rang. He picked up the receiver.

"Wallander."

There was a scratching and scraping noise. He repeated his name.

"Are you the one who's dealing with that life raft?"

Wallander didn't recognize the voice. It was a man speaking quickly and under pressure.

"Who am I speaking to?"

"That's irrelevant. This is about that life raft."

Wallander reached for his notebook.

"Did you phone us the other day?"

"Phone you?" The man seemed genuinely surprised.

"It wasn't you who phoned and warned us that a life raft would be washed ashore somewhere not far from Ystad?"

There was a long silence. Wallander waited.

"Forget it," the man said, and hung up.

Wallander wrote down details of the conversation. He knew that he had made a mistake. The man had called because he wanted to talk about the bodies in the life raft, but when he heard there had already been a call, he was surprised, perhaps frightened, and decided to hang up. It was obviously not the same man Martinsson had spoken to. So there was more than one person with information. Martinsson was right: whoever had seen something must have been onboard a ship. They must have been crew, since nobody went out alone in a boat during the winter. But which ship? It could have been a ferry, or a fishing boat, or perhaps a freighter or one of the oil tankers that were forever traversing the Baltic.

Martinsson appeared in the doorway.

"Are you ready?" he asked.

Wallander decided not to mention the phone call just yet. He'd tell his colleagues when he'd had time to think the whole thing through.

"I haven't spoken to Björk," was all he said. "We can meet in half an hour."

Martinsson disappeared, and he rang Björk's number.

"Björk."

"Wallander. How's it going?"

"Come by and I'll fill you in."

Wallander was surprised by what Björk had to say.

"We're going to have a visitor," Björk told him. "The foreign ministry is going to send us someone who will assist us in our investigation."

"Someone from the foreign ministry? What will they know about a murder investigation?"

"I have no idea, but he'll be arriving this afternoon. I thought it would be good if you picked him up. His flight is due at Sturup at 5:20."

"For God's sake!" Wallander said. "Is he coming to help us, or to keep an eye on us?"

"I have no idea," Björk said again. "Besides, that's just the beginning. Guess who else has been in touch."

"The national police commissioner?"

Björk gave a start. "How did you know that?"

"My guesses are sometimes right. What does he want?"

"To be kept informed. And to send us a couple of officers, one from serious crime and one from narcotics."

"Do they need to be met at the airport too?"

"No. They can look after themselves."

Wallander thought for a moment.

"This seems odd," he said. "Not least the official from the foreign ministry. Why is he coming? Have they been in touch with the Soviet police? And the Eastern bloc?"

"Everything is according to the book, or so the foreign ministry people tell me—whatever that means." Björk flung out his arms. "I've been chief of police long enough to know how things are done in this country. Sometimes I'm the one who's kept in the dark. Other times it's the minister of justice. Mostly, though, it's the Swedish people who aren't told what's really going on."

Wallander was well aware of the many scandals involving justice in recent years, which had exposed the network of tunnels linking the basements of state organizations. Tunnels linking ministries and institutions. What had been thought to be mere suspicions, or accusations dismissed as the fantasies of the lunatic fringe, had now been confirmed. A large proportion of the real power was practiced in dimly lit secret corridors, far beyond the control regarded as essential in a state governed by the rule of law.

There was a knock on the door, and Björk shouted "Come in!" It was Svedberg, with an evening paper in his hand.

"I thought you might like to see this," he said.

Wallander gave a start when he saw the front page. Bold headlines announced the sensational discovery of bodies on the Scanian coast. Björk jumped up from his chair and grabbed the newspaper, and they all read it over each other's shoulders. To his surprise, Wallander recognized his own anxious face in a blurred photograph. It must have been taken at the time of the Lenarp murder, he thought quickly.

"The investigation is being led by criminal inspector Knut Wallman."

Björk flung the paper down. He had the red patch on his brow that foreshadowed a furious outburst. Svedberg sidled towards the door.

"It's all there," Björk snarled. "Just as if it had been written by you, Wallander, or you, Svedberg. The paper knows the foreign ministry is involved, and that the national police commissioner is keeping an eye on developments. They even say that the life raft was made in Yugoslavia, which is more than anyone has told me. Is this true?"

"It's true," Wallander said. "Martinsson told me this morning."

"This morning? For Christ's sake! When is this damned paper printed?"

Björk was pacing up and down. Wallander and Svedberg looked at each other. When Björk lost his temper he could go on and on forever.

Björk grabbed hold of the newspaper again and read aloud,

"'Soviet death patrols. The new Europe has exposed Sweden to crime with a political slant.' What do they mean by that? Can anybody explain? Wallander?"

"I have no idea. I figure the best policy is to take no notice of what they say in the press."

"How can anybody take no notice? We'll be besieged by the media after this."

As if he had just uttered a prophecy, the phone rang. It was a *Daily News* reporter asking for a comment. Björk put his hand over the receiver.

"We'd better call another press conference. Or shall we issue a statement? What's best? What do you think?"

"Both," Wallander answered. "But wait until tomorrow for the press conference. That man from the foreign ministry might have something to say."

Björk informed the journalist and hung up without answering any questions. Svedberg left the room while Björk and Wallander put together a short press release. When Wallander stood up to go, Björk asked him to stay.

"We'll have to do something about these leaks," he said. "I've obviously been far too naïve. I remember you complaining about it last year, when you were busy with that murder in Lenarp, but I dismissed it as an overreaction. What can I do about it now?"

"I wonder whether it's possible to do anything," Wallander said. "That's a lesson I learned last year. I think we're just going to have to put up with this sort of thing from now on."

"You know, it'll be a great relief to retire," Björk said after a moment's thought. "I sometimes get the feeling the world is leaving me behind."

"We all feel like that," Wallander said. "I'll go and get that man from the foreign ministry. What's his name?"

"Törn."

"First name?"

"Nobody mentioned one."

Wallander found Martinsson and Svedberg waiting for him in his office. Svedberg was describing Björk's outburst. Wallander decided to keep the meeting brief. He told them about the telephone call and his conclusion that more than one person had seen the life raft.

"Was he a local?" Martinsson asked.

Wallander nodded.

"We ought to be able to trace them in that case," Martinsson said. "We can eliminate oil tankers and freighters. What does that leave?"

"Fishing boats," Wallander said. "How many fishing boats are working off the south coast of Skåne?"

"A lot," Martinsson said. "Of course, it's February and quite a few will be docked in the harbor. Tracking them down will be a lot of work, but I think it can be done."

"We can decide on that tomorrow," Wallander said. "Things may have changed altogether by then."

He told them what he'd heard from Björk. Martinsson reacted more or less as he had, but Svedberg simply shrugged.

"We're not going to get any further today," Wallander said, wrapping up the meeting. "I have to write a report on what's happened so far. You'd better do the same. Then we can see what we make of the people from serious crime and narcotics tomorrow. Not to mention Mr. Törn from the foreign ministry."

Wallander was early to the airport. He had coffee with the immigration control officers, and listened to the usual complaints about working hours and wages. At 5:15 p.m. he took a seat on a bench outside the passenger lounge and stared halfheartedly at the ads on a television suspended from the ceiling. The Stockholm flight was announced, and Wallander realized that the man from the foreign ministry might be expecting to be met by a police officer in uniform. If I stand with my hands behind my back and sway backwards and forwards, he thought, perhaps that will do.

He studied the passengers streaming past: none of them seemed to be looking around for someone. When the stragglers had gone by and the stream eventually dried up altogether, he realized he had missed his man. What do foreign ministry officials look like? he wondered. Like ordinary people, or like diplomats? But then, what does a diplomat look like?

"Kurt Wallander?" said a voice behind him.

He spun around and his eyes fell on a youngish woman.

"Yes," he said, "I'm Kurt Wallander."

The woman removed her glove and held out her hand. "Birgitta Törn," she said. "Foreign ministry. Perhaps you were expecting a man?"

"I was, actually," he said.

"There are still not all that many female career diplomats," Birgitta Törn said, "but that doesn't prevent a large proportion of the Swedish foreign ministry from being in the hands of women."

"Well," Wallander said. "Welcome to Skåne."

As they waited at the baggage carousel, he watched her discreetly. She was not especially striking, but there was something about her eyes that caught his attention. When he picked up her suitcase and turned to look at her, he could see what it was. She wore contact lenses. Mona had worn them during the last few years of their marriage.

They went out to the car. Wallander asked about the weather

in Stockholm, and if she'd had a pleasant flight. She answered him, but he sensed that she was holding him at arm's length.

"I'm booked into a hotel called the Century," she told him as they drove to Ystad. "I'd like to go through all the investigation reports so far. I take it you've been advised that all the material should be placed at my disposal?"

"No," Wallander said. "Nobody's said anything about that, but since none of it is secret, you can have it. There's a folder on the backseat."

"Good thinking," she said.

"When all's said and done, I have only one question," Wallander said. "Why are you here?"

"The unstable situation in the East means that the foreign ministry is monitoring all abnormal incidents. In addition to this, we can help with the formal inquiries that may have to be made in countries that are not members of Interpol."

She talks like a politician, thought Wallander. There's no room for doubt in what she says.

"Abnormal incidents," he said. "That's one way of putting it. If you like I can show you the life raft at the police station."

"No, thank you," Törn said. "I don't want to interfere in police work, but it would be useful if we could arrange a meeting for tomorrow morning. I'd appreciate a briefing on where things stand."

"The best time would be 8 a.m.," said Wallander. "Maybe you don't know that we're being sent some extra men by the police commissioner? I assume they'll be here tomorrow."

"I had been informed," Törn answered.

The Century Hotel was in a street off the main square. Wallander parked outside and reached for the folder of reports. Then he took her suitcase out of the trunk.

"Have you been to Ystad before?" he asked.

"I don't think so."

"Then perhaps I could suggest that the Ystad police should invite you to dinner."

There was a faint trace of a smile as she answered.

"That's very kind of you," she said, "but I have a lot of work to do."

Wallander could feel himself getting annoyed. Perhaps a police officer in a small provincial town wasn't good enough company.

"The Continental Hotel would be the best place for a meal," he said. "Turn right from the square. Would you like me to pick you up tomorrow morning?"

"I'll find my own way," she said. "Thank you all the same. And thank you for meeting me."

Wallander drove home. It was 6:30 p.m. He felt thoroughly dissatisfied with every aspect of his life. It wasn't just the emptiness of coming home to an apartment with nobody to welcome him. There was also the feeling that it was getting more and more difficult to cope with his working environment. And now his body had started acting up. He used to be secure in his work as a detective, but not anymore. His insecurity had developed when he was struggling to solve the brutal double murder in Lenarp the year before. He and Rydberg had often discussed how Sweden, a country that was changing rapidly, becoming unfamiliar and uncertain, needed a new kind of police officer. He felt more inadequate as the days passed. It wasn't a kind of insecurity that any of the courses offered by the Swedish police board could help to cure.

He took a beer from the fridge, switched on the television and slumped down on the sofa. The screen was occupied by one of the endless streams of talk shows that seemed to be served up every day.

His mind wandered back to the job at the Trelleborg Rubber Company. Maybe that was the opportunity for change that he so needed? Maybe one should only be a police officer for a limited number of years, and then devote one's life to something entirely different?

He made no move to go to bed until nearly midnight.

He'd just turned off the light when the phone rang. Oh no, not tonight as well, he thought. Not another murder. He picked up the receiver, and immediately recognized the voice of the man who'd called earlier in the afternoon.

"Could be I know something about that life raft," the man said.

"We're interested in any information that might be of assistance to us."

"I can only tell you what I know if I have a guarantee that the police will never tell anybody that I phoned."

"You can be as anonymous as you like."

"That's not enough. I must have a guarantee that nothing will be said about this call."

Wallander thought for a moment, then gave the man his word. He still seemed hesitant. He's scared of something, Wallander thought.

"You have my word as a police officer."

"I don't put much faith in that."

"You should," Wallander said. "There's not a credit institution in the world that can come up with anything negative about me."

There was a pause, and Wallander could hear the man's breathing.

"Do you know where Industry Road is?" the man asked suddenly.

Wallander did know. It was on an industrial estate on the eastern edge of the town.

"Drive there now," the man said. "It's one-way, but that doesn't matter, there's no traffic at this time of night. Switch off your engine and turn off your lights."

"Where do you want me to stop? It's a long road."

"Just go there. I'll find you. And be alone. Otherwise, forget it."

He hung up.

Wallander felt worried. He knew he ought to phone Martinsson or Svedberg and ask for backup. But he forced himself to ignore his anxiety. What could happen, anyway?

He flung back the duvet and got up. The temperature had fallen below freezing, and he shuddered as he got into the car in the deserted street.

When he turned into Industry Road, which was lined with car showrooms and small business premises, there was no sign of any lights. He drove halfway down the road, then switched off his lights and engine and settled down in the darkness to wait. The fluorescent clock on his dashboard showed just past midnight.

At 12:30, nothing had happened. He made up his mind to go back home if nobody had appeared by 1 a.m.

He didn't notice the man until he was standing next to the car. He quickly rolled down the window. The man's face was in darkness, and Wallander couldn't make out his features. He did recognize the voice, though.

"Drive after me," the man said, and disappeared.

A few minutes later a car approached from the opposite direction and flashed its lights. Wallander followed, and they drove out of town to the east.

Suddenly, he realized he was scared.

CHAPTER 5

The harbor at Brantevik was deserted. Only a few, isolated lights were reflected in the dark, stagnant waters of the basin. Wallander wondered whether the lights had been broken, or if, as part of its cuts, the local government wasn't replacing burned-out bulbs. The future of our society gets gloomier and gloomier, he thought. A symbolic image is becoming more and more real.

The lights of the car ahead of him went out. Wallander switched off his own and sat there in the darkness. The clock on the dashboard marked off time in a series of electronic jerks—1:25 a.m. A flashlight suddenly illuminated the darkness, dancing around like a glowworm. Wallander opened his car door and clambered out, shivering as the cold night air struck him. The man with the flashlight stopped a few yards short of him. Wallander still couldn't make out his features.

"Let's go out onto the quay," the man said.

He spoke in a broad Scanian dialect. It was impossible to sound threatening with an accent like that, Wallander thought. He knew of no other dialect with so much gentleness built into it. Even so, he was hesitant.

"Why?" he asked. "Why do we have to go out onto the quay?"

"Are you scared?" the man said. "We're going out onto the quay because there's a boat moored there."

He turned around and set off, with Wallander following him. A gust of wind clawed at his face. They stopped beside the dark silhouette of a fishing boat. The smell of sea and oil was very strong. The man handed Wallander the flashlight.

"Aim it at the mooring ropes," he said.

Wallander caught sight of him for the first time. A man in his 40s, possibly slightly older. A weather-beaten face with the rough skin of somebody who leads an outdoor life. He was dressed in dark blue overalls and a gray jacket, with a black knitted cap pulled down over his eyes. The man took hold of a mooring rope and clambered onboard. He melted into the darkness in the direction of the wheelhouse, and Wallander waited. A gas lantern was lit, and the man returned over the creaking deck to the prow.

"Welcome aboard," he said.

Wallander fumbled for the frozen rail and heaved himself aboard. He followed the man across the sloping deck, stumbling over a coiled hawser.

"Don't fall in," the man said. "The water's cold."

Wallander followed him into the cramped wheelhouse and then down into the engine room. The place stank of diesel and lubricating oil. The man hung the lantern on a hook in the ceiling and turned down the light.

Wallander realized that the man was scared to death. He was all fingers and thumbs, and in a hurry. Wallander sat down on the uncomfortable bunk covered with a dirty blanket.

"You keep your promises, I trust," the man said.

"I always keep my promises," Wallander replied.

"Nobody does that," the man said. "I'm thinking about what will happen to me."

"What is your name?"

"That's irrelevant."

"But you did see the life raft with two dead bodies?"

"Could be."

"You wouldn't have phoned us otherwise."

The man reached for a grimy chart beside him on the bunk.

"Here," he said, pointing. "That's where I saw it. It was just before 2 p.m. when I noticed it, the twelfth. Last Tuesday, that is. I've been trying to guess where on earth it could have come from."

Wallander searched through his pockets for a pencil and something to write on, but of course he found nothing.

"Let's take it slowly," Wallander said. "Start at the beginning. Where were you when you noticed the raft?"

"I've written it down," the man answered. "Just over six nautical miles off Ystad, in a straight line to the south. The raft was drifting towards the northwest. I've written down the exact position."

He handed Wallander a crumpled scrap of paper. Wallander had the impression the location was exact, even though the figures meant nothing to him.

"The life raft was drifting," he said. "I wouldn't have noticed it if it had been snowing."

We'd never have noticed it, thought Wallander. Every time he says *I*, he hesitates almost imperceptibly, as if he had to keep reminding himself to tell only part of the truth.

"It was drifting to port," the man continued. "I towed it towards the Swedish coast and let it go when I could see land."

That explains the severed rope, Wallander thought. They were in a hurry and they were nervous. They didn't hesitate to sacrifice a bit of rope.

"Are you a fisherman?" he asked.

"Yes."

No, thought Wallander. You lied again, you're a bad liar, and I wonder what you're afraid of.

"I was coming home," the man said.

"You must have a radio onboard," Wallander said. "Why didn't you alert the coastguard?"

"I have my reasons."

Wallander could see that he would have to break down the man's fear or he would never get anywhere. Confidence, he thought. He must feel he really can trust me.

"I have to know more," Wallander said. "Obviously I'll be making use of whatever is said here in the investigation, but nobody will know it was you who said it."

"Nobody has said anything. Nobody has telephoned."

It dawned on Wallander that there was a perfectly simple explanation for the man's anxious determination to be anonymous. He'd realized before, during his conversation with Martinsson, that the man he was talking to had not been alone on the boat; but now he knew exactly how many crewmen there had been. Two. Not three, not more, just two. And it was this second man that he was afraid of.

"Nobody's telephoned," Wallander said. "Is it your boat?"

"What difference does that make?"

Wallander started all over again. He was certain now that the man had nothing to do with the men's death but had only been onboard the vessel that discovered the life raft and towed it towards the shore. That made things simpler, although he couldn't understand why the witness was quite so scared. Who was the other man?

Then it came to him. Smugglers. Trafficking in refugees or booze. This boat is being used for smuggling. That's why there's no smell of fish.

"Did you notice any other vessels nearby when you saw the life raft?"

"No."

"Are you absolutely sure?"

"I only say what I know."

"But you said you'd been guessing?"

The answer Wallander received was definite.

"The raft had been in the water for a long time. It couldn't have been cast off recently."

"Why not?"

"It had already started to collect algae."

Wallander couldn't remember seeing any algae when he'd inspected the raft himself.

"There was no sign of any algae when we found it."

The man thought for a moment.

"It must have been washed off when I towed it towards the shore. The raft was bobbing up and down in my wash."

"How long do you think it had been in the water?"

"Maybe a week. Hard to say."

Wallander sat watching the man. He was restless and seemed to be straining to hear any sound as they spoke.

"Is there anything else you want to tell me?" Wallander asked him. "Every little thing could be significant."

"I think the raft had drifted from one of the Baltic countries."

"Why do you think that? Why not Germany?"

"I know these waters. I think that raft had come from the Baltic states."

Wallander tried to picture a map of the region.

"That's a long way," he said. "Past the whole of the Polish coast, and right into German waters. I find that hard to believe."

"During the Second World War mines could drift a very long way in a short time. The winds we've had lately would make it quite possible."

The light from the lantern suddenly started to die down.

"I've got nothing more to say," the man said, folding up the chart. "You remember what you promised?"

"I know exactly what I promised. I have one more question, though. What are you frightened of? Why did we have to meet in the middle of the night?"

"I'm not frightened," the man said, as he put the chart away. "And if I was, that would be my business."

Wallander tried to think of any other questions he should ask before it was too late.

Neither of them noticed the slight movement of the boat. It was a gentle dip, so gentle it was no wonder that it passed unnoticed, like a faint swell that only just reached land.

Wallander climbed up from the engine room and shone his flashlight quickly over the walls of the wheelhouse. He couldn't see anything that would make it easy to identify the boat again later.

"Where can I get in touch with you if I need to?" he asked when they were back on the quay.

"You can't," the man said. "And in any case, you won't need to. There's nothing more I can tell you."

Wallander counted his paces as he walked along the quay. When he put his foot down for the 73rd time he felt the gravel of the harbor square. The man had been swallowed up by the shadows: he'd taken his flashlight and disappeared without another word. Wallander sat in his car without switching on the engine. For a moment he thought he saw a shadow moving in the darkness, but then decided he'd imagined it. It dawned on him that he was meant to drive away first. When he came out onto the main road he slowed down, but no headlights appeared in his rearview mirror.

It was 2:45 a.m. when he reached home. He sat at his kitchen table and noted down the details of the conversation he had had in the fishing boat. The Baltic states, he thought. Can the life raft really have drifted all that way? He went to the living room and found his tattered school atlas in a cupboard among piles of old magazines and opera programs. Southern Sweden and the Baltic Sea. The Baltic states seemed quite close and yet far away at the same time. I know nothing about the sea, he thought, about currents and winds. Perhaps the man was right? And why would he have told me something he knew was untrue? Once again, he thought of the man's fear, and the other crew member, the unknown man, of whom he was so afraid.

It was 4 a.m. by the time he went back to bed. He lay awake for a long time before he managed to fall asleep.

He awoke with a start. The clock on his bedside table said 7:46 a.m. He cursed, jumped out of bed and dressed. He stuffed his tooth-brush and toothpaste in his jacket pocket and parked outside the station just before 8 a.m. In reception, Ebba beckoned to him.

"Björk wants to see you," she said. "You're a sight! Did you over-sleep?"

"And how," Wallander said, darting into the bathroom to brush his teeth. At the same time he tried to gather his thoughts in preparation for the meeting. How on earth was he going to deal with his nocturnal excursion to a fishing boat in Brantevik harbor?

When he got to Björk's office, there was nobody there. He made his way to the largest of the station's conference rooms and knocked on the door, feeling like a schoolboy turning up late for classes.

There were six people sitting around the oval table, and they all stared at him.

"I'm a few minutes late, I'm afraid," he said, sitting down on the nearest empty chair. Björk was looking at him sternly, but

Martinsson and Svedberg grinned and looked as if they wondered where he'd been. He thought Svedberg might even be sneering at him. Birgitta Törn was on Björk's left, inscrutable as ever. Next to her were two other people who Wallander didn't know. He stood up and went to greet them. Both men were in their 50s, surprisingly alike, well-built and with friendly faces. The first one introduced himself as Sture Rönnlund, the other was Bertil Lovén.

"I'm from serious crime," Lovén said. "Sture's from narcotics."

"Kurt is our most experienced officer," Björk said. "Please help yourselves to coffee."

When everybody had fetched a cup, Björk started the meeting.

"Needless to say, we're grateful for all the help we can get," he began. "None of you can have failed to noticed the stir caused in the media by the discovery of these bodies. That is why we need to conduct this investigation with extra vigor and commitment. Birgitta Törn has joined us primarily as an observer and to be of assistance when it comes to making contacts with countries where Interpol has no influence, but that doesn't prevent us from taking advantage of her expertise."

Then it was Wallander's turn. Everybody had copies of the case documents, so he didn't bother to go into detail, but simply summarized what had happened. He spent some time on the results of the forensic examination. When he'd finished, Lovén asked for clarification on a few points. That was all. Björk looked around the room.

"Well," he said, "what next?"

Wallander could feel himself getting annoyed at the way Björk was deferring to the woman from the foreign ministry and the two Stockholm detectives. He couldn't resist firing a shot across their bows, and indicated to Björk that he wanted to speak.

"Too much of this is unclear," he said, "and I don't just mean the case itself. I don't understand why the foreign ministry has considered it necessary to send Birgitta Törn to Ystad. I can't believe the ministry simply wants to help us in establishing contacts with the Russian police. It seems to me that the foreign ministry has decided to keep an eye on our investigation, and if so, I'd like to know just what is going to be watched. And most of all, of course, why the ministry has reached such a decision. For obvious reasons, I can't help feeling that Stockholm knows something we don't. Or perhaps it isn't the foreign ministry that has reached this conclusion—maybe it's somebody else?"

There was a deathly silence when Wallander had finished. Björk was staring at him in horror.

Finally Birgitta Törn spoke.

"There's no reason to doubt the explanation we've given for our coming to Ystad," she said. "The unstable situation in Eastern Europe requires us to keep a very close eye on developments there."

"We don't even know for sure that the men are from an Eastern bloc country," Wallander said, interrupting her. "Or do you know something we don't? In that case, I'd like to know."

"I think perhaps we should calm down a bit," Björk said.

"I want an answer to my questions," Wallander said. "I'm not going to be fobbed off with nonsense about the unstable political situation."

The inscrutable mask was suddenly gone from Birgitta Törn's face. She glared at Wallander, her expression indicating an increasing contempt and a wish to keep him at bay. Hmm, I'm awkward, Wallander thought, one of those ever-so-troublesome peasants.

"The situation is as I've described it," Törn said. "If you had any sense, you would realize there was no need to go on like this."

Wallander shook his head and turned to Lovén and Rönnlund.

"What about your instructions?" he asked. "Stockholm doesn't usually send out people unless there's been a formal request for assistance, and we haven't made such a request, so far as I know. Or have we?"

Björk shook his head.

"Okay, so Stockholm has decided this on its own initiative. I'd like to know why, if we're going to be working together. I'm assuming the ability of our force to conduct its business efficiently hasn't been impugned before we've even started."

Lovén was shuffling uneasily, but it was Rönnlund who answered. Wallander detected a note of sympathy in his voice.

"The commissioner thought you might need a bit of help," he said. "Our job is to place ourselves at your disposal. That's all. You're in charge of the investigation, and if we can be of assistance, so much the better. Neither Bertil nor I have any doubts about your ability to conduct this case on your own, and for myself, I think you've acted speedily and decisively over the last few days."

Wallander nodded in appreciation. Martinsson was grinning, and Svedberg was picking thoughtfully at his teeth with a splinter he'd broken from the conference table.

"Well, perhaps we can consider where to go from here," Björk said.

"Indeed," Wallander said. "I have a few theories I'd like to test out on you, but first I'd like to tell you about a little adventure I had during the night."

He felt calm again. He'd pitted himself against Birgitta Törn and not been vanquished. He'd find out what she was really doing here soon enough. Rönnlund's support had made him feel better. He told them about his telephone call and his visit to the fishing boat in Brantevik. He stressed that the man had been certain the life raft could have drifted from as far as one of the Baltic states. Björk was inspired to take unexpected initiatives, and asked reception to arrange for charts of the whole area to be sent up immediately. Wallander imagined Ebba collaring the next officer that sauntered through reception, instructing him to produce the maps without delay. He poured himself another cup of coffee and started to explain his theories.

"The evidence points to the men having been murdered onboard a ship," he said. "You would expect the bodies to have been disposed of in the ocean, but I suspect that the killers wanted the bodies to be found. I find it difficult to explain why that should be so, not least because it must have been very uncertain where and when the life raft would wash ashore. Anyway, the men were shot at close range after being tortured. People are tortured as punishment, or to extract information. The next thing to bear in mind is that both men were under the influence of drugs, amphetamines, to be precise. Somehow or other, drugs are involved in this case. I have the distinct impression these men were not short of money—their clothes make that clear. By Eastern European standards they must have been pretty well off if they could afford to buy the shoes and clothes they were wearing. I'd never be able to afford their clothes."

Lovén burst out laughing at his final remark, but Birgitta Törn continued staring doggedly down at the table.

"We know quite a lot, even if we can't fit the bits of the jigsaw together to produce a picture that gives us the sequence of events and the reason the men were murdered. There's one thing we need to establish immediately: who were these men? That's what we must concentrate on. And we must also get a ballistics report without delay on the bullets that killed them. I want a check on all missing or wanted persons in Sweden and Denmark. Fingerprints,

photos and descriptions of the men must be sent immediately
to Interpol. Maybe we'll find something in our criminal records.
And we need to contact the police in the Soviet Union and the
Baltic states, assuming that hasn't happened already. Perhaps
Birgitta Törn can fill us in on this?"

"That will happen later today," she said. "We'll be contacting
the international division of the Moscow police."

"The police in Estonia, Latvia and Lithuania must be contacted
as well."

"That will happen via Moscow."

Wallander looked questioningly at her, then turned to Björk.
"Didn't we have a visit from the Lithuanian police last autumn?"

"What Birgitta Törn says is no doubt correct," Björk said. "The
Baltic states have their own national police forces, but it's still the
Soviet police that makes the formal decisions."

"I wonder," Wallander said. "Still, I dare say that the foreign
ministry knows more about this than I do."

"Yes," Törn said, "no doubt we do."

Björk brought the meeting to a close, and immediately disappeared with Birgitta Törn. A press conference had been arranged
for 2 p.m. Wallander stayed behind in the conference room and
went over the various tasks with the others. Svedberg fetched the
plastic bag containing the bullets, and Lovén undertook to make
sure that the ballistic examination happened quickly. The others
split the enormous job of going through the lists of missing and
wanted persons. Martinsson had contacts in the Copenhagen
police, and started to get in touch with them.

"You don't need to bother about the press conference,"
Wallander said. "That'll be a headache for Björk and myself."

"Are they as unpleasant here as they are in Stockholm?"
Rönnlund asked.

"I don't know what press conferences are like in Stockholm," Wallander told him, "but they're not exactly fun here."

The rest of the day was spent sending descriptions of the dead men to all police districts in Sweden and the Scandinavian countries, and working their way through various records and registers. It was soon clear that the men's fingerprints weren't in the Swedish or Danish records, but Interpol would take longer to give an answer. Wallander and Lovén weren't sure whether the East German police records had been incorporated into Interpol. Had their criminal records been transferred to a central database covering the whole of unified Germany? Come to that, had there actually been any normal criminal records in the German Democratic Republic? Had there been a distinction between the vast archives of the security services and criminal records? Lovén agreed to find the answers to these questions, while Wallander prepared himself for the press conference.

When he and Björk met before the briefing was due to begin, Wallander noticed that his boss was very quiet. Why doesn't he say anything, he wondered. Did he think I was rude to that elegant lady from the foreign ministry?

A large number of journalists and television reporters gathered in the room where the press conference was going to take place. Wallander looked for the young reporter from the *Express*, but couldn't see him.

Björk started proceedings, as usual, launching an unexpected attack on the "incomprehensibly irresponsible" reports published by the press. Wallander's thoughts wandered to his nighttime meeting with the frightened man at Brantevik harbor. When it was his turn to speak, he began by repeating his appeal for the public to contact the police if they had any information that might be relevant. A reporter asked if there had been any response so far, and

74 HENNING MANKELL

Wallander said there had not. The press conference was surprisingly low key, and Björk expressed his satisfaction as they left the room.

"What's the lady from the foreign ministry doing?" Wallander asked as they walked down the corridor.

"She's on the phone nearly all the time," Björk said. "No doubt you think we ought to bug her calls."

"It wouldn't be a bad idea," Wallander muttered.

The day passed without significant developments. It was a question of being patient, of seeing whether any fish would swim into the nets they'd put out.

Shortly before 6 p.m. Martinsson popped his head in Wallander's office and asked if he'd like to come to dinner at his place that evening. He'd already invited Lovén and Rönnlund, who seemed to be feeling homesick.

"Svedberg's busy," he said. "Birgitta Törn told me she was going to Malmö tonight. What about you?"

"Sorry, I can't," Wallander said. "I've got an appointment, I'm afraid."

It was partly true. He hadn't absolutely made up his mind whether to drive again to Brantevik and take a closer look at the fishing boat.

At 6:30 p.m. he phoned his father as usual, and was instructed to buy a new pack of cards and bring it with him the next time he came. As soon as he'd hung up, he left the station. The wind had dropped, and the sky was clear. He stopped on the way home to buy some food. By 8:30 p.m., when he'd finished eating and was waiting for the coffee to brew, he still hadn't made up his mind. No doubt it could wait until tomorrow. Besides, he was exhausted from the previous night's exertions.

He sat for a long time at his kitchen table over his coffee, trying to imagine Rydberg opposite him, discussing the day's events. He went through what had happened step by step with his invisible visitor. It was three days since the life raft had beached at Mossby Strand. They weren't going to get any further until they established who the dead men were, but even if they did that, the riddle might remain unsolved.

He put his cup in the sink. He noticed a drooping plant on his windowsill, and watered it before going to the living room and choosing a Maria Callas recording of *La Traviata*. He had made up his mind to postpone the visit to the fishing boat.

Later that evening he tried to call his daughter at her college near Stockholm, but nobody answered. At 10:30 p.m. he went to bed and fell asleep almost at once.

The following day, the fourth day of the investigation, just before 2 p.m., what everybody had been expecting finally came to pass. Birgitta Törn went to Wallander's office with a telex. The police in Riga had informed the Swedish foreign ministry, via their superiors in Moscow, that it was likely that the men were Latvian citizens. In order to facilitate further investigations, Major Litvinov of the Moscow police suggested that his Swedish colleagues might like to establish direct contact with the serious crimes unit in Riga.

"So, they do exist after all," Wallander said. "The Latvian police, I mean."

"Who said they didn't?" she answered. "If you'd gotten in touch with Riga directly, though, there could have been diplomatic repercussions. I'm not sure we'd have received a response at all. I take it you are aware that the situation in Latvia is rather tense."

Wallander knew that. It was barely a month since the Soviet elite troops had attacked the ministry of the interior in central Riga and killed many innocent people. Wallander had seen newspaper pictures of barricades made of stone blocks and iron poles. All the same, he wasn't quite clear what was going on. As usual, he felt he didn't know enough about what was happening around him.

"What do we do now, then?" he asked tentatively.

"We establish contact with the police in Riga. The main thing is to make sure we really are dealing with the people indicated in the telex."

Wallander read the message again. The man in the fishing boat had been right: the life raft had indeed drifted the whole way from the Baltic coast.

"We still don't know who they were," he said.

But he did know three hours later. A call from Riga had been announced, and the investigation team gathered in the conference room. Björk was so on edge that he spilled coffee down his jacket.

"Is there anybody here who speaks Latvian?" Wallander asked. "I don't."

"The call will be in English," Birgitta Törn said. "We asked for this."

"You take it," Björk said to Wallander.

"My English isn't all that good."

"No doubt his won't be either," Rönnlund said. "What was his name? Major Litvinov? It'll even itself out, I figure."

"Major Litvinov is stationed in Moscow," Birgitta Törn pointed out. "We'll be talking to the police in Riga, in Latvia."

The call came at 5:19 p.m. The line was surprisingly clear. A man introduced himself as Major Liepa from the Riga police. Wallander made notes as he listened, occasionally answering a question. Major Liepa spoke very bad English, and Wallander was not at all confident that he understood everything he said. Nevertheless, when the call was over he felt he had the most important information jotted down in his notebook.

Two names, two identities: Janis Leja and Juris Kalns.

"Riga had their fingerprints," Wallander said. "According to Major Liepa there was no doubt that the bodies we found are these two."

"Excellent," Björk said. "What sort of men were they?"

Wallander read from his notes.

"Notorious criminals," he said.

"Did he have any idea why they might have been murdered?" Björk asked.

"No, but he didn't seem particularly surprised. If I understood him, he said that he'll be sending over some documentation. He also wondered if we were interested in inviting over any Latvian police officers to assist with the investigation."

"That would be an excellent idea," Björk said. "The quicker we can get this case out of the way, the better."

"The foreign ministry will support any such move, of course," Birgitta Törn said.

So it was agreed. The next day Major Liepa sent a telex announcing that he personally would be flying to Arlanda the following afternoon, and would get the first connection to Sturup.

"A major," Wallander said. "What does that mean?"

"I've no idea," Martinsson said. "I generally feel like a corporal in this business myself."

Birgitta Törn went back to Stockholm. Now that she was gone, Wallander had difficulty recalling the sound of her voice, or even what she looked like. That's the last I'll see of her, he thought, and I don't suppose I'll ever discover why she came here in the first place.

*

Björk had taken it upon himself to meet the Latvian major at the airport, which meant that Wallander could spend the evening playing canasta with his father. As he drove out to Löderup, he thought to himself that the case would soon be solved. The Latvian police would presumably supply a plausible motive, and then the whole investigation could be transferred to Riga. That was no doubt where the murderer would be found. The life raft had been washed up on the Swedish coast, but the origins of it all, of the murders, were on the other side of the sea. The bodies of the dead men would be sent back to Latvia and there the case would be resolved.

In this judgment, Wallander was completely wrong. The case had scarcely begun. What had begun in Skåne, and in earnest, was winter.

CHAPTER 6

Wallander had expected Major Liepa to be in uniform when he arrived at the police station in Ystad, but the man Björk introduced him to on the sixth day of the investigation was wearing a baggy gray suit and a badly knotted tie. Moreover, he was short, with hunched shoulders that seemed to suggest he had no neck at all, and Wallander could see no trace of any military bearing. Major Liepa's first name was Karlis, and he was a chain-smoker: his fingers were yellow with nicotine stains from his extra-strong cigarettes.

The morning was gray and windy. A snowstorm was expected over Skåne towards evening, and since a particularly nasty flu virus had gained a foothold among the police, Björk felt he had to release Svedberg from the case for the time being: there was an urgent list of other crimes awaiting immediate attention. Lovén and Rönnlund had gone back to Stockholm, and as Björk was not feeling too well, he left Martinsson and Wallander to get on with the investigation with Major Liepa. They were sitting around the conference room, and Major Liepa was chain-smoking.

The major's smoking habits presented a serious problem at the station. Anti-smoking agitators protested to Björk that Liepa smoked all the time, particularly in smoke-free areas of the station. Björk urged his colleagues to display a degree of tolerance that guests had a right to expect, but he also asked Wallander to find a tactful way of explaining that the smoking ban must be observed.

When Wallander summoned up his shaky English and explained how important it was for Swedish rules regarding smoking to be observed, Liepa shrugged and stubbed out his cigarette without further ado. From then on he made an effort to avoid smoking anywhere other than in Wallander's office and the conference room, but even Wallander was finding it hard to put up with the smoke, and he asked Björk that Major Liepa be given an office of his own. In the end, Svedberg moved in with Martinsson, and Liepa was installed in Svedberg's office.

Major Liepa was very near-sighted. His rimless spectacles seemed to be much too weak, and when he was reading he held documents only a couple of inches in front of his eyes. He seemed to sniff the paper, rather than scrutinizing it, and anyone watching found it hard not to laugh out loud. Wallander occasionally heard officers making disparaging remarks about the little hunchbacked Latvian major, but he felt no hesitation in discouraging such condescending behavior. He had found Liepa an extremely shrewd and perceptive police officer—not unlike Rydberg, not least in being passionate in his enthusiasm. Criminal cases might nearly always be subject to standard procedures, but Wallander knew that was no reason to let one's thoughts get into a rut. Major Liepa was an inspired detective, and his colorless appearance camouflaged a clever man and an experienced investigator.

The previous evening Wallander had played canasta with his father, and then set his alarm clock for 5 a.m. so he would have time to read a brochure about Latvia that a local bookseller had found for him. It had occurred to him that it would be a good idea to begin by informing each other as to how the police forces in their respective countries actually worked. The fact that the Latvian police used military ranks indicated big differences between the two forces. Over his morning coffee Wallander had tried to formulate some general principles in English concerning the working methods of the Swedish police, but it struck him that he didn't really know how the Swedish police force worked. Things weren't made any easier by the fact that the national police commissioner had recently introduced wide-ranging reforms, and Wallander seemed to be endlessly reading badly written memos describing the changes. When he asked Björk what these changes really meant, he had been given vague, evasive replies. Now, sitting opposite the chain-smoking major, he decided he might as well forget all such matters—if any misunderstanding arose they would sort it out.

When Björk had excused himself, coughing away heartily, Wallander decided that it was time to break the ice. He asked Major Liepa where he was staying in Ystad.

"In a hotel," Liepa replied. "I don't know what it's called."

Wallander was disconcerted. Liepa seemed to have no interest in anything other than the case in hand.

Better leave the polite chitchat until later, he thought. All we have in common is an investigation into a double murder, nothing else.

Major Liepa embarked on a long and detailed account of how the Latvian police had been able to establish the identity of the two dead men. His English was not good, and this obviously irritated him. During one of their breaks, Wallander called his bookseller friend and asked whether he had an English-Latvian dictionary in stock, but he didn't. They were going to have to undertake a difficult journey together with very little of a common language.

After more than nine hours of intensive reading of reports—Martinsson and Wallander staring at their copies of an incomprehensible, stencilled document in Latvian while Major Liepa translated, pausing all the while to try to find the right word before continuing—Wallander thought he had more or less grasped what had happened. Despite their comparative youth, Leja and Kalns had made a name for themselves as a pair of volatile and predatory criminals. Wallander noted the contempt with which Major Liepa described them as members of the Russian minority in his country. He had known that the large group of ethnic Russians that had lived in Latvia since Russia annexed the Baltic states at the end of the Second World War were opposed to the campaign for national liberation, but he hadn't been aware of the extent of the problem. He simply didn't have the political insight, he told himself. Major Liepa made no attempt to conceal his disgust at this situation, making it plain on several occasions.

"These Russians were bandits," he said, "members of our eastern Mafia."

Leja was 28 and Kalns barely 30, but they each had substantial criminal records: robbery, assault, smuggling and illegal currency transactions. The Riga police suspected that at least three murders could be attributed to the pair, but it had not been possible to bring charges.

When Major Liepa finished translating the reports and extracts from criminal records, Wallander asked a question that seemed to him crucial.

"These men have committed many big crimes," he said. (Martinsson interjected, suggesting that a better word in English might be "serious.") "What appears odd is the fact that they have only been in prison for very short periods. I mean, they were convicted criminals and had been sentenced."

Major Liepa's face broke into a broad smile, and he seemed keen to respond. That was a question he was hoping for, Wallander thought. It was worth more than all the polite exchanges he could have mustered.

"I have to explain the situation in my country," Major Liepa said, lighting another cigarette. "No more than 15 percent of the population of Latvia are Russians, but even so, Russians have controlled our country in every way since the end of the war. The sending in of Russian nationals is one way used by Moscow to suppress us—it might be the most effective method used. You ask me why Leja and Kalns have spent so little time in prison when they should really have been there for life, even executed. Well, I do not say that all public prosecutors and judges are corrupt: that would be an oversimplification, it would be a controversial and unethical claim. What I say is that Leja and Kalns had powerful protectors behind them."

"The Russian Mafia," Wallander said.

"Yes and no. The Mafia in our country also needs subtle protectors. I'm convinced that Leja and Kalns spent a lot of their time serving the KGB. The secret police never likes to see its own men in prison, unless they are traitors or defectors. The shadow of Stalin has always hovered over the heads of people like that."

The same is true of Sweden, was Wallander's immediate reaction. We might not be able to refer to such a monster in our recent history, but a complicated network of interdependent individuals is not the exclusive preserve of a totalitarian state.

"The KGB," Major Liepa said. "And the Mafia. They're linked. Everything is connected by links only the initiated can see."

"The Mafia," Martinsson interrupted, who so far had remained silent, apart from helping Wallander with his English. "That's something new for us in Sweden, the concept of well-organized Russian or East European crime syndicates. A few years ago the Swedish police became aware of gangs of Russian origin, in Stockholm especially: we still know very little about them. There have been isolated incidents of brutality warning us that something of this kind was appearing in Sweden, and we are aware that over the next few years this type of criminal will seek to infiltrate our own underworld, and establish themselves in key positions."

Wallander was jealous of the fluent way that Martinsson could express himself in English. His pronunciation might be awful, but his vocabulary was much richer than Wallander's. Why didn't the national police board provide courses in English, instead of all those silly jamborees about staff development and internal democracy?

"I'm sure you're right," Major Liepa said. "As the Communist states start to disintegrate, they behave like shipwrecked sailing boats: the criminals are the rats, the first to leave the sinking ship. They have contacts; they have money; they also have access to advice. A lot of the refugees from the Eastern bloc are nothing but criminals. Not fleeing oppression, but seeking new territory. It's easy for them to forge a new past and identity."

"Major Liepa," Wallander said. "You say that this is what you believe the situation to be. You do not know for certain?"

"I'm certain," replied Major Liepa, "but I can't prove it. Not yet."

Wallander realized that in Major Liepa's words were references and significance he couldn't recognize or understand. In Major Liepa's country, criminal activities were linked with a political elite that had the authority to overrule and directly influence the sentencing of criminals. The two dead men had criminal backgrounds. Who would want them dead? And why?

It occurred to Wallander that as far as Major Liepa was concerned every criminal investigation involved his search for proof of a political implication: maybe that's how we should approach things in Sweden, he thought. Maybe we have to accept that we just aren't digging deeply enough into the criminal activity all around us.

"The men," Martinsson asked. "Who killed them?"

"I don't know," Major Liepa replied. "They were executed, of course—but why tortured? What did the killers want to know before they silenced Leja and Kalns? Did they find out what they wanted to know? I also have many unanswered questions."

"We're hardly going to find the answers here in Sweden," Wallander said.

"I know," Major Liepa said. "The solution might possibly be found in Latvia."

Wallander pricked up his ears. Why had he said "possibly"?

"If we can't find the answer in Latvia, where can we find it?" he asked.

"Further away."

"Further to the east?" suggested Martinsson.

"Or possibly further south," Major Liepa said hesitantly, and both Martinsson and Wallander recognized that he didn't want to reveal what he was thinking for the moment.

They decided they had done all they could for the day. Thanks to all the sitting down and the laborious discussions they'd had with the major, Wallander could feel the repercussions of an old lumbago attack. Martinsson promised to help Major Liepa change some currency at the bank, and Wallander suggested that he also get in touch with Lovén in Stockholm, to find out the latest on the ballistic investigation. Wallander's own task was to write a report on what had happened at the meeting. The prosecutor, Anette Brolin, had let it be known that she would appreciate an update as soon as possible.

La Brolin, thought Wallander as he left the smoke-filled conference room and set off down the corridor. This is a case you're not going to be able to take to court. We'll off-load it to Riga as soon as we can, together with two corpses and a red life raft. Then we can put the rubber stamp on our own investigation, and maintain that we've done all we can and have "no reason to initiate further investigation."

Wallander wrote his report after lunch, while Martinsson looked after Major Liepa, who had expressed a desire to buy some clothes for his wife. Wallander had just phoned the prosecutor's office and had been told that Anette Brolin was free and would see him, when Martinsson strode into his office.

"What have you done with the major?" Wallander asked.

"He's in his room, smoking," Martinsson said. "He's already dropped ashes all over Svedberg's fancy carpet."

"Has he had anything to eat?"

"I treated him to the lunch of the day at the Hornblower. Dumplings. I don't think he liked them—he spent most of the time smoking and drinking coffee."

"Did you reach Lovén?"

"He's out with the flu."

"Have you talked to anybody else?"

"It's impossible to reach anybody by phone, nobody's in. Nobody knows when they're coming back. Someone promises that they'll call back, but no one ever does."

"Maybe Rönnlund could give you a hand?"

"I tried him as well, but he was out on business. Nobody knew what business, where he was, or when he was coming back."

"Better try again. I have to see the prosecutor about this report. I'm assuming we can hand the case over to Major Liepa rather soon—the bodies, the life raft and the documentation. He's welcome to take the whole mess back to Riga with him."

"That's what I came to talk to you about."

"What is?"

"The life raft."

"What about it?"

"Major Liepa wanted to examine it."

"Well, all he had to do was to go down to the basement."

"It's not quite as simple as that."

Wallander could feel himself getting annoyed. Martinsson sometimes took forever to get to the point.

"What's so difficult about walking down the stairs to the basement?"

"The raft's not there."

Wallander stared at Martinsson in astonishment. "What do you mean 'not there'?"

"Not there."

"What on earth do you mean? It's on a couple of trestles, where you and Captain Österdahl examined it. By the way, we ought to write to him and thank him for his help—good that you reminded me of that."

"The trestles are still there," said Martinsson, "but the life raft isn't."

Wallander put his papers down on his desk and hurried down into the basement, closely followed by Martinsson. He was right. The two wooden trestles had been overturned and were lying there on the concrete floor, and the life raft was nowhere to be seen.

"What the hell's going on?" Wallander shouted.

Martinsson was hesitant, as if he didn't really believe what he was saying.

"There's been a break-in. Hansson was down here last night, and the life raft was here then. This morning one of the traffic police noticed that the door had been forced, so it must have been stolen during the night."

"That's impossible," Wallander said. "How can the police station have been burgled? There are people here around the clock, for God's sake. Is anything else missing? Why hasn't anybody said anything about this?"

"A patrol officer reported it to Hansson, but he forgot to tell you. There was nothing here apart from the raft, and all the other doors were locked. None of them has been forced. Whoever did this was after the life raft, and nothing else."

Wallander stared at the overturned trestles. Somewhere deep down he could feel a worry starting to gnaw away at him.

"Martinsson," he said slowly, "can you remember off the top of your head whether any of the newspapers reported that the life raft was in the basement at the police station?"

"Yes," he said. "I remember reading that. I also seem to remember there was a photographer down here. But who would take the risk of breaking into a police station to get their hands on a life raft?"

"You've hit the nail on the head," Wallander said. "Who would take a risk like that?"

"I'm lost," Martinsson said.

"Maybe Major Liepa will have the answer," Wallander said. "Bring him here. Then we'll have a thorough search. And tell somebody to get ahold of the patrol officer. Who was it?"

"I think it was Peters. He's probably at home now, in bed. If it snows tomorrow night, he's going to have a hard shift."

"We'll have to wake him," Wallander said. "We have no alternative."

When Martinsson left, Wallander inspected the door. It was a thick steel door with a double lock, but the burglars had gotten in without doing any visible damage to the door itself. Obviously the lock had been picked. These people knew what they were doing,

Wallander thought. They knew how to pick a lock at any rate. He took another look at the overturned trestles. He'd inspected the life raft himself, and had been absolutely certain he hadn't missed anything. Martinsson and Österdahl had also examined the raft, and so had Rönnlund and Lovén.

What didn't we notice? There has to be something, he thought.

Martinsson reappeared with the major, cigarette in hand. Wallander switched on all the lights, and Martinsson explained to the major what had happened. Wallander was watching him. As he'd expected, Liepa showed no surprise. He only nodded slowly, then turned to Wallander.

"You had examined the life raft," he said. "A retired captain had specified that it had been made in Yugoslavia, I think. That's no doubt correct—there are many Yugoslavian life rafts on Latvian vessels, including police boats. But you had examined the raft, I believe?"

"Yes," Wallander answered. And then he realized the fatal error he'd made. Nobody had let the air out of the rubber boat, nobody had looked inside it. It had not occurred to him to do so. Major Liepa seemed to have understood already, and Wallander felt embarrassed. How could he have failed to open the raft up? He would have thought of it sooner or later, of course, but he ought to have done it immediately. It would be a waste of time to explain to Major Liepa what he'd already worked out for himself.

"What could have been inside?" he asked.

Major Liepa shrugged.

"Drugs, I suppose," he said.

Wallander thought for a moment.

"That doesn't follow. Two corpses are dumped in a life raft filled with drugs? Then left to drift wherever the wind takes it?"

"That's right," said Major Liepa. "Perhaps a mistake had been made. The person who collected the life raft was given the task of putting it right."

They made a minute inspection of the whole basement. Wallander hurried up to reception and asked Ebba to devise a plausible emergency that had prevented him from presenting his report to Anette Brolin. The news that the police station had been burgled spread like wildfire, and Björk came storming down the stairs.

"If this gets out," he said, "we'll be the laughing stock of the whole country."

"This won't be leaked," Wallander said. "It's too painful."

Wallander told Björk what he guessed had happened, realizing that Björk would have serious reservations as to whether he was competent to run a serious crime investigation. It had been an inexcusable lapse.

Have I grown complacent? he wondered. Am I even up to being a security officer at the Trelleborg Rubber Company? Maybe the best thing would be for me to go back on the beat again in Malmö?

They found not a single clue. No fingerprints, no footprints on the dusty floor. The gravel outside the forced door had been churned up by police cars, and there was nothing to indicate that any of the tire tracks weren't from the police's own cars. Eventually they agreed that there was nothing more they could do, and they went back to the conference room. Peters had turned up, sullen and angry at having been called in. All he could contribute was the exact time that he had discovered the break-in. Wallander had also checked with the night duty staff, but nobody had seen or heard anything. Nothing. Nothing at all. Wallander suddenly felt very tired. He had a headache from Major Liepa's cigarettes. What should I do now? he wondered. What would Rydberg have done?

*

Two days later the missing life raft was still a mystery. Major Liepa had advised that trying to track it down would waste resources. Wallander had to agree, however reluctantly, but he couldn't shake off the sense of having made an unforgivable mistake. He was despondent, and woke every morning with a headache.

Skåne was in the grip of a fierce snowstorm. The police were warning people via the radio to stay at home and venture out onto the roads only if it was absolutely essential. Wallander's father was snowed in, but when he phoned, his father told him he hadn't even noticed that the road was deep in snow drifts. The chaos caused by the blizzard meant that more or less no progress was made with the case. Major Liepa had shut himself in Svedberg's office and was studying the ballistics report. Wallander had a long meeting with Anette Brolin. Every time he met her he was stung by the memory of the crush he had on her the year before, but the memory seemed unreal, as if he'd imagined it all. Brolin contacted the director of public prosecutions, and the legal section of the foreign ministry, to get approval to close the case in Sweden and hand it over to the police in Riga. Major Liepa had also arranged for his headquarters to make a formal request to the foreign ministry.

On an evening when the blizzard was at its height, Wallander invited Major Liepa to his apartment. He'd bought a bottle of whisky, which they emptied during the course of the evening. Wallander started feeling drunk after a couple of glasses, but Major Liepa appeared completely unaffected. Wallander had started addressing him simply as "major," and he didn't seem to object. It wasn't easy to hold a conversation with the Latvian police officer. Wallander couldn't decide whether this was due to shyness, if his poor English embarrassed him, or if he might have a touch of aristocratic reserve. Wallander told him about his family, chiefly Linda and the college she was at in Stockholm. For his part, Major Liepa said simply that he was married to a woman named Baiba, but that they had no children. As the evening wore on, they sat for long intervals holding their glasses, saying nothing.

"Sweden and Latvia," Wallander said, "are there any similarities? Or is everything different? I try to picture Latvia, but I just can't. And yet we're neighbors."

The moment he'd uttered the question, Wallander realized it was pointless. Sweden was not a country governed as a colony by a foreign power. There were no barricades in the streets of Sweden. Innocent people were not shot or run over by military vehicles. Surely everything was different?

The major's reply was surprising.

"I'm a religious man," he said. "I don't believe in a particular God, but even so one can have a faith, something beyond the limits of rationality. Marxism has a large element of built-in faith, although it claims to be a science and not merely an ideology. This is my first visit to the West: until now I have only been able to go to the Soviet Union or Poland or the Baltic states. In your country I see an abundance of material things. It seems to be unlimited. But there's a difference between our countries that is also a similarity. Both are poor. You see, poverty has different faces. We lack the abundance that you have, and we don't have the freedom of choice. In your country I detect a kind of poverty, which is that you do not need to fight for your survival. For me the struggle has a religious dimension, and I would not want to exchange that for your abundance."

Wallander knew the major had prepared this speech in advance: he hadn't paused to search for words. But what exactly had he said? Swedish poverty? Wallander felt he must protest.

"You're wrong, major," he said. "There's a struggle going on in this country too. A lot of people here are excluded—was that the right word?—from the abundance you describe. Nobody starves to death, it is true, but you are wrong if you think we don't have to fight."

"One can only fight for survival," the major said. "I include the fight for freedom and independence. Whatever a person does beyond that is something they choose to do, not something they have to do."

Silence followed. Wallander would have liked to ask so many questions, not least about recent events in Riga, but he didn't want to reveal his ignorance. Instead, he got up and put on a Maria Callas record.

"*Turandot*," the major said. "Very beautiful."

The snow and wind raged outside as Wallander watched the major striding away towards his hotel soon after midnight. He was hunched into the wind, wearing his cumbersome overcoat.

The snowstorm had blown itself out by the following morning, and blocked roads could be reopened.

When Wallander woke up, he had a hangover, but he'd made a decision. While they were awaiting the decision from the director of public prosecutions, he would take Major Liepa with him to Brantevik to see the fishing boat he'd visited one night the week before.

Just after 9 a.m. they were in Wallander's car, heading east. The snow-covered landscape glittered in the bright sunshine: it was −3°C.

The harbor was deserted. Several fishing boats were moored at the jetty furthest out, but Wallander couldn't immediately tell which one he'd been on. They walked out along the jetty, Wallander counting 73 steps.

The boat was called *Byron*. It was timber-built, painted white, and about 40 feet long. Wallander grasped the thick mooring rope and closed his eyes: did he recognize it? He couldn't say. They clambered aboard. A dark red tarpaulin was lashed over the hold. As they approached the wheelhouse, which was secured by a large padlock, Wallander tripped over a coiled hawser and knew he was on the right boat. The major pulled loose a corner of the tarpaulin and shone a flashlight into the hold: it was empty.

"No smell of fish," Wallander said. "No sign of any fish scales, no nets. This boat is used for smuggling. But what are they smuggling? And where to?"

"Everything," said the major. "There has been an acute shortage of everything in the Baltic states up until now, and so smugglers can bring us anything at all."

"I'll find out who owns the boat," Wallander said. "Even if I've made a promise, I can still find out who owns it. Would you have made the promise I did, major?"

"No," Major Liepa replied. "I'd never have done that."

There wasn't much more to see. When they got back to Ystad Wallander spent the afternoon trying to establish who owned the *Byron*. It wasn't easy. It had changed owners numerous times in the last few years, and one of the many owners had been a trading company in Simrishamn with the imaginative name *Wankers' Fish*. Next the boat had been sold to a fisherman by the name of Öhrström, who had sold it after only a few months. Wallander eventually managed to establish that a Sten Holmgren, who lived in Ystad, now owned the boat. Wallander was surprised to find that they actually lived on the same street, Mariagatan. He looked up Sten Holmgren in the phone book, but didn't find him. There were no records of a company owned by Sten Holmgren at the county offices in Malmö. To be on the safe side Wallander also checked the county offices in Kristianstad and Karlskrona, but there was no trace of a Sten Holmgren there either.

Wallander flung down his pencil and went for a cup of coffee. The phone started ringing as he returned to his office. It was Anette Brolin.

"Guess what I have to tell you," she said.

"That you're dissatisfied with one of our investigations again?"

"Of course I am, but that's not what I was going to say."

"Then I've no idea."

"The case is to be closed, and the whole matter will be transferred to Riga."

"Is that definite?"

"The director of public prosecutions and the foreign ministry are in complete agreement. They both say the case should be abandoned. I've just heard. The formalities seem to have been sorted out in double time. Your major can go home now, and take the bodies with him."

"He'll be glad about that," Wallander said. "Going home, that is."

"Any regrets?"

"None at all."

"Ask him to come and see me. I've told Björk. Is Liepa around?"

"He's in Svedberg's office, smoking his head off. I've never met a heavier smoker."

Early the next day Major Liepa caught a flight to Stockholm with a connection to Riga. The two zinc-lined coffins went to Stockholm in a hearse, and onwards by air cargo.

Wallander and Major Liepa said their goodbyes at the check-in at Sturup. Wallander had bought an illustrated book on Skåne as a farewell present—it was the best he could think of.

"I'd like to hear how things turn out," he said.

"You'll be kept informed," the major told him.

They shook hands, and Major Liepa went on his way.

A strange man, Wallander thought as he drove away from the airport. I wonder what he really thought of me.

The next day was Saturday. Wallander had a nap, then drove to Löderup to see his father. He had his supper at a pizzeria, with a few glasses of red wine. All the time he was wondering whether or not he should apply for the post at the Trelleborg Rubber Company. The closing date was fast approaching. He spent Sunday morning first in the laundry room, then applying himself to the unwelcome task of cleaning his apartment. In the evening he went to the last cinema left in Ystad. It was showing an American police thriller, and he had to admit to himself that it was exciting, despite its unrealistic exaggerations.

On Monday he was in his office shortly after 8 a.m., and had just taken off his jacket when Björk came marching in.

"We've had a telex from the Riga police," he said.

"From Major Liepa? What's he got to say?"

Björk seemed embarrassed.

"I'm afraid Major Liepa is not able to write anything at all," Björk said uneasily. "He has been murdered. The day he got home. A police colonel, name of Putnis, signs this telex. They're asking for our assistance, and I imagine that means you'll have to go there."

Wallander sat at his desk and read the telex.

The major dead? Murdered?

"I'm sorry about this," Björk said. "It's awful. I'll call the police commissioner and ask him to respond to their request."

Wallander flopped back in his chair. Major Liepa murdered? He could feel a lump in his throat. Who could have killed the short-sighted, chain-smoking little man? And why? His thoughts went to Rydberg, who was also dead. Suddenly he felt very lonely.

Three days later he left for Latvia. It was shortly before 2 p.m. on February 28. As the Aeroflot plane swung left and flew over the Gulf of Riga, Wallander stared down at the sea and wondered what lay in store for him.

CHAPTER 7

The first thing Wallander noticed was the cold. He could feel no difference between standing in line at passport control and walking from the plane to the terminal. He had landed in a country where it was just as cold inside as it was out, and he regretted not having packed a pair of long johns.

The shivering passengers moved slowly through the grim arrivals area. Two Danes distinguished themselves by complaining in loud voices about what they expected to find in Latvia. The older one had been to Riga before, and was instructing his younger colleague about the wretched atmosphere of apathy and insecurity that was characteristic of the country. These noisy Danes annoyed Wallander. It was as though he felt they should have more respect for a short-sighted police officer that had been murdered a few days earlier.

Ten days ago he would hardly have been confident of placing the three Baltic states on the map. Tallinn could have been the capital of Latvia for all he knew, and Riga a major Estonian port. He remembered little more than bits and pieces of a geographical survey of Europe from his schooling. Before leaving Ystad he had spent two days reading up on Latvia and had gained the impression of a little country that had been oppressed by the whims of history, repeatedly falling victim to the sparring of the big powers. Even Sweden had marched triumphantly into this country, bloodstained and ruthless. But it seemed to him that the key moment had been in 1945, when the German war machine was crippled and the Soviet army marched into Latvia and annexed it without encountering real opposition. The attempt to set up an independent Latvian government had been savagely suppressed, and the so-called liberation army from the East, in one of the cynical twists history loves to impose, had turned into its exact opposite: a regime that ruthlessly snuffed out the sovereignty of the Latvian people.

The two loud-mouthed Danes, who were in Riga to deal in agricultural machinery, had just reached the passport control window, and Wallander was reaching into his inside pocket for his own passport, when he felt a tap on the shoulder. He flinched, as if he'd been afraid of being exposed as a criminal, turned and was confronted by a man in a gray-blue uniform.

"Are you Kurt Wallander?" the man asked him. "My name is Jazeps Putnis. I'm late, I'm sorry, but your flight was early. Obviously you should not be inconvenienced by the formalities. Follow me."

According to the telex from Riga, Jazeps Putnis held the rank of colonel. His impeccable English reminded Wallander of Major Liepa's constant struggle for the right words and correct pronunciation. He followed Putnis through a door guarded by a soldier, and they emerged into another reception area just as shabby and dark as the last, where suitcases were being unloaded from a trolley.

"Let's hope there's no delay with your luggage," Putnis said. "May I be so bold as to bid you welcome to Latvia. And more especially, to Riga! Have you ever been here before?"

"No," Wallander said. "I'm afraid I never have been."

"Needless to say, I'd have preferred the circumstances to be different," Putnis said. "The death of Major Liepa was very sad."

Wallander waited for him to elaborate, but he didn't. Putnis strode over to a man in faded blue overalls and a fur hat leaning against a wall. The man stood to attention when Putnis addressed him, and disappeared through one of the doors leading out into the airport.

"It's taking an awfully long time," Putnis said with a smile. "Do you have the same problem in Sweden?"

"Sometimes," Wallander said. "Yes, occasionally we do have to wait."

Colonel Putnis was the polar opposite of Major Liepa. He was very tall, decisive and energetic in his movements, and his direct gaze seemed to go straight through Wallander. He was clean-cut, with gray eyes that appeared to take in everything that was going on around him. He reminded Wallander of an animal—a lynx, perhaps, or a leopard, in a gray-blue uniform. He tried to guess his age: 50 perhaps? Possibly older.

A luggage trailer came clattering up, pulled by a tractor belching exhaust fumes. Wallander recognized his suitcase immediately and failed to prevent Colonel Putnis from carrying it for him. A black Volga police car was waiting for them alongside the taxi ramp, and a chauffeur saluted as he opened the door. Wallander was astonished, but managed a hesitant salute in return. Pity Björk couldn't have seen that, he thought. I wonder what Major Liepa made of the police officers in jeans, none of whom saluted him, when he landed in the insignificant little Swedish town of Ystad.

"We've booked you into the Latvia Hotel," Colonel Putnis said as they drove away from the airport. "It's the best hotel in town. It has more than 25 floors."

"I have no doubt it's excellent," Wallander said. "I'd like to pass on greetings and sympathy from my colleagues in Ystad. Major Liepa was only with us for a few days, but he was very well liked."

"Thank you," Colonel Putnis said. "The major's death is a great loss for all of us."

Why doesn't he say more, Wallander wondered. Why doesn't he describe what happened? Why was the major murdered? By whom? How? Why have they asked me to come here? Is there some suspicion that the major's death might be connected with his visit to Sweden?

He looked out over the countryside: deserted fields with irregular patches of snow; here and there an isolated gray dwelling surrounded by an unpainted fence; here and there a pig rooting in a dunghill. He had the impression of endless misery, making him think of the trip he'd recently made to Malmö with his father. Skåne might look inhospitable in winter, but what he was seeing here suggested a desolation that was beyond anything he'd ever imagined.

As he contemplated the countryside, Wallander was overcome by sadness. It was as if the country's painful history had covered the fields in gray paint. He felt an impulse to act: he hadn't come to Riga just to be depressed by a grim winter landscape.

"I'd like to see a report as soon as possible," he said. "What actually happened? All I know is that Major Liepa was murdered the day he got back to Riga."

"Once you've settled into your room I'll come and collect you," Colonel Putnis said. "We've planned a meeting for this evening."

"All I need to do is to dump my suitcase," Wallander said. "I'll only need a couple of minutes."

"The meeting is arranged for 7:30 p.m.," Colonel Putnis said. It was clear to Wallander that his eagerness would make no difference. The plan had already been decided on.

It was starting to get dark as they drove through Riga's suburbs towards the center of town. Wallander took in the dreary housing estates stretching away on both sides of the road. He couldn't make up his mind how he felt about what might lie in store for him.

The hotel was in the city center, at the end of a wide esplanade. Wallander caught sight of a statue and realized it must be of Lenin. The Latvia Hotel stuck up into the night sky like a dark-blue column. Colonel Putnis led him through a deserted foyer to reception. Wallander felt as though he was on the ground floor of a multi-storied car park that had been turned into a hotel entrance hall as an emergency measure. A row of elevators lined one of the narrow walls, and overhead were staircases leading in all directions.

To his astonishment he found he didn't need to register. Colonel Putnis collected his room key from the female receptionist, then escorted him into one of the cramped elevators and up to the 15th floor. Wallander's room was number 1506, with a view over the city's rooftops. He wondered if he'd be able to see the Gulf of Riga in daylight.

Colonel Putnis left after establishing that Wallander was satisfied with the room, and telling him he would collect him in two hours' time and take him to the meeting at police head-quarters.

Wallander stood at the window gazing out over the rooftops. A truck clattered past in the street below. Cold air was seeping in through the drafty windows, and when he felt the radiator he found that it was barely lukewarm. Somewhere in the background a telephone rang unanswered.

Long johns, he thought. That's the first thing I'll buy tomorrow morning.

He unpacked his case and placed his toiletries in the spacious bathroom. He'd bought a bottle of whisky at the airport and, after a few moments' hesitation, poured a good measure into his toothbrush mug. There was a Russian-made radio on the bedside table, and he switched it on. A man was speaking very quickly, sounding excited, as if he were commenting on some sports event in which the action was very fast and unpredictable. He turned down the bedcover and lay down on the bed.

Well, here I am in Riga, he thought. I still have no idea what happened to Major Liepa. All I know is that he's dead. Most importantly of all, I don't know what this Colonel Putnis expects me to be able to do.

It was too cold to lie on the bed, so he decided to go down to reception and change some money. Perhaps the hotel would have a café where he could get a cup of coffee.

When he got to reception he was surprised to see the two Danish businessmen he'd been annoyed by at the airport. The older one was standing at the desk waving a map angrily. It looked as though he was trying to show the girl how to make a paper kite or perhaps a glider, and Wallander couldn't stop himself from laughing. He saw a sign announcing that he was welcome to change some money. An elderly lady nodded at him in a friendly way as he handed over two hundred-krona bills, and received an enormous pile of Latvian bills in return. When he got back to reception the two Danes had left. He asked the receptionist where he could get a cup of coffee, and was pointed in the direction of the big dining room where a waiter escorted him to a table by a window and gave him a menu. He decided on an omelette and a cup of coffee. Clanking streetcars and people dressed in fur coats flitted past the high window, and the heavy curtains swayed in the draft from the ill-fitting frames.

He looked around the deserted dining room. At one table an elderly couple were having dinner in total silence; at another a man in a gray suit was drinking tea by himself. That was all.

Wallander thought back to the previous evening when he'd
arrived in Stockholm on an afternoon flight from Sturup. His
daughter Linda was waiting for him when the airport bus pulled
up at Central Station, and they walked to the Central Hotel nearby.
She was staying in Bromma, close to the college, so he'd booked
her a room in his hotel. That evening he'd taken her to dinner at a
restaurant in the Old Town. It was a long time since they'd seen
each other, and the conversation seemed to him stilted, with lots
of changes of subject. Again, he wondered if what Linda had put
in her letters was the truth. She'd written that she was enjoying
college life, but when he asked her about it her replies were very
terse. He couldn't hide his irritation when he asked if she had any
plans for the future, and she replied that she had no idea what
she was going to do.

"Isn't it about time you had?" he asked.

"What's that got to do with you?" she said.

Then they'd argued, without raising their voices. He insisted
that she couldn't just carry on vaguely wandering from one educational establishment to another, and she'd said she was old enough
to do whatever she liked.

It had dawned on him that Linda was very much like her father.
He couldn't put his finger on it, but he had the feeling he could
hear his own voice as he listened to her. History was repeating
itself: he recognized his own complicated relationship with his
father echoed in his conversation with his daughter.

The meal dragged on and they drank their wine; gradually the
tension and the friction faded away. Wallander told her about
the journey he was about to make, and for a brief moment toyed
with the idea of inviting her to come with him. Time started to
race by, and it was after midnight when he paid the bill. It was
cold outside, but they walked back to the hotel even so, then sat

talking in his room until after 3 a.m. When she finally went to bed, Wallander felt that it had been a successful evening despite the awkward start, but he couldn't quite shake off the nagging worry caused by not being clear about the way his daughter was leading her life.

When he checked out in the morning, Linda was still asleep. He paid for her room and left her a note that the receptionist promised to pass on.

He was roused from his reveries by the departure of the silent elderly couple. There were no new diners, and the only other person in the room was the man drinking tea. He glanced at his watch: nearly an hour to go before Colonel Putnis was due to pick him up.

He paid his bill, did some rapid sums in his head and registered that the meal had been extremely cheap. When he got back to his room he went through the papers he had brought with him. He was slowly beginning to get back into the case—the case he had thought he'd consigned to the oblivion of the archives. He could even smell the acrid tang of the major's strong cigarettes in his nostrils again.

Colonel Putnis knocked on his door at 7:17 p.m. The car was waiting in front of the hotel, and they drove through the dark streets to police headquarters. It had grown much colder during the evening, and the city was almost deserted. The streets and squares were poorly lit, and Wallander had the impression of a town built up of silhouettes and stage sets. They drove through an archway and drew up in what looked like a walled courtyard. Colonel Putnis hadn't spoken during the journey, and Wallander was still waiting to hear why he'd been called over to Riga. They walked along empty, echoing corridors, down a staircase and then

along another corridor, and eventually came to a door which
Colonel Putnis opened without knocking.

Wallander entered a large, warm but poorly lit room dominated
by an oval conference table covered in a green felt cloth. There
were twelve chairs at the table, and a jug of water and some glasses
in the center. A man was waiting deep in the shadows, and he
turned and approached as Wallander came in.

"Welcome to Riga," the man said. "My name's Juris Murniers."

"Colonel Murniers and I have joint responsibility for solving
the murder of Major Liepa," Putnis said.

Wallander sensed right away that there was tension between the
two men. Something in Putnis's tone of voice gave it away. There
was also something hidden in the brief exchange.

Colonel Murniers was in his 50s, with closely cropped gray
hair. His face was pale and bloated, as if he was diabetic. He was
short, and Wallander observed that he moved around without the
slightest sound. Another cat-creature. Two colonels, two cats, both
in gray uniforms.

Wallander and Putnis hung up their overcoats and sat at the
table. The waiting time is over, Wallander thought. What happened
to Major Liepa? Now I'm going to find out. Murniers did the
talking. Wallander noticed he had positioned himself so that
his face was almost all in shadow, and when he spoke in fluent,
well-formulated English, his voice seemed to come from an
endless darkness. Colonel Putnis sat staring straight ahead, as if
he couldn't really be bothered to listen.

"It's very mysterious," Murniers said. "The very day Major Liepa
returned from Stockholm, he gave his report to Colonel Putnis
and me. We sat in this room and discussed the case. He was going
to be responsible for continuing the investigation here in Latvia.
We broke up at about 5 p.m., and we later learned that Major

Liepa went straight home to his wife. They live in a house behind
the cathedral. She has said that he seemed perfectly normal,
although of course he was pleased to be home. They had dinner,
and he told her about his experiences in Sweden. Incidentally,
you seem to have made a very good impression on him, Inspector
Wallander. Shortly before 11 p.m. the phone rang—Major Liepa
was just getting ready for bed. His wife didn't know who called,
but the major got dressed again and told her that he would have to
go back to police headquarters immediately. There was nothing
unusual about that, although she may have been disappointed that
he had been called out the same night he'd returned from abroad.
He didn't give any reason for his having to go on duty."

Murniers fell silent and reached for the water jug. Wallander
glanced at Putnis, who was staring straight ahead.

"After that, everything is very confused," Murniers continued.
"Early the next morning some dockers found Major Liepa's body
at Daugavgriva—that's at the far end of the big harbor here
in Riga. The major was lying on the wharf, dead. We were able
to establish that the back of his skull had been smashed in with
a heavy implement, perhaps an iron bar or a wooden club. The
postmortem revealed that he had been murdered an hour or two
hours at the most after leaving home. That's really all we know.
We have no witnesses who saw him leaving home, nor out at
the harbor. It's all very mysterious. It's very rare for a police officer
to be killed in this country. Least of all one of Major Liepa's rank.
Naturally, we're very keen for the murderer to be found as soon as
possible."

That was all Murniers had to say, and he sank back into the
shadows.

"So in fact, nobody had telephoned and summoned him here,"
Wallander said.

"No," Putnis said quickly. "We've looked into that. The duty officer, a Captain Kozlov, has confirmed that no one was in contact with Major Liepa that evening."

"That leaves only two possibilities, then," Wallander said.

Putnis nodded. "Either he lied to his wife, or he was tricked."

"In the latter case, he must have recognized the voice," Wallander said. "Either that, or whoever called expressed himself in a way that didn't arouse suspicion."

"We have also come to those conclusions," Putnis said.

"Of course, we can't exclude the possibility that there is a connection between his work in Sweden and his murder," Murniers said from the shadows. "We can't exclude anything, and that's why we've asked for assistance from the Swedish police. From you, Inspector Wallander. We are grateful for any thoughts, any ideas you might have that can help us. You will receive all the assistance you require."

Murniers got to his feet.

"I suggest we leave it at that for tonight," he said. "I imagine you're tired after your journey."

Wallander didn't feel the slightest bit tired. He'd been prepared to work all night if necessary, but as Putnis had also stood up, he had to accept that the meeting was closed.

Murniers pressed a bell fixed to the edge of the table, and almost immediately the door opened and a young police officer in uniform appeared.

"This is Sergeant Zids," Murniers said. "He speaks excellent English, and will be your chauffeur while you are in Riga."

Zids clicked his heels and saluted, but Wallander couldn't bring himself to do more than nod in return. As neither Putnis nor Murniers had invited him to dinner, he realized that he would have the evening to himself. He followed Zids out into the courtyard, and after the well-heated conference room the dry cold struck him with full force. Zids opened the back door of a black car for him, and Wallander clambered in.

"It's cold," Wallander said as they drove out through the archway.

"Yes, Colonel," Sergeant Zids said. "It is very cold in Riga just now."

Colonel, thought Wallander. He can't imagine that the Swedish police officer could have a lower rank than Putnis and Murniers. The thought amused him, but at the same time he could see that there was nothing so easy to get used to as privileges. Your own car, your own driver, plenty of attention.

Sergeant Zids drove fast through the empty streets. Wallander didn't feel tired at all, and the thought of the chilly hotel room scared him.

"I'm hungry," he said to the sergeant. "Take me to a good restaurant that isn't too expensive."

"The dining room at the Latvia Hotel is best," Zids said.

"I've already been there," Wallander said.

"There's no other restaurant in Riga where the food is as good," Zids said, braking sharply as a streetcar came clattering around a corner.

"There must be more than one good restaurant in a city with a million inhabitants," Wallander said.

"The food isn't good," the sergeant said, "but it is at the Latvia Hotel."

That's obviously where I'm supposed to go, Wallander thought, settling back in his seat. Maybe he's been ordered not to let me loose in the town? In certain circumstances having your own driver can mean the opposite of freedom.

Zids pulled up at the hotel entrance, and before Wallander had managed to reach for the door handle, the sergeant had opened it for him.

"What time would you like me to collect you tomorrow morning, Colonel?" he asked.

"Eight o'clock will be fine," Wallander replied.

The foyer was even more deserted now. He could hear music somewhere in the background. He collected his key from the receptionist and asked if the dining room was open. The man, who had heavy eyelids and pale features reminiscent of Colonel Murniers, nodded. Wallander asked where the music was coming from.

"We have a nightclub," the receptionist said glumly.

As Wallander left reception, he thought he recognized the man who'd been drinking tea in the dining room earlier: now he was sitting in a worn leather sofa, reading a newspaper. Wallander was certain it was the same man.

I'm being watched, he thought. Just like the worst of those Cold-War novels, there's a man in a gray suit pretending to be invisible. What on earth do Putnis and Murniers think I'm going to do?

The dining room was almost as empty as it had been earlier in the evening. A group of men in dark suits were sitting around a long table at the far end of the room, speaking in low voices. To his surprise, Wallander was shown to the same table as before. He had vegetable soup, and a chop that was tough and overdone, but the Latvian beer was good. He was feeling restless so didn't bother about coffee, and instead paid his bill and went in search of the hotel's nightclub. The man was still on the sofa.

Wallander had the impression of walking through a labyrinth. Various half-flights of stairs that seemed to lead nowhere brought him back to the dining room. He tried to follow the sound of the music, and eventually came upon an illuminated sign at the end of a dark corridor. A man said something Wallander didn't understand and opened the door for him, and he found himself in a dimly lit bar. In sharp contrast to the dining room, the bar was jam-packed. Behind a curtain separating the bar from the dance floor a band was blaring away, and Wallander thought he recognized an Abba song. The air was fetid, and he was reminded once again of the major's cigarettes. He noticed a table that seemed to be empty, and elbowed his way through the throng. All the time he had the feeling he was being watched, and realized there was every reason for him to be cautious. Nightclubs in the Eastern bloc countries were often the haunts of gangs who made a living robbing visitors from the West.

He managed to bawl out an order to a waiter through all the noise, and a few minutes later a glass of whisky landed on the table in front of him. It cost almost as much as the meal he'd had earlier. He sniffed at the contents of the glass, imagining a plot involving spiked drinks, and drank a depressed toast to himself.

A girl, who never told him her name, emerged from the shadows and sat down on the chair next to him. He didn't notice her until she leaned her head over towards him, and he could smell her perfume, reminiscent of winter apples. She spoke to him in German, and he shook his head; her English was awful, worse than the major's was, but she offered to keep him company and asked for a drink. Wallander felt at a loss. He realized she was a prostitute, but tried to put that fact out of his mind: Riga was dreary and cold, and he had an urge to talk to somebody who wasn't a colonel. He could buy her a drink; he was the one calling the shots after all. Only very occasionally when he was extremely drunk was he likely to lose control. The last time that had happened was the previous winter, when he'd thrown himself at the public prosecutor, Anette Brolin, in a moment of anger and lust. He shuddered at the memory. That must never happen again. Not here in Riga, at least. Nevertheless, he felt flattered by the girl's attention. She's come to my table too soon, he thought. I've only just arrived, and I haven't gotten used to this strange country yet.

"Maybe tomorrow," he said. "Not tonight."

It struck him that she was barely 20. Behind all that make-up was a face that reminded him of his own daughter. He emptied his glass, stood up and left. That was a close call, he thought. Much too close. The man in the gray suit was still in the foyer, reading his newspaper.

Sleep well, Wallander said to himself. I'll see you again tomorrow, no doubt.

He slept badly. The duvet was heavy and the bed uncomfortable. Through the mists of his sleep he could hear a telephone ringing constantly. He wanted to get out of bed and answer it, but when he woke up everything was silent.

The next morning he was woken up by a knock on the door. Only half-awake, he shouted, "Come in." When the knock came again, he realized he'd left the key in the lock. He pulled on his trousers and opened the door to find a woman in a maid's apron with a breakfast tray. He was surprised, since he hadn't ordered breakfast, but perhaps that was just part of the normal service? Maybe Sergeant Zids had arranged it?

The chambermaid said good morning in Latvian, and he tried to memorize the expression. She placed the tray on a table, gave him a shy little smile and went towards the door. He followed in order to lock it after her but instead of leaving the room, the chambermaid closed the door and put her finger to her mouth.

Wallander stared at her in surprise. She slowly took a sheet of paper from the pocket of her apron, and Wallander was about to speak when she put her hand over his mouth. He could sense her fear, and knew she wasn't a chambermaid at all, but he could also see she that she wasn't a threat. She was just scared. He took the paper and read what it said, in English. He read it twice in order to memorize it, then looked up at her. She put her hand in her other pocket and produced something that looked like a crumpled poster. She handed it over, and when he unfolded it he realized it was the dust jacket of the book about Skåne he'd given her husband, Major Liepa, the week before. He looked up at her again. Besides the fear, her face also indicated something else— determination perhaps, or maybe obstinacy. He walked across the cold floor and fetched a pencil from the desk. On the inside of the dust jacket, which had a photograph on it of the cathedral in Lund, he wrote: *I have understood.* He gave her back the dust jacket, and it struck him that Baiba Liepa looked nothing like what he had imagined. He couldn't remember what the major had said when he was sitting on Wallander's sofa in Mariagatan in Ystad, listening to Maria Callas and talking about his wife, but the impression he'd formed was different, not of a face like hers.

He cleared his throat as he carefully opened the door, and she melted away.

She had come to him because she wanted to speak to him about her dead husband, the major. And she was terrified. When somebody called his room and asked for a Mr. Eckers, he was to take the elevator to the foyer, then go down the steps leading to the hotel sauna and look for a gray-painted, steel door next to the dining room's loading bay. It should be unlocked, and when he came out into the street behind the hotel, she'd be waiting for him and would tell him about her dead husband.

Please, she'd written. *Please, please.* Now he was quite certain that there had been more than mere fear in her face: there was defiance as well, perhaps even hatred. There's something going on here that's bigger than I'd suspected, he thought. It needed a messenger in a chambermaid's uniform to make me realize. I'd forgotten that I'm in an alien world.

Just before 8 a.m. he emerged from the elevator on the ground floor. There was no sign of a man reading a newspaper, but there was a man looking at postcards on a stand. Wallander went out into the street. It was warmer than the previous day. Sergeant Zids was sitting in the car, waiting for him, and bade him good morning. Wallander climbed into the backseat and the sergeant started the engine. Day was slowly breaking over Riga. The traffic was heavy, and the sergeant was unable to drive as fast as he would have liked. All the time Wallander could see Baiba Liepa's face in his mind's eye. Suddenly, without warning, he felt scared.

CHAPTER 8

Shortly before 8:30 a.m., Wallander discovered that Colonel
Murniers smoked the same extra-strong cigarettes as Major
Liepa. He recognized the packet, with the brand name
"PRIMA," that the colonel took out of his uniform pocket and
placed on the table in front of him.

Wallander felt as though he was in the middle of a labyrinth.
Sergeant Zids had led him up and down stairs around the appar-
ently endless police headquarters before stopping at a door that
turned out to be to Murniers's office. It seemed to Wallander
that there must surely be a shorter and more straightforward way
to Murniers's office, but he was not allowed to know it.

The office was sparsely furnished, not especially big, and what
immediately caught Wallander's interest was the fact that it had
three telephones. On one wall was a dented filing cabinet, with
locks. Besides the telephones there was a large cast-iron ashtray
on his desk, decorated with an elaborate motif that Wallander
thought at first was a pair of swans, then realized was a man with
bulging muscles carrying a flag into a headwind.

Ashtray, telephones, but no papers. The venetian blinds for
the two high windows behind Murniers's back were either half-
lowered or broken, Wallander couldn't make up his mind which.
He stared at the blinds as he digested the important news
Murniers had just imparted.

"We've arrested a suspect," the colonel had said. "Our investigations during the night have produced the result we'd been hoping for."

At first Wallander thought he was referring to the major's murderer, but then it came to him that Murniers meant the dead men in the life raft.

"It was a gang," Murniers said. "A gang with branches in both Tallinn and Warsaw. A loose collection of criminals who make a living out of smuggling, robbery, burglary, anything that makes money. We suspect that they've recently started to profit from the drug-dealing that has unfortunately penetrated Latvia. Colonel Putnis is interrogating the man at this very moment. We shall soon know quite a lot more."

The last few sentences were delivered as a calm, factual and measured statement. Wallander could see Putnis in his mind's eye, slowly extracting the truth from a man who'd been tortured. What did he know about the Latvian police? Was there any limit to what was permitted in a dictatorship? Come to that, *was* Latvia a dictatorship? He thought of Baiba Liepa's face. Fear, but also the opposite of fear. *When somebody telephones and asks for Mr. Eckers, you must come.*

Murniers smiled at him, as if it was obvious he could read the Swedish police officer's thoughts. Wallander tried to hide his secret by saying something quite untrue.

"Major Liepa led me to understand that he was worried about his personal safety," he said, "but he gave no reason for his anxiety. That's one of the questions Colonel Putnis ought to try and find an answer to—whether there's a direct connection between the men found dead in the life raft and the murder of Major Liepa."

Wallander thought he could detect an almost invisible shift in Murniers's expression. So, he'd said something unexpected. But was it his insight that was unexpected, or that Major Liepa really had been worried and Murniers already knew?

"You must have asked the key questions," Wallander said. "Who could have enticed Major Liepa out in the middle of the night? Who would have had a reason to murder him? Even when a controversial politician is murdered one has to ask whether there might have been a private motive. That's what happened when Kennedy was assassinated, and the same was the case when the Swedish prime minister was shot down in the street some years ago. You must have thought of all this, I take it? You must also have concluded that there was no credible private motive, or you wouldn't have asked me to come to Riga."

"That is correct," Murniers said. "You are an experienced police officer and your analysis is accurate. Major Liepa was happily married. He was not in financial difficulties. He didn't gamble, he didn't have a mistress. He was a conscientious police officer who was convinced that the work he did was helping our country to develop. We think his death must be connected with his work. Since he was working on no other case apart from the death of the men found in the life raft, we asked for help from Sweden. Perhaps he said something to you that didn't appear in the report he handed in the day he died? We need to know, and we hope you can help us."

"Major Liepa talked about drugs," Wallander said. "He referred to the spread of amphetamine factories in Eastern Europe. He was convinced that the two men died as a result of an internal dispute within a syndicate involved in drug smuggling. He devoted much energy to trying to discover whether the men had been killed for revenge, or because they had refused to reveal something. Furthermore, there were good reasons to believe the life raft itself had been carrying a cargo of drugs, since it was stolen from our police station. What we never managed to work out was how these various things might be linked."

"Let's hope Colonel Putnis gets an answer to that," Murniers said. "He's a very skilled interrogator. In the meantime I thought I might suggest that I should show you the place where Major Liepa was murdered. Colonel Putnis takes his time over an interrogation, if he thinks it's worth it."

"Is the place where he was found the actual place where he was killed?"

"There's no reason to suppose otherwise. It's a remote spot. There are not many people around the docks at night."

That's not true, Wallander thought. The major would have put up a struggle. It can't have been easy to drag him out onto a quay in the middle of the night. Saying the place is remote isn't a good enough explanation.

"I would like to meet the major's widow," he said. "A conversation with her could be important for me as well. I assume you've spoken to her several times?"

"We've had a very detailed conversation with Baiba Liepa," Murniers said. "Of course we can arrange for you to meet her."

They drove along by the river in the gray light of the winter morning. Sergeant Zids was instructed to track down Baiba Liepa while Wallander and Colonel Murniers drove out to where the body had been found, the place Murniers also claimed was the scene of the murder.

"What's your theory?" Wallander asked as they lounged in the backseat of Murniers's car, which was bigger and plusher than the one Wallander had been allocated. "You must have one, you and Colonel Putnis."

"Drugs," Murniers answered without hesitation. "We know the big bosses in the drug business surround themselves with bodyguards, men who are nearly always addicts themselves, prepared to do anything in order to get their daily fix. Maybe those bosses thought Major Liepa was getting a bit close for comfort?"

"Was he?"

"No. If that theory were correct, at least a dozen officers here in the Riga police force would have come before Major Liepa on a death list. The odd thing about this is that Major Liepa had never been involved in investigating drug crimes before. It was pure coincidence that he seemed to be the most appropriate officer to send to Sweden."

"What kind of cases had Major Liepa been dealing with?"

Murniers gazed vacantly out of the car window. "He was a very skilled all-around detective. We had some robberies in Riga recently that involved murder as well: Major Liepa handled the case brilliantly and arrested those responsible. When other investigators, at least as experienced as he was, had run up against a brick wall, Major Liepa was often the officer we turned to."

They sat in silence as the police car stopped at some traffic lights. Wallander watched a group of people hunched against the cold at a bus stop and had the distinct impression no bus would ever come and open its doors for them.

"Drugs," he said. "That's old hat for us in the West, but it's something new for you."

"Not completely new," Murniers said, "but we've never seen it before on the scale that is normal today. Opening up our borders has produced opportunities and a market on a completely different scale. I don't mind admitting that we've sometimes felt helpless. We'll need to develop cooperation with police forces in the West because a lot of the drugs that pass through Latvia are actually destined for Sweden. Hard currency is the bait. It's quite clear to us that Sweden is one of the markets that the gangs here

in Latvia are most interested in. For obvious reasons. It's not far
from Ventspils to the Swedish coast, and moreover, that coast is
long and difficult to patrol. You could say that they've taken
over classical smuggling routes—they used to transport barrels
of vodka the same way."

"Tell me more," Wallander said. "Where are the drugs manufactured? Who's behind it all?"

"You must understand that we are living in an impoverished
country," Murniers said. "Just as impoverished and decrepit as
our neighbors. For many years we've been forced to live as if
we were shut in a cage. We've only been able to observe the riches
of the West from a distance. Now, all of a sudden, everything
is obtainable. But there's one condition: you need money. For
someone who's prepared to go to any lengths, who's totally lacking
in scruples, the quickest way to get that money is through drugs.
When you helped us to dismantle our walls and open the gates
to the countries that had been shut away, you also opened up the
sluices for all manner of appetites that need satisfying. Hunger
for all those things we'd been forced to observe from a distance but
forbidden or prevented from touching. Needless to say, we've still
no idea how things are going to work out."

Murniers leaned forward and said something to the driver, who
immediately braked and came to a halt by the curb.

Murniers pointed at the façade of the building opposite them.

"Bullet holes," he said. "About a year old."

Wallander leaned forward to look. The wall really was riddled
with bullet holes.

"What is this building?" he asked.

"One of our ministries," Murniers said. "I'm showing you this
to help you to understand. To understand why we still don't know
what's going to happen. Will we get more freedom? Or will the

freedom we have be restricted? Or disappear altogether? We still don't know. You have to understand, Inspector Wallander, that you are in a country where nothing is yet decided."

They drove on until they came to a vast area of dockland. Wallander tried to digest what Murniers had said. He'd started to sympathize with the pale man with the bloated features, to feel that everything he said involved Wallander as well—indeed, maybe involved him more than anybody else.

"We know there are laboratories making amphetamines and maybe other drugs like morphine and ephedrine," Murniers said. "We also suspect that Asian and South American cocaine cartels are trying to establish new networks in the former Eastern bloc. The idea is that they should replace the previous routes that went straight to Western Europe. Many of these have been closed down by the European police, but the cartels believe that in the virginal East European territories they might be able to evade keen-eyed police officers. Let's say they find us easier to corrupt and bribe."

"Officers like Major Liepa?"

"He would never have stooped to accepting a bribe."

"I mean that he was a keen-eyed police officer."

"If his eyes were too keen, if that's what sent him to his death, I trust Colonel Putnis will establish this shortly."

"Who is this man that you've arrested?"

"Someone we've often come across in circumstances in which the two dead men were involved. A former butcher from Riga who has been one of the leaders of the organized crime we've been fighting against constantly. Remarkably enough, he's always managed to avoid going to prison—but maybe we can nail him this time."

The car slowed down and stopped by a wharf with piles of scrap iron and abandoned cranes. They got out of the car and walked to the water's edge.

"That's where Major Liepa was found."

Wallander looked around, trying to establish basic facts.

How had the murderers and the major gotten here? Why just here? It wasn't good enough to say that this part of the docks was remote. Wallander inspected the remains of what had once been a crane. *Please*, Baiba Liepa had written. Murniers had lit a cigarette and was stamping his feet rhythmically to keep warm.

Why doesn't he want to tell me about where the crime actually took place? Wallander thought. Why does Baiba Liepa want to meet me in secret? *When somebody telephones and asks for Mr. Eckers. . . .* What am I really doing here in Riga?

The anxiety he'd felt that morning had returned. He wondered whether it had to do with the fact that he was a stranger in an unknown country. The job of a police officer was to deal with circumstances of which oneself was a part. Here, he was an outsider. Perhaps he could penetrate this foreign environment in the guise of Mr. Eckers? Kurt Wallander was a Swedish police officer, and he felt helpless in these alien circumstances. He went back to the car.

"I'd like to study your documentation," he said. "The post-mortem, forensic reports, photos."

"We shall have all the papers translated," Murniers said.

"It might be quicker if I have an interpreter," Wallander suggested. "Sergeant Zids speaks excellent English."

Murniers smiled wryly and lit another cigarette.

"You are in a hurry," he said. "You're impatient. Of course Sergeant Zids can translate the reports for you."

When they got back to police headquarters, they'd gone behind a curtain and watched Colonel Putnis and the man he was interrogating through a two-way mirror. The interrogation room was cold and furnished with only a small wooden table and two chairs. Colonel Putnis had taken off his tunic. The man sitting opposite him was unshaven and looked exhausted. His answers to Putnis's questions were very slow.

"This will take some time," Murniers said pensively, "but we'll get to the truth sooner or later."

"What truth?"

"Whether or not we're right."

They returned to the inner sanctum of the labyrinth, and Wallander was shown to a small office in the same corridor as Murniers's. Sergeant Zids arrived with a file on the investigation into the major's death. Before Murniers left them to get on with it, he and the sergeant exchanged a few words in Latvian.

"Baiba Liepa will be brought here for an interrogation at 2 p.m. this afternoon," said Murniers.

Wallander was horrified. *You have betrayed me, Mr. Eckers. Why did you do that?*

"What I had in mind was a conversation," Wallander said. "Not an interrogation."

"I shouldn't have used the word 'interrogation,' " Murniers said. "Allow me to explain that she indicated she would be delighted to see you."

Murniers left, and two hours later Zids had translated all the documents in the file. Wallander had examined the blurred photographs of Liepa's body, and his feeling that something vital was missing was reinforced. Since he knew he could think more clearly when he was doing something else, he asked the sergeant to drive him to a shop where he could buy long johns. The sergeant didn't appear surprised at his request. Wallander was struck by the absurdity of the whole situation as he marched into the clothing store selected by the sergeant: it was as if he were buying underpants with a police escort. Zids did the talking for him, and insisted that Wallander should try on the long johns before paying for them. He bought two pairs, and they were duly wrapped up in brown paper and tied with string. When they emerged into the street, he suggested they should have lunch.

"Not at the Latvia Hotel, though," he said. "Anywhere else, but not there."

Sergeant Zids turned off the main street and drove into the old town. It seemed to Wallander that he was entering a new labyrinth he would never be able to find his way out of alone.

They stopped at the Sigulda restaurant. Wallander had an omelette, and the sergeant a bowl of soup. The atmosphere was stifling and heavy with cigarette smoke. The place was full when they arrived, and Wallander had noted that the sergeant had demanded a table.

"This would have been impossible in Sweden," he said as they were eating. "I mean, a police officer marching into a crowded restaurant and demanding a table."

"It's different here," Sergeant Zids said, unconcerned. "People prefer to keep on the good side of the police."

Wallander could feel himself getting annoyed. Sergeant Zids was too young for such arrogance.

"I don't want to cut any lines in the future," he said.

The sergeant stared at him in astonishment.

"Then we won't get any food," he said.

"The dining room at the Latvia Hotel is always empty," Wallander replied curtly.

They were back at police headquarters just before 2 p.m. During the meal Wallander had sat there without speaking, trying to establish in his mind just what was wrong with the report Zids had translated. He had concluded that what worried him was the very *perfection* of the whole thing—it was as if it had been written in such a way as to make questions unnecessary. That was as far as he had gotten, and he wasn't sure he was right. Maybe he was seeing ghosts where there weren't any?

Murniers wasn't in his office and Colonel Putnis was still busy with his interrogation. The sergeant went to fetch Baiba Liepa, leaving Wallander alone in his office. He wondered if it was bugged, if someone was observing him through a two-way mirror. As if to assert his innocence, he took off his trousers and put on his long johns. He had just noticed how his legs were starting to itch when there was a knock on the door. He shouted, "Come in," and the sergeant ushered in Baiba Liepa. *I'm not Mr. Eckers. There's no such person as Mr. Eckers. That's exactly why I want to talk to you.*

"Does Major Liepa's widow speak English?" he asked the sergeant.

Zids nodded.

"Then you can leave us alone."

He had tried to prepare himself. *I must remember that everything I say and do can be monitored. We can't even put our fingers over our lips, let alone write notes. But Baiba Liepa has to understand that Mr. Eckers still exists.*

She was dressed in a dark overcoat and a fur hat. Unlike earlier in the day, she was wearing glasses. She took off her hat, and shook out her dark hair.

"Please sit down, Mrs. Liepa," Wallander said. She immediately smiled, a quick smile, as if he'd sent her a secret signal with a flashlight. He noted that she accepted it with no trace of surprise, but rather as if she'd expected nothing different. He knew he had to put to her all the questions he already had answers to. Perhaps she could send him a message through her responses, some insight into what was being held back for the eyes of Mr. Eckers only?

He expressed his sympathy—formally, but sincerely even so. Then he asked the questions that were natural in the circumstances, bearing in mind all the time that some unknown person would be monitoring them.

"How long were you married to Major Liepa?"

"For eight years."

"If I understand correctly, you didn't have any children."

"We wanted to wait. I have my career."

"What is your career, Mrs. Liepa?"

"I'm an engineer. But these last few years I've spent most of my time translating scientific papers. Some of them for our technical university."

How did you arrange serving me breakfast? he wondered. Who is your contact at the Latvia Hotel? The thought distracted him. He asked his next question.

"And you thought you couldn't combine that with having children?"

He regretted asking that question right away. That was a private matter, irrelevant. He apologized by not waiting for an answer, but just pressing on.

"Mrs. Liepa," he said. "You must have thought, worried, wondered about what really happened to your husband. I've had the interrogations you had with the police translated. You say you don't know anything, don't understand anything, have no idea about anything. I'm sure that's the case. Nobody wants your husband's murderer to be caught and punished more than you do. Nevertheless, I'd like you to think back one more time, to the day when your husband got back from Sweden. There might be something you overlooked because of the shock of hearing that your husband had been murdered."

Her reply gave him the first coded signal for him to interpret.

"No," she said. "I haven't forgotten anything. Nothing at all." *Herr Eckers, I wasn't shocked by something unexpected. What happened was what we'd feared.*

"Maybe a bit earlier, then," Wallander said. He would have to tread very carefully now, so as not to make it too difficult for her.

"My husband didn't speak about his work," she said. "He would never break the oath of silence he'd taken when he became a police officer. I was married to a man whose morals were of a very high standard."

Absolutely, Wallander thought. It was the very high standard of his morals that killed him. "I had exactly the same impression of Major Liepa," he said, "despite the fact that we only met for a couple of days in Sweden."

Did she understand now that he was on her side? That he'd asked her to come and see him for that very reason? So that he could lay out a smokescreen of questions that didn't mean anything?

He repeated his request for her to search again through her recollections. They batted questions and answers to and fro for a while until Wallander decided it was time to stop. He rang a bell, assuming that Sergeant Zids would be listening for it, then stood up and shook her hand.

How did you know I'd come to Riga, he wondered. Somebody must have told you. Somebody who wanted us to meet. But why? What is it you think a police officer from an insignificant little Swedish town will be able to do to help you?

The sergeant appeared to escort Baiba Liepa to some distant exit. Wallander stood at the drafty window and looked into the courtyard. Sleet was falling over the city, and beyond the high wall he could see church steeples and the occasional high-rise building. He suddenly had the feeling that he'd let himself get carried away without allowing his reason to come up with objections, that it was all in his imagination. He was suspecting conspiracies where there weren't any, he'd swallowed the unfounded myth about the Eastern bloc dictatorships being based on the pitting of one citizen against another. What justification had he for mistrusting Murniers and Putnis? The fact that Baiba Liepa had turned up at his hotel disguised as a chambermaid could have an explanation that proved to be much less dramatic than he'd imagined.

His train of thought was broken by a knock on the door. It was Colonel Putnis. He seemed tired, and his smile was strained.

"The interrogation of the suspect has been temporarily adjourned," he said. "Unfortunately the suspect has not made the confessions we had hoped for. We are now checking various pieces of information he has given us, and then I'll resume the cross-examination."

"What are you basing your suspicions on?" Wallander asked.

"In the past he often used Leja and Kalns as couriers and henchmen," Putnis said. "We hope to be able to prove that they've been drug smuggling this last year. Hagelman, as he's called, is the type who wouldn't hesitate to torture or murder his colleagues if he thought it necessary. He hasn't been acting alone, of course: we're looking for other members of his gang at present. Many of them are Soviet citizens, so they might well be in their own country now, unfortunately. But we're not going to give up. We've also found several weapons Hagelman had access to, and we're looking into whether the bullets that killed Leja and Kalns came from any of them."

"What about the connection with Major Liepa's murder," Wallander asked. "Where does that fit in?"

"We don't know," Putnis replied, "but it was a planned killing, an execution. He wasn't even robbed. We have to conclude that it had something to do with his work."

"Could Major Liepa have been leading a double life?" Wallander asked.

Putnis smiled wearily.

"We live in a country where awareness of what our fellow citizens do has become an art form," he said. "That is no less true in the case of fellow police officers. If Major Liepa had been leading a double life, we'd have known about it."

"Unless somebody was protecting him," Wallander said.

Putnis stared at him in astonishment.

"Who could have been protecting him?"

"I don't know," Wallander said. "Just thinking aloud. Not a particularly well-founded thought, I'm afraid."

Putnis got up to leave.

"I had intended to invite you to our house for dinner this evening," he said, "but unfortunately that won't be possible as I have to go on with the interrogation. Perhaps Colonel Murniers had the same idea? It would be most impolite of us to leave you to your own devices in a strange town."

"The Latvia Hotel is splendid," Wallander said. "Besides, I'd planned to summarize the thoughts I've had about the death of Major Liepa. That will take all evening."

Putnis nodded.

"Tomorrow evening, then," he said. "I'd like you to come and meet my family. Ausma, my wife, is an excellent cook."

"I'd like that," Wallander said. "That would be very nice."

Putnis left, and Wallander rang the bell. He wanted to get out of the police headquarters before Murniers had a chance to invite him home, or maybe to some restaurant or another.

"I'd like to go back to the hotel now," Wallander said when

Zids appeared in the doorway. "I have quite a lot of notes to write up in my room this evening. You can come and collect me at 8 a.m. tomorrow."

When the sergeant had left him at his hotel, Wallander bought some postcards and stamps in reception. He also asked for a map of the city, but the map the hotel had was not detailed enough, and he was directed to a bookstore not far away.

Wallander looked around in the foyer, but couldn't see anyone drinking tea or reading a newspaper. That means they're still here, he thought. One day they'll be obvious, the next they'll be invisible. I'm supposed to doubt whether the shadows exist.

He left the hotel and went in search of the bookstore. It was already dark, and the pavement was wet from sleet. There were a lot of people about, and Wallander stopped now and then to look in shop windows. The goods on display were limited, and hard to tell apart. When he got to the bookstore, he glanced back over his shoulder: there was no sign of anybody hesitating mid-stride.

An elderly gentleman who didn't speak a word of English sold him a map of Riga. He went on and on in Latvian, as if he took it for granted that Wallander could understand every word. He returned to his hotel. Somewhere in front of him was a shadow he couldn't see. He made up his mind to ask one of the colonels the next day why he was being watched. He thought he'd broach the subject in a friendly fashion, without sarcasm or aggression.

He asked at reception if anybody had tried to contact him. "No calls, Mr. Wallander, no calls at all," was the answer.

He went up to his room and sat down to write his postcards, moving the desk away from the window, to avoid the draft. He chose a card with a picture of Riga Cathedral to send to Björk. Baiba Liepa lived somewhere not far from there; late one evening the major had taken a telephone call and been summoned. *Who made that call, Baiba? Mr. Eckers is in his room, waiting for an answer to that question.*

He wrote cards to Björk, Linda and his father. He hesitated about the last of his cards, then decided to send greetings to his sister, Kristina.

It was 7 p.m. now. He filled his bath with lukewarm water, and balanced a glass of whisky on the edge of the tub. Then he closed his eyes and started to go through the whole thing, from the very beginning. The life raft, the dead men, the peculiar embrace they were in. He tried to find something he'd missed earlier. Rydberg used to talk about the ability to see *what was invisible.* Observing what was odd in what seemed to be natural. He went methodically through the whole case. Where were the clues he just couldn't see?

When he'd finished his bath he sat at his desk and started to make more notes. He felt sure the two Latvian police colonels were on the right track. There was nothing to contradict the theory that the men in the life raft had been punished for an internal indiscretion. It didn't really matter that they had been shot in their shirtsleeves and then flung into a life raft. He didn't believe any more that whoever did this intended the bodies to be found.

Why was the life raft stolen? he wrote. *By whom? How was it possible for Latvian criminals to get to Sweden so easily? Was the theft carried out by Swedes, or by Latvians in Sweden with Swedish contacts?* Major Liepa had been murdered the very night he got back from Sweden. There was plenty to suggest he'd been silenced. *What did Major Liepa know?* he wrote. *And why am I being given a thoroughly unsatisfactory account of the case, which avoids establishing where the murder took place? Baiba Liepa,* he wrote. *What does she know but doesn't want to tell the police?*

He slid his notes to one side and poured himself another glass of whisky. It was nearly 9 p.m., and he was hungry. He picked up the telephone receiver to check that it was working, then went down to reception and informed them he was in the dining room if anybody called. When he got to the dining room, he was shown to the same table as before. Maybe there's a microphone in the ashtray, he thought ironically. Maybe there's somebody under the table, taking my pulse? He drank half a bottle of Armenian wine with his roast chicken and potatoes. Every time the swing doors opened, he thought it might be the receptionist coming to tell him somebody had phoned. He took a glass of brandy with his coffee, and looked around the dining room. Quite a few of the tables were occupied tonight. There were some Russians in one corner, and a party of Germans at a long table together with their Latvian hosts. It was nearly 10:30 p.m. when he paid his incredibly low bill, and he wondered for just a moment whether he ought to look in at the nightclub. Then he thought better of it and walked up the stairs to the 15th floor.

Just as he was inserting his key into the lock, he heard the telephone ring. Cursing aloud, he flung open the door and grabbed the receiver. *Can I speak to Mr. Eckers?* It was a man speaking, and his English was very poor. Wallander responded as he was supposed to do, saying there was no Mr. Eckers here. *Oh, I must have made a mistake.* The man apologized, and hung up. *Use the back door. Please, please.*

He put on his overcoat and his knitted cap—then changed his mind and put it in his pocket. When he reached the foyer he made sure he couldn't be seen from reception. The party of Germans was just leaving the dining room as he approached the revolving doors. He hastened down the stairs to the hotel sauna and a corridor leading to the restaurant's service entrance. The gray steel door was exactly as Baiba Liepa had described it. He opened it carefully, feeling the wind in his face, then made his way down the loading ramp and soon found himself at the rear of the hotel.

The street was lit by only a few lamps, and he glided into the shadows. The only person he saw was an old man walking his dog. He stood motionless in the darkness, waiting. Nobody came. The man stood patiently by a trash can while his dog cocked its leg, then as the man walked past he told Wallander to follow him once they'd turned the corner. A streetcar clattered somewhere in the distance as Wallander waited. He put on his knitted cap: it had stopped snowing and was growing colder. The man disappeared around the corner, and Wallander walked slowly after him. When he turned the corner, he found himself in another alley; there was no sign of the man and his dog. Without a sound, a car door opened right beside him. *Mr. Eckers,* said a voice from the darkness inside, *we ought to be going right away.* As Wallander climbed into the backseat, it struck him that what he was doing was all wrong. He remembered the feeling he'd had that very morning, when he was in another car being driven by Zids. He could remember the fear. Now it had returned.

CHAPTER 9

The pungent smell of damp wool.

That was how Kurt Wallander would remember his nighttime drive through Riga. He had crouched down and clambered into the backseat, and before his eyes had grown used to the dark, unknown hands had pulled a hood over his head. It smelled of wool, and when he began to sweat he could feel his skin start to itch. Nevertheless, his fear, the intense conviction that everything was wrong, as wrong as could be, had disappeared the moment he got into the car. A voice he assumed belonged to the hands that had pulled the hood over his head had tried to calm him down. *We are not terrorists. We just have to be cautious.* He recognized the voice from the telephone, the voice that had inquired about Mr. Eckers and then apologized for getting the wrong room. The soothing voice had been absolutely convincing, and afterwards it occurred to him that perhaps this was something people in the chaotic, broken-down Eastern-bloc countries had to learn: how to sound convincing in claiming there was no threat, when really everything was threatening.

The car was uncomfortable. The sound of the engine told him it was Russian—presumably a Lada. He couldn't work out how many people there were in the car, just that there were at least two: in front of him was the driver, who kept coughing, and the man beside him who had spoken so soothingly. Now and again his face was hit by a draft of cold air as somebody rolled down a window to let the cigarette smoke out. For a moment he thought he could detect a faint trace of perfume in the car, Baiba Liepa's perfume, but he realized it was only his imagination, or perhaps a hope. It was impossible to judge how fast they were going, but when there was a sudden change of road surface he assumed they had left the city behind them. The car occasionally slowed down and turned left or right, and once they negotiated a rotary. He tried to keep a check on the time, but soon gave up. Finally, the car took one last turn and started bumping and jumping about in a way that suggested they had left the road altogether, and the journey came to an end. The driver switched off the engine, the doors were opened, and he was helped out of the car.

It was bitterly cold, and he thought he could smell conifers. Someone was holding him by the arm to prevent him from falling. He was led up some steps, a door creaked, he entered a warm room, there was a smell of kerosene, then the hood was removed. He gave a start. He could see again—and the shock was greater than when the hood had first been pulled over his head. The room was oblong, with rough wooden walls, and his immediate impression was that he was in some kind of hunting lodge. There was a stag's head mounted over an open fireplace, all the furniture was made of pale wood, and the only light came from a couple of kerosene lamps.

The man with the soothing voice began to speak. He face was nothing like Wallander had imagined—insofar as he had imagined him at all. He was short, and astonishingly thin, as if he had endured terrible hardship or been on a hunger strike. His face was pale, his horn-rimmed glasses seemed far too big and heavy for his cheekbones, and Wallander thought he could be anything from 25 to 50. He smiled, indicated a chair, and Wallander sat down. Without a sound another man emerged from the shadows with a thermos flask and some cups. Maybe it's the driver, Wallander thought. He was older, swarthy, and definitely the kind of person who rarely smiled. Wallander was poured a cup of tea, the two men sat down on the opposite side of the table, and the driver turned up a kerosene lamp with a white porcelain globe that stood on the table. An almost inaudible sound came from the shadows beyond the light of the kerosene lamp, and Wallander realized there were other people present. Somebody's been waiting for me, and made the tea.

"We can only offer you tea, Mr. Wallander," the man said. "But you had dinner shortly before we collected you, and we shan't keep you long."

There was something about what the man said that annoyed Wallander. As long as he'd been Mr. Eckers, he'd felt it was nothing to do with him personally; but now he was Mr. Wallander, and they had been watching him from some invisible spy-hole, observed him having dinner, and the only mistake they'd made was to phone his room a few seconds too early, before he'd managed to open the door.

"I have every reason to distrust you," he said. "I don't even know who you are. Where's Baiba Liepa, the major's widow?"

"Please excuse my impoliteness. My name is Upitis. You can be completely calm. The moment our conversation is over, you can return to your hotel, I promise you."

Upitis, thought Wallander. It's like Mr. Eckers. Whatever his name is, you can be sure it's not that.

"A promise from an unknown person is worthless," Wallander said. "You drove me off with a hood over my head. (Is *hood* really the right word?) I agreed to meet Mrs. Liepa on her terms, because I knew her husband. I assumed she might be able to tell me something that could help the police to throw light on why Major Liepa was killed. I've no idea who you are. In other words, I have every reason to distrust you."

Upitis thought for a moment, and nodded in agreement.

"You're right," he said. "Please don't think we are being so cautious without good reason. I'm afraid it's essential. Mrs. Liepa was unable to be with us tonight, but I'm speaking on her behalf."

"How can I be sure of that? What is it that you want, in fact?"

"We want your help."

"Why do you have to give me a false identity? Why this secluded meeting place?"

"As I've already said, I'm afraid it is necessary. You haven't been in Latvia very long yet, Mr. Wallander—you'll understand eventually."

"How do you think I could help you?"

Once again he heard an almost imperceptible noise from the shadows beyond the faint light of the kerosene lamp: Baiba Liepa, he thought. She's not coming out, but she's there all right, very close to me.

"You must be patient for a few minutes," Upitis said. "Let me begin by explaining what Latvia really is."

"Is that necessary? Latvia's a country like any other country, though I have to admit I don't know what your flag looks like."

"I think it is necessary for me to explain. The very fact that you say our country is just like all the others means that there are certain things you really do have to understand."

Wallander took a sip of tea. He tried to penetrate the shadows with his gaze: maybe there was a hint of a beam of light he could see from the corner of his eye, as if from a door that wasn't properly closed.

The driver was warming his hands around his mug. His eyes

were closed, and it was clear to Wallander that the conversation was to be between himself and Upitis.

"Who are you?" he asked. "Tell me that at least."

"We're Latvians," Upitis answered. "We happened to be born in this stricken country at a very unfortunate time, our paths have crossed, and we have realized that both we and you are involved in a mission that simply must be carried out."

"Major Liepa?" Wallander asked, but left his question unfinished.

"Let me start at the beginning," Upitis said. "You have to understand that our country is on the verge of total collapse. Just as in the other two Baltic states, not to mention the other countries that were treated as colonies by the Soviet Union, people are trying to recover the freedom they lost after the Second World War. But freedom is born of chaos, Mr. Wallander, and monsters bent on achieving ghastly aims are lurking in the shadows. Assuming that one can be either for or against freedom is a catastrophic error. Freedom has many faces. The large number of Russians who were moved here in order to dilute the Latvian population and bring about our ultimate demise are not only worried about their presence being questioned, but naturally enough they're also frightened of losing all their privileges. There is no historical precedent of people voluntarily surrendering their privileges, and so they are arming themselves to defend their position, and doing so in secret. That's why what happened here last autumn came about: the Soviet army seized control and declared a state of emergency. It is an illusion to suppose that one can emerge as a unified nation from a brutal dictatorship, and proceed easily to something like democracy. As far as we are concerned, freedom is alluring, like a beautiful woman one cannot resist. But others regard freedom as a threat that must be opposed at all costs."

Upitis fell silent, as if what he had said was a revelation that shook even him.

"A threat?" Wallander said.

"We could be faced with civil war," Upitis said. "Political dialogue might be replaced with a situation in which people bent only on revenge run amok. The desire for freedom could turn into a horrific state of affairs that no one can foresee. Monsters are hovering in the wings, knives are being sharpened in the night. It's just as difficult to say how the showdown will turn out as it is to predict the future."

A mission that simply must be carried out. Wallander tried to decide exactly what Upitis meant by that, but he knew in advance that he was wasting his time. His ability to grasp what was happening in Europe was practically nonexistent: political goings-on had never had any place in his police officer's world. He usually voted when elections came around, but haphazardly, without any committed interest. Changes which had no immediate effect on his own life left him unmoved.

"Chasing after monsters is hardly the kind of thing police officers get up to," he said tentatively, trying to excuse his ignorance. "I investigate real crimes that have been committed by real people. I agreed to become Mr. Eckers because I assumed Baiba Liepa wanted to see me with nobody else present. The Latvian police have asked me to help them to track down Major Liepa's murderer, primarily by trying to find out if there is any link with the two Latvian citizens whose bodies were washed ashore on the Swedish coast in a life raft. And now, all of a sudden, you seem to be the ones asking me for help—is that right? If so, it must be possible to put the request more simply, without making long speeches about social problems I can't understand."

"That is correct," Upitis said. "But let's say we shall be helping each other."

Wallander couldn't remember the English word for "riddle," and had to express himself in a roundabout way.

"It's not clear enough," he said. "Can't you say exactly what it is you want, come straight to the point?"

Upitis slid over his notebook, which had been hidden behind the kerosene lamp, and produced a pen from the pocket of his shabby jacket.

"The bodies of two Latvian citizens drifted ashore on the Swedish coast," he said. "Major Liepa went over to Sweden. Did you work with him?"

"Yes. He was a good police officer."

"But he was only in Sweden for a few days?"

"Yes."

"How could you know he was a skillful investigator after such a short time?"

"Thoroughness and experience are almost always immediately evident."

It was clear to Wallander that the questions seemed innocent enough, but that Upitis was quite sure of what he was after. The questions were a way of spinning an invisible web. He was like a skillful investigator himself, heading for a specific goal right from the start. The simplicity of the questions was an illusion. Perhaps he's a police officer, Wallander thought. Maybe it isn't Baiba Liepa hiding in the shadows? Maybe it's Colonel Putnis? Or Colonel Murniers?

"So you thought highly of Major Liepa's work?"

"Of course. Isn't that what I said?"

"If you discount Major Liepa's experience and thoroughness as a police officer?"

"How can one discount that?"

"What impression did you have of him as a man?"

"The same as I had of him as a police officer. He was calm, thorough, very patient, knowledgable, intelligent."

"Major Liepa had the same opinion of you, Mr. Wallander. He thought you were a good police officer."

Alarm bells rang in Wallander's mind. It was only a vague feeling, but he suspected Upitis was coming around to his important questions. At the same time he realized something was wrong. Major Liepa had only been home for a few hours before he was murdered, but even so here was this Upitis, obviously knowing details of the major's trip to Sweden. Only the major could have passed on that kind of information, either directly or via his wife.

"That was nice of him," Wallander said.

"Were you very busy during the time Major Liepa spent in Sweden?"

"There's always a lot to do when you're investigating a murder."

"So you didn't have time to socialize?"

"I beg your pardon? I don't understand the question."

"Socialize. Relax. Laugh and sing. I've heard the Swedes like singing."

"Major Liepa and I didn't start a choir, if that's what you mean. I invited him to my home one evening, but that was all. We emptied a bottle of whisky and listened to music. It was snowing heavily that night. He went back to his hotel afterwards."

"Major Liepa was very fond of music. He sometimes complained at how rarely he had time to go to concerts."

The alarm bells rang louder. What the hell is he trying to find out, he wondered. Who is this Upitis? And where's Baiba Liepa?

"May I ask what the music was you listened to?" Upitis asked.

"Maria Callas. I don't remember which opera. *Turandot*, I think."

"I'm not familiar with it."

"It's one of Puccini's most beautiful operas."

"And you drank whisky?"

"Yes."

"And it was snowing hard?"

"Yes."

He's coming to the point now, Wallander thought feverishly. What does he want me to say without my realizing I've said it?

"What brand of whisky were you drinking?"

"JB, I think."

"Major Liepa was very moderate when it came to strong liquor. Mind you, he did occasionally like to relax over a drink."

"Really?"

"He was moderate in all respects."

"I think I was probably more affected by the drink than he was. If that's what you want to know."

"Nevertheless, you seem to have a clear memory of the evening."

"We listened to music. Sat there with glasses in our hands. Chatted. Sat quietly. Why shouldn't I remember that?"

"No doubt you continued discussing the bodies in the life raft?"

"Not as far as I remember. Major Liepa probably did most of the talking, about Latvia. It was only then that I discovered he was married, by the way."

Wallander noticed a sudden change in atmosphere. Upitis was observing him intently, and the driver changed his position on his chair almost imperceptibly. Wallander was so sure his intuition was reliable that he had no doubt they had just passed the point in the conversation that Upitis had been working towards all the time. But what was it, exactly? In his mind's eye he could see the major sitting on his sofa, resting the glass of whisky on one knee, listening to the music. There must have been something more to it, something that justified the creation of Mr. Eckers as a secret identity for a Swedish police officer.

"You presented Major Liepa with a book as he was leaving, is that right?"

"I bought him a book of photographs of Skåne. Not very imaginative, perhaps, but I couldn't think of anything better."

"Major Liepa much appreciated the gift."

"How do you know?"

"His wife told me."

Now we're on the way out, thought Wallander. These questions are just to distract attention from the real point of the conversation.

"Have you had dealings with police officers from the Eastern bloc before?"

"We were once visited by a Polish detective. That's all."

Upitis pushed his notebook to one side. He hadn't made a single note so far, but Wallander was certain Upitis had found out what he wanted to know. What was it, he wondered. What am I telling him without realizing it?

Wallander took a sip of tea, which was by now icy cold. Now it's my turn. Now I must stand this conversation on its head.

"Why was the major killed?" he asked.

"Major Liepa was very worried about the way things were going in this country," Upitis replied hesitantly. "We often talked about it, wondering what could be done."

"Was that why he was killed?"

"Why else would anyone want to murder him?"

"That's not an answer. It's a different question."

"We are afraid it's the truth."

"Who would have any reason to kill him?"

"Remember what I said earlier. About people who are afraid of freedom."

"Who sharpen their knives under the cover of night?"

Upitis nodded slowly. Wallander tried to think, to take in everything he'd heard.

"If I understand correctly, you're members of an organization," he said.

"Rather a loosely connected circle of people. An organization is far too easy to track down and crush."

"What are you trying to achieve?"

Upitis seemed to hesitate. Wallander waited.

"We are free human beings, Mr. Wallander, in the midst of this un-freedom. We are free in the sense that we're able to analyze what's going on all around us in Latvia. Perhaps one should add that most of us are intellectuals. Journalists, academics, poets. Perhaps we form the core of what can become the political move-ment that could save our country from ruin. If chaos breaks out. If the Soviet Union launches an invasion. If a civil war cannot be avoided."

"Major Liepa was one of you?"

"Yes."

"A leader?"

"We don't have any leaders, Mr. Wallander, but Major Liepa was an important member of our circle. Given his position, he had an excellent overview. We think he was betrayed."

"Betrayed?"

"The police force in this country is entirely under the control of the occupying power. Major Liepa was an exception. He was playing a double game with his colleagues. He ran great risks."

Wallander thought for a moment. He recalled something one

of the colonels had said. *We are very good at keeping an eye on one another.*

"Are you suggesting someone in the police force might be behind the murder?"

"We can't be sure, of course, but we suspect that is the case. There's no other satisfactory explanation."

"Who can it have been?"

"That's what we hope you can help us to find out."

It struck Wallander that here at last was the first sign that a solution to the jigsaw puzzle might be at hand. He thought about the suspiciously inadequate examination of the place where the major's body had been found. He thought about the way he had been followed from the moment he set foot in Riga. Suddenly, he saw there was a pattern behind all the diversions that had been following each other thick and fast.

"One of the colonels?" he said. "Putnis or Murniers?"

Upitis replied without hesitation. It would occur to Wallander later that there was a ring of triumph in his voice.

"We suspect Colonel Murniers."

"Why?"

"We have our reasons."

"What reasons?"

"Colonel Murniers has distinguished himself as the loyal Soviet citizen he is in many ways."

"Is he a Russian?" Wallander asked in astonishment.

"Murniers came to Latvia during the war. His father was in the Red Army. He joined the police in 1957, when he was young. Very young and very promising."

"So you're saying he has killed one of his own subordinates?"

"There's no other explanation, but we cannot know whether Murniers committed the murder himself."

"Why was Major Liepa murdered the night he got back from Sweden?"

"Major Liepa was an uncommunicative man," Upitis said. "He didn't waste words. That's a habit you acquire in this country. Although I was a close friend of his, he never said anything more to me than he had to. You learn not to burden your friends with too many confidences. Nevertheless, he did occasionally indicate he was onto something."

"What?"

"We don't know."

"You must have some idea, surely?"

Upitis shook his head. He suddenly looked very tired. The driver was motionless on his chair.

"How do you know you can trust me?" Wallander asked.

"We don't, but we have to take the risk. We imagine a Swedish police officer is not interested in getting too involved in the terrible chaos that is the norm in our country."

Absolutely, Wallander thought. I don't like being followed, I don't want to be driven off at night to secret meetings in hunting lodges. What I want most of all is to go back home.

"I must see Baiba Liepa," he said.

Upitis nodded.

"We'll phone you and ask for Mr. Eckers," he said. "Maybe as soon as tomorrow."

"I can ask for her to be brought in for questioning."

Upitis shook his head. "Too many people would be listening," he said. "We'll arrange a meeting."

That was the end of the discussion. Upitis seemed to be lost in thought. Wallander glanced into the shadows: the faint beam of light was no longer to be seen.

"Did you find out what you wanted to know?" he asked.

Upitis smiled, without replying.

"During the evening when Major Liepa was round at my place, drinking whisky and listening to *Turandot*, he said nothing that could have had a bearing on his murder. You could have asked me right away."

"There are no shortcuts in this country of ours," Upitis said. "The roundabout route is most often the only accessible one, and the safest."

He put his notebook away and got to his feet. The driver jumped up from his chair.

"I'd rather not have to wear the hood on the way back," Wallander said. "It makes me itchy."

"Of course," Upitis said. "You must realize, though, that it is also in your interests to be cautious."

It was moonlit and cold as they drove back to Riga. Through the car windows Wallander could see the silhouettes of dark villages flashing by. They continued through the suburbs, in the shadow of countless tower blocks and unlit streets.

Wallander got out of the car in the same place as he'd clambered in. Upitis had told him to use the hotel's back entrance. When he tried the door, he found it was locked. He was wondering what to do next when he heard the door being unlocked carefully from the inside. To his surprise he recognized the man who had opened the door to the hotel's nightclub a few days earlier. Wallander followed him up a fire escape and was accompanied until he'd opened the door of room 1506. It was just after 2 a.m.

The room was freezing. He poured whisky into his toothbrush mug, wrapped himself in a blanket and sat down at the desk. Although he was tired he knew he wouldn't be able to sleep until he'd written a summary of what had just happened. The pen felt cold in his hand. He pulled towards him the notes he'd made earlier, took a sip of whisky, and started to think.

Go back to the beginning, Rydberg would have said. *Forget all the gaps and the puzzles. Start with what you know for certain.*

But what did he know for certain, in fact? Two murdered Latvians drift ashore near Ystad in a life raft manufactured in Yugoslavia. That was one starting point beyond question. A major from the Riga police force spends a few days in Ystad, in order to assist in the investigation. Wallander himself makes the inexcusable error of not examining the life raft thoroughly enough. And then it is stolen. *Stolen by whom?* Major Liepa goes back to Riga. He submits a report to the two colonels, Putnis and Murniers. Then he goes home and shows his wife the book he'd been given by the Swedish police officer, Wallander. *What does he discuss with his wife?* What makes her turn to Upitis after having disguised herself as a hotel chambermaid? *Why does she invent Mr. Eckers?*

Wallander emptied his glass and poured out some more whisky. The tips of his fingers were white, and he put his hands inside the blanket to warm them up.

Look for a connection even where you don't think there can be one, Rydberg often used to say. But were there any connections? The only common denominator was Major Liepa. The major had talked about smuggling, and about drugs. So had Colonel Murniers. But there was no proof, only speculation.

Wallander read through what he had written, at the same time thinking about what Upitis had said, *Major Liepa was onto something.* But what? One of the monsters Upitis had spoken of? Deep in thought, he contemplated the curtains wafting gently in the draft from the ill-fitting window. *Somebody betrayed him. We suspect Colonel Murniers.*

Could that be possible? Wallander's mind went back to the

previous year, when a police officer in Malmö had shot down an asylum-seeking refugee in cold blood. Was there really any such thing as an impossibility?

He continued writing. *Dead men in life raft—drugs—Major Liepa—Colonel Murniers.* What did that chain indicate? What had Upitis wanted to know? Did he think Major Liepa had given something away that night, as he sat on my sofa listening to Maria Callas? Did he want to know what had been said? Or did he just want to know *if* Major Liepa had confided anything at all to me?

It was nearly 3:15 a.m. Wallander sensed he'd gotten about as far as he was going to get. He went to the bathroom and brushed his teeth. In the mirror he saw that his face was still red and blotchy from the woollen hood.

What does Baiba Liepa know? What is it that I can't see?

He got undressed and flopped into bed after setting his alarm for just before 7 a.m., but he couldn't sleep. He looked at his watch: 3:45 a.m. He could see the hands of the alarm clock in the darkness: 3:35 a.m. He adjusted his pillow and shut his eyes. Suddenly he gave a start and looked at his watch again: 3:51 a.m. He stretched out his hand and switched on the bedside light. The alarm clock said 3:41 a.m. He sat up. Why was the alarm clock slow? Or was his wristwatch fast? Why the difference? It had never happened before. He picked up the alarm clock and adjusted the hands to show the same time as his wristwatch: 3:44 a.m. Then he switched off the light and closed his eyes. As he was on the point of dozing off, he was jerked back into consciousness. He lay quite still in the darkness, telling himself it was all in his imagination. In the end, though, he switched the light on once more, sat up in bed and unscrewed the back of his alarm clock.

The microphone was about as big as a penny, three or four millimeters thick. It was jammed between the two batteries. At first, Wallander thought it was a lump of fluff, or a piece of gray tape; but when he tilted the lamp and examined the clock's mechanism closely, he saw that what was stuck between the batteries was a cordless microphone. He sat there for a long time, staring at the clock he was holding in his hand. Then he screwed the back on again. Shortly before 6 a.m. he sank into restless slumber, leaving the bedside light on.

CHAPTER 10

Wallander woke in a state of irrepressible fury. He felt humili-
ated and shaken by the fact that somebody had placed a microphone in his alarm clock. He took a shower to wash away the
weariness that had taken hold of his body, and decided to discover
at once why he was being both bugged and followed. He assumed
that the colonels were responsible, but why had they invited him to
come and help them, and then immediately demonstrated how
little they trusted him by keeping him under observation? He
could understand the man in the gray suit. He imagined surveil-
lance was par for the course in a country still so obviously behind
the iron curtain. But breaking into his hotel room and planting a
microphone!

At 7:30 a.m. he ordered a cup of coffee in the dining room. He
looked around to see if there was any sign of a shadow, but he was
alone apart from a couple of Japanese people conversing quietly
and anxiously at a table in the corner. He went out into the street
just before 8 a.m. The air was milder—perhaps spring was on the
way. Sergeant Zids was standing by the car, waving to him. As a
sign of his displeasure Wallander sat grim and silent all the way
to the fortified police headquarters. When Sergeant Zids made to
see him to his office in Murniers's corridor, Wallander waved him
away—he knew the way by now. But, to his great annoyance, he
got lost and had to ask for directions. He stopped at Murniers's
door and raised his hand to knock, then changed his mind and

went to his own office. He was tired still, and felt he needed to pull himself together before venting his rage on Murniers. He had barely taken off his jacket when the phone rang.

"Good morning," Colonel Putnis said. "I hope you slept well, Mr. Wallander."

No doubt you know perfectly well that I've hardly slept at all, Wallander thought. The microphone must have told you I didn't snore even once. I'll bet there's a report on your desk already.

"I can't complain," he said. "How's the interrogation going?"

"Not very well, I'm afraid, but I'll try again this morning. We shall confront the suspect with a lot of new material that may encourage him to reconsider his position."

"I feel rather redundant," Wallander said. "I can't really see how I can be of any help."

"Good police officers are always impatient," Colonel Putnis said. "I thought I might stop by, if you don't mind."

"I'm here," Wallander said.

Colonel Putnis arrived 15 minutes later. He had with him a young police officer carrying a tray with two cups of coffee. Putnis had bags under his eyes.

"You look tired, Colonel Putnis."

"The air in the interrogation room is always bad."

"Maybe you smoke too much?"

Putnis shrugged. "I'm sure you're right," he said. "I've heard that Swedish police officers seldom smoke. I find it hard to contemplate an existence without cigarettes."

Major Liepa, thought Wallander. Had he managed to describe that peculiar police station in Sweden where no smoking was allowed except in designated areas?

Putnis had taken out a packet of cigarettes.

"Do you mind?" he asked.

"Please go ahead. I don't smoke myself, but I'm not irritated by cigarette smoke."

Wallander tried the coffee. It had a bitter aftertaste and was very strong. Putnis sat deep in thought, watching the smoke floating up to the ceiling.

"Why are you keeping watch on me?" Wallander asked him.

Putnis stared questioningly.

"I beg your pardon?"

He knows how to put on an act, thought Wallander, and could feel his indignation flood back.

"Why are you keeping watch on me? I've known that you're having me followed; but why do you consider it necessary to hide a microphone in my alarm clock?"

Putnis studied him thoughtfully.

"The microphone in your alarm clock can only be due to an unfortunate misunderstanding," he said. "Some of my subordinates can be over-enthusiastic at times. The plainclothes police officers who are keeping an eye on you are there for your own safety."

"Why? What could happen to me?"

"We don't want anything to happen to you. Until we know why Major Liepa was murdered, we are being extra careful."

"I can look after myself," Wallander said dismissively. "I'd be grateful if you'd refrain from planting any more microphones. If I find another one, I shall return to Sweden immediately."

"I apologize," Putnis said. "I shall ensure that whoever was responsible receives a severe reprimand."

"But you are the one who issued the orders, surely?"

"Not for the microphone," Putnis insisted. "That must have been one of my captains taking a regrettable initiative."

"The microphone was very small," Wallander said. "Very advanced. I take it somebody will have been sitting in a neighboring room, listening?"

Putnis nodded.

"Of course," he said.

"I thought the Cold War was over," Wallander said.

"When one historical period is replaced by another, there is always a group of people left over from the old society," Putnis said philosophically. "I'm afraid that's true even of police officers."

"Will you allow me to ask some questions not directly linked to the investigation?" Wallander asked.

Putnis's weary smile returned. "Of course," he said, "but I'm not sure if I will be able to give you satisfactory answers."

It occurred to Wallander that Putnis's exaggerated politeness was out of step with the impression he had of police officers in the Eastern bloc countries. When he had first met Putnis he had been reminded of a big cat. A smiling beast of prey. A polite, smiling beast of prey.

"I don't mind admitting that I haven't much idea of what's happening in Latvia," he began, "but I do know what happened here last autumn. Tanks in the streets, people lying dead in the gutter. The dreaded advance of the Russian 'Black Berets.' I've seen the remains of the barricades in the streets. I've seen bullet holes in house walls. There is a widespread desire to break away from the Soviet Union, to finally put an end to the occupation. That determination is coming up against opposition."

"There are different ways of looking at that opposition," Putnis said hesitantly.

"Where do the police stand in this situation?"

Putnis stared at him in surprise. "We keep order, of course," he replied.

"How does one keep tanks in order?"

"What I mean is that we make sure people keep calm. Ensure that nobody gets hurt unnecessarily."

"But surely the tanks must be regarded as the cause of the disorder?"

Putnis carefully stubbed out his cigarette before replying. "You and I are both police officers," he said. "We have the same elevated goal: to combat crime and ensure that people feel safe. But we work in different circumstances, and that affects the way in which we go about our business."

"You said there are different ways of looking at things. I suppose there are different views inside the police force as well?"

"I know that in the West, the police are regarded as apolitical civil servants. The police force has to be neutral towards whatever government happens to be in power. In principle the same applies in our country as well."

"But there is only one party here, isn't there?"

"Not anymore. Certain new political organizations have emerged in recent years."

Wallander could see that Putnis was skillfully avoiding answering any of his questions. He decided to take the bull by the horns.

"What do you think yourself?" he asked.

"What about?"

"About independence. Breaking free."

"A colonel in the Latvian police force has no business commenting on that question. Certainly not to a stranger."

"I hardly think there are any hidden microphones in here," Wallander insisted. "Your reply will go no further. Besides, I'll be back in Sweden shortly. I'm hardly going to get on a soap box in the town square and announce what you've told me in strict confidence."

Putnis eyed him up and down for some time before replying.

"I trust you, Inspector Wallander, of course. Allow me to say that I sympathize with what is happening in this country—and in our neighboring countries, and the Soviet Union; but I'm afraid not all of my colleagues share that view."

Colonel Murniers, for instance, Wallander thought. But he won't admit as much, of course.

Colonel Putnis got to his feet. "That was a thought-provoking conversation," he said. "But now I have to confront an unpleasant person in an interrogation room. The reason I stopped by was to say that my wife Ausma wonders if it will be convenient for you to have dinner with us tomorrow evening. I had forgotten that we had a previous engagement tonight."

"That would be splendid," Wallander said.

"Colonel Murniers would like you to be in touch with him this morning. He thought you and he could discuss the areas the investigation should be concentrating on. Obviously, I'll let you know if my interrogation achieves a breakthrough."

Putnis left the room. Wallander read through the notes he'd made the night before, when he'd gotten back from the hunting lodge in the forest. *We suspect Colonel Murniers*, Upitis had said. *We think Major Liepa was betrayed. There's no other explanation.*

He stood at the window, gazing out over the rooftops. He'd never been involved in an investigation quite like this one. People leading lives he had absolutely no conception of occupied the territory he found himself in. How should he proceed? Perhaps he might just as well go home? And yet, he couldn't deny that he was curious. He wanted to know why the short-sighted little major had been murdered. Where were the connections? He went back to the desk and started going through his notes one more time. The telephone rang, and he lifted the receiver, expecting to hear Murniers's voice. All he could hear at first was a deafening crackle, and then he realized it was Björk trying to make himself understood in his poor English.

"It's me!" he yelled into the mouthpiece. "Wallander. I can hear you."

"Kurt!" Björk shouted. "Is that you? I can hardly hear you. I'm only on the other side of the Baltic—why is the line so awful? Can you hear me?"

"I can hear you. You don't need to shout."

"What did you say?"

"Stop shouting! And don't speak so fast!"

"How's it going?"

"Slowly. I don't even know if we're getting anywhere."

"Hello?"

"I said it's going slowly. Can you hear me?"

"Only just. Don't speak so fast. Stop shouting. Are you okay?"

All of a sudden the connection was crystal clear—Björk might have been in the neighboring room.

"That's better. I didn't hear what you said."

"It's going slowly, and I don't know if we're getting anywhere. A colonel by the name of Putnis has been questioning a suspect since yesterday, but I've no idea where that will lead."

"Do you think you can be of use?"

Wallander hesitated, then replied confidently. "Yes," he said. "I think it's good for me to be here—if you can spare me for a bit longer."

"There's been nothing special here. It's pretty quiet. You can concentrate on what you're doing."

"Any leads on the life raft?"

"Not a thing."

"Is there anything else I ought to know? Have you got Martinsson there?"

"Martinsson's in bed with flu. We've dropped the preliminary

investigation now that Latvia's taken over. We've got nothing new
to contribute."

"Have you had any snow?"

Wallander didn't hear Björk's reply. The telephone link was
cut off, as if somebody had taken a pair of scissors to it. Wallander
replaced the receiver, and it occurred to him that he ought to
phone his father. He still hadn't sent the postcards he'd written.
Maybe he ought to buy some souvenirs of Riga? What on earth
could one take home from Latvia? He pushed away a vague feeling
of homesickness, drank the remains of his cold coffee and went
back to his notes. After half an hour he leaned back in his creaking
desk chair and stretched. At last he was beginning to feel less
tired. The first thing I must do is talk to Baiba Liepa, he thought.
Until I do that, everything is based on guesswork. She must have
information of crucial significance. I have to know why Upitis
arranged the meeting last night, what he wanted me to tell him
or feared I might know.

He wrote her name on a piece of paper and drew a ring round it.
He put an exclamation mark after her name. Then he wrote
Murniers's name and put a question mark after it. He gathered
his papers together, stood up and went out into the corridor. When
he knocked on Murniers's door, he heard a grunting noise and on
entering found Murniers on the phone. The colonel pointed to one
of the uncomfortable visitors' chairs, and Wallander sat down and
waited. He listened to what Murniers was saying. It seemed to be a
heated conversation, and occasionally the colonel's voice rose to a
bellow. Wallander realized there was considerable strength confined
within that swollen, neglected body. He couldn't understand a word
of what was being said, but it suddenly dawned on him that
Murniers was not speaking Latvian—the intonation was different. It
was a while before it occurred to him that Murniers must be speak-

ing Russian. The conversation ended with Murniers firing off a salvo that sounded like a string of peremptory orders, then slamming down the receiver.

"Idiots," he muttered, wiping his face with his handkerchief. He turned to Wallander, cool and collected once more, and smiled. "It's always difficult when one's subordinates don't do what they're supposed to do. Do you have the same problem in Sweden?"

"Often," Wallander replied politely.

He watched the man sitting opposite. Could he have murdered Major Liepa? Of course he could! The experience he'd gained during his years in the police force had given him this unambiguous answer: there are no murderers. Only ordinary people who commit murder.

"I thought perhaps we could go through all the material one more time," Murniers said. "I'm convinced the man Colonel Putnis is interrogating is involved in some way or other, but while the questioning is going on perhaps we might be able to find some new angles?"

Wallander decided to take the bull by the horns.

"I feel that the investigation of the crime scene is inadequate," he said.

Murniers raised an eyebrow.

"In what way?"

"Sergeant Zids translated the report for me, and several details didn't ring true. To start with, nobody seems to have bothered to search the quay itself."

"What might have been found there?"

"Tire marks. Major Liepa would hardly have walked out to the harbor that night."

Wallander waited for Murniers to comment, but as the colonel said nothing, he continued.

"Nobody seems to have looked for a murder weapon either. My overall impression is that the murder couldn't have been committed where the body was found. The reports that Sergeant Zids translated for me state that the scene of the crime and the place where the body was found are identical, but they provide no evidence to support this. What strikes me as oddest of all, though, is that no witnesses have been questioned."

"There were no witnesses," Murniers said.

"How do you know?"

"We've spoken to the security officers at the harbor. Nobody saw anything. Besides, Riga is a city that sleeps at night."

"I was thinking rather about the district where Major Liepa lived. It was late at night when he left the house. Somebody might have heard a door closing and checked to see who was going out so late. A car might have stopped. There's nearly always somebody who saw or heard something, if only you dig deep enough."

Murniers nodded. "That's exactly what we're doing just now," he said. "A number of police officers are currently knocking on doors with a photo of Major Liepa."

"Don't you think that's a bit late? People soon forget. Or they mix up days and dates. Major Liepa used to go up and down those stairs to his apartment every day."

"Sometimes it can be advantageous to wait a little," Murniers answered. "When the rumor that Major Liepa had been murdered started to spread, people claimed to have seen all kinds of things. Or they imagined they had. Waiting for a few days can be a way of getting people to reflect, to sort out the difference between what they imagined they might have seen, and accurate observations."

Wallander knew that Murniers had a point, but his own experience was that it could be helpful to conduct two door-to-door exercises, with a few days between visits.

"Is there anything else that concerns you?" Murniers asked.

"What did Major Liepa have on?"

"What do you mean?"

"Was he in uniform, or in civilian clothes?"

"In uniform. He'd told his wife he had to go on duty."

"What did they find in his pockets?"

"Cigarettes and matches. Some small change. A pen. Nothing that had no business to be there. There was nothing missing, either. His identity card was in his breast pocket, and he'd left his wallet at home."

"Was he carrying his gun?"

"Major Liepa preferred not to carry a gun unless there was a real risk that he might be forced to use it."

"How did he generally get to the police station?"

"He had a car with a driver, of course, but often he chose to walk. God knows why."

"In the case notes it says that Baiba Liepa doesn't recall having heard a car stop outside."

"Of course not. He wasn't going on duty—he'd been tricked."

"He didn't know that at the time, though. Since he didn't go back inside, he must have assumed something had happened to the car. What did he do then?"

"Presumably he started walking. We can't be sure."

Wallander had no more questions, but was now certain that the investigation had been conducted badly. So badly that it gave the impression of having been set up. But in order to conceal what?

"I'd like to spend some hours nosing around his home and the surrounding streets," Wallander said. "Sergeant Zids can help me."

"You won't find anything," Murniers assured him, "but you're welcome to. If anything crucial comes out of the interrogation, I'll send for you."

He pressed the bell; Sergeant Zids appeared in the doorway. Wallander asked him to start by showing him the town. He felt he needed to give his brain an airing before getting to grips with the fate of Major Liepa.

Sergeant Zids seemed to relish the task of showing off his city to the visitor. He described the streets and parks they passed at length, and Wallander could see how proud he was. They drove down Aspasias Boulevard, with the river on the left, and the sergeant pulled up by the curb to show Wallander the tall monument to freedom. Wallander tried to work out what the gigantic obelisk represented, and recalled Upitis saying that one could long for freedom, but also be scared of it. Some disreputable-looking men were squatting at the foot of the monument, shabbily dressed, shivering with cold. Wallander watched one of them pick up a cigarette end from the street. Riga is full of contrasts, he thought. Everything I see, and think I'm beginning to understand, is immediately followed by its opposite. Unpainted high-rise buildings soar above highly decorated but decrepit blocks of flats built before the war. Huge esplanades end up either as narrow alleys or as splendid squares—the Cold-War parade grounds of gray concrete and granite monuments.

When the sergeant stopped at a red light Wallander watched the endless stream of people flowing down the pavements. Were they happy? Were they any different from people back home? He couldn't judge.

"Verman's Park," Sergeant Zids said. "There are a couple of cinemas over there, the Spartak and the Riga. That's the Esplanade to the left. Now we're turning into Valdemar Street. When we've crossed the bridge over the municipal canal, you'll see the Dramatic Theater on your right. Now we're turning left again, into November 11th Quay. Shall we keep going, Colonel Wallander?"

"No, that'll be enough," Wallander said, not feeling in the least like a colonel. "You can help me buy some souvenirs later on, but now I'd like you to stop somewhere near Major Liepa's house."

"Skarnu Street," Sergeant Zids told him, "in the heart of the oldest part of Riga."

He parked behind a truck that was belching out exhaust fumes while the driver unloaded some sacks of potatoes. Wallander hesitated for a moment over whether or not to take the sergeant along with him. Without him he wouldn't be able to ask any questions, but even so, he felt a need to be alone with his observations and thoughts.

"That's Major Liepa's house," Sergeant Zids said, pointing at a building crammed between two tower blocks that appeared to be holding it up.

"Did his apartment overlook the street?" asked Wallander.

"Yes, on the second floor, those four windows to the left."

"Wait here," Wallander told him.

It was the middle of the day, but the street was quiet. Wallander walked slowly to the house Major Liepa had emerged from when he went out for that last, solitary walk. He remembered Rydberg saying that a police officer had to be an actor, to approach the unknown by trying to get inside it, under the skin of a criminal or a victim, imagining their thoughts and reactions. Wallander went up to the entrance door and opened it. It was dark on the staircase and there was an acrid smell of urine. He let go of the door and it closed with no more than a slight click.

He could not trace where the insight came from, but as he stood peering up the dim stairs, something suddenly became clear to him. It was as if a little gleam of light had spread out and he could remember everything he'd seen flashing before his eyes. *There was something beforehand*, he thought. When Major Liepa came to

Sweden a lot had already happened. The life raft Mrs. Forsell had
come upon at Mossby Strand was only a small part of a chain of
events that Major Liepa was tracking. That was what Upitis had
wanted to know. Had Major Liepa revealed any of his suspicions,
had he said anything about what he knew or suspected of a crime
back in his homeland? Wallander could now see quite clearly that
he'd missed a line of thought he ought to have caught onto sooner.
If Upitis was right and Major Liepa had been betrayed by one
of his colleagues, possibly Colonel Murniers, wasn't it possible
that others besides Upitis might be asking the same question? *How
much does this Swedish police officer actually know? Is it possible that
Major Liepa has passed on to Wallander some of what he knows or
suspects?*

It had occurred to him that the fear he had experienced several
times since arriving in Riga had been a warning signal. Perhaps
he ought to be more on his guard than he had hitherto realized?
There was no doubt whoever was behind the murders of the
men in the life raft and Major Liepa would have no hesitation in
killing again.

He crossed the street and looked up at the windows. Baiba
Liepa must know, he thought. But why didn't she go to the
hunting lodge herself? Is she being watched? Is that why I've
become Mr. Eckers? Why did I agree to talk to Upitis? Who is
Upitis? Who was it listening in the doorway beyond the dim light
of that kerosene lamp?

Getting under the skin, he thought—now Rydberg would have
started his solitary role-playing game.

*Major Liepa returns from Sweden. He delivers his report to
Colonel Putnis and Colonel Murniers, then goes home. Something
he said while accounting for his activities in Sweden resulted in
somebody pronouncing an immediate death sentence. He goes home,*

has dinner with his wife and shows her the book he's been given by the Swedish police officer Inspector Wallander. He's glad to be home again, and has no idea that this is the last evening of his life. Once he's dead, his wife tries to establish contact with the Swedish police officer: she invents Mr. Eckers, and a man calling himself Upitis questions him in an attempt to find out what Wallander knows, or what he doesn't know. The Swedish police officer is asked to help, although it is not at all clear how he can help. Nevertheless, it is obvious that the crime is connected with the political unrest in Latvia, and that at the heart of it is a dead major of the police force by the name of Liepa. In other words, there is an extra link to add to the chain already established: politics. Is that what the major discussed with his wife the final evening of his life? The phone rings just before 11 p.m. Nobody knows where the call came from, but Major Liepa appears to have no sense of it being connected with the carrying out of the death sentence. He says he's been called in for night duty, and leaves his apartment. He never comes back.

No car ever turned up, Wallander thought. He waits for a few moments, of course. He doesn't suspect there's anything wrong. After a while it occurs to him the car may have broken down, so he decides to walk. Wallander took his map of Riga from his pocket, and started walking. Sergeant Zids was sitting in the car, watching him. Who is he reporting to, Wallander wondered. Colonel Murniers?

The voice on the phone calling him out in the middle of the night must have inspired confidence, he thought. Major Liepa can't have suspected anything. On the other hand, he must have had reason to be extremely suspicious about everybody. Who was there whom he could trust? The answer was obvious. Baiba Liepa, his wife.

It was clear to Wallander that he wasn't going to get anywhere by wandering around with a map in his hand. The people—there must have been more than just one of them—who had set up the major would have planned it pretty carefully. If he were going to get anywhere he would have to explore different avenues.

When he returned to the car, it struck Wallander that it was odd there was no written report of the major's trip to Sweden. Wallander had seen for himself how the major had been making notes during his time in Ystad. On several occasions he'd commented on how important it was to write detailed reports.

But Sergeant Zids had not translated any such written report for him. It was either Putnis or Murniers who had given an account of their last meeting with the major.

He could see Major Liepa in his mind's eye. The moment the plane left Sturup, he would have folded out the little table in the back of the seat in front and started writing his report. He would have continued writing while waiting for his transfer at Arlanda, and kept on working at it during the last part of his journey—the flight to Riga.

"Didn't Major Liepa submit a written report on his work in Sweden?" he asked after getting into the car.

Sergeant Zids stared at him in surprise. "How would he have had time for that?"

Oh, he'd have made time, Wallander thought to himself. That report must exist, but perhaps there's somebody who doesn't want me to see it.

"Souvenirs," Wallander said. "I'd like to go to a department store, and then we can have lunch. But remember, no cutting in line."

They parked outside the central department store. Wallander spent an hour wandering around with the sergeant in tow. The store was packed, but there were not many goods on display.

It was only when he came to the books and CDs section that his interest was aroused. He found some opera recordings with Russian singers and orchestras, and they were very cheap. He also bought some art books at similarly low prices. He wasn't really sure who he was going to give them to, but he had them gift-wrapped and the sergeant guided him to and fro between the various registers. It was all so complicated that Wallander broke out in a sweat.

When they emerged into the street again, he proposed without more ado that they should eat at the Latvia Hotel. The sergeant nodded his approval, as if to indicate that the point he'd been trying to make all along had gotten through at last.

Wallander went up to his room with his presents, took off his jacket, and washed his hands in the bathroom. He hoped in vain that the phone would ring and somebody would ask for Mr. Eckers, but nobody did. He locked his room door behind him and took the elevator down to the ground floor. Even though Sergeant Zids had been with him, he had asked if there were any messages when he collected his room key: the receptionist shook her head. He looked around in reception for any of the colonels' men, but saw no one. He had sent Sergeant Zids ahead to the dining room, in the hope that this might result in their being seated at a different table from the usual one.

A woman waved to him. She was at a counter that sold news-papers and postcards. He had to look around before being sure he was the one she was beckoning to. He walked over to her.

"Would you like to buy some postcards, Mr. Wallander?" she asked.

"Not just now," Wallander said, wondering how she knew his name. The woman was wearing a gray dress and was probably in her 50s. She had made the mistake of painting her lips bright red, and it occurred to Wallander that what she needed was an honest girlfriend to tell her how awful it looked.

She held out some cards for him to look at. "Beautiful, aren't they?" she said. "Wouldn't you like to see a bit more of our country?"

"I don't think I have time, I'm afraid," he said. "Otherwise I'd love to make a tour of Latvia."

"I'm sure you can find time for an organ concert, though," said the woman. "You're fond of classical music after all, Mr. Wallander."

He gave an almost imperceptible start. How could she know his taste in music?

"There's an organ concert tonight in St. Gertrude's Church," she told him. "It starts at 7 p.m. I've drawn a map for you, in case you want to go."

She handed it over to him, and he noticed it said *Mr. Eckers* in pencil on the back.

"The concert is free," the woman said, when she saw him fumbling in his inside pocket for his wallet.

Wallander nodded and put the map in his pocket. He bought some of the postcards, then went into the dining room. This time he was certain he was going to meet Baiba Liepa.

Sergeant Zids was sitting at the same old table, signaling to him. The dining room was unusually full, and the waiters seemed to be busy for once. Wallander sat down and showed Zids his postcards.

"We live in a very beautiful country," the sergeant said.

An unhappy country, Wallander thought. Wounded, crippled, like an injured animal. This evening I'll meet one of those birds with injured wings. Baiba Liepa.

CHAPTER 11

Wallander left the hotel at 5:30 p.m. He figured that if he couldn't shake off the shadows during the next hour, then he never would. When he said goodbye to Sergeant Zids after their lunch together—he had excused himself by saying he had some paperwork to deal with and preferred to do it in his hotel room—he had spent the rest of the afternoon trying to resolve how to get rid of the men tailing him.

He had no experience of being shadowed, and only very rarely had he done any shadowing of a suspect himself. He ransacked his memory to try to recall any words of wisdom from Rydberg about the difficulties of tailing people, but was forced to conclude he had not expressed any views on the art of shadowing. Wallander also realized that he could not plan any surprise maneuvers since he wasn't familiar with the streets of Riga. He would have to seize any opportunity that arose, and he was not confident of succeeding, but he felt bound to try. Baiba Liepa wouldn't have gone to such lengths to ensure that they met in secret unless she had good reason. Wallander couldn't imagine someone married to the major would be prone to overly dramatic gestures.

It was already dark when he left the hotel, and it had started to get windy. He left his key at reception without saying where he was going or when he would be back. St. Gertrude's Church, where the concert was to take place, was not far from the Latvia

Hotel. He had a vague hope of being able to lose himself among all the people hurrying home from work.

Out in the street, he buttoned up his jacket and glanced quickly around, but couldn't see anybody who looked as if they were following him. Perhaps there was more than one of them? He knew that experienced shadows never trailed their target but always tried to position themselves ahead. He walked slowly, stopping frequently to look at shop windows. He hadn't been able to think of a better ploy than pretending to be a foreigner who was looking for suitable souvenirs to take back home with him. He crossed the broad Esplanade and walked down the street behind the government offices. He thought of hailing a taxi and asking to be taken somewhere and then transferring to another one, but decided that would be far too easy a ruse for a pursuer to see through. No doubt whoever was following him could very quickly establish who had used the city's taxis and where they had gone.

He stopped at a window display of drab-looking clothes for men. He didn't recognize any of the people passing by behind him, whose reflections he could see in the glass. What am I doing, he wondered. *Baiba, you should have told Mr. Eckers how he could find his way to the church without being followed.* He set off again. His hands were cold, and he regretted not bringing any gloves with him.

On the spur of the moment he went into a café, and entered a smoke-filled room crammed with people that smelled strongly of beer and tobacco and sweat, and looked around for a table. There wasn't an empty one, but he could see a vacant chair right at the back in a corner. Two old men, each with a glass of beer in front of him, were deep in conversation and merely nodded when Wallander pointed inquiringly at the chair. A waitress with damp patches under her arms shouted something at him, and he pointed at one of the beer glasses. All the time, he was keeping an eye on the entrance: would his shadow follow him in? The waitress came with his frothing glass. He gave her a bill and she put his change on the sticky table. A man in a worn black leather jacket came in. Wallander watched him make his way to a group that seemed to have been waiting for him, and sit down. Wallander took a sip of beer and glanced at his wristwatch: 5:55 p.m. Now he would have to make up his mind how to proceed. The door to the bathroom was diagonally behind him—every time the door opened, he was assailed by the stench of urine. When he had half-emptied his glass, he got up and went to the bathroom. He found himself in a narrow corridor with cubicles on each side and a urinal at the end, lit by a single bulb. He thought there might be a back door he could use, but the corridor was closed off by a brick wall. That's no good, he thought: no point in even trying. How do you get away from something you can't even see? *Unfortunately Mr. Eckers will have unwelcome company when he goes to the concert.* His inability to find a solution was irritating him. As he was standing at the urinal, the door opened and a man came in and locked himself in one of the cubicles.

Wallander knew immediately that it was somebody who'd arrived at the café after him—he had a good memory for faces. He didn't hesitate, knowing he would just have to risk making a mistake. He hurried back through the smoky café and out the door. Out in the street, he looked around, peering into doorways, but could see no one. Quickly he retraced his steps, turned into a narrow alley and ran as fast as he could until he emerged once more into the Esplanade. A bus was standing at a stop, and he managed to board it just before the doors closed. He got off at the next stop without having been asked for the fare, left the main road and went down one of the numerous alleys. He paused in the light from a streetlamp to check the map. He still had some

time, and he ducked into a dark entrance to wait. For the next ten
minutes nobody he judged to be a possible shadow went by. He
knew he might still be watched, but he felt he had now done all he
could.

He reached the church just before 7 p.m. It was already quite full,
but he found a space by one of the side aisles, and watched the
people still streaming into the church. He couldn't see anyone who
might be his shadow; nor could he see Baiba Liepa.

The sound of the organ shocked him. It was as if the whole
church was about to be shattered by the sheer power of the music.
Wallander remembered an occasion when, as a child, his father
had taken him to church. The organ music had frightened him
so much that he'd burst into tears. Now, he recognized something
soothing in the music. Bach has no homeland, he thought. His
music belongs everywhere. Wallander let the music seep into his
consciousness.

*Murniers might have been the one who phoned Major Liepa.
Something the major said when he got back from Sweden might have
driven Murniers to silence him swiftly. Major Liepa might have been
ordered to report for duty. He might even have been murdered at
the police station itself.*

He was suddenly shaken out of his train of thought by the
sensation of being watched. He looked to either side of him but
could see only faces concentrating on the music. In the broad
central choir all he could see were people's backs. He continued
looking around until his gaze reached the aisle opposite.

There was Baiba Liepa, in the middle of a pew, amidst a group
of old people. She was wearing her fur hat, and looked away once
she was certain Wallander had recognized her. For the next hour
he tried to avoid looking at her again, but now and then he

couldn't resist glancing in her direction, and he could see she was sitting with her eyes closed, listening to the music. Wallander was overcome by a feeling of unreality. Only a few weeks ago her husband had been sitting on his sofa while they'd listened to Maria Callas singing in *Turandot*, with a blizzard raging outside the windows. Now he was in a church in Riga, the major was dead, and his widow was sitting with her eyes closed, listening to a Bach fugue.

She must know how we're going to get away from here, he thought. She chose the church as a meeting place, not me.

When the concert was over everyone stood up to leave immediately, and there was a bottleneck at the exit. The rush astonished Wallander. It was as if the music had never existed, and the congregation was trying to flee from a bomb scare. He lost sight of Baiba Liepa in the crush, and allowed himself to be carried along by the crowd. Just as he reached the porch, he caught sight of her in the shadows of the north transept. He saw her beckoning to him, and turned away from the throng of people elbowing their way towards the door.

"Follow me," she said. Behind an ancient burial vault was a narrow door, which she opened with a key bigger than her hand. They emerged into a churchyard, she looked around quickly, then hurried on through the decrepit headstones and rusty iron crosses. They left the churchyard through a gate into a back street, and a car with its lights off started its noisy engine, and they scrambled in. This time Wallander was certain the car was a Lada. The man behind the wheel was very young and smoking one of those extra-strong cigarettes. Baiba Liepa smiled quickly at Wallander, shy and uncertain, and they drove out into a wide main thoroughfare Wallander guessed must be Valdemar. They continued north, past a park Wallander remembered from the tour he'd made with

Sergeant Zids, and then turned left. Baiba Liepa asked the driver
something, and received a shake of the head by way of reply.
Wallander noticed the driver checked his rearview mirror constantly. They turned left again, and suddenly the driver accelerated
and made a U-turn. They passed the park again, and Wallander
was now sure it was the Verman's Park; then they drove back
towards the city center. Baiba Liepa was leaning forward in her
seat, as if giving the driver silent instructions by breathing down
the back of his neck. They went along Aspasias Boulevard, passed
another of those deserted squares, and crossed a bridge whose
name Wallander didn't know.

They came to a district of ramshackle factories and grim
housing estates. They seemed to be going more slowly now; Baiba
Liepa was leaning back in her seat, and Wallander assumed they
were confident that nobody had managed to get on their trail.

Minutes later they drew up outside a rundown, two-story
building. Baiba nodded to Wallander, and they got out. She led
him swiftly through an iron gate, up a gravel path, and unlocked a
door. Wallander heard the car driving off behind them. He entered
a hall that smelt faintly of disinfectant, noting that it was lit by
just one dim bulb behind a red cloth shade, and it occurred to
him that they could well be at the entrance to a disreputable nightclub. He hung up his thick overcoat, put his jacket over the back
of a chair, then followed her into a living room where the first
thing he saw was a crucifix hanging on one wall. She switched on
some lights, and all at once she seemed quite calm. She signaled
him to sit down.

Afterwards, long afterwards, he would be astonished to find he
could remember nothing at all about the room in which he had
his meetings with Baiba Liepa. The only thing that stuck in his
memory was the black, meter-high crucifix hanging between two

windows whose curtains were carefully drawn, and the lingering smell of disinfectant in the hall. But as for the worn armchair in which he sat, listening to Baiba Liepa's horrific story—what color was it? He couldn't remember. It was as if they had talked in a room with invisible furniture. The black crucifix could just as well have been suspended in mid-air, held up by a divine force.

She had been wearing a russet-colored dress which he later learned the major had bought for her in a department store in Ystad. She had put it on in order to honor his memory, she said, and she'd also thought it would be a reminder of the crime she herself had suffered through the betrayal and murder of her husband. Wallander did most of the talking, asking questions which she answered in her restrained voice.

The first thing they did was to do away with *Mr. Eckers.*

"Why that particular name?" he had asked.

"It's just a name," she said. "Maybe there is such a person, maybe not. I made it up. It was easy to remember."

At first she spoke in a way that reminded Wallander of Upitis. It was as if she needed time to close in on the point she may well have been frightened of reaching. He listened attentively, afraid of missing any implied significance—something he had discovered was a feature of Latvian society, but she confirmed Upitis's account of the struggle that was taking place in Latvia. She spoke of revenge and hatred, of a fear that was slowly starting to lose its grip, of a post-war generation that had been suppressed. It seemed to Wallander that she was anti-communist, of course, anti-Soviet, one of the friends of the West that, paradoxically, the Eastern bloc countries had always managed to produce to give succor to their imagined enemies. Nevertheless, she never resorted to making claims she could not support by detailed argument. He realized afterwards that she was trying to get him to *understand.*

She was his teacher, and she didn't want to leave him in ignorance about the circumstances that lay behind the current situation, that explained the events of which it was too soon to establish an overall view. He realized that he had been far too ignorant of what was really going on in Eastern Europe.

"Call me Kurt," he had said, but she shook her head and continued to keep him at the distance she'd settled on from the start. He would continue to be Mr. Wallander.

He had asked her where they were.

"In an apartment belonging to a friend," she told him. "To endure, and to survive, we have to share everything—the more so as we are living in a country and at a time when everyone is being urged to think only of themselves."

"As far as I can see, communism is the opposite of that," Wallander said. "I thought it claimed that only things thought and carried out collectively were acceptable."

"That's the way it used to be," she said. "But everything was different in those days. It might be possible to recreate that dream some time in the future—perhaps it's impossible to resurrect dead dreams? Just as once you're dead, you're dead forever."

"What exactly happened?" he asked.

At first she seemed not to understand what he meant, but then she understood that he was asking about her husband.

"Karlis was betrayed and murdered," she said. "He had penetrated too far under the surface of a crime too massive, that involved too many important people, for him to be allowed to go on living. He knew he was living dangerously, but he hadn't yet been exposed as a defector. A traitor inside the nomenklatura."

"He came back from Sweden," Wallander said. "He went straight to police headquarters to deliver his report. Did you meet him at the airport?"

"I didn't even know he was coming home," she answered. "Perhaps he'd tried to phone, I'll never know. Maybe he'd sent a telegram to the police headquarters and asked them to inform me. I'll never know that either. He didn't call me until he was in Riga. I didn't even have the right food to celebrate his return. One of my friends gave me a chicken. I'd only just finished preparing the meal when he turned up with that beautiful book."

Wallander felt a little guilty. The book he had bought, in great haste and without much thought, was lacking in emotional significance. Now, when he heard her speaking of it like this, he felt as if he had deceived her.

"He must have said something when he came home," Wallander said, painfully aware of the limitations of his English vocabulary.

"He was elated," she said. "Naturally, he was also worried and furious; but what I shall remember above all is how elated he was."

"What had happened?"

"He said something had become clear at last. 'Now I'm sure I'm on the right track,' he said, again and again. Since he suspected our apartment was bugged, he took me out into the kitchen, turned on the faucet, and whispered in my ear. He said he had exposed a conspiracy that was so gross and so barbaric that you people in the West would finally be forced to recognize what was happening in the Baltic countries."

"Is that what he said? A conspiracy in the Baltic states? Not just in Latvia?"

"I'm quite certain of it. He often grew irritated because the three Baltic countries tend to be regarded as one entity, despite the big differences between them, but this time he wasn't only talking about Latvia."

"He actually used the word 'conspiracy'?"

"Yes."

"Did you realize what was implied?"

"Like everybody else, he'd known for a long time that there were direct links between certain criminals, politicians and even police officers. They protected each other in order to facilitate all kinds of criminal activity, and then shared the proceeds. Karlis himself had been offered bribes on many occasions, but he had too much self-respect to consider accepting any. For a long time he'd been working undercover, trying to track down what was happening and who was involved. I knew all about it, of course. I knew we lived in a society that was fundamentally nothing but a conspiracy. A collective philosophy of life had turned into a monster, and in the end the conspiracy was the only valid ideology."

"How long had he been investigating this conspiracy?"

"We were married for eight years, but he'd started those investigations long before we met."

"What did he think he was going to achieve?"

"At first, nothing more than the truth."

"The truth?"

"For posterity. For a time he was certain would eventually come. A time when it would be possible to reveal what had really being going on during the occupation."

"So he was an opponent of the communist regime? In that case, how could he become a high-ranking police officer?"

Her response was angry, as if he were guilty of serious slander of her husband.

"But don't you understand? A communist is precisely what he was! What made him so disappointed was the massive betrayal! The corruption and indifference. The dream of a new kind of society that had been turned into a lie."

"So he led a double life?"

"You can hardly be expected to understand what that involves, year after year being forced to pretend you are somebody you are not, professing beliefs you abominate, defending a regime you hate. It didn't only affect Karlis, though. It affected me as well, and everybody else in this country who refused to give up the hope of a new world."

"What had he discovered that made him so elated?"

"I don't know. We didn't have time to talk about it. We had our most intimate conversations under the covers, where no one could hear us."

"He said nothing at all?"

"He was hungry. He wanted to eat and drink wine. I think he felt that at long last, he could relax for a few hours. Give in to his feelings of elation. If the phone hadn't rung, I believe he'd have burst into song with his wine glass in his hand."

She broke off, and Wallander waited. It occurred to him that he didn't even know whether Major Liepa had been buried yet.

"Think back," he said gently. "He might have hinted at something. People who've made an important breakthrough can sometimes let slip something they don't intend to say."

She shook her head. "I have thought," she said. "And I'm quite certain he didn't. Maybe it was something he'd learned in Sweden? Maybe he'd worked out in his head the solution to a crucial problem?"

"Did he leave any papers at home?"

"I have looked. He was very careful, though. The written word could be far too dangerous."

"Did he give anything to his friends? Upitis?"

"No. I'd have known if he had."

"Did he confide in you?"

"We confided in each other."

"Did he confide in anyone else?"

"Obviously he trusted his friends; but we have to understand that every secret we confide in another person can be a burden to them. I'm quite sure nobody else knew as much as I did."

"I must know everything," Wallander said. "Every little detail you know about this conspiracy is important."

She sat in silence for a while before she spoke. Wallander realized he'd been concentrating so hard that he'd broken into a sweat.

"Some years before we met, at the end of the 1970s, something happened that really opened his eyes to what was going on in this country. He often spoke of it, saying that every person's eyes need to be opened in an individual way. He used a metaphor I didn't understand at first. 'Some people are woken up by cocks crowing, others because the silence is too great.' Now I know what he meant. What happened, more than ten years ago, was that he'd been involved in a long and meticulous investigation that eventually led to his arrest of the culprit. It was a man who had stolen many icons from our churches, irreplaceable works of art that had been smuggled out of the country and sold for huge sums of money. Karlis had no doubt the man would be found guilty. But he wasn't."

"Why not?"

"He wasn't even taken to court. The case was abandoned. Karlis couldn't understand what was going on, of course, and demanded a trial—but without warning the man was released and all the documents on the case declared secret. Karlis was ordered to forget the whole business. The man who issued that order was his superior. I can still remember his name, Amtmanis. Karlis was convinced that Amtmanis was himself protecting the criminal, and may even have been sharing the spoils. That incident hit him very hard."

Wallander's mind went back to that snowy night when the near-sighted little major was sitting on his sofa. "*I'm a religious man,*" he had said. *"I don't believe in a particular God, but even so one can still have a faith."*

"And then?"

"I still hadn't met Karlis then, but I think he went through a serious crisis. Maybe he thought of resigning from the police. As a matter of fact, I believe it was me who convinced him he should continue in his job."

"How did you meet?"

She looked at him in surprise. "Does that matter?"

"It might. I don't know. All I do know is I have to keep asking questions if I'm going to be able to help you."

"How do people meet?" she said with a sad smile. "Through friends. I'd heard about this young police officer who wasn't like the others. He didn't look like much, but I fell in love with him the first time I saw him."

"So you got married? He kept on working?"

"He was a captain when we met, but he was promoted unusually quickly. Every time he took another step up the ladder, he would come home and say that another invisible little funeral wreath had been hung on his shoulder straps. He continued to try to find proof of a link between the leading politicians of our country, the police, and various gangs. He had made up his mind to pin down all the contacts, and he once talked about a secret government department here in Latvia whose only purpose was to coordinate contacts between the underworld and the politicians and police officers involved. About a year ago I heard him use the word 'conspiracy' for the first time. You mustn't forget that he had the feeling then that he was in step with the times: *perestroika* in Moscow had spread as far as Latvia, and we'd begun to meet more often and to discuss more openly what needed to be done in our country."

"Was his boss still Amtmanis?"

"Amtmanis had died. Murniers and Putnis had become his immediate superiors. He distrusted both of them, and had the definite feeling that one of them was involved in, and possibly even the leader of the conspiracy he was trying to penetrate. He said there was a 'condor' and a 'lapwing' in the police force, but he didn't know which was which."

"A condor and a lapwing?"

"The condor is a vulture, but the lapwing is an innocent wader. When Karlis was a boy, he was very interested in birds and had even dreamed of becoming an ornithologist."

"But he didn't know which was which? I thought he had decided it was Colonel Murniers?"

"That was much later, about ten months ago. Karlis was on the trail of a huge drug-trafficking ring. He said it was a devilish plan that would be able to kill us twice."

"What did he mean by that?"

"I don't know." She stood up quickly, as if she were suddenly scared of going any further. "I can offer you a cup of tea," she said. "I'm afraid I don't have any coffee."

"I'd love a cup of tea," Wallander said.

She disappeared to the kitchen and Wallander tried to decide the most important questions to ask next. He was sure that she was being honest with him, but he still didn't know what she and Upitis thought he could do to help them. He doubted he'd be able to fulfill the expectations they had of him. I'm just a simple police officer from Ystad, he thought. What you people need is a man like Rydberg—but he's dead, like the major. He can't help you.

She came back with a teapot and cups on a tray. There must be somebody else in the apartment, he thought—the water couldn't possibly have boiled as quickly as that. Wherever I go there's a hidden guard keeping watch on me, and I understand very little of what's really going on.

He could see she was tired.

"How long can we go on?" he asked.

"Not much longer. My house is bound to be under observation— I can't stay away too long, but we can continue here tomorrow night."

"I'm invited to Colonel Putnis's then."

"I understand. What about the following night?"

He nodded, took a sip of tea (which was weak), and continued asking his questions. "You must have wondered what Karlis meant by the drug-smuggling ring killing twice," he said. "You must have discussed it with Upitis, surely?"

"Karlis once said that you can use anything at all for blackmail purposes," she answered. "When I asked what he meant by that, he said it was something one of the colonels had told him. Why I remember that particular detail, I have no idea. Maybe because Karlis was very quiet and withdrawn at the time."

"Blackmail?"

"That was the word he used."

"Who was going to be blackmailed?"

"Latvia."

"Did he really say that? A whole country could be subjected to blackmail?"

"Yes. If I weren't certain, I wouldn't say it."

"Which of the colonels had used the word 'blackmail'?"

"I think it was Murniers, but I'm not sure."

"What did Karlis think of Colonel Putnis?"

"He said Putnis wasn't among the worst."

"What did he mean by that?"

"He observed the law. He didn't take bribes from just anyone."

"But he did take bribes?"

"They all do."

"Not Karlis, though?"

"Never. He was different."

Wallander could see she was starting to get restless. The rest of his questions would have to wait.

"Baiba," he said—and that was the first time he used her first name—"I want you to think over everything you've told me this evening. The day after tomorrow I might ask you the same questions again."

"Yes," she said. "All I do is think."

For a moment he thought she was going to cry, but she regained her self-control and got to her feet. She drew back a curtain hanging on one wall to reveal a door, which she opened. A young woman entered, smiled and began to clear away the tea things.

"This is Inese," Baiba Liepa told him. "You went to visit her this evening. That's your explanation if you're asked. You met her in the nightclub at the Latvia Hotel, and she's become your lover. You don't know exactly where she lives, only that it's on the other side of the bridge. You don't know her second name as she's only your lover for the few days you're in Riga. You think she's a filing clerk."

Wallander listened open-mouthed. Baiba Liepa said something in Latvian, and Inese struck a pose for him.

"Remember her face," Baiba Liepa said. She'll be collecting you the day after tomorrow. Go to the nightclub after 8 p.m., and you'll find her there."

"What's your own alibi?"

"I went to an organ concert, then visited my brother."

"Your brother?"

"He was the one driving the car."

"Why did you put a hood over my head when I went to meet Upitis?"

"His judgment is better than mine—we didn't then know if we could trust you."

"What do you really think I can do to help?"

"See you the day after tomorrow," she said evasively. "We have no time to lose."

The car was at the gate. She didn't say a word during the drive back to the city center. Wallander suspected she was crying. When they dropped him not far from the hotel, she shook his hand. She muttered something in Latvian, and Wallander scrambled out of the car, which disappeared in a flash. He was hungry, but even so he went straight up to his room. He poured himself a glass of whisky, then lay down on the bed, under the covers.

He could think only of Baiba Liepa.

It was after 2 a.m. before he undressed and got into bed. In his dreams, someone was lying at his side. It wasn't his "lover" Inese, but somebody else, someone the colonels directing his dreams never allowed him to see.

Sergeant Zids collected him the next morning at exactly 8 a.m. At 8:30 a.m. Colonel Murniers came to his office.

"We think we've found Major Liepa's murderer," he said.

Wallander looked at him in astonishment.

"You mean the man Colonel Putnis has been interrogating these last couple of days?"

"No, not him. He's no doubt a slimy criminal who's also involved in some way or another—but we've got another man. Come and see!"

They went down to the basement. Murniers opened the door

to an antechamber with a two-way mirror on one wall. Murniers beckoned to Wallander, inviting him to take a look.

The room behind the mirror had bare walls, a table and two chairs. On one of the chairs was Upitis. He had a dirty bandage on his forehead. He was wearing the same shirt he'd had during their nighttime conversation in the unknown hunting lodge.

"Who is he?" Wallander asked, without taking his eyes off Upitis. He was afraid his shock might betray him. On the other hand, maybe Murniers knew already.

"He's a man we've had our eyes on," Murniers said. "A failed academic, poet, butterfly collector, journalist. Drinks too much, talks too much. He's spent quite a few years in prison, for all kinds of offenses. We've known for some time that he was involved in serious crime, although we could never prove it. We had an anonymous tip suggesting he might have something to do with Major Liepa's death."

"Is there any proof?"

"Needless to say, he doesn't confess to anything at all—but we have evidence as significant as a voluntary confession."

"What?"

"The murder weapon."

Wallander turned to look at Murniers.

"The murder weapon," Murniers repeated. "Perhaps we should go up to my office so that I can give you the background to this arrest. Colonel Putnis ought to be there as well by now."

Wallander followed Murniers up the stairs. He noticed the colonel was humming to himself. Somebody's been leading me up the garden path, he thought, horrified. Somebody's been leading me up the garden path—but I don't know who. I don't know who, and I don't know why.

CHAPTER 12

Upitis was charged. When the police searched his apartment they found an old wooden club with strands of hair stuck to it. Upitis didn't have an alibi for the night of Major Liepa's murder. He claimed he was drunk, had been with some friends, but couldn't remember whom. In the course of the morning Murniers sent out a squad of officers to question people who might have been able to supply Upitis with an alibi, but nobody remembered having seen or been visited by him. Murniers expended an enormous amount of energy on the search, while Colonel Putnis seemed more inclined to wait and see what developed.

Wallander did everything he could to discover the truth. His first reaction when he saw Upitis through the two-way mirror was that Upitis had been betrayed, but then he started to have doubts. Too much was still unclear. Baiba Liepa's description of living in a society where conspiracy was the highest common denominator echoed in his ears. Even if Major Liepa's suspicions had been correct and Murniers was a corrupt police officer, if he was the person behind the major's death, the whole case seemed to be descending into the unreal. Was Murniers prepared to risk sending an innocent man to court merely in order to get rid of him? Wasn't that an act of extraordinary arrogance?

"If he's found guilty," he asked Putnis, "what punishment will he get?"

"We are sufficiently old-fashioned to have retained the death penalty," Putnis said. "Murdering a high-ranking police officer is just about the worst crime you can commit. I would expect him to be shot. Personally, I think that would be an appropriate punishment—what is your view, Inspector Wallander?"

Wallander made no reply. That he was in a country where they executed criminals was so horrific that he was rendered temporarily speechless.

Putnis was playing a waiting game, and Wallander realized that the two colonels often went in different directions without telling each other. Putnis had not even been informed of Murniers's anonymous tip. In the course of one of Murniers's most frenzied moments of hyperactivity during the morning, Wallander had invited Putnis into his office, asked Sergeant Zids to fetch some coffee, and tried to get Putnis to explain to him what was actually going on. From the start he had observed a certain tension between the colonels, and now, when he was more confused than ever, he thought he had nothing to lose by putting his misgivings to Putnis.

"Is this really the right man?" he asked. "What motive could he have? A wooden club with some bloodstains and strands of hair—how can that be proof before anybody has even carried out forensic tests? The hair could be from a cat, couldn't it?"

Putnis shrugged. "We shall see," he said. "Murniers is pretty sure of what he's doing. He very seldom arrests the wrong man—he's much more efficient than I am. But you seem to have misgivings, Mr. Wallander. Might I ask on what grounds?"

"I just wonder, that's all," Wallander said. "All too often I've arrested a criminal who seemed to be the most unlikely of suspects."

They sat in silence, drinking their coffee.

"Of course, it would be marvelous if Major Liepa's murderer

could be caught," Wallander said, "but this guy doesn't look like the leader of a criminal network that made up its mind to dispose of a police officer."

"Possibly he's a drug addict," Putnis said hesitantly. "Drug addicts can be driven to do anything at all. Somebody in the background might have given him an order."

"To kill a senior police officer with a wooden club? A knife or a pistol, okay—but a wooden club? And how did he manage to carry the body to the harbor?"

"I don't know. That's what Murniers is going to find out."

"How's it going with that man you are interrogating?"

"Well. He hasn't admitted anything yet, but he will. I'm convinced he's been part of the drug smuggling that the men who drifted ashore in the life raft were involved in. Just now I'm keeping him waiting, giving him time to think over the situation he's in."

Putnis went back to his office, and Wallander sat perfectly still in his chair, trying to get a fix on the situation. He wondered whether Baiba Liepa knew that her friend Upitis had been arrested for the murder of her husband. He returned in his mind's eye to the hunting lodge in the forest, and realized it was conceivable that Upitis might have been afraid that Wallander knew something which might also have forced him to smash a Swedish police officer's head with a wooden club. Wallander could see that all theories were crumbling, all the trails getting cold, one by one. He tried to reassemble the pieces to see if there was anything he could salvage.

After an hour of quiet contemplation, he concluded there was only one thing for him to do—go back to Sweden. He had come to Riga because the Latvian police had asked for his assistance. He hadn't been able to give them any help, and now that a culprit seemed to have been arrested, there was no longer any reason for him to stay. He had no choice but to accept his own confusion, accept that he had actually been interrogated at night by a man who might turn out to be the person he'd been looking for. He had played the role of *Mr. Eckers* without knowing anything about the play he assumed he was taking part in. The only sensible thing to do was to go home as soon as possible and forget the whole business. And yet, he was reluctant to do that. Beyond all the uneasiness and confusion there was something else: Baiba Liepa's fear and defiance, Upitis's weary eyes. It occurred to him that much about Latvian society was beyond his comprehension; it might also be that he could see things the others couldn't see.

He decided to give it a few more days. As he felt the need to do something practical, instead of just sitting and brooding in his office, he asked Sergeant Zids, who had been waiting patiently in the corridor, to fetch the documentation for all the cases Major Liepa had been concerned with over the past twelve months. He could see no obvious way forward, so he decided to go backwards for a while, into the major's recent past. Perhaps he might be able to find something in the archives that could provide a lead.

Sergeant Zids demonstrated his usual efficiency by returning after half an hour with a bundle of dusty files. Six hours later Sergeant Zids was hoarse and complaining of a headache. Wallander had allowed neither Zids nor himself a lunch break: they had gone through the files one by one, and Sergeant Zids had translated, explained, answered Wallander's questions, then gone on translating. Now they had come to the last page of the last report in the last file, and Wallander had to face his disappointment. He knew that during the last year of his life Major Liepa had arrested a rapist, a robber who had been terrorizing one of Riga's suburbs for ages, solved two cases of postal forgery, and cracked three murders of which two had taken place in families where the murderer and the victim had known each other. He had found no trace of what Baiba Liepa had maintained was her husband's real task. There was no doubt that Major Liepa had been a conscientious and at times even pedantic investigator, but that was all Wallander had been able to glean from the day's work. As he sent Zids off to return the files, it occurred to him that the only remarkable thing about them was what wasn't there. Major Liepa must have saved his data from the covert investigation somewhere, Wallander was certain of it. He couldn't have carried it all in his head. He had no doubt there was a risk of being caught out, so how could he seriously contemplate conducting an investigation aimed at the future without leaving a testimony somewhere or another? He could have been run over by a bus, and there would be no record. There must be a written record somewhere, and somebody must know where it was. Did Baiba Liepa know? Or Upitis? Was there some other person in the major's background, somebody the major had even kept secret from his wife? "Every secret we confide in another person can be a burden to them," Baiba Liepa had said, and those were certainly her husband's words.

Sergeant Zids came back from the archives.

"Did Major Liepa have any family apart from his wife?" Wallander asked him.

"I don't know," he replied, "but no doubt Mrs. Liepa will."

Wallander didn't want to ask Baiba Liepa that question just yet. He thought that from now on, he had no alternative but to follow what seemed to be the normal procedure here, and not to pass on any unnecessary information or confidences, but act on his own according to a private agenda.

"There must be a personal dossier on Major Liepa," he said. "I'd like to see it."

"I don't have access to that," Sergeant Zids said. "Only a few people can access the personal archives."

Wallander pointed to the telephone. "Call somebody who does have that access," he said. "Tell them that the Swedish police officer wants to see Major Liepa's personal dossier."

Sergeant Zids finally managed to contact Colonel Murniers, who promised that Major Liepa's dossier would be produced immediately. Three quarters of an hour later it was on Wallander's desk. It was in a red file, and the first thing he saw on opening it was the major's face. It was an old photograph, and he was surprised to see that the major's appearance had hardly changed in over ten years.

"Translate!" he told Zids.

The sergeant shook his head. "I don't have the authority to see the contents of red files," he said.

"If you're allowed to collect the file, surely you're allowed to translate the contents for me?"

Sergeant Zids shook his head sadly. "I don't have the authority," he said.

"I'm giving you the authority. All you need to do is to tell me if Major Liepa had any other family besides his wife. Then I'll order you to forget everything."

Reluctantly, Sergeant Zids sat down and leafed through the papers. Wallander had the impression that Zids was handling the papers with as much distaste as if they were dead bodies.

Major Liepa had a father. According to the dossier he had the same first name as his son, Karlis, and was a retired postmaster with an address in Ventspils. Wallander recalled the brochure the red-lipped lady at the hotel had shown him: it contained details of an excursion to the coast and the town of Ventspils. Major

Liepa's father was 74, and a widower. Wallander studied the major's face one more time, and pushed the file to one side. At that moment Murniers entered the room. Sergeant Zids hurriedly got to his feet and tried to put as much distance as possible between himself and the red file.

"Have you found anything interesting?" Murniers asked. "Anything we've overlooked?"

"Nothing. I was just going to send the dossier back to the archive."

The sergeant took the file and left the room.

"How is the interrogation of the man you've arrested?" Wallander asked.

"We'll break him," Murniers said coldly. "I'm sure we've got the right man, even if Colonel Putnis seems to have his doubts."

I also have my doubts, Wallander thought. Maybe I can talk to Putnis about it when we meet tonight? Try to find out what grounds we have for our doubts?

He decided there and then that it was the time to set off on a lonely march out of his confusion. There was no reason any longer to keep his thoughts to himself. In the realm of lies, perhaps the half-truth is king, he told himself. Why stick to the facts when all around the truth is being twisted every which way?

"I've been very puzzled by something Major Liepa said to me during his stay in Sweden," he said. "It wasn't clear what he meant. He had drunk a good deal of whisky, but he seemed to be suggesting he was worried that some of his colleagues might not be totally reliable."

Murniers showed no sign of surprise at what Wallander said.

"He was a bit drunk, of course," Wallander went on, feeling a little uneasy about slandering a dead colleague, "but I think he suspected that one of his superiors was in collusion with various criminal networks here in Latvia."

"An interesting claim, even if it did come from a drunk man," Murniers said thoughtfully. "If he used the word 'superiors,' he could only have been referring to Colonel Putnis and myself."

"He didn't name any names," Wallander said.

"Did he give any reasons for his suspicions?"

"He spoke about drug smuggling. About new routes through Eastern Europe. He thought it would be impossible to exploit these trafficking routes without some highly placed person protecting the activity."

"That's interesting," Murniers said. "I always regarded Major Liepa as an unusually rational person. A man with a very special conscience."

He's unconcerned, Wallander thought. Would that be possible if Major Liepa was right?

"What conclusions do you draw yourself?" Murniers asked.

"None at all. I just thought I'd mention it."

"You were right to," Murniers said. "Perhaps you should mention it to my colleague Colonel Putnis as well."

Murniers left. Wallander put on his jacket and found Sergeant Zids in the corridor. When he got back to the hotel he lay on the bed and slept for an hour. He forced himself to take a quick, cold shower and put on the dark blue suit he had brought with him from Sweden. Shortly after 7 p.m. he went down to the foyer where Sergeant Zids was leaning on the reception desk, waiting for him.

Colonel Putnis lived in the country, quite a way south of Riga. It occurred to Wallander during the journey that he was always being driven through Latvia at night. He was moving in the dark, and thinking in the dark. Sitting in the back of the car, he suddenly felt pangs of homesickness. He realized that what caused it was the vagueness of his mission. He stared out into the darkness, and decided he had better phone his father the next day. His father was bound to ask when he was coming home. Soon, he'd say. Very soon.

Sergeant Zids turned off the main road and drove through tall iron gates. Colonel Putnis's driveway was the best cared for stretch of road Wallander had encountered during his stay in Latvia. Sergeant Zids pulled up alongside a terrace lit by spotlights. Wallander had a strong sense of finding himself in a different land. When he got out of the car and everything around him was no longer dark and decrepit, he had left Latvia behind.

Colonel Putnis was on the terrace to welcome them. He had discarded his police uniform in favor of a well-cut suit that reminded Wallander of the clothes worn by the dead men in the life raft. Standing by his side was his wife, a woman much younger than her husband. Wallander guessed she was not yet 30. When they were introduced it emerged that she spoke excellent English, and Wallander strode into the handsome mansion with that special kind of well-being one only gets on completing a long and strenuous journey. Colonel Putnis, crystal whisky glass in hand, showed him around the house, and the colonel made no attempt to conceal his pride. Wallander could see that the rooms were furnished with pieces imported from the West, giving the house a luxurious, yet restrained air.

No doubt I'd have been just like this couple if I lived in a country where everything seems nearly to be on the point of running out or breaking down, he thought. But the house must have cost a great deal of money, and he was surprised that a police colonel could earn as much. Bribes, he thought. Bribes and corruption. But then he quashed the thought immediately. He didn't know Colonel Putnis and his wife, Ausma. Perhaps there were still such things as family fortunes in Latvia, despite the fact that those in government had had nearly 50 years in which to change all the financial norms? What did he know about it? Nothing.

They dined by the light of a tall candelabra. Wallander gathered from the conversation that Ausma also worked for the police, but in a different sector. He had the impression that her work was top secret, and it occurred to him that she might belong to the local section of the Latvian KGB. She asked him a lot of questions about Sweden, and the wine encouraged him to be expansive, despite his efforts to control himself.

After dinner Ausma disappeared into the kitchen to make coffee. Putnis served cognac in a living room where attractive leather armchairs stood in various groups. Wallander would never be able to afford furniture like that no matter how long he worked, and the thought made him aggressive. He felt a vague personal responsibility. It was as if—by not protesting—he would have contributed to the bribes that made Colonel Putnis's home affordable.

"Latvia is a land of enormous contrasts," he said, stumbling over the English words.

"Isn't Sweden as well?"

"Of course—but not as obviously as here. It would be unthinkable for a Swedish police officer to live in a house like yours."

Colonel Putnis stretched out his hands as if to excuse himself.

"My wife and I are not rich," he said, "but we have lived frugally for many years. I'm 55 now, and would like to live in comfort in my old age. Is there anything wrong with that?"

"I'm not talking about rights and wrongs," Wallander said, "I'm talking about differences. When I met Major Liepa, it was the first time I'd come across anybody from one of the Baltic states. I had the impression he came from a country with much poverty."

"There are a lot of poor people here, I'm not denying that."

"I'd like to know how things really stand."

Colonel Putnis's gaze was penetrating. "I don't think I understand your question."

"With regard to bribes. Corruption. Links between criminal organizations and politicians. I'd like to know the answer to something Major Liepa said when he came to my apartment in Sweden. Something he said when he was about as drunk as I am now."

Colonel Putnis observed him with a smile. "Of course," he said. "Of course I shall explain if I can—but first I need to know what Major Liepa actually said."

Wallander repeated the invented quotation he'd presented to Colonel Murniers a few hours earlier.

"Irregularities do occur, even in the Latvian police force," Putnis said. "Many police officers receive low wages, and the temptation to accept bribes can be great. At the same time, though, I have to say that Major Liepa had a tendency to exaggerate the prevailing circumstances. His honesty and industry were admirable, of course, but occasionally he may have been guilty of confusing facts with emotional misconceptions."

"You mean he was exaggerating?"

"Unfortunately I think he was."

"Even when he claimed that a high-ranking police officer was deeply embroiled in criminal activity?"

Colonel Putnis warmed his cognac glass in his hands. "He must have been referring to either Colonel Murniers or myself," he said. "That surprises me. His accusation was both inaccurate and irrational."

"But there must have been some explanation?"

"Perhaps Major Liepa thought Murniers and I were getting old too slowly," Putnis said with a smile. "Perhaps he was dissatisfied by the fact that we stood between him and his own promotion?"

"Major Liepa didn't give me the impression of being especially concerned with his own career."

Putnis nodded sagely. "Let me suggest a plausible explanation," he said, "but I must stress it is strictly between ourselves."

"I do not normally betray confidences."

"About ten years ago Colonel Murniers succumbed to an unfortunate weakness," Putnis said. "He was caught taking a bribe from a director of one of our textile factories who had been arrested on suspicion of embezzlement. The money taken by Murniers was seen as compensation for his turning a blind eye to the fact that some of the arrested man's fellow criminals had been given the opportunity to conceal certain documents that could have provided crucial proof."

"What happened next?"

"The matter was hushed up. The businessman was given a symbolic sentence, and within a year he was appointed head of one of the country's biggest sawmills."

"What happened to Murniers?"

"Nothing. He was full of remorse. He had been overworked at the time, and had gone through a painful and lengthy divorce. The tribunal assigned the task of judging the case decided that the offense should be forgiven. Perhaps Major Liepa had assumed, wrongly, that a temporary weakness was in fact a chronic character defect? That's the only explanation I can give you. Can I pour you some more cognac?"

Wallander held out his glass. Something Colonel Putnis had said, and also Murniers earlier, nagged at him, although he couldn't put his finger on it. Just then Ausma came in with the coffee tray, and began to tell Wallander with great enthusiasm about all the sights he must see before leaving Riga. As he listened to her, his anxiety nagged away in the back of his mind. Something crucial had been said, something barely noticeable: but it had caught his attention even so.

"The Swedish Gate," Ausma said. "You haven't even seen our monument from the time when Sweden was one of the great powers of Europe?"

"I must have missed it."

"Sweden is still a great power even today," Colonel Putnis said. "A small country, but much envied on account of its great riches."

Afraid of losing the thread of the vague suspicion he had intuitively registered, Wallander excused himself and went to the bathroom. He locked the door and sat down. Many years ago, Rydberg had taught him the importance of immediately following up on a clue that seemed to dangle so close to his eyes that it was difficult to see. It dawned on him. Something Murniers had said, that had been contradicted by Colonel Putnis only moments ago, using almost the same words.

Murniers had spoken of Major Liepa's rationality, and Colonel Putnis about his irrationality. In view of what Putnis had vouchsafed about Murniers, perhaps that wasn't difficult to understand; but as Wallander sat there on the toilet seat, he realized that he would have expected the pair to have precisely the opposite views.

"We suspect Murniers," Baiba Liepa had said. "We suspect he was betrayed."

Maybe I've got it all wrong, Wallander thought. Maybe I'm seeing in Murniers what I ought to be looking for in Colonel Putnis? The one who spoke of Major Liepa as rational was the one I'd have expected to think the opposite. He tried to recall Murniers's voice, and it came to him that the colonel had possibly implied something more. Major Liepa is a rational person, a rational police officer: that would suggest his suspicions are correct.

He considered that proposition, and realized he had been far too ready to accept suspicions and information passed on to him at second and third hand. He flushed the toilet and returned to his coffee and cognac.

"Our daughters," Ausma said, holding out two framed portraits. "Alda and Lija."

"I have a daughter too," Wallander said. "She's called Linda."

For the rest of the evening the conversation meandered aimlessly back and forth, and Wallander wished he could make a move to leave without appearing impolite. Nevertheless, it was almost 1 a.m. by the time Zids pulled up outside the Latvia Hotel. Wallander had dozed in the back seat, and he realized he had drunk more than he should have. The next day he would be exhausted, and he'd have a hangover in the bargain.

He lay in bed staring out into the darkness for a long time before falling asleep. The two colonels melted into a single image. He would never be able to reconcile himself to going home until he'd done everything in his power to shed some light on Major Liepa's death. There are links, he thought. Major Liepa, the dead men in the life raft, the arrest of Upitis. It's all connected. It's just that I can't see the chain yet. And behind my head, on the other side of that thin wall, there are invisible people registering every breath I take. Perhaps they will take down and report the fact that I'm lying here wide awake for hours before falling asleep? Maybe they think that enables them to read my thoughts? A solitary truck trundled past in the street below. Just before he dozed off it occurred to him that he'd been in Riga for six days already.

CHAPTER 13

When Wallander woke the next morning he was just as tired and hungover as he had feared. His temples were throbbing, and when he brushed his teeth he thought he was going to be sick. He dissolved two headache tablets in a glass of water, and bemoaned the fact that his capacity for drinking strong liquor in the evening was a thing of the past.

He examined his face in the mirror and saw that he was getting more and more like his father. His hangover was not only making him feel miserable, that something was now lost forever, but he was also noticing the first vestiges of age in his pale, puffy face. He went down to the dining room at 7:30 a.m., had a cup of coffee and forced down a fried egg. He felt rather better once he had some coffee inside him. He had half an hour to himself before Sergeant Zids was due to collect him, and he rehearsed once more the facts in this complicated chain of events that had begun when two well-dressed, dead men drifted ashore at Mossby Strand. He tried to digest the discovery he had made the previous night, the possibility that it might well be Putnis and not Murniers who was pulling the strings in the background, but this thought merely led him back to square one. Nothing was clear. He had gathered that an investigation in Latvia was conducted in circumstances entirely different from those applying in Sweden. The amassing of facts and the establishing of a chain of proof was so very much more complicated against the shadowy backdrop of a totalitarian state.

Perhaps the first thing that had to be decided here was whether
a crime should be investigated at all, he thought, or whether it
might come into the category of "non-crimes." It seemed to him
that he should redouble his efforts to extract explanations from
the two colonels. As things stood at the moment, he couldn't
know whether they were opening or closing invisible doors in
front of him.

Eventually he got up and went out to find Sergeant Zids. As they
drove through Riga, the combination of decrepit buildings and
dreadful, grim squares filled him once more with a special kind
of melancholy he had never before experienced. He imagined
that the people he saw standing at bus stops or scurrying along
the sidewalks felt the same desolation, and he shuddered at the
thought. He felt homesick again, although he was not sure what
there was about home that filled him with longing.

The phone rang as he opened the door of his office. He had
sent Sergeant Zids to fetch some coffee.

"Good morning," Murniers said, and Wallander could tell that
the gloomy colonel was in a good mood. "Did you have a pleasant
evening?"

"I enjoyed the best food I've had since coming to Riga,"
Wallander replied, "but I'm afraid I had too much to drink."

"Moderation is a virtue unknown in this country," Murniers
said. "As I understand it, the success of Sweden is based on an
ability to live with restraint."

Before Wallander could think of a suitable response, Murniers
continued. "I have a most interesting document on my desk here
in front of me," he said. "I think it will help you to forget drinking
too much of Colonel Putnis's excellent cognac."

"What kind of document?"

"Upitis's confession. Written and signed during the night."

Wallander said nothing.

"Are you still there?" Murniers asked. "Perhaps you ought to come to my office right away."

In the corridor Wallander bumped into Sergeant Zids, and, cup in hand, he entered Murniers's office. The colonel was sitting at his desk, wearing that weary smile of his, and he picked up a file from his desk as Wallander sat down.

"So, here we have a confession from the criminal, Upitis," he said. "It will be a real pleasure for me to translate it for you. You seem surprised?"

"I am," Wallander said. "Was it you who interrogated him?"

"No. Colonel Putnis had ordered Captain Emmanuelis to take charge of the interrogation. He has done even better than we had expected. Emmanuelis is clearly a police officer with a bright future."

Did Wallander detect a note of irony in Murniers's voice? Or was it just the normal tone of voice of a tired, disillusioned police officer?

"So, Upitis, the drunken butterfly collector and poet, has decided to make a full confession," Murniers continued. "Together with two others, Bergklaus and Lapin, he admits to having murdered Major Liepa in the early hours of February 23. The three men had undertaken to carry out a contract placed on the life of Major Liepa. Upitis claims he doesn't know who was behind the contract, and that is probably true. The contract passed through many hands before ending up at the right address. Since it was placed on the life of a senior police officer, the sum involved was considerable. Upitis and the other two gentlemen shared the reward, which corresponds to about a hundred years' wages for a worker here in Latvia. The contract was placed well over two months ago—long before Major Liepa left for Sweden. The person commissioning the murder did not lay down a deadline: the key thing was that Upitis and his accomplices didn't fail. Then, suddenly, that changed. Three days before the murder, when Major Liepa was still in Sweden, that is, Upitis was contacted by an intermediary and instructed that he must be disposed of immediately upon his return to Riga. No reason for this urgency was given, but the sum of money involved was increased and a car was put at Upitis's disposal. Upitis was to visit a cinema in the city, the Spartak to be exact, every day, in the morning and in the evening. On one of the black columns supporting the roof of the building someone would place an inscription—the kind of thing you in the West call graffiti—and when it appeared Major Liepa was to be liquidated straight away. That inscription appeared in the morning of the day Major Liepa was due back. Upitis immediately contacted Bergklaus and Lapin. The intermediary had told them that Major Liepa would be lured out of his apartment late that evening. What happened next was up to them. This evidently caused the three murderers considerable problems. They assumed Major Liepa would be armed, that he would be on the alert, and that he would probably resist. This meant they would have to strike the moment he left the building. Naturally, there was every chance that they would make a mess of it."

Murniers broke off abruptly and looked at Wallander.

"Am I going too fast?" he asked.

"No. I think I can follow."

"They drove to the street where Major Liepa lived," Murniers went on. "They had taken out the bulb of the lamp by the front door, and they hid in the shadows, armed with various weapons. Earlier, they had been to a bar and fortified themselves with large amounts of strong liquor. When Major Liepa stepped through the door, they attacked. Upitis maintains it was Lapin who struck him on the back of the head. When we bring in Lapin and Bergklaus, no doubt they will all blame each other. Unlike Swedish law, ours permits us to condemn more than one man if it proves not to be possible to decide which of them was the actual killer. Major Liepa slumped down on to the pavement, the car drove up, and the body was crammed into the backseat. On the way to the harbor he came around, whereupon Lapin is said to have struck him on the head again. Upitis claims Major Liepa was dead when they carried him out to the quayside. The intention was to give the impression that Major Liepa had been the victim of some kind of accident—that was doomed to failure, but it seems that Upitis and his accomplices didn't make much of an effort to mislead the police."

Murniers tossed the report back onto his desk.

Wallander thought back to the evening he had spent at the hunting lodge, Upitis and all his questions, the strip of light from the door where somebody had been listening.

"*We think Major Liepa was betrayed, we suspect Colonel Murniers.*"

"How could they know Major Liepa would come back home on that day?" he asked.

"Possibly somebody working for Aeroflot had been bribed. There are passenger lists, after all. Certainly we shall be looking into that."

"Why was the major murdered?"

"Rumors spread quickly in a society like ours. Perhaps Major Liepa was being too awkward for certain powerful criminals to tolerate."

Wallander thought for a moment before putting his next question. He had listened to Murniers's account of Upitis's confession, and realized that something was wrong—terribly wrong. Even though he knew it was a fabrication, he couldn't guess at the truth.

The lies complemented each other, and what had really happened and the reasons for it were impossible to see.

He realized he didn't have any questions to ask. There were no more questions, just vague, helpless statements.

"You must know that not a word of Upitis's confession is true," he said.

Murniers gave him a searching look. "Why shouldn't it be true?"

"For the simple reason that Upitis didn't kill Major Liepa, of course. The whole confession is made up. He must have been forced to make it. Unless he's gone insane."

"Why couldn't a criminal like Upitis have murdered Major Liepa?"

"Because I've met him," Wallander said. "I've spoken to him. I'm convinced that if anybody in this country can be excluded from suspicion of having murdered Major Liepa, it's Upitis."

Murniers's astonishment couldn't possibly have been an act. So, it wasn't him standing in the shadows at the hunting lodge, listening, Wallander registered. Who was it, then? Baiba Liepa? Or Colonel Putnis?

"You say you've met Upitis?"

Wallander made a snap decision to go once again for a half-truth. He had no choice, he had to protect Baiba Liepa.

"He came to my hotel room and introduced himself. I recognized him when Colonel Putnis pointed him out through the two-way mirror in the interrogation room. When he came to see me, he said he was a friend of Major Liepa's."

Murniers was sitting tense and erect in his chair, all his attention concentrated on what Wallander had just said.

"Strange," he said. "Very strange."

"He came to see me because he wanted to tell me he thought Major Liepa had been murdered by one of his colleagues."

"By the police?"

"Yes. Upitis hoped I would be able to help him to work out what had happened. How he knew there was a Swedish police officer in Riga I have no idea."

"What else did he say?"

"That Major Liepa's friends didn't have any proof, but that the major had said that he felt under threat."

"Threatened by whom?"

"By somebody in the police. Perhaps also by the KGB."

"Why should he feel threatened?"

"For the same reason that Upitis believes criminals in Riga had decided the major should be liquidated. There is an obvious link."

"What link?"

"The fact that Upitis was right on two counts, although he must have lied on one occasion."

Murniers leapt to his feet. Wallander wondered whether he, the police officer from Sweden, had overstepped the mark, pushed his luck too far, but the way Murniers looked at him suggested he was almost pleading with him.

"Colonel Putnis must hear this," Murniers said.

"Indeed," Wallander said. "He must."

Ten minutes later Putnis strode through the door. Wallander had no opportunity to thank him for the dinner before Murniers, speaking excitedly and forcefully in Latvian, recounted what Wallander had just told him about his meeting with Upitis. Wallander was certain that Putnis's expression would reveal whether he had been the one in the shadows that night in the hunting lodge, but he gave nothing away. Wallander tried to think of a plausible explanation for Upitis having made a false confession, but everything was so confused and obscure that he gave up the attempt.

Putnis's reaction was very different from that of Murniers.

"Why didn't you tell anybody before that you had met this criminal Upitis?" he asked.

Wallander didn't know what to say. He could tell that he had broken the bond of trust between them, but at the same time he wondered whether it was a coincidence that he had been having dinner with the Putnises the night Upitis made his alleged confession. Was there any such thing as a coincidence in a totalitarian society? Hadn't Putnis also said he always preferred to interrogate his prisoners alone?

Putnis's indignation subsided as quickly as it flared up. He was smiling again, and put his arm on Wallander's shoulder.

"Upitis, the butterfly collector and poet, is a crafty fellow," he said. "One has to admit it is a very clever move to divert suspicion from himself by going to see a Swedish police officer who happens to be visiting Riga, but there is nothing false about his confession. I've been expecting him to cave in. The murder of Major Liepa is solved. That means there is no longer any reason why you should stay in Riga. I'll see about arranging for your journey home right away. We will express our thanks to the Swedish foreign ministry through the official channels."

It was then that it dawned on Wallander just how the whole of this gigantic conspiracy must be organized. He could see not just the scope of it, and the ingenious mixture of truth and lies, false trails and genuine chains of cause and effect, but it was also clear to him that Major Liepa had been the skillful and honorable police officer he had thought him to be. He understood Baiba Liepa's fear just as well as he understood her defiance. Although he was now going to be forced to go home, he knew he would have to see her again. He owed her that, just as he knew he had an obligation to the dead major.

"Of course I'll go home," he said, "but I'll stay until tomorrow.

I've had far too little time to see the beautiful city I've been staying in—that's something I realized last night, talking to your wife."

He had been addressing both the colonels, apart from this last bit, which was directed at Putnis.

"Sergeant Zids is an excellent guide," he continued. "I trust I can make use of his services for the rest of today, even though my work here is now finished."

"Of course," Murniers said. "Perhaps we ought to celebrate the fact that this peculiar business is about to be solved. It would be impolite of us to allow you to fly back home without our presenting you with a souvenir, or drinking one another's health."

Wallander thought about the coming evening. Inese would be waiting for him in the hotel nightclub and pretending to be his mistress, to take him to his appointment with Baiba Liepa.

"Let's keep it low key," he said. "We're police officers after all, not actors celebrating a successful opening night. Besides, I've already got something arranged for tonight. A young lady has agreed to keep me company."

Murniers smiled and produced a bottle of vodka from one of his desk drawers.

"That's something we wouldn't want to spoil," he said. "Let's drink a toast here and now!"

They're in a hurry, Wallander thought. They can't get me out of the country quickly enough.

They drank one another's health. Wallander raised his glass to the two colonels, and wondered if he would ever discover which one had signed the order leading to the murder of the major. That was the only thing he was still doubtful about, the only thing he couldn't know. Putnis or Murniers? What was quite certain now was that Major Liepa had been right. His secret investigations had led him to a truth he had taken with him to the grave, unless he had left a record. That is what Baiba Liepa would have to find if she wanted to know who had killed her husband, if it was Murniers or Putnis. Only then would she discover why Upitis had made a false confession in a desperate attempt to find out which of the colonels was responsible for the major's death.

Here I am drinking with one of the worst criminals I've ever come across, Wallander thought. The only thing is, I don't know which one it is.

"We shall accompany you to the airport in the morning, of course," Putnis said when the toasts were over.

Wallander left police headquarters feeling like a newly released prisoner, marching a few paces behind Sergeant Zids. They drove through the streets with the sergeant pointing out various places of interest. Wallander looked and nodded, muttering "yes" and "very pretty" when it seemed appropriate. But his thoughts were miles away. He was thinking about Upitis, and the choice he'd obviously been given. What had Murniers or Putnis whispered in his ear? What had they produced from their store of threats, the scope of which Wallander hardly dared imagine? Perhaps Upitis had a Baiba Liepa of his own, perhaps he had children. Did they still shoot children in Latvia? Or was it sufficient just to threaten that every door would be closed to them in the future, that their future would be over before it had even started? Was that how a totalitarian state functioned? What choice did Upitis have? Had he saved his own life, his family, Baiba Liepa, by pretending to be the murderer? Wallander tried to recall the little he knew about the show trials that had led to a series of appalling injustices throughout the history of communism. Upitis fitted into that pattern somewhere or another. Wallander knew he would never be able to comprehend how people could be forced to admit to crimes they could never have committed, admit to murdering their best friend deliberately and in cold blood.

I'll never know, he thought. I'll never know what happened, and that's just as well because I'd never be able to understand it anyway. But Baiba Liepa would understand, and she has got to know. Someone is in possession of the major's last will and testimony, his investigation is not dead, it's still alive but it is outlawed and hiding somewhere where not only the major's soul is keeping watch over it.

What I'm looking for is the "Guardian," and that's something Baiba Liepa must know. She must know that somewhere, there is a secret that mustn't be lost. It's so cleverly hidden that nobody but her will be able to find it and interpret it. She was the person he trusted, she was the major's angel in a world where all the other angels had fallen.

Sergeant Zids stopped before a gate in the ancient city wall of Riga, and Wallander got out of the car, realizing it must be the Swedish Gate that Mrs. Putnis had spoken about. He shivered. It had grown cold again. He inspected the cracked brick wall absentmindedly, and tried to decipher some ancient symbols carved into it. He gave up more or less immediately, and went back to the car.

"Shall we go on?" the sergeant asked.

"Yes," said Wallander. "I want to see all there is to see."

He had realized that Zids liked driving, and all alone in the backseat, despite the cold, despite the sergeant's constant glances in the rearview mirror, he preferred the car to his hotel room. He was thinking about the evening, about how essential it was that nothing should prevent his meeting with Baiba Liepa. For a moment he considered contacting her at the university and telling her what he knew in a deserted corridor. But he had no idea what subject she taught, and he didn't even know if there was more than one university in Riga.

There was also something else that had begun to form in his mind. The brief meetings he had had with Baiba Liepa, although fleeting and overshadowed by the grim point of departure, had been more than mere conversations about a sudden death. They had an emotional content far beyond what he was used to. Deep down he could hear his father's tetchy voice bewailing his son who had gone astray and not only become a police officer but had also been stupid enough to fall for the widow of a dead Latvian police officer.

Is that the way it was? Had he really fallen in love with Baiba Liepa?

As if Sergeant Zids could read his thoughts, he stuck out his arm and pointed to a long, ugly building, telling him that it was a part of Riga University. Wallander contemplated the grim brick edifice through the misted-up car window. Somewhere in there was Baiba Liepa. All official buildings in this country looked like prisons, and it seemed to Wallander their occupants really were prisoners. Not the major, and not Upitis, although he was now a real prisoner and not just one trapped in an endless nightmare.

He suddenly felt tired of driving around with the sergeant, and requested him to return to the hotel. Without knowing why, he asked him to come back at 2 p.m.

He spotted one of the men in gray immediately, and it occurred to him that the colonels no longer needed to pretend. He went into the dining room and deliberately sat down at a different table, ignoring the anxious face of the waiter who came to attend to him. I can really stir things up by refusing to cooperate with the government department that takes care of table placing, he thought, feeling furious. He slammed himself into the chair, ordered a beer and schnapps, and then noticed that the boil he got on his buttock from time to time had reappeared, making him even angrier. He stayed in the dining room for more than two hours, and whenever his glass was empty he beckoned the waiter and ordered a refill. As he grew more and more drunk, he staggered around in his mind and, in a burst of sentimentality, he imagined taking Baiba Liepa back to Sweden with him. As he left the dining room, he couldn't help waving to the man in gray who was keeping watch from one of the sofas. He took the elevator to his room, lay down on the bed and fell asleep. Much later somebody started knocking on a door somewhere inside his head. It took him a while to realize that it was the sergeant knocking on his door. Wallander jumped out of bed, yelled at him to wait, and doused his face with cold water. He asked the sergeant to take him out of town to a forest where he could go for a walk and prepare for his meeting with the lover who would take him to Baiba Liepa.

It was cold in the forest, the ground was hard under his feet and it seemed to Wallander he was in an impossible situation. We live in an age when the mice are hunting the cats, he thought. But that isn't true either, as nobody knows any more who are the mice and who the cats. That sums up my situation precisely. How can I be a police officer when nothing is what it seems to be anymore, nothing makes sense. Not even Sweden, the country I once thought I understood, is an exception. A year ago I drove a car in an advanced state of intoxication, but I wasn't punished because my colleagues rallied to protect me—just another case of the criminal shaking hands with the man who's chasing him.

As he walked through the fir trees while Zids waited in the black limousine, he made up his mind to apply for the job at the Trelleborg Rubber Company. He'd come to the point where a decision like this was inevitable. Without any doubt, without needing to convince himself, he realized it was time to get out.

The thought put him in a good mood, and he returned to the car. They drove back to Riga. He said goodbye to the sergeant and went to the reception desk for his key, where he was handed a letter from Colonel Putnis informing him that his flight to Helsinki would leave at 9:30 a.m. the next morning. He went up to his room, took a bath in the lukewarm water, and went to bed. There were three hours to go before he was due to meet Inese, and he ran through everything that had happened once more. He tried to put himself in the major's position, and imagined the extent of the loathing Karlis Liepa must have felt. The loathing and also the feeling of impotence at having access to proof, but not being able to do anything about it. He had seen into the very heart of the corruption, which involved either Putnis or Murniers or possibly both of them, meeting criminals and creating a situation not even the Mafia had managed to achieve: state-controlled crime. Liepa had seen, and he'd seen too much, and he'd been murdered. Somewhere or other was his testimony, records of his investigation and his proof.

Wallander sat bolt upright in bed. He had overlooked the most serious consequence of this testimony. It must have occurred to Putnis or Murniers as well. They would have reached the same conclusion and be just as keen to find the proof that Major Liepa had hidden. His fear returned. Nothing could be easier than arranging for a Swedish police officer to disappear. There could be an accident, a criminal investigation that was in fact just a game with words, and a zinc coffin could be sent back to Sweden, with deepest regrets.

Possibly they already suspected that he knew too much. Or was the rapid decision to send him back home a sign that they were confident that he knew nothing at all?

There's nobody here I can trust, Wallander thought. I'm all on my own, and I must do as Baiba Liepa, decide who to confide in, and risk making a decision that might turn out to be wrong. But I'm isolated, while all around me are eyes and ears that would have no hesitation in sending me down the same road as the major. Perhaps another conversation with Baiba Liepa would be too risky.

He got out of bed and stood at the window, looking out over the rooftops. It had grown dark, it was nearly 7 p.m., and he would have to make up his mind.

I am not a courageous man, he thought. Least of all am I a police officer with a disregard for death, who takes risks without hesitation. What I would most like to be doing is investigating bloodless burglaries and frauds in some quiet corner of Sweden.

Then he thought of Baiba, her fear and her defiance, and he knew he would never be able to live with himself were he to fail her now. He put on his suit and went downstairs shortly after 8 p.m. There was a different man in gray with a different newspaper in the foyer, but this time Wallander didn't bother to wave. Although it was quite early in the evening, the nightclub was already packed. He elbowed his way through the throng, past several women giving him come-hither smiles, and finally reached an empty table. He knew he shouldn't have anything to drink, but when a waiter came to his table he ordered a whisky even so. There was no band on the platform, but music was blaring out of loudspeakers suspended from the black ceiling. He tried to make out people in this murky, twilight world, but everything was just shadows and voices drowned by the awful music.

Inese appeared from nowhere, and she played her part with an assurance that surprised him. There was no sign of the shy lady he had met a couple of days earlier. She was heavily made up and provocatively dressed in a miniskirt, and he realized he hadn't prepared himself at all for this charade. He held out his hand to greet her, but she ignored it and stooped down to kiss him.

"We can't go just yet," she said. "Order me a drink. Laugh. Look as if you're pleased to see me."

She drank whisky, smoking nervously, keeping an eye on the nightclub entrance. Wallander tried to play the part of a middle-aged man flattered by the attention of a young woman. He tried to pierce the wall of sound, and told her about his long tour of the city with the sergeant as his guide. When Wallander said he would be going back home the next day, she started. He wondered how deeply involved she was, whether she was one of the "friends" Baiba Liepa had referred to, the friends whose dreams were the guarantee that the future of their country wouldn't be thrown to the dogs. But I can't trust her either, Wallander thought. She too might be leading a double life, having been given no choice, or as a last desperate ploy.

"Pay now," she said. "We'll be leaving in a moment."

Wallander noticed that the lights had gone on over the platform and the band in their pink silk jackets were starting to tune their instruments. He paid the waiter, and Inese smiled, pretending to whisper sweet nothings in his ear.

"There's a back door next to the bathrooms," she said. "It's locked, but if you knock somebody will open it. You'll come out into a garage. There'll be a white Moskvitch standing there with a yellow mudguard over the right front wheel. The car isn't locked. Get into the backseat. I'll be there shortly after you. Smile now, whisper in my ear, give me a kiss. Then go."

He did as he was told, then stood up. Next to the bathrooms he knocked on a metal door and heard a key turn immediately. People were going in and out of the bathrooms, but nobody seemed to pay any attention as he slipped through the door into the garage. I'm in a country full of secret entrances and exits, he thought. Nothing seems to happen in the open.

The garage was cramped and dimly lit, and smelled of engine oil and gas. Wallander could see a truck with one wheel missing, some bicycles, and then the white Moskvitch. There was no sign of the man who had opened the door for him. Wallander tried the car door. It was unlocked. He got into the backseat and waited. Shortly afterwards Inese appeared. She was clearly in a hurry. She started the engine, the garage doors slid open, and she drove out of the hotel, turning left away from the wide streets surrounding the block with the Latvia Hotel at its core. He noticed that she was keeping a constant lookout in the rearview mirror, and kept changing direction, following some invisible map. After about 20 minutes of twisting and turning, she seemed satisfied they were not being followed. She asked Wallander for a cigarette, and he lit one for her. They crossed over the long iron bridge and into a maze of dirty factories and endless clusters of barrack-like blocks of flats. Wallander was not sure if he recognized the building outside which she came to a halt.

"Hurry up," she said. "We don't have much time."

Baiba Liepa let them in, and exchanged a few hurried words with Inese. Wallander wondered if she had already been told he would be leaving Riga the next morning, but she said nothing, merely taking his jacket and putting it over a chair back. Inese had disappeared, and they were once again alone together in the quiet room with the heavy curtains. Wallander had no idea how to start, what he ought to say, and so he did what Rydberg had so often told him to do: tell it how it is, it can't make things any worse, just tell it how it is!

She slumped back in the sofa as if struck by a terrible pain when Wallander told her Upitis had confessed to murdering her husband.

"It's not true," she whispered.

"I've had his confession translated for me," he said. "It claims he had two accomplices."

"It's not true!" she screamed, and it was as if a floodgate had finally burst. Inese appeared in the shadows and looked at Wallander: he knew immediately what he should do. He moved over to the sofa and put his arms around Baiba, who was shivering and sobbing. Wallander had time to register that she might be crying because Upitis had committed an act of betrayal that was so outrageous, it was impossible to comprehend, or she could be crying because the truth was about to be suppressed by means of a false, forced confession. She was sobbing frantically, and clinging on to him as if she were seized with pain.

Looking back, it seemed to Wallander that was the moment when he burned his boats and began to accept that he was in love with Baiba Liepa. He had realized the love he now felt had its origins in another person's need of him. He asked himself briefly if he had ever felt anything like it before.

Inese came in with two cups of tea. She briefly stroked Baiba Liepa's head, and the major's widow stopped crying almost immediately. Her face was ashen.

Wallander told her all that had happened, and that he would be returning to Sweden in the morning. He told her the whole story he had managed to piece together, and was surprised how convincing it sounded. He eventually got around to mentioning the secret which must exist somewhere or other, and she nodded to show that she understood.

"Yes," she said. "He must have hidden something away. He must have made notes. A true testimony can never consist of unwritten thoughts."

"But you don't know where it is?"

"He never said anything about it."

"Is there anybody else who might know?"

"Nobody. I was the only one he confided in."

"He has his father in Ventspils, doesn't he?"

She looked at him in surprise.

"I found out about him," he said. "I thought he might be a possibility."

"He was very fond of his father," she said, "but he would never have trusted him with documents."

"Then where can he have hidden them?"

"Not in our apartment. That would have been too dangerous. The police would have torn the whole building apart if they thought there might be anything hidden there."

"Think," Wallander said. "Put yourself back in time, try to remember. Where could he possibly have hidden them?"

She shook her head. "I don't know."

"He must have foreseen that something like this could happen. He must have assumed you would understand, would have known there was proof waiting for you to find. It must be somewhere that only you would think of."

She suddenly grabbed hold of his hand. "You must help me," she said. "You can't leave."

"It's impossible for me to stay," he said. "The colonels would never understand why I hadn't gone back to Sweden, and how would I be able to stay here without their knowing?"

"You can come back," she said, still clinging on to his hand. "You've got a girlfriend here. You can come as a tourist."

But you're the one I'm in love with, he thought. Not Inese.

"You've got a girlfriend here," she repeated.

He nodded. He did have a girlfriend in Riga, but it wasn't Inese. He said nothing, and she didn't try to make him. She seemed convinced he would return. Inese came back into the room, and by now Baiba Liepa had gotten over the shock of hearing that Upitis had made a confession.

"In our country you can die if you say something," she said, "and you can die if you don't say anything. Or say the wrong things. Or talk to the wrong people. But Upitis is strong. He knows we won't abandon him. He knows we know his confession isn't true. That's why we will win in the end."

"Win?"

"All we ask for is the truth," she said. "All we ask for is decency, something fundamental. The freedom to live in the freedom we choose to live in."

"That's too big a thing for me," Wallander said. "I want to know who murdered Major Liepa. I want to know why two dead men drifted ashore on the Swedish coast."

"Come back here and I'll teach you about my country," Baiba Liepa said. "Not just me, but Inese as well."

"I don't know," Wallander said.

Baiba Liepa looked at him. "You can't be a man who lets people down," she said. "If you were, Karlis would have been wrong. And he was never wrong."

"It's not possible," Wallander repeated. "If I were to come back here, the colonels would know about it immediately. I'd have to have a false identity, a false passport."

"That can be arranged," Baiba Liepa said eagerly. "Provided I know you'll come back."

"I'm a police officer," Wallander said. "I can't risk my very existence by traveling around the world on a forged passport."

He regretted saying it the moment the words had crossed his lips. He looked Baiba Liepa in the eye and saw the dead major's face.

"All right," he said slowly. "I'll come back."

The night wore on and it turned midnight. Wallander was trying to help Baiba Liepa locate some clue as to where the major could have hidden his proof. Her concentration was unshakeable, but nowhere could they find any traces. In the end their conversation simply petered out.

Wallander thought of the dogs that were looking out for him somewhere out there in the darkness—the colonels' dogs that never ceased to look for him. With a growing feeling of unreality, he saw that he was being drawn into a plot that would bring him back to Riga to conduct a criminal investigation in secret. He would be a non-police officer in a country with which he was completely unfamiliar, and this non-police officer would be trying to establish the truth about a crime that many people already regarded as solved, finished and done with. He knew the whole venture was mad, but he couldn't take his eyes off Baiba Liepa's face, and her voice had been so full of conviction he had been unable to withstand it.

It was nearly 2 a.m. when Inese announced they would have to call a halt. She left him alone with Baiba Liepa, and they bade farewell to each other in silence.

Baiba leaned forward and kissed him on the cheek. "We have friends in Sweden," she said. "They'll be in touch with you. They'll help to organize your return."

Inese drove him back to the hotel. As they approached the bridge, she nodded at the rearview mirror.

"Now they're tailing us. We must look as though we're very much in love and can't bear to part when we say goodbye outside the hotel."

"I'll do my best," Wallander said. "Maybe I should try and persuade you to come up to my room."

She laughed.

"I'm a good girl," she said, "but when you come back maybe we can let things go that far."

She left, and he stood for a while in the bitter cold, trying to look as if he were devastated by her going.

The next day he flew home via Helsinki.

The colonels escorted him through the airport and bade him a hearty farewell. One of these men murdered the major, Wallander said to himself. Or was it both of you? But how could a police officer from Ystad be expected to discover what really happened?

It was late evening when he got back home and unlocked the door of his apartment in Mariagatan. Already the whole episode had begun to fade and take on the nature of a dream, and it seemed to him that he would never see Baiba Liepa again. She would have to mourn the death of her husband without ever discovering what happened.

He took a sip of the whisky he had bought during the flight. Before going to bed he spent a considerable time listening to Maria Callas, feeling tired and uneasy. He wondered how it was all going to end.

CHAPTER 14

Six days after he returned he received a letter.

He found it on the floor in the hall when he returned home after a long and difficult day at the station. Sleet had been falling all afternoon, and he spent some time on the landing shaking his clothes and stamping his feet before opening the door.

He thought later that it was as if he'd been steeling himself for the moment when they contacted him. Deep down he'd known all along that they would, but he still didn't feel ready for it.

The envelope on his doormat was an ordinary brown one—at first he thought it was some kind of advertising material as there was a company name printed on the front. He put it on the hall table and forgot all about it. It wasn't until he'd finished his dinner, a fish gratin that had been in the freezer too long, that he remembered the letter and went to fetch it. It was from "Lippman's Flowers," and it struck him that this was an odd time of year for a garden center to be sending a catalogue. He very nearly put it straight into the trash, but he could never resist taking a look at even the most uninteresting junk mail before throwing it away. It was a bad habit picked up from his job: there might be something hidden among the colorful brochures. It sometimes seemed to him that he lived the life of a man compelled to turn over every stone he found. He always needed to know what was underneath it.

He opened the envelope and saw that it contained a handwritten letter: he realized they had contacted him. He left the letter on the kitchen table while he made a cup of coffee. He needed to give himself a bit of time before reading it. When he'd left the plane at Arlanda a week ago, he had felt vaguely uneasy, but relieved to no longer be in a country where he was being watched all the time, and in a flash of unaccustomed spontaneity he'd tried to start a conversation with the woman at immigration control when he handed his passport in through the window. "It's good to be home," he'd said, but she had glanced dismissively at him and shoved the passport back without even opening it.

This is Sweden, he'd thought. Everything is bright and cheerful on the surface, our airports are built so that no dust or shadows could ever intrude. Everything is visible, nothing is any different from what it seems to be. Our national aspiration, our religion, is that security written into the Swedish constitution, which informs the whole world that starving to death is a crime. But we don't talk to strangers unless we have to, because anything unfamiliar can cause us harm, dirty our floors and dim our neon lights. We never built an empire and so we've never had to watch one collapse, but we persuaded ourselves that we'd created the best of all possible worlds, and that even if small, we were the privileged keepers of paradise. Now that the party's over we take our revenge by having the least friendly immigration control officers in the world.

His feeling of relief was replaced almost immediately by depression. In Kurt Wallander's world, this worn-out or at least partially demolished paradise, there was no place for Baiba Liepa. He couldn't imagine her here, in all this light, under all these neon strips that never failed. Nevertheless, he was already beginning to pine for her, and when he'd lugged his suitcase down the long, prison-like corridor to the domestic terminal where he would wait for his connection to Malmö, he was already starting to dream of his return to Riga, to the city where the invisible dogs had been spying on him. The Malmö flight was delayed, and he had been issued a coupon that entitled him to a sandwich. He had sat for ages in the café, watching airplanes taking off and landing in the light snow. All around him men in smart suits were chattering away into mobile phones, and to his astonishment he actually heard an overweight washing-machine salesman jabbering into his monstrous plaything, telling the story of Hansel and Gretel to a child. He found a pay phone and dialed his daughter's number. To his amazement he got through to her, and felt immediate pleasure on hearing her voice. He toyed briefly with the idea of staying on for a few days in Stockholm, but realized that she was very busy and he didn't raise the subject. Instead, he thought of Baiba, about her fear and her defiance, and he wondered if she really dared to believe that the Swedish police officer wouldn't let her down. What could he possibly do, though? If he were to go back the dogs would pick up his scent, and he would never be able to shake them off.

It was late in the evening by the time he landed at Sturup. There was nobody there to meet him, so he took a taxi into Ystad and from the dark backseat chatted about the weather to the driver, who was going far too fast. When there was nothing more to say about the fog and the snowflakes dancing in the headlights, he suddenly imagined he could smell Baiba Liepa's perfume in the car, and felt anguish at the thought of not seeing her again.

The next day he drove out to see his father at Löderup. The home help had cut his hair for him, and it seemed to Wallander that he was looking healthier than he had for years. He'd brought him a bottle of cognac, and his father nodded approvingly when he saw the label.

To his surprise, he'd told his father about Baiba Liepa. They'd been sitting in the old shed his father used as a studio. There was an unfinished canvas on the easel, the unchanging landscape. Wallander could see that it was going to be one with a grouse in the bottom left-hand corner. When he'd arrived with his bottle of cognac, his father had been coloring the grouse's beak, but he'd put down his brush and wiped his hands on a rag smelling of turpentine. Wallander told him about his trip to Riga and then, without really understanding why, he stopped describing the city and told him about the meeting with Baiba Liepa. He didn't mention that she was the widow of a police officer who had been murdered, he only told him her name, said he'd met her and that he missed her.

"Does she have any children?" his father asked.

Wallander shook his head.

"Can she have children?"

"I suppose so. How on earth should I know?"

"You must know how old she is, surely?"

"Younger than I am. About 33, perhaps."

"Then she can have children."

"Why do you want to know if she can have children?"

"Because I think that's what you need."

"I've got Linda."

"One's not enough. A person has to have at least two children in order to understand what it's all about. Bring her over to Sweden. Marry her!"

"It's not as easy as that."

"Do you have to make everything so damned complicated just because you're a police officer?"

Here we go, Wallander thought. He's off again. The moment you start having a conversation with him he finds some excuse for getting at me because I joined the police force.

"Can you keep a secret?" he asked the old man.

His father eyed him suspiciously. "How could I avoid being able to?" he asked. "Who is there I could tell it to?"

"I'm thinking of quitting being a police officer," Wallander said. "I might apply for a different job. As a security officer at the rubber factory in Trelleborg. I only said I might."

His father stared at him for some time before replying.

"It's never too late to see sense," he said eventually. "The only thing you'll regret is that it took you so long to make up your mind."

"I only said I might. I didn't say it was definite."

But his father wasn't listening. He'd gone back to the easel and was finishing the grouse's beak. Wallander sat on an old sleigh and watched him for a while in silence. Then he went home, thinking how he had nobody to talk to. He was 43 years old and missed having somebody to confide in. When Rydberg died, he'd become lonelier than he could ever have imagined. The only person he had was Linda. He couldn't talk to Mona, his ex-wife. She'd become a stranger to him, and he knew next to nothing about her life in Malmö.

As he drove past the turning to Kåseberga, he thought of going to Kristianstad to pay a visit to Göran Boman in the police there. Maybe he could talk to him about everything that had happened. But he didn't. He returned to duty after writing a report for Björk. Martinsson and his other colleagues asked him a few questions over coffee in the canteen, but it was soon clear they weren't really interested in anything he had to say. He mailed his application to the factory in Trelleborg and rearranged the furniture in his office in an attempt to revive some enthusiasm for work. Björk seemed to have noticed his heart wasn't really in it, and made a well-meaning but vain effort to cheer him up by asking him to stand in for him and give a lecture to the Rotary Club. He agreed to do it, and gave an unsuccessful talk on technology in police work over lunch at the Continental Hotel. He forgot every word he'd said the moment he sat down.

One morning he woke up and was convinced he was ill. He went to the police doctor and was given a thorough examination. The doctor could find nothing wrong with him, but advised him to continue to keep an eye on his weight. He had returned from Riga on Wednesday, and on Saturday evening he drove to a restaurant in Åhus where there was a dance band. After a couple of dances a physiotherapist from Kristianstad called Ellen invited him to join her at her table, but he couldn't get Baiba Liepa's face out of his mind, she was following him around like a shadow, and he made his excuses and left early. He took the coast road from Åhus and stopped at the deserted field where the flea markets are held every summer—the previous year he had set off there like a madman, gun in hand, in pursuit of a murderer. The field was lightly covered in snow, the full moon was shining over the sea, and he could see Baiba Liepa standing before him. He drove back to his apartment in Ystad and drank himself into a stupor. He turned his stereo up so loud that the neighbors started thumping on the walls.

He woke on the Sunday morning with palpitations, and the day developed into a long drawn-out wait for something unidentifiable, something unreachable.

The letter arrived on Monday. He sat at his kitchen table, reading the neat handwriting. It was signed by somebody calling himself Joseph Lippman.

You are a friend of our country, wrote Joseph Lippman. *We have been informed from Riga of your marvelous work there. You will shortly be hearing from us with more details of your return journey. Joseph Lippman.*

Wallander wondered what his "marvelous work" consisted of. And who were the "us" who were going to get in touch again?

He was annoyed by the brevity of the message, and the tone that sounded almost like an order. Did he have no say in the matter? He had certainly not agreed to enter any secret service run by invisible people. His anguish and doubt were stronger than his resolve and willpower. He wanted to see Baiba Liepa again, that was true; but he didn't trust his motives, and knew he was behaving like a lovelorn teenager.

Nevertheless, when he woke up on Tuesday morning he suspected that deep down, he had made up his mind. He drove to the station, took part in a dismal union meeting and then went in to see Björk.

"I was wondering if I might take some of the leave I'm due for," he said.

Björk stared at him with a mixture of envy and deep sympathy.

"I wish I could do the same," he said gloomily. "I've just been reading a long memo from the national police board. I've imagined all my colleagues up and down the country doing exactly the same thing, every one of them hunched over his desk. I read it through, then sat there thinking that I haven't a clue what it's all about. We are expected to pass comment on various earlier documents about some big reorganization plan, but I've no idea which of all those documents this memo is referring to."

"Go on leave," Wallander suggested.

Björk petulantly shoved aside a paper lying on the desk in front of him.

"Out of the question," he said. "I'll be able to go on leave when I retire. If I live that long. Of course, it would be very stupid to die at my desk. You want to go on leave, you said?"

"I'm thinking of having a week's skiing in the Alps. If I do

it could help solve some of your problems regarding work over
midsummer—I can work then and wait until the end of July
before going on holiday."

Björk nodded. "Have you really managed to find a package trip
at this time of year? I thought they were all fully booked by now."

"No."

Björk raised an eyebrow. "That sounds a bit iffy, doesn't it?"

"I'll take the car down to the Alps. I don't like package holidays."

"Who does?"

Björk suddenly assumed the formal expression he wore when
he considered it necessary to remind everyone who was the boss.

"What cases have you got on your desk at the moment?"

"Surprisingly few. That assault business out at Svarte is the most
pressing of them, but that's something any of the others can take
over."

"When are you thinking of leaving? Today?"

"Thursday will do."

"How long had you thought of staying away?"

"I have ten days coming to me."

Björk nodded and made a note.

"I think it's a good idea for you to take some leave. You've
been looking a bit out of sorts."

"You can say that again," Wallander said, as he made his escape.

He spent the rest of the day working on the assault case. He
made several telephone calls and also managed to reply to an
inquiry from the bank about some muddle with his salary pay-
ments. All the time he was expecting something to happen. He
looked up the Stockholm telephone directory and found several
people called Lippman, but there was nothing in the Yellow Pages
about "Lippman's Flowers."

Shortly after 5 p.m. he cleared his desk and went home. He made a little detour and pulled up outside the new furniture store, went inside and found a leather armchair he rather liked for his apartment, but was horrified by the price. He stopped at the grocer's in Hamngatan to buy some potatoes and bacon. The young girl at the checkout smiled and seemed to recognize him, and he recalled that a year or so previously he'd spent a day trying to track down a man who'd robbed the shop. He drove home, made the dinner, and then plopped himself down in front of the television.

They contacted him shortly after 9 p.m.

The telephone rang, and a man speaking broken Swedish asked him to come to the pizzeria across the road from the Continental Hotel. Wallander suddenly felt sick and tired of all this secrecy business, and asked for the man's name.

"I have every reason to be suspicious," he explained. "I want to know what I'm letting myself in for."

"My name is Joseph Lippman. I wrote to you."

"Who are you?"

"I run a little business."

"A nursery?"

"I suppose you could call it that."

"What do you want from me?"

"I think I expressed myself quite clearly in the letter."

Wallander hung up. He wasn't getting any answers anyway. He was infuriated at being constantly surrounded by invisible faces who expected him to be interested and prepared to cooperate. What evidence was there to prove that this Lippman wasn't one of the Latvian colonels' henchmen?

He didn't take the car but walked down Regementsgatan to the center of town. It was 9:30 p.m. by the time he reached the pizzeria. There were people at about ten of the tables, but he

couldn't see a man who could possibly be Lippman. He remembered something Rydberg had once taught him. You should always
decide whether it would be better to be the first or the last person
to arrive at a predetermined meeting place. He didn't know if it
was of any importance in this case. He sat at a table in the corner,
ordered a glass of beer, and waited.

Joseph Lippman turned up just before 10 p.m. By then Wallander
had begun to wonder whether the intention had been to lure
him away from his apartment, but the moment the door opened and
the man entered, Wallander had no doubt the new arrival was Joseph
Lippman. He was in his 60s, and wearing an overcoat far too big
for him. He moved slowly and cautiously among the tables, as
if he were afraid of falling or treading on a mine. He smiled at
Wallander, took off his overcoat and sat down opposite him. He
was nervous, and kept glancing around the room. At one of the
tables sat a couple of men who were being terribly rude about a
third, who wasn't with them.

Wallander guessed that Joseph Lippman was Jewish. At least,
he looked like what Wallander thought of as a typical Jew. His
cheeks were covered in tough gray stubble, and his eyes were dark
behind rimless spectacles. But then, what did Wallander know
about what Jews looked like? Nothing.

The waitress approached, and Lippman ordered a cup of tea.
He was so excessively polite that Wallander suspected he had
endured many humiliations in his life.

"I'm most grateful that you came," Lippman said quietly.
Wallander had to lean forward in order to hear what he was
saying.

"You didn't give me any choice," he said. "First a letter, then
a telephone call. Maybe you should start by telling me who you
are."

Lippman shook his head. "Who I am is of no significance. You are the important one, Mr. Wallander."

"No," Wallander said, feeling himself getting annoyed again. "You must understand that I've no intention of listening to what you've got to say if you're not even prepared to confide in me who you are."

The waitress arrived with the tea, and they waited until they were alone again.

"My role is merely that of organizer and messenger," Lippman said. "Who wants to know the name of the messenger? It doesn't matter. We are meeting here tonight, and then I shall disappear. We will probably never meet again. The important thing, therefore, is not confiding in you, but practical decisions. Security is always a practical matter. In my view the business of trust is also a practical matter."

"In that case we might just as well conclude the conversation now," Wallander said.

"I've got a message for you from Baiba Liepa," Lippman said hastily. "Don't you even want to hear that?"

Wallander relaxed. He observed the man sitting opposite him, strangely hunched up, as if his health were so fragile he might collapse any moment.

"I don't want to hear anything until I know who you are," he said eventually. "It's as simple as that."

Lippman took off his glasses and carefully poured some milk into his tea.

"I'm merely thinking of your own best interests, Mr. Wallander," Lippman said. "In this day and age it's often best to know as little as possible."

"I've been to Latvia," Wallander said. "I've been there, and I think I know what it is to be constantly under observation, forever being checked. But we're in Sweden now, not Riga."

Lippman nodded pensively. "You may be right," he said, "Perhaps I am an old man who can no longer discern how reality is changing."

"A nursery," Wallander said, in an attempt to help him out. "I don't suppose they have always been like they are now?"

"I came to Sweden in the autumn of 1941," Lippman said, stirring his tea. "I was a young man then, and I had the naïve ambition of becoming an artist, a great artist. It was freezing cold as dawn broke and we caught sight of the Gotland coast. That was the moment we knew we'd made it, despite the fact that the boat had sprung a leak and several of my companions on board were seriously ill. We were undernourished, we had tuberculosis. Nevertheless, I have a clear memory of that freezing cold dawn. It was the beginning of October, and I made up my mind I was going to paint a picture of the Swedish coast that would symbolize freedom. That's what it might look like, the gates of paradise. Cold and frozen, a few black cliffs barely visible through the mist. But I never did paint that picture. I became a gardener instead. Now I make a living by suggesting appropriate decorative plants for various Swedish firms. I've noticed how people, and especially people working for the new information technology companies, have an insatiable need to hide their machines among green plants. I shall never paint that picture of paradise. I'll just have to make do with the fact that I've seen it. I know paradise has many gates, just as hell does. One has to learn to distinguish between them, or one is lost."

"And that is something Major Liepa could do?"

Lippman did not react to Wallander's mention of the major.

"Major Liepa knew what the gates looked like," he said, "but that's not why he had to die. He died because he had seen who was going in and out through those gates. People who are afraid of the light, because the light makes them visible to people like Major Liepa."

Wallander had the impression that Lippman was a deeply religious man. He expressed himself like a priest standing before a congregation.

"I have lived the whole of my life in exile," Lippman continued. "For the first ten years, until the middle of the 1950s, I believed I would one day be able to return to my home country. Then came the interminable 1960s and 70s, when I'd completely given up hope. Only very ancient Latvians living in exile, only the really old and the really young and the really crazy Latvians believed the world would change so that we might one day be able to return to our homeland. They believed in a dramatic turning point, while I was expecting a long drawn-out conclusion to the tragedy that even then seemed to be complete. But very suddenly things began to happen. We received mysterious reports from our homeland, optimistic reports. We saw the gigantic Soviet Union beginning to tremble, as if some latent fever had at last begun to take hold. Could it really be that what we had never dared to believe might actually happen? We still don't know the answer to that question. We realize that we might yet again be tricked out of our freedom. The Soviet Union is weakened, but that could be a temporary condition. We do not have much time at our disposal. Major Liepa knew that, and that is what drove him on."

"We?" Wallander said. "Who are we?"

"All Latvians in Sweden belong to an organization," Lippman answered. "We have joined various organizations as a substitute for our lost homeland. We have tried to help people retain their culture, we have constructed various lifelines, we have established foundations. We have listened to cries for help and we have attempted to respond to them. We have fought constantly to avoid being forgotten. Our exile organizations have been our way of replacing the cities and villages we have lost."

The glass door opened and a man entered. Lippman reacted immediately. Wallander recognized the man—his name was Elmberg and he was the manager of one of the local gas stations.

"There's no cause for alarm," he said. "That man hasn't hurt a fly since the day he was born. I doubt if he's ever given a thought to the existence of Latvia. He's the manager of a gas station."

"Baiba Liepa has sent a cry for help," Lippman said. "She is asking you to come. She needs your assistance."

He took an envelope from his inside pocket. "From Baiba Liepa," he said. "For you."

Wallander took the envelope. It was not sealed, and he carefully extracted the thin writing paper. Her message was brief, and written in pencil, as if in a hurry.

There is a testimony and a guardian, she had written, *but I'm afraid I shall be unable to discover the right place on my own. Trust the messenger as you once trusted my husband, Baiba.*

"We can supply everything you need in order to get to Riga," Lippman said when Wallander put the letter down.

"You can hardly make me invisible!"

"Invisible?"

"If I go to Riga I must become somebody new. How will you manage that? How can you guarantee my safety?"

"You will have to trust us, Mr. Wallander. But we don't have much time."

Wallander could see that Lippman was anxious. He tried to convince himself that none of what was happening all around him was real. But he knew that this was what the world was like. Baiba Liepa had made one of the thousands of cries for help that are constantly sent across continents. This one was meant for him, and he was obliged to answer.

"I've requested leave from Thursday onwards," he said. "Officially I'm going skiing in the Alps. I can be away for just over a week."

Lippman slid his cup to one side. His weak, melancholy expression had been replaced by fierce determination.

"That's an excellent idea," he said. "Naturally, a Swedish police officer goes to the Alps every winter to try his luck on the piste. What route are you travelling?"

"Via Sassnitz, then by car through the old East Germany."

"What's the name of your hotel?"

"I've no idea. I've never been to the Alps before."

"But you can ski?"

"Yes."

Lippman was deep in thought. Wallander beckoned the waitress and ordered a cup of coffee. Lippman shook his head absent-mindedly when Wallander asked him if he wanted any more tea. Eventually he removed his glasses and rubbed them carefully against the sleeve of his jacket.

"Going to the Alps is an excellent idea," he repeated. "But I need a bit of time to make the necessary arrangements. Tomorrow evening somebody will phone you and inform you which of the morning ferries you should take from Trelleborg. Whatever else you do, don't forget to put your skis on the roof rack. Pack everything as if you really were going to the Alps."

"How do you think I'm going to be able to enter Latvia?"

"You'll find out all you need to know on the ferry. Somebody will make contact with you. You will have to trust us."

"I can't guarantee that I'll accept your plan."

"There's no such thing as a guarantee in this world of ours,

Mr. Wallander. All I can do is promise that we shall do our best to excel ourselves. Perhaps we ought to pay and go now?"

They took leave of each other outside the pizzeria. The wind had come up and was squalling. Joseph Lippman bade him a hasty farewell before disappearing in the direction of the railway station. Wallander walked home through the deserted town, thinking over what Baiba Liepa had written.

The dogs are on her trail, he thought. She's scared and worried. The colonels have also caught on to the fact that the major must have left a testimony somewhere. It dawned on him that there was no time to lose. There was no longer any place for fear or second thoughts. He had to respond to her cry for help.

The next day he prepared for the journey.

Shortly after 6 p.m. a woman called to say he'd been booked on the ferry leaving Trelleborg at 5:30 a.m. the next morning. To Wallander's astonishment, she announced herself as a representative for "Lippman's Travel Agency."

He went to bed at midnight. His last thought before going to sleep was how crazy the whole scheme was. He was on the point of getting involved voluntarily in something that was doomed to fail. At the same time, Baiba's cry for help was real, and he felt bound to answer it.

Early the next morning he drove onto the ferry in Trelleborg harbor. One of the passport officials waved to him and asked where he was going.

"To the Alps," Wallander told him.

"Sounds great."

"Does you good to get away occasionally."

"That's what we all need to do."

"I couldn't have kept going a single day longer."

"Well, you can forget all about being a police officer for a few days."

"I will," Wallander said, but knew that was definitely not true. He was about to embark on his toughest assignment. An assignment that didn't even exist.

The dawn skies were gray. He went up on deck as the ferry pulled away. He shivered as he watched the open sea slowly grow as the ship moved further from land and the Swedish coast disappeared from view.

He was in the cafeteria having a bite to eat when a man in his 50s, with a ruddy face and shifty eyes, approached him and introduced himself as Preuss. Preuss had written instructions from Joseph Lippman, and a brand new identity that Wallander was to use from now on.

"Let's take a walk up on deck," Preuss suggested.

There was thick fog over the Baltic the day Wallander went back to Riga.

CHAPTER 15

The border was invisible.

It was there nevertheless, inside him, like a coil of barbed wire, just under his breastbone. Kurt Wallander was scared. He would look back on the final steps he took on Lithuanian soil to the Latvian border as a crippling trek towards a country from where he would find himself shouting Dante's words: Abandon hope, all ye who enter here! Nobody returns from here—at least, no Swedish police officer will get out alive.

The night sky was filled with stars. Preuss had been with him from the moment he had made contact onboard the Trelleborg ferry, and he didn't seem unmoved by what was in store. Through the darkness Wallander could hear that his breathing was fast and irregular.

"We must wait," Preuss whispered in his barely comprehensible German. "*Warten, warten.*"

At first, Wallander had been furious at being supplied with a guide who didn't speak a word of English. He wondered what Joseph Lippman had been thinking of, assuming that a Swedish police officer, barely able to string together a few words of English, would be a German speaker. Wallander had come very close to calling off the whole thing, which now appeared to be the triumph of wild fantasy over his own common sense. It seemed to him that the Latvians had been living in exile for too long and had lost all touch with reality. Twisted by grief, over-optimistic or just plain crazy. How could this man Preuss, this skinny little man with the scarred face, inspire Wallander with sufficient courage, and not least provide sufficient security, to enable him to return to Latvia as an invisible, non-existent person? What did he actually know about Preuss, who had simply appeared in the ferry cafeteria? That he might be a Latvian citizen living in exile, that he might be earning his living as a coin dealer in the German city of Kiel—but what else? Absolutely nothing.

Nevertheless, something had made him keep going, and Preuss had sat beside him in the passenger seat, dozing all the time, while Wallander sped on following the directions Preuss gave him by pointing at a road atlas. They traveled eastwards through the former East Germany and by 5 p.m. were five kilometers short of the Polish border, where Wallander backed his car into a rickety barn next to a decaying farmhouse. The man who met them was yet another exiled Latvian, but he spoke good English. He promised that the car would be kept completely safe until Wallander returned. They waited until nightfall, then stumbled through a dense spruce forest until they reached the border, and crossed the first invisible line on the route to Riga. In a little town whose name Wallander quickly forgot, they were met by Janick, a man with a heavy cold, who picked them up in an old, rusty truck. A bumpy, jerky ride over the Polish steppe ensued. Wallander caught the driver's cold, and longed for a decent meal and a bath, but all he was offered were cold pork chops and camp beds in freezing houses out in the Polish hinterland. Progress was slow. Generally they traveled at night or just before dawn. The rest of the time was passed in sleep or in uncomfortable silence. He tried to understand why Preuss was being so cautious. What had they to fear, as long as they were in Poland? He was given no explanation. Preuss understood little of what Wallander was saying, and

Janick hummed an English pop song from the war years, when he
wasn't sniffing and snivelling and spreading germs in Wallander's
direction. When they finally got to the Lithuanian border
Wallander had started to hate "We'll Meet Again." He could just as
easily have been somewhere in the heart of Russia as in Poland.
Or Czechoslovakia, or Bulgaria. He had completely lost all sense
of where Sweden was in relation to where they were. The lunacy of
the whole undertaking became more obvious with every kilometer
that the truck took him deeper into the unknown. They traveled
through Lithuania on a series of buses, none of which had any
springs, and now, four whole days after Preuss had first contacted
him on the ferry, they were close to the Latvian border, in the
middle of a forest smelling strongly of resin.

"*Warten,*" Preuss kept repeating, and Wallander sat down obedi-
ently on a tree stump and waited. He was cold, and felt sick.

I'll have pneumonia by the time I get to Riga, he thought
desperately. Of all the stupid things I've done in my life, this is
the stupidest, and it deserves no respect, nothing more than a
loud guffaw of scorn. Here, on a tree stump in a Lithuanian forest,
sits a Swedish police officer in early middle age, one who has
completely lost his sense of judgment and gone out of his
mind.

But there was no going back. Clearly he would never be able
to retrace his steps without help. He was totally dependent on
the confounded Preuss, who the idiot Lippman had allocated to
him as a guide, and there was no alternative but to keep going,
further and further away from the dictates of reason, until they
came to Riga.

On the ferry, just as the Swedish coastline disappeared from
view, Preuss had introduced himself as Wallander was having
coffee in the cafeteria. They had gone out on deck in the biting

wind. Preuss had with him a letter from Lippman, and to his astonishment Wallander found himself assuming yet another new identity. This time he wasn't to be "Mr. Eckers," but Herr Hegel, Herr Gottfried Hegel, a German sales representative for a sheet music and fine art book publisher. He was amazed when, as if it were the most natural thing in the world, Preuss handed over a German passport with Wallander's photograph duly glued in place and stamped. He recognized it as a photograph Linda had taken of him several years earlier—how Lippman had got hold of it was a mystery. He was now Herr Hegel, and eventually realized from Preuss's stubborn talk and gesticulating that he should hand over his Swedish passport for the time being. Wallander gave him the document, knowing he was insane to do so.

It was now four days since he had been confronted by his new identity. Preuss had scrambled onto an uprooted tree, and Wallander could just see his face through the darkness. The man seemed to be peering into the east. It was a few minutes past midnight. Suddenly Preuss raised his hand and pointed eagerly to the east. They had hung a kerosene lamp on a branch so that Wallander wouldn't lose contact with Preuss. He stood up and squinted in the direction Preuss was pointing. He made out a faint, blinking light as if a motorcyclist with a faulty engine was coming towards them.

"*Gehen!*" he whispered. "*Schnell, nun. Gehen!*"

Twigs and branches poked and scratched at Wallander's face. I'm crossing the final border, he thought, but I have barbed wire in my stomach.

They came to a boundary line cut through the forest like a street. Preuss held Wallander back briefly while he listened attentively, then he dragged him across the empty space and into the cover of the dense forest on the other side. After about ten minutes they came upon a muddy cart track and found a car waiting. Wallander could see the glow from a cigarette inside. Somebody got out and came towards him with a hooded flashlight. All of a sudden, he realized Inese was standing before him.

It would be a long time before he forgot the surge of joy and relief at seeing her, at encountering something familiar after all the unknown. She smiled at him in the faint light from the flashlight, but he couldn't think of anything to say. Preuss stretched out his skinny hand in farewell, then was swallowed up by the forest before Wallander even had time to say goodbye.

"It's a long way to Riga," Inese said. "We must get going."

Occasionally they left the road so that Inese could have a rest, and they also had a puncture in one of the tires, which Wallander had managed to change with enormous effort. He had suggested he might do some of the driving, but she had merely shaken her head, without giving any explanation.

He realized right away that something had happened. There was something hardened and determined about Inese that couldn't simply be explained by exhaustion. He sat beside her in silence, unsure whether she'd have the strength to answer questions. He had been told that Baiba Liepa was expecting him, and that Upitis was still in prison, that his confession had been reported in the newspapers.

"My name's Gottfried Hegel this time," he said when they'd been on their way for two hours and had stopped to fill up with gas from a spare can he'd gotten from the backseat.

"I know," Inese answered. "It's not a very attractive name."

"Tell me why I'm here, Inese. How am I to help you?"

She didn't answer. Instead, she asked him if he was hungry and passed him a bottle of beer and two meat sandwiches in a paper bag. Then they continued their journey. At one point he dozed off, but shook himself awake, worried that she might fall asleep at the wheel.

They reached the outskirts of Riga shortly before dawn. It was March 21, his sister's birthday. In an attempt to embellish his new identity, he decided that Gottfried Hegel had a large number of brothers and sisters, and that his youngest sister was called Kristina. He could see Mrs. Hegel in his mind's eye, a rather masculine woman with the beginnings of a moustache, and their house in Schwabingen built of red brick with a well-kept but characterless back garden. The story Lippman had supplied as background to the passport had been sketchy in the extreme. Wallander imagined it would take an experienced interrogator no more than a minute to demolish Gottfried Hegel, and expose the passport as fake.

"Where are we going?" he asked.

"We're nearly there," she replied.

"How can I be at all useful if nobody tells me anything?" he asked. "What are you keeping from me? What's happened?"

"I'm tired," she said, "but we're pleased you've come back. Baiba is happy. She'll burst into tears when she sees you."

"Why won't you answer my questions? Something's happened, I can see you're scared to death. What is it?"

"Everything has become much more difficult these last two weeks, but it's better if Baiba tells you herself. Anyway, there's a lot I don't know either."

They were driving through the endless suburbs. The silhouettes of factories were vaguely visible against the yellow, streetlit sky. The deserted streets were shrouded in fog, and it occurred to Wallander that this was how he'd imagined the countries of Eastern Europe, countries that called themselves socialist and declared themselves to be paradise on earth.

Inese stopped outside an oblong warehouse, switched off the engine, and pointed to a low, iron door at one gable end.

"Go there," she said. "Knock, and they'll let you in. I must go."

"Will I see you again?"

"I don't know. That's up to Baiba."

"Aren't you forgetting you're my girlfriend?"

She smiled fleetingly before answering. "I might have been Mr. Eckers's girlfriend," she said, "but I'm not sure I'm as fond of Herr Hegel. I'm a good girl and I don't run off with just any man."

Wallander got out and she drove off immediately. Just for a moment he considered trying to find a bus stop and traveling into the city center, where he'd be able to look for a Swedish consulate or embassy and get help to return home. He didn't dare to imagine how a Swedish diplomat would react to the story the Swedish police officer would have to tell. He could only hope that handling acute mental derangement was one of the skills a diplomat possessed. But it was too late for that. He would have to go through with what he'd embarked on.

He marched over the crunchy gravel and knocked on the iron door. A bearded man Wallander had never seen before opened it. He was cross-eyed, but gave him a friendly nod, peered over Wallander's shoulder to make sure he hadn't been followed, then ushered him quickly in and closed the door.

Wallander found himself in a warehouse full of toys. Wherever he looked were wooden shelves piled high with dolls. It was as if he'd descended into an underground catacomb with dolls' faces grinning at him like evil skulls. It was like a dream. Maybe he was in bed at his Mariagatan apartment in Ystad and nothing that surrounded him was real? All he needed to do was to breathe steadily and wait until he woke up. But there was no welcome awakening to look forward to. Three more men emerged from the shadows, followed by a woman. Wallander recognized the driver who had sat in silence in the shadows when he had spoken to Upitis.

"Mr. Wallander," the man who had opened the door for him said, "we're so pleased you've come to assist us."

"I've come because Baiba Liepa asked me to," Wallander answered. "Not for any other reason. She's the one I want to meet."

"That's not possible just now," said the woman, in faultless English. "Baiba is being watched constantly, but we think we know how we can get you to her."

Wallander sat down on a rickety wooden chair, and was handed a cup of tea. He had difficulty making out the men's faces in the dim light. The cross-eyed man, who seemed to be the leader of the welcoming committee, squatted down in front of Wallander.

"We are in a very difficult position," he said. "We're all under constant observation because the police know there is a risk that Major Liepa has hidden away some documents that could threaten their existence."

"So Baiba hasn't found the papers?"

"Not yet."

"Has she any idea at all where he might have hidden them?"

"No. But she believes you will be able to help her."

"How will I be able to do that?"

"You are on our side, Mr. Wallander. You're a police officer and used to solving riddles."

They're insane, Wallander thought indignantly. They're living in a dream world, and I'm the last straw they have to clutch at. All at once he could understand what oppression and fear did to people. They put their hope in some unknown savior who would spring from nowhere and redeem them.

Major Liepa had not been like that. He trusted no one but

himself and his close friends and confidants. For him the alpha and omega of all the injustices forced upon the Latvian nation was reality. He was religious, but had refrained from allowing his religious ideals to be obscured by a god. Now the major was gone, and they no longer had a central point from which to orientate themselves: Kurt Wallander, the Swedish police officer, would have to enter the arena and shoulder the fallen mantle.

"I must see Baiba Liepa as soon as possible," he insisted. "That's the only thing that really matters."

"That will happen during the course of today," the cross-eyed man said.

Wallander felt exhausted. What he would most like to do would be to have a bath and then climb into bed and sleep. He didn't trust his own judgment when he was overtired, and he was afraid that he would make a mistake that would have fatal consequences.

The cross-eyed man was still squatting at his feet. Wallander noticed he had a revolver tucked inside his trousers.

"What will happen when Major Liepa's papers are found?" he asked.

"We shall have to find ways of publishing them," the man replied, "but the main thing is that you should get them out of the country and publish them in Sweden. That will be a revolutionary event, a historic occasion. The world will realize what has been going on in this stricken land of ours."

Wallander felt an overwhelming need to protest, to guide these confused people back to the path beaten by Major Liepa, but his weary brain was unable to conjure up the English word "savior," and all he could manage to think was how incredible it was that he was here in Riga, in a toy warehouse, and that he didn't have the slightest idea what he was going to do next.

*

Then everything happened very fast. The warehouse door was flung open, Wallander got up from his chair and he saw Inese running between rows of shelves, screaming. He had no idea what was happening, but then came a violent explosion and he threw himself headlong behind some shelves crammed with dolls' heads.

The building was flooded with searchlights and there was a series of loud bangs, but it was only when he saw the cross-eyed man had taken out his revolver and fired that he realized the place was being subjected to intensive gunfire. He crawled further back behind the shelving but came up against a wall. The noise was unbearable. He heard a scream, and when he turned to look he saw that Inese had fallen over the chair he had just been sitting on. Her face was covered with blood and it seemed she had been shot straight through the eye. She was dead. At that very moment the cross-eyed man raised an arm to his head: he'd been hit, but Wallander couldn't tell whether he was alive. He knew he must escape, but he was trapped in a corner and now the first of the men in uniform came racing up, machine guns in hand. Without hesitating, he knocked over a rack of Russian dolls which rained down on him, and he lay down on the floor, allowing himself to be immersed in a flood of toys. All the time he was thinking he would be discovered at any moment and shot—his false passport wouldn't help him. Inese was dead, the warehouse had been surrounded, and the insane, daydreaming people inside had no chance to resist.

The gunfire ceased as abruptly as it had started. The silence was deafening, and he tried not to breathe. He could hear voices, soldiers or police officers talking to one another, and then he recognized one of them: there was no doubt at all, it was Sergeant Zids. He could just see the uniformed men through his covering of dolls. All the major's friends appeared to be dead and were being carried out on gray canvas stretchers. Then Sergeant Zids emerged from the shadows and ordered his men to search the warehouse. Wallander closed his eyes, thinking it would soon be over. He wondered if Linda would ever know what had happened to her father, who disappeared while holidaying in the Alps, or whether his disappearance would become a mystery in the annals of the Swedish police force.

But nobody came to kick the dolls away from his face. The echoing jackboots slowly faded away, the sergeant's irritated voice ceased to urge on his men, and only silence and the acrid stench of spent ammunition were left behind. Wallander had no idea how long he lay there, motionless. Eventually the cold of the concrete floor made him shiver so much that the dolls started rattling. He sat up carefully. One of his feet had gone to sleep, or been frozen stiff, he wasn't sure which. The floor was spattered with blood, there were bullet holes everywhere, and he forced himself to take a series of deep breaths so as not to start vomiting.

They know I'm here, he thought. It was me Sergeant Zids ordered his soldiers to look for. Or maybe they thought I hadn't arrived yet? Perhaps they thought they had moved in too soon?

He forced himself to think, even though he couldn't get the image of Inese out of his mind. He would have to get out of this house of death, he would have to accept the fact that he was on his own now. There was only one thing to do: find the Swedish embassy. His heart was pounding violently, and he feared he was suffering a heart attack that he would never recover from. Tears streamed down his face as he thought of Inese lying dead. Looking back, he could never work out how long it took for him to regain his self-control and start to think rationally again.

The iron door was locked. He assumed the whole warehouse was under observation. He would never be able to get away in daylight. Behind one of the overturned racks was a window, almost completely obscured by dust. He picked his way over to it through the broken and shattered toys, and looked out. Two jeeps were parked, facing the warehouse. Four soldiers were keeping watch on the building, their weapons at the ready. Wallander stepped back from the window and explored the building. He was thirsty—there must be water somewhere. While he was looking, his mind was working overtime. He was a hunted man, and the hunters had introduced themselves with shattering brutality. There was no question of establishing contact with Baiba Liepa. He might as well arrange his own execution. The two colonels, or at least one of them, would stop at nothing in order to prevent the major's discoveries from being published. Shy, modest Inese had been gunned down in cold blood, like vermin. Perhaps it had been friendly Sergeant Zids who had fired the shot that had passed straight through her eye.

His fear was now coupled with violent hatred. If he had a weapon in his hand, he would not have hesitated to use it. For the first time in his life he was prepared to kill another human being, without even trying to excuse it as self-defense.

There's a time to live, and a time to die, he thought. That was the mantra he had repeated to himself when he'd been stabbed by a drunk in Pildamm Park in Malmö. Now it had acquired extra meaning.

He came upon a dirty bathroom with a dripping tap. He rinsed his face and quenched his thirst, then found a part of the warehouse that was cut off from the rest, unscrewed the light bulb, and sat down in the dark to wait for nightfall. It would have to come eventually.

To keep his fear under control, he tried to concentrate on working out a plan of escape. Somehow or other he must reach the city center and find the Swedish embassy. He would have to count on every single police officer, every single "Black Beret," knowing what he looked like and having orders to watch out for him. Without help from the Swedish embassy, he would be lost. He figured that remaining undetected for more than a very short time was out of the question. He must also assume the Swedish embassy would be under observation.

The colonels must suppose that I already know the major's secret, he thought, or they wouldn't have reacted as they did. I say the colonels, because I still don't know which of them is behind everything that has happened.

He dozed off for a few hours, only to wake up with a start when he heard a car drawing up outside the warehouse. Occasionally, he went back to the dirty window. The soldiers were still there, on the alert. Wallander felt sick the whole of that never-ending day. He couldn't get over the evil of it all. He forced himself to his feet and searched the whole building, looking for a way out. The main door was out of the question. Eventually, he found a grille in a wall close to the ground, covering a hole that may once have contained some kind of ventilator. He pressed his ear to the cold brick wall to discover whether he could hear any sign of soldiers on this side of the building as well, but he could hear nothing. What he would do if he did eventually get out of the warehouse, he had no idea. He tried to rest as much as he could, but was unable to sleep. Inese's crumpled body, her blood-covered face, wouldn't go away. Dusk fell, and with it a sharper cold.

Shortly before 7 p.m. he decided he would have to leave. With great care, he started to ease off the rusty grill. At any moment he expected a searchlight to be switched on, excited voices to shout out commands, and a hail of bullets to smash into the wall. Eventually he managed to detach the grill, slide it carefully to one side and scramble through. There was a faint yellow light from an adjacent factory illuminating the wasteland outside the warehouse, and he tried to get his eyes used to the near-darkness. There was no sign of the soldiers. About ten meters away was a row of rusting trucks, and he decided to start by trying to get as far as that without being noticed. He took a deep breath, crouched down, and ran as fast as he could to the old wrecks. As he came to the first of them, he stumbled over an old tire and hit his knee against a broken bumper. The pain was excruciating, and he thought the noise would immediately attract the attention of the soldiers on the other side of the warehouse. But he lay still and nothing happened. The pain in his knee was unbearable, and he could feel blood running down his leg.

What next? He thought of the Swedish embassy, but then he realized he neither could nor wanted to give up. He had to contact Baiba Liepa, and it was no good sending up a private distress signal. Now that he had escaped the warehouse where Inese and the cross-eyed man had met their deaths, he had enough strength to think differently. He had come here for Baiba Liepa, and she was the person he should try to find, even if it was the last thing he did in this life.

He crept through the shadows, following a fence around the factory and eventually coming to the street. He still didn't know where he was, but he could hear the muffled drone that sounded like a highway in the distance, and he headed for the noise. He occasionally passed other people, and he sent a silent "thank you" to Joseph Lippman who had been far-sighted enough to insist that Wallander should put on the clothes Preuss had brought with him in a shabby suitcase. He walked for over half an hour, cowering in the shadows to avoid police cars, and all the while

trying to work out what to do. He had to accept that there was
only one person he could turn to. It would involve a major risk,
but he had no choice. It also meant he would have to spend
another night in hiding. It was chilly, and he would have to find
something to eat if he were going to survive the night.

He realized that he would never have the strength to walk all
the way to the center of Riga. His knee was hurting badly, and
he was so tired he couldn't think straight. He would have to steal
a car. The very thought of the risks involved horrified him, but
it was his only chance. He had noticed a Lada parked in a street
he had just passed—it hadn't been standing outside a house, but
seemed strangely deserted. He retraced his steps. He tried to recall
how to open locked car doors and short-circuit engines. But what
did he know about a Lada? Maybe it wasn't possible to start one
of those using the methods perfected by Swedish car thieves.

The car was gray and its bumpers were dented. Wallander stood
in the shadows, observing the car and the surroundings. All he
could see were factories with all the lights out. He went over to a
broken-down fence around a loading bay in the ruins of what had
once been a factory. His fingers were frozen stiff, but he managed
to break off a length of wire about two feet long. He made a loop
at one end, then hastened over to the car.

Sliding the wire in through the car window and manipulating
the door handle was easier than he had expected. He scrambled
into the driver's seat and hunted for the ignition lock and the
cables. He cursed the fact that he didn't have any matches. Sweat
was pouring down the inside of his shirt, but he was so cold that
he was shivering. Eventually, out of sheer desperation, he ripped
the whole bundle of wires out from behind the ignition, pulled
the lock away, and connected up the loose ends. The car was in
gear, and leapt forward when the ignition produced a spark. He

shifted into neutral, then connected the loose ends again. The engine started, he fumbled for the handbrake without finding it, pressed all the buttons in sight on the dashboard in an attempt to find the lights, then engaged first gear.

This is a nightmare, he thought. I'm a Swedish police officer, not a madman with a German passport stealing cars in the Latvian capital of Riga. He drove in the direction he'd been heading on foot, working out which gear was which, wondering why there was such a stench of fish in the car.

After a short while he reached the highway he'd previously heard the noise from. The engine almost stopped as he turned onto it, but he managed to keep it going. He could see the lights of Riga. He had already made up his mind to try to find his way to the district around the Latvia Hotel and go to one of the little restaurants he'd seen there. Once again he sent a silent "thank you" to Joseph Lippman, who had made sure Preuss provided him with some Latvian currency. He had no idea how much money he had, but hoped it would be enough for a meal. He crossed the river and turned left onto the riverside boulevard. There was not a lot of traffic, and he got stuck behind a streetcar and was immediately subjected to some furious honking from a taxi just behind him that had been forced to brake suddenly. He was getting nervous, stripping the gears, and only managed to get away from the streetcars by turning onto a side street. He discovered too late that he had driven onto a one-way street. A bus was coming towards him, the street was very narrow, and no matter how hard he tried and fiddled with the gear lever, he couldn't find reverse. He was on the brink of abandoning the car in the middle of the street and running away when he finally managed to engage reverse gear and back out of the way. He turned into one of the streets near the Latvia Hotel and parked in a legal parking spot.

He was soaked in sweat and knew that he ran the risk of pneumonia if he couldn't soon have a hot bath and change his clothes.

A church clock tolled 8:45 p.m. He crossed the street and went
into a smoke-filled café. He was lucky and found an empty table.
The men deep in conversation over their beer glasses didn't seem
to notice him, there was no sign of anybody in uniform, and
he was now able to assume the role of Gottfried Hegel, traveling
salesman. Once, when he and Preuss had stopped for a meal
in Germany, he had noticed that the German for menu was
Speisekarte so that was what he asked for. Unfortunately, it was
all in incomprehensible Latvian, and so he just pointed to one of
the dishes. He was served a plate of beef stew, and ordered a glass
of beer to help wash it down. For a short while, his mind was
completely blank.

He felt better when he'd eaten. He ordered coffee and felt his
mind working again. He realized how he should spend the night.
All he needed to do was to take advantage of what he had discovered about this country—that is, that everything has its price.
While he was here before he had noticed that just behind the
Latvia Hotel were several guesthouses and scruffy hotels. He would
go to one of them, brandish his German passport, then put a
few Swedish hundred-krona notes on the desk, thus buying some
peace and quiet and avoiding unnecessary questions. There was a
risk that the police had instructed every hotel in Riga to look out
for him, but that was a risk he would just have to take. His German
identity should get him through one night at least. With a bit of
luck he might manage to find a receptionist whose first instinct
wasn't to go running off to the police.

He drank his coffee and thought about the two colonels. And
Sergeant Zids, who might have been personally responsible for
murdering Inese. Somewhere out there in this awful darkness

was Baiba Liepa, and she was waiting for him. "Baiba Liepa will be very pleased." Those were just about the last words Inese had spoken in her short life.

He looked at the clock over the bar counter. Nearly 10:30 p.m. He paid his bill and calculated that he had more than enough money to pay for a hotel room. He left the café and stopped outside the Hermes Hotel not far away. The outside door was open, and he tramped up a creaking staircase to the upper floor. A curtain was drawn aside, and he found an old, hunchbacked woman peering at him from behind thick glasses. He smiled the friendliest smile he could conjure up, said "*Zimmer,*" and put his passport on the desk. The old woman nodded, said something in Latvian, and gave him a card to fill in. As she hadn't even bothered to look at his passport, he made up his mind on the spot to change his plans and signed himself in under an invented name. He was so flustered that the only name he could think of was Preuss. He gave himself the first name Martin, claimed he was 37 years old, from Hamburg. The woman gave him a friendly smile, handed over the key, and pointed to a corridor behind his back. Unless the colonels are so desperate to find me that they organize raids on every single hotel in Riga tonight, I'll be able to spend a quiet night here, Wallander thought. Needless to say, they will eventually realize that Martin Preuss is in fact Kurt Wallander, but by then I should be miles away. He unlocked his door, was delighted to find there was a bathroom, and could hardly believe his luck when the water gradually became warm. He undressed and slumped into the bath. The heat seeping into his body made him feel drowsy, and he nodded off.

When he woke, the water was stone cold. He got out of the bath, dried himself and went to bed. A streetcar clattered by in the street. He stared into the darkness and felt his fear returning. He must stick to his plan. If he lost control over his own judgment, the dogs on his trail would soon catch his scent. Then he would be sunk. He knew what he had to do. He would look for the only person in Riga who might possibly be able to put him in touch with Baiba Liepa. He had no idea what her name was, but he did remember that she had red lips.

CHAPTER 16

Inese returned just before dawn.

She came to him in a nightmare in which both colonels were keeping watch over him from somewhere in the shadows, though he couldn't see them. She was still alive, and he tried to warn her, but she didn't hear what he said and he knew he wouldn't be able to help her. He woke with a start and found himself in his room in the Hermes Hotel.

He'd put his wristwatch on the bedside table. It was just after 6 a.m. A streetcar clattered past in the street below. He stretched out in bed, feeling thoroughly rested for the first time since he'd left Sweden.

He lay in bed and relived with agonizing clarity the events of the previous day. His mind was now fully alert, and the horrific massacre seemed unreal. The indiscriminate killing was incomprehensible. He was filled with despair at the death of Inese and didn't know how he would be able to cope with the knowledge that he had been unable to help her, or the cross-eyed man and the others, the people who had been waiting for him but whose names he didn't even know. His agitation drove him out of bed. He left his room shortly before 6:30 a.m., went out to reception and paid his bill. The old woman took his money, and a quick check revealed that he had enough left to spend another few nights in a hotel, should it prove necessary.

It was a cold morning. He turned up the collar of his jacket and decided to get some breakfast before putting his plan into operation. After wandering the streets for 20 minutes or so, he found a café. It was half empty, but he went in and ordered coffee and some sandwiches, then sat down at a corner table that was hidden from the entrance. By 7:30 a.m. he knew he could wait no longer. Now it was make or break time.

Half an hour later he was standing outside the Latvia Hotel, exactly where Sergeant Zids had waited for him in his car. He hesitated. Maybe he was too early. Maybe the woman with the red lips hadn't arrived yet? He went in, glanced over at reception, where several early birds were paying their bills, passed the sofa where his shadows had sat buried in their newspapers, and discovered that the woman actually was there, standing at her counter, carefully setting out various newspapers in front of her. What if she doesn't recognize me, he wondered. Perhaps she's just a messenger who doesn't know anything about the errands she is running?

At that very moment she saw him, standing next to one of the big columns in the foyer. He could tell that she recognized him immediately, knew who he was, and wasn't frightened to see him again. He went over to her table, reached out his hand, and explained loudly in English that he wanted to buy postcards. In order to give her time to get used to his sudden appearance, he kept on talking. Did she happen to have any postcards of old Riga? There was nobody nearby, and when he thought he'd been talking for long enough he leaned forward, as if to ask her to explain some detail or other on one of the postcards.

"You recognize me," he said. "You gave me a ticket for the organ concert where I met Baiba Liepa. Now you must help me to see her again. You're the only person who can help me. It's very important for me to meet Baiba, but at the same time, you ought to be clear that it is very dangerous, as she's being watched. I don't know if you are aware of what happened yesterday. Show me something in one of your brochures, pretend you are explaining it to me, but answer my question."

Her bottom lip started trembling, and he could see her eyes filling with tears. As he couldn't risk her crying and drawing attention to them, he quickly explained how he was very interested in postcards not only of Riga, but also of the whole of Latvia. A good friend of his had said there was always an excellent selection of cards at the Latvia Hotel.

She pulled herself together, and he told her he realized she must know what had happened. But did she also know he had returned to Latvia? She shook her head.

"I have nowhere to go," he said. "I need somewhere to hide while you arrange for me to meet Baiba."

He didn't even know her name. Did he have any right to ask her to do this for him? Wouldn't it be better if he gave up and went looking for the Swedish embassy? Where do you draw the line on what is reasonable and decent in a country where innocent people are gunned down indiscriminately?

"I don't know if I can arrange for you to meet Baiba," she said in a low voice. "I've no idea if it's still possible. But I can hide you in my home. I'm much too insignificant a person for the police to be interested in me. Come back in an hour. Wait at the bus stop on the other side of the street. Go now."

He stood up again, thanked her like the satisfied customer he was pretending to be, put a brochure in his pocket, and left the hotel. He spent the next hour among the crowd of customers at one of the big department stores, and bought himself a new hat in an attempt to change his appearance. After an hour he went to stand at the bus stop. He saw her emerge from the hotel, and when she came to stand beside him, she pretended he was a total stranger. A bus came after a few minutes, they got on, and Wallander sat a couple of rows behind her. For over half an hour the bus circled around the city before heading off in the direction of the suburbs. He tried to make a note of the route, but the only landmark he recognized was the enormous Kirov Park. They came to a huge, drab housing estate, and when she pressed the bell to stop the bus he was taken by surprise, and almost didn't get off in time. They walked through a frosty playground where some children were climbing on a rusty frame. Wallander trod on the swollen body of a cat lying dead on the ground. He followed the woman into a dark, echoing entrance. They emerged into an open atrium where the cold wind bit into their faces. She turned to face him.

"My apartment is very small," she said. "My father lives with me; he's very old. I'll just tell him you're a homeless friend. Our country is full of homeless people, and it's only natural for us to help each other. Later on my two children will come home from school. I'll leave them a note to say they should make you some tea. It's very cramped, but it's all I can offer you. I must go straight back to the hotel."

The apartment consisted of two small rooms, a kitchenette and a minuscule bathroom. An old man lay resting on a bed.

"I don't even know your name," Wallander said, accepting the coat-hanger she held out for him.

"Vera," she said. "You're called Wallander."

She said his surname as though it had been his first name, and it occurred to him that he barely knew what to call himself at the moment. The old man on the bed sat up, but when he was about to stand up with the aid of his walking stick and shake hands, Wallander protested. That wasn't necessary, he didn't want to cause any inconvenience. Vera produced some bread and cold meat in the little kitchen, and he protested again: what he was looking for was somewhere to hide, not a restaurant. He felt embarrassed at having to ask her to help him out like this, and guilty about the fact that his own apartment in Mariagatan was three times the size of the space she had at her disposal. She showed him the other room where most of the space was taken up by a large bed.

"Close the door if you want some peace," she said. "You can rest here. I'll try to get back from the hotel as soon as I can."

"I don't want to put you in any danger," he said.

"When something is necessary, it has to be done," she said. "I'm glad you came to me."

Then she left. Wallander slumped down on the edge of the bed. He'd gotten this far. Now all he needed to do was to wait for Baiba Liepa.

Vera got back from the hotel just before 5 p.m. By then Wallander had had tea with her two children, Sabine aged twelve and her elder sister Ieva, 14. He had learned some Latvian words, they had giggled at his hopeless rendition of "This little piggy went to market," and Vera's father had even sung an old soldier's ballad for them in a shaky voice. Wallander had managed to forget his mission and the image of Inese shot through the eye and the brutal massacre. He had discovered that normal life existed away from the clutches of the colonels, and that was precisely the world Major Liepa had been defending. People were meeting in remote hunting lodges and warehouses for the sake of Sabine and Ieva and Vera's ancient father.

When Vera got back she hugged her daughters, then shut herself in her bedroom with Wallander. They were sitting on her bed, and the situation suddenly seemed to embarrass her. He touched her arm in an effort to express his gratitude for what she had done, but she misunderstood the gesture and pulled away. He realized it would be a waste of time trying to explain, and instead asked whether she had managed to contact Baiba Liepa.

"Baiba is crying," she said. "She is mourning her friends. Most of all she is crying for Inese. She had warned them the police had stepped up their activities, and pleaded with them to be careful. Even so, what she most dreaded came to pass. Baiba is crying, but she is also possessed by fury, just like me. She wants to meet you tonight, Wallander, and we have a plan for how to proceed. But before we do anything else, we must have something to eat. If we don't eat, we have as good as given up all hope."

They managed to fit themselves around a dining table that she folded down from one of the walls in the room where her father had his bed. It seemed to Wallander that it was as if Vera and her family lived in a trailer. In order to make room for everything, meticulous organization was essential, and he wondered how it was possible to live a whole life in such cramped conditions. He thought of the evening he had spent in Colonel Putnis's mansion outside Riga. It was in order to protect their privileges that one of the colonels had instructed his subordinates to undertake an indiscriminate witch-hunt for people like the major and Inese. Now he could see how great the differences were in their lives. Every transaction between these people left blood on their hands.

The meal consisted of vegetable stew produced by Vera on her tiny stove. The girls set the table with a loaf of coarse bread and beer. Wallander could sense the tremendous tension in Vera, but she succeeded in concealing it from her family. Yet again he asked himself what right he had to expose her to such risks. How would he ever be able to live with himself if anything happened to her?

After the meal the girls cleared the table and did the dishes, while the old man went back to bed to rest.

"What's your father's name?" Wallander asked.

"He has a strange name," Vera told him. "He's called Antons. He's 76 years old and has bladder trouble. He's spent the whole of his life working as a foreman at a printing works. They say old typographers can be affected by some kind of lead poisoning that makes them absentminded and confused. Sometimes he seems to be living in another world. Maybe he's been affected by the disease."

They were sitting on the bed in her room again, and she had drawn the door curtain. The girls were whispering and giggling in the tiny kitchen, and he knew the moment had come.

"Do you remember the church where you met Baiba after a concert?" she asked. "St. Gertrude's?"

He nodded; he remembered.

"Do you think you could find your way back there?"

"Not from here."

"But from the Latvia Hotel? From the city center?"

"Yes, I could."

"I can't go to the center of town with you, it's too dangerous. But I don't think anybody suspects you are here in my apartment. You must take the bus back to the city center on your own. Don't get off at the stop outside the hotel—use the one before or the one after. Find the church and wait until 10 p.m. Do you remember the back gate in the churchyard you used when you left the church that first time?"

Wallander nodded. He thought he remembered it, even if he wasn't quite sure.

"Go in through that gate when you're absolutely certain nobody is looking. Wait there. If it's at all possible, Baiba will come
to you."

"How did you contact her?"

"I phoned her."

Wallander looked skeptical.

"The telephone must be bugged."

"Of course it's bugged. I called her and said the book she'd
ordered had arrived. That meant she knew she should go to a
certain bookshop and ask for a certain book. I'd left a note there
telling her you had arrived and were in my apartment. Some hours
later I went to a store where one of Baiba's neighbors usually
shops. There was a note from Baiba saying she'd try to get to the
church tonight."

"But what if she can't make it?"

"Then I can't help you any more. You can't come back here
either."

Wallander could see she was right. This was his only chance of
meeting Baiba Liepa again. If it didn't work, he had no choice but
to find his way to the Swedish embassy and get help in fleeing
the country.

"Do you know where the Swedish embassy is in Riga?"

She thought for a moment before answering. "I don't even know
if Sweden has an embassy here," she said.

"There must be a consulate, though?"

"I don't know where."

"It must be in the telephone directory. Write down the Latvian
for 'Swedish embassy' and 'Swedish consulate.' There must be a
telephone directory in a restaurant. Write the Latvian for 'telephone directory' as well."

She wrote down what he was asking for on a sheet of paper torn out of one of the girl's exercise books, and taught him the correct pronunciation for the words.

Two hours later he said goodbye to Vera and her family, and set off. She had given him one of her father's old shirts and a scarf, so that he could change his appearance a bit more. He had no idea if he would ever see them again, and he was already beginning to miss them.

As he walked to the bus stop, he saw the dead cat, lying at his feet like an ominous symbol of what was to come.

When he was on the bus he suddenly had the feeling once again that he was being watched already. There were not many passengers going into town in the evening, and he had sat right at the rear of the bus so that he could see everybody's back in front of him. He looked now and then through the filthy back window, but couldn't see a car following them.

Nevertheless, his instinct made him anxious. He couldn't shrug off the feeling that they were tailing him. He tried to work out what to do. He had about a quarter of an hour in which to make up his mind. Where should he get off? How should he go about shaking off the shadows? It seemed an impossible situation, but he suddenly had an idea that was bold enough to have a slight chance of succeeding. He assumed it wasn't just him they were keeping an eye on. It must be at least as important for them to follow him until he met up with Baiba Liepa, and then to wait for the moment when they could be certain of finding the major's testimony.

He ignored the instructions given him by Vera, and got off the bus outside the Latvia Hotel. Without looking around, he strode into the hotel, marched up to the reception desk, and asked if they had a room for one or possibly two nights. He spoke clearly in English, and when the receptionist said they did indeed have a room, he produced his German passport and signed himself in as Gottfried Hegel. He explained that his luggage would be arriving later, and then, in as loud a voice as he dared use without giving the impression he was purposely setting a false trail, he asked to be woken up a few minutes before midnight as he was expecting an important telephone call. He hoped this would give him a start of four hours. As he didn't have any luggage, he accepted the key himself and walked over to the elevator. He had been given a room on the fourth floor, and now it was essential for him to act decisively without any hesitation. He tried to remember from his first visit where the back staircase was, and when he got out of the elevator on the fourth floor he knew immediately where to go. He went down into the gloom of the back staircase and hoped they hadn't had time to put guards around the whole hotel. He went right down to the basement and found his way to the door that opened out onto the rear of the hotel. Just for a moment he was afraid it might not be possible to open the door without a key, but he was lucky. The key was in the lock. He stepped out into the murky back street, stood absolutely still for couple of seconds and looked around. It was deserted, and he couldn't hear any hurried footsteps. He kept close to the walls, turned off onto side streets, and didn't stop running until he was at least three blocks from the hotel. He was out of breath by then and withdrew into a doorway while he got his breath back to see if he was being followed. He tried to imagine how, at this very moment in some other part of the city, Baiba Liepa was also trying to shake off the dogs that one of the colonels had put on her tail. He had no doubt she would succeed, because her tutor had been one of the best, the major himself.

He managed to find his way to St. Gertrude's church just before

10 p.m. There was no light coming from the church's enormous windows, and he found a nearby yard where he could wait unseen. Somewhere inside the building he could hear people quarrelling, a long, relentless flood of excited words culminating in a loud noise, a scream and then silence. He stamped his feet in order to keep warm, and tried to remember what date it was. From time to time a car drove past in the street outside, and he half expected one of them to stop and for the passengers to find him hiding among the dustbins.

The feeling that they already knew where he was kept returning, and he wondered if his attempt to break free by registering at the Latvia Hotel had failed. Had he made a mistake in assuming that Vera wasn't in the pay of the colonels? Perhaps they were waiting for him in the shadows of the churchyard, waiting for the moment when the major's testimony would be revealed? He pushed the thought away. His only alternative would be to flee to the Swedish embassy, and he knew he couldn't do that.

The clock in the church tower struck 10 p.m. He emerged from the yard, looked carefully for any sign of life in the street, and hurried over to the little iron gate. Although he opened it extremely carefully, there was a slight squeaking noise. A few street lamps cast a faint glow over the churchyard wall. He stood absolutely still, listening. Not a sound. He cautiously walked along the path to the side door he had used last time to leave the church with Baiba. Once again he had the feeling he was being watched, that his pursuers were somewhere ahead of him, but he continued as far as the church wall, then settled down to wait.

Without a sound, Baiba Liepa appeared by his side, as if she had materialized out of the darkness. He gave a start when he saw her. She whispered something he didn't catch, then led him quickly through the door that was standing ajar, and he realized she had been inside the church, waiting for him. She locked the door with the enormous key and went over to the altar. It was very dark inside the church, and she led him by the hand as if he were blind, he couldn't understand how she could find her way through the darkness. Behind the sacristy was a windowless storeroom, and a kerosene lamp was standing on a table. That was where she had been waiting for him, her fur coat was lying over a chair, and he was surprised and touched to note that she had placed a photograph of the major next to the lamp. There was also a thermos flask, some apples and a hunk of bread. It was as if she had invited him to the last supper, and he wondered how long it would be before the colonels tracked them down. He wondered about her relationship with the church, whether she had a god unlike her late husband, and he realized that he knew just as little about her as he once had about her husband.

When they were safely inside the room behind the sacristy, she put her arms around him and hugged him tightly. He could feel she was crying, and that her fury was so great, her hands were like iron claws digging into his back.

"They killed Inese," she whispered. "They killed all of them. I thought you were dead as well. I thought it was all over, and then Vera contacted me."

"It was terrible," Wallander said. "But we mustn't think about that now."

She stared at him in astonishment. "We must always think about that," she said. "If we forget that, we forget we are human."

"I didn't mean that we should forget it," he explained. "I just meant that we have to move on. Mourning prevents us from acting."

She flopped down onto a chair, and he could see she was haggard from pain and exhaustion. He wondered how much longer she would be able to keep going.

The night they spent in the church became the point in Kurt Wallander's life when he felt he had penetrated to the very center of his own existence. He had never previously looked at his life from an existential point of view. It was possible that at moments of deep depression—when he had seen the body of someone murdered, a child killed in a traffic accident, or a desperate suicide case—he might have been struck by the thought that life is so very short when death strikes. One lives for such a short time, but will be dead forever. But he had become adept at brushing aside such thoughts. He tried to regard life as mainly a practical business, and he doubted his ability to enrich his existence by adjusting his life in accordance with any particular philosophy. Nor had he ever worried about the particular span of time that fate had ordained he should live. One was born at such and such a time, and one died at such and such a time: that was about as far as he had ever gotten when it came to contemplating his earthly existence. The night he spent with Baiba Liepa in the freezing cold church made him look deeper into himself than he had ever done before. He realized that the world at large bore very little resemblance to Sweden, and that his own problems seemed insignificant compared with the savagery that was characteristic of Baiba Liepa's life. It was as if it was only now he could accept as fact the massacre in which Inese had died, only now that it became real. The colonels did exist, Sergeant Zids had fired a murderous volley from a real weapon, bullets that could split open hearts and in a fraction of a second create an abandoned universe. He wondered about how intolerable it must be, always to be afraid. The age of fear, he thought: that is my age, and I have never understood that before, even though I am into my middle years.

She said they were safe in the church, as safe as they could ever be. The vicar had been a close friend of Karlis Liepa, and hadn't

hesitated to provide Baiba with a hiding place when she had asked
for his help. Wallander told her about his instinctive feeling that
they had already tracked him down, and were waiting somewhere
in the shadows.

"Why should they wait?" Baiba objected. "For people like that
there is no such thing as waiting when it comes to arresting and
punishing those who threaten their existence."

Wallander thought she could well be right. At the same time, he
was certain the most important thing was the major's testimony:
what frightened them was the evidence the major had left behind,
not a widow and, as far as they were concerned, a harmless Swedish
police officer who had set out on his own private vendetta.

Something else occurred to him. It was so astounding that he
decided not to say anything about it to Baiba yet. It had suddenly dawned on him that there could be another reason why
their shadows had not revealed themselves and simply arrested
them and carted them off to the fortified police headquarters.
The more he thought about it during the long night in the church,
the more plausible it became. But he said nothing, mainly in
order not to subject Baiba to any more strain than was absolutely
necessary.

He recognized that her despondency was as much due to the
fact that she couldn't understand where Karlis had hidden his
testimony as to her shock at the death of Inese and her other
friends. She had tried everything she could think of, attempted to
put herself inside her husband's mind, but still she hadn't found
the answer. She had removed tiles in the bathroom and ripped
the upholstery off their furniture, but found nothing except dust
and the bones of dead mice.

Wallander tried to help her. They sat opposite each other across
the table, she poured out tea, and the light from the kerosene

lamp transformed the gloomy room into a warm, intimate room. Wallander would have liked most of all to hug her and share her sorrow, and again he considered the possibility of taking her with him to Sweden, but he knew she wouldn't be able to contemplate that, not yet in any case. She would rather die than abandon hope of finding the testimony her husband must have left behind.

At the same time, however, he also considered the third possibility—the reason why the shadows were not moving in to arrest them. If his suspicions were correct, and he was becoming increasingly convinced they might well be, there was not just an enemy lurking in the shadows, but also the enemy's enemy who was actually standing guard over them. The condor and the lapwing. He still didn't know which of the colonels had which plumage, but perhaps the lapwing was aware of the condor, and wanted to protect its intended prey?

The night in the church was like a journey to an unknown continent, where they would try to find something but didn't know what they were looking for. A brown paper parcel? A suitcase? Wallander was convinced the major was a wise man who knew that a hiding place was useless if it was too cleverly concealed. In order to break into the major's way of thinking, however, he would have to find out more about Baiba Liepa. He asked questions he didn't want to ask, but she insisted that he do so, begging him not to spare her feelings.

With her help he explored their lives in intimate detail. Occasionally they would come to a point where he thought they had cracked it, but then it would transpire that Baiba had already been down that trail and found it was cold. By 4:30 a.m. he was on the point of giving up. He looked wearily into her exhausted face.

"What else is there?" he asked. "What else is there we can do? A hiding place must exist somewhere, must be embodied in some kind of space. A motionless space, waterproof, fireproof, theft-proof. Where else is there?"

He forced himself to go on. "Is there a cellar in your block of apartments?" he asked.

She shook her head.

"We've already talked about the attic. We've been over every inch of the apartment. Your sister's summer cottage. His father's house in Ventspils. Think, Baiba. There must be another possibility."

He could see she was close to the breaking point.

"No," she said, "there is nowhere else."

"It doesn't need to be indoors. You said you sometimes used to drive out to the coast. Is there a rock you used to sit on? Where did you pitch your tent?"

"I've told you all that already. I know Karlis would never have hidden anything there."

"Did you really always pitch your tent at exactly the same spot? For eight summers in a row? Maybe you chose a different site on one occasion?"

"We both enjoyed the pleasure of returning to the same place."

She wanted to go on, but he was driving her backwards all the time. It seemed to him the major would never have chosen a place randomly. Wherever it was, it had to be part of their joint past.

He started all over again. The lamp was beginning to run out of kerosene, but Baiba found a church candle. Then they set out on yet another journey through the life she and the major had shared. Wallander was afraid Baiba would collapse with exhaustion, wondered when she had last had any sleep, and tried to cheer her up by trying to appear optimistic, even though he wasn't optimistic at all. He started with the apartment they had shared. In spite of everything, was there any possibility at all that she might have overlooked something? After all, a house consists of innumerable cavities.

He dragged her through room after room, and in the end she was so tired she was yelling out her answers.

"There is nowhere!" she screamed. "We had a home, and apart from the summers, that's where we lived. During the day I was at the university, and Karlis went to police headquarters. There is no testimony. Karlis must have thought he was immortal."

Wallander understood that her anger was also directed at her husband. It was a lament that reminded him of the previous year when a Somali refugee had been brutally murdered, and Martinsson had tried to soothe the desperate widow. We are living in the age of the widow, he thought. Our homes are the dwellings of fear and widows. . . .

He broke off. Baiba could see that he had hit upon a new train of thought.

"What is it?" she whispered.

"Just a minute," he replied, "I've got to think."

Was it possible? He tested it from various angles, and tried to discard it as a pointless exercise. But he couldn't shake it off.

"I'm going to ask you a question," he said slowly, "and I want you to answer right away, without thinking. Answer without hesitation. If you do start thinking, it's possible your answer might be wrong."

She stared intently at him in the flickering candlelight.

"Is it possible that Karlis might have chosen the most unthinkable of all hiding places?" he asked. "Inside police headquarters?"

He could see a glint come into her eye.

"Yes," she said without hesitation. "He might well have done that."

"Why?"

"Karlis was like that. It would fit with his character."

"Where?"

"I don't know."

"His own office is a possibility. Did he ever talk to you about the police headquarters?"

"He hated it. Like a prison. It was a prison."

"Think hard, Baiba. Was there any room in particular he talked about? Somewhere that meant something special to him? That he hated more than any other room? Or somewhere he even liked?"

"The interrogation rooms made him feel sick."

"It's not possible to hide anything there."

"He hated the colonels' offices."

"He couldn't have hidden anything there, either."

She was thinking so hard that she closed her eyes. When she returned from her thoughts and reopened her eyes, she had found the answer.

"Karlis often used to talk about somewhere he called 'The Evil Room,'" she said. "He used to say that room contained all the documents describing the injustices that afflicted our country. That's where he's hidden his testimony of course—in the midst of the memories of all those who have suffered so agonizingly and so long. He's deposited his papers somewhere in the police head-quarters archives."

Wallander looked at her. There was no sign of her former exhaustion.

"Yes," he said. "I think you're right. He's chosen a hiding place hidden inside a hiding place. He's chosen the Chinese puzzle. But how has he coded his testimony so that only you would be able to find it?"

She suddenly started laughing and crying at the same time.

"I know," she sobbed. "Now I can see the way he did it. When we first met, he used to perform card tricks for me. As a young man he had dreamed of becoming an ornithologist, but he also dreamed of becoming a magician. I asked him to teach me some tricks. He refused. It became a sort of game between us. He did show me how to do one of his card tricks, the simplest of all. You split the pack up into two parts, one containing all the black cards and the other all the red cards. Then you ask somebody to pick a card, memorize it, and put it back into the pack. By switching the two halves, you make a red card appear among the black ones, and vice versa. He often used to say that the world was a gray sequence of misery, but I would light up his existence. That's why we always used to look for a red flower among all the blue ones or yellow ones, and we went out of our way to find a green house in among all the white ones. It was a sort of game we used to play in secret. That's what he must have been thinking of when he hid his testimony. I imagine the archives are full of files in different colors. Somewhere or other there'll be one that's different, different in color or maybe even in size. That's where we'll find what we're looking for."

"The police archives must be enormous," Wallander said.

"Sometimes when he had to go away, he used to put the pack of cards on my pillow with the red card inserted among all the black ones," she said. "I've no doubt there is a file on me in the archives. That's where he'll have inserted his wild card."

It was 5:30 a.m. They hadn't quite reached their destination, but at least they now thought they knew where it was. Wallander stretched out his hand and touched her arm.

"I'd like you to come back to Sweden with me," he said in Swedish.

She stared uncomprehendingly at him.

"I said we'd better get some rest," he explained. "We've got to get away from here before dawn. We don't know where we should be heading, nor do we know how we're going to pull off the biggest trick of all—breaking into the police headquarters. That's why we've got to get some rest."

There was a blanket in a cupboard, rolled up under an old mitre. Baiba spread it out on the floor. As if it were the most natural thing in the world, they clung tightly to each other to keep warm.

"Get some sleep," he said. "I just need to rest. I'll stay awake. I'll wake you up when we have to leave."

He waited for a moment, but got no answer. She was asleep already.

CHAPTER 17

They left the church shortly before 7 a.m.

Wallander had to help Baiba, who was so exhausted she was barely conscious. It was still dark when they set off. While she was asleep on the floor beside him, he had lain awake and thought about what they should do. He knew he was obliged to have a plan ready. Baiba would hardly be able to help him any more: she had burned her bridges, and was now as much of an outlaw as he was. From now on he was also her savior, and it seemed to him as he lay there in the darkness that he was no longer capable of making any plans; he'd run out of ideas.

However, the thought that there might be a third possibility kept him going. He could see that it was extremely risky to rely on any such thing. He might be wrong, in which case they would never be able to evade the major's murderer. But by the time they left the church, he was convinced there was no alternative.

It was a cold morning. They stood completely still in the darkness outside the door. Baiba was clinging on to his arm. Wallander detected an almost inaudible sound in the darkness, as if somebody had changed position and accidentally scraped a foot against the frozen gravel. Here they come, he thought. The dogs will be released now. But nothing happened, everything remained very still, and he led Baiba towards the gate in the churchyard wall. They emerged into the street, and now Wallander was certain their pursuers were close at hand. He thought he could see a shadowy movement in a doorway, and heard a slight creaking noise as the gate opened behind them for a second time. The dogs one of the colonels has on his leash are not especially skillful, he thought ironically. Unless they want us to know they have their eye on us all the time.

Baiba had been brought to her senses again by the cold of the morning. They paused at a street corner, and Wallander knew he had to think of something.

"Do you know anybody who has a car we could borrow?" he asked.

She thought for a while, then shook her head.

His fear suddenly made him feel annoyed. Why was everything so difficult in this country? How would he be able to help her when nothing was normal, nothing was like he was used to?

Then he remembered the car he had stolen the previous day. The chances of it still being where he had left it were small, but it seemed to him that he had nothing to lose by going to find out. They came to a café that had opened early, and he hustled Baiba inside, thinking how that would confuse the pack of dogs behind them. They would have to split into two groups, and they must be constantly on their guard in case he and Baiba had already found the proof. That thought put Wallander in a much better mood. There was a possibility he hadn't thought of before. He might be able to lay false trails for their pursuers. He hurried along the street. First of all he must establish whether the car was still there.

It was still where he had left it. Without a pause for thought he climbed in behind the wheel, noticing again the smell of fish, joined the electric cables, this time remembering to put the gear shift into neutral first. He pulled up outside the café and left the engine running while he went in to fetch Baiba. She was sitting at a table over a cup of tea, and it occurred to him that he was also hungry, but that would have to wait. She had already paid, and they went straight out to the car.

"How did you manage to get the car?" she asked.

"I'll explain another time," he said. "For the moment just tell me how to get out of Riga."

"Where are we going?"

"I don't know yet. To start with, just let's get out into the country."

There was more traffic on the roads now, and Wallander moaned and groaned about the lack of power in the engine, but at last they reached the outskirts of the city and were in flat countryside with farms here and there among the fields.

"Where does this lead to?" Wallander asked.

"Estonia. It ends up in Tallinn."

"We're not going that far."

The pointer on the fuel gauge had started jerking up and down, and he turned into a gas station. An old man, blind in one eye, filled the tank, and when Wallander came to pay, he found he didn't have enough money. Baiba was able to make up the difference, and they drove off. Wallander had been keeping his eye on the road, and noticed a black car of a make he didn't recognize pass by, followed closely by another. As they had emerged from the gas station, he had glanced in the rearview mirror and seen another car parked on the hard shoulder behind them. So, three of them, he thought. At least three cars, maybe more.

They came to a town whose name Wallander never discovered. He stopped the car in a square where a group of people were gathered around a stall selling fish. He was very tired. If he didn't get some sleep soon, his brain would no longer function. He noticed a hotel sign on the far side of the square, and made up his mind on the spot.

"I have to get some sleep," he said to Baiba. "How much money have you got on you? Enough for a room?"

She nodded. They left the car where it was, crossed the square and checked into the little hotel. Baiba said something in Latvian that made the girl at the reception desk blush, but she didn't ask them to fill in any registration forms.

"What did you tell her?" Wallander asked when they were safely inside their room overlooking a courtyard.

"The truth," she said. "That we are not married and are only going to stay for a few hours."

"She blushed, didn't she? Did you see her blush?"

"I would have too."

Just for a moment the tension was relieved. Wallander burst out laughing and Baiba blushed. Then he turned serious again.

"I don't know if you realize this, but this is the craziest escapade I've ever been involved in," he said. "Nor do I know if you realize I'm at least as scared as you are. Unlike your husband, I'm a police officer who has spent the whole of his life working in a town not much bigger than the one we're in now. I have no experience with complicated criminal networks and police massacres. Now and then I have to solve a murder, of course, but I spend most of my time chasing drunken burglars and escaped bulls."

She sat beside him on the edge of the bed.

"Karlis said you were a good police officer," she said. "He said you had made a careless mistake, but nevertheless you were a good police officer."

Wallander reluctantly recalled the life raft.

"Our two countries are so different," he said. "Karlis and I had completely different starting points for the work we had to do. He would no doubt have been able to operate in Sweden as well, but I could never be a police officer in Latvia."

"That's exactly what you are now," she said.

"No," he objected. "I'm here because you asked me to come. Maybe I'm here because Karlis was who he was. I don't actually know what I'm doing here in Latvia. There's only one thing I do know for certain, and that's that I want you to come back to Sweden with me. When all this is over."

She looked at him in astonishment. "Why?" she asked.

He realized he wouldn't be able to explain it to her, as his own feelings were so contradictory and uncertain.

"Never mind," he said. "Forget it. I have to get some sleep now if I'm going to be able to think clearly. You also need some rest. Maybe it's best if you ask the receptionist to knock on the door in three hours."

"The girl will start blushing again," Baiba said as she got up from the bed.

Wallander curled up under the quilt. He was already asleep when Baiba came back from reception.

When he woke up three hours later, it felt as if he'd only been asleep for a couple of minutes. The knocking on the door had not disturbed Baiba, who was still sleeping. Wallander forced himself to take a cold shower in order to drive the tiredness from his body. When he'd finished dressing, he thought he'd let her go on sleeping until he had worked out what they were going to do next. He wrote her a message, saying that she should wait for him to come back, that he wouldn't be long.

The girl in reception smiled hesitantly at him, and Wallander thought that there was a trace of sensuousness in her eyes. She turned out to understand a little English, and when he asked where he could get a bite to eat she pointed to the door of a little dining room that formed part of the hotel. He sat down at a table with a view of the square. People were still crowded around the fish stall, bundled up against the cold morning. The car was where Wallander had left it.

On the other side of the square was one of the black cars he had seen pass by the petrol station. He hoped the dogs were freezing as they sat on guard in their cars. The girl in reception also acted as waitress, and came in with a plate of sandwiches and a pot of coffee. He kept glancing out at the square as he ate, and all the time he was working out a plan of action. It was so outrageous, it might just have a chance of succeeding.

When he had finished eating he felt better. He returned to the room and found Baiba awake. He sat down on the bed and began to explain what he had decided to do.

"Karlis must have had somebody he trusted among his colleagues," he said.

"We never socialized with other police officers," she said. "We had friends from different circles."

"Think hard," he urged her. "There must have been somebody he had coffee with now and then. It doesn't need to have been a friend. It'll be enough if you can remember somebody who wasn't his enemy."

She tried to think, and he gave her time. His plan depended on the major having had somebody he might not have trusted, exactly, but didn't distrust.

"He sometimes mentioned Mikelis," she said, still thinking hard. "A young sergeant who wasn't like the rest of them. But I don't know anything about him."

"You must know something, surely? Why did Karlis talk about him?"

She had propped the pillow up against the wall, and he could see she was doing her best to remember.

"Karlis used to go on about how horrified he was by his

colleagues' nonchalance," she began. "Their cold-blooded reaction to any kind of suffering. Mikelis was an exception. I think he and Karlis had once been delegated to arrest a poor man with a large family, and afterwards, he'd said to Karlis that he thought it was awful. Maybe Karlis mentioned him in some other context as well, but I don't remember."

"When was that?"

"Quite recently."

"Try and be more precise. A year ago? More?"

"Less. It can't have been as long as a year ago."

"Mikelis must have been working with the serious crimes squad if he was working together with Karlis?"

"I've no idea."

"He must have been. You must phone Mikelis and tell him you need to talk to him."

She stared at him in horror. "He'll have me arrested."

"Don't tell him you're Baiba Liepa. Just say you've something to tell him that could be useful for his career prospects, but you must be granted anonymity."

"It's not easy to fool the police in this country."

"You have to sound convincing. You mustn't give up."

"But what should I say?"

"I don't know. You'll have to help me to work something out. What is the biggest temptation a Latvian police officer can be confronted with?"

"Money."

"Foreign currency?"

"A lot of people in my country would sell their own mother for American dollars."

"You must tell him you know some people who have lots of American dollars."

"He'll ask where it all comes from."

Wallander thought for a moment, and remembered something that had happened recently in Sweden.

"You must phone Mikelis and tell him you know two Latvians who have robbed a bank in Stockholm and acquired a large amount of foreign currency, mainly American dollars. They raided an exchange bureau at the central station in Stockholm, and the Swedish police never managed to solve the crime. The two robbers are back here in Latvia now, and they have all the foreign currency with them. That's what you must say."

"He'll ask who I am and how I know about it."

"Give him the impression you've been the girlfriend of one of the men, but that he's jilted you. You want revenge, but you're afraid of them and don't dare to give your name."

"I'm so bad at lying."

He was suddenly angry.

"Then you'd better learn. Right now. This Mikelis is our only hope of getting into the archives. I have a plan, and it might just work. If you can't think of any suggestions, then I have to."

He got up from the bed. "We're going back to Riga now, I'll tell you all about it in the car."

"Do you mean Mikelis is going to look for Karlis's papers?"

"No, not Mikelis," he replied solemnly. "I'll do that. But Mikelis has to let me into the police headquarters."

They had returned to Riga, and Baiba had telephoned from a post office and managed to lie successfully. Then they'd gone to the indoor market. Baiba had told him to wait in the big hangar-like hall where they sold fish. He watched her disappear into the throng, and he knew he might never see her again. She returned, however, having met Mikelis in the meat section. They had wandered from stall to stall, examining the meat and talking. She told him there were no bank robbers in fact, and no American dollars. During the drive back to Riga Wallander had told her not to hesitate but to jump in with both feet and tell him the whole story. There was no other option. It was all or nothing.

"He'll either arrest you," he'd told her, "or he'll play along with us. If you start hesitating, he might suspect it's a plot against him, maybe something being tried on by one of his superiors who is testing his loyalty. You must be able to prove that you are Karlis's widow if he doesn't recognize your face. You must say and do exactly what I've told you."

A good hour later Baiba returned to where Wallander was waiting. He could see immediately that she had pulled it off. Her face radiated happiness. He was reminded again how beautiful she was.

She reported in a low voice that Mikelis had been very scared. His whole career as a police officer was on the line. He might even be risking his life. Nevertheless, she suspected he was also feeling relief.

"He's one of us," she said. "Karlis was not mistaken."

There were still some hours to go before Wallander could put his plan into operation, and to fill in the time they wandered through the city, fixed two alternative meeting places, and then continued to the university where she worked. In a deserted biology lecture room smelling of ether, Wallander fell asleep with his head resting on a showcase containing the skeleton of a seagull. Baiba curled up on a broad window ledge, contemplating the park outside. There was nothing to do but wait, silent and exhausted.

Shortly before 8 p.m. they parted outside the biology theater. A caretaker was doing his rounds, checking that lights were switched off and doors locked, and Baiba talked him into switching off the light above one of the back doors for a moment.

When the light went out, Wallander slipped out the door, ran through the grounds in the direction Baiba had indicated, and when he paused to catch his breath he was sure the pack was still gathered around the university building.

The moment the clock in the church tower behind the police headquarters struck 9 p.m., Wallander walked in through the well-lit doors and into the section of the fortress that was accessible to the public. Baiba had described in detail what Mikelis looked like, and the only thing that surprised Wallander when he found him was how young he was. Mikelis was waiting behind a desk, and Wallander wondered how on earth he had explained away his presence there. In a loud, shrill voice he protested in English about having been mugged in the street. The bastards had not only taken his money, but they'd also stolen his holy of holies, his passport.

For one desperate moment it struck him that he might have made a fatal error. He'd forgotten to tell Baiba to find out if Mikelis spoke English. What if he only spoke Latvian? He could hardly avoid bringing in somebody who did speak English, and then Wallander would really be in trouble.

To his relief Mikelis did speak a little English, better than the major in fact, and when one of the other duty officers came over to the desk to see if he could take this troublesome Englishman off Mikelis's hands, he was sent away. Mikelis ushered Wallander into an adjacent room. The other officers displayed some curious interest, but hardly of the kind that suggested that they were suspicious and about to sound the alarm.

The interrogation room was bare and cold. Wallander sat down on a chair, and Mikelis observed him unsmilingly.

"At 10 p.m. the night shift will take over," said Mikelis. "By then

I ought to have filled in a report form on the assault. I'll send out a car to search for some suspects whose appearance we can invent. We have exactly one hour."

As Wallander had expected, Mikelis told him that the archives were huge. He would have no chance of going through even a tiny portion of all the shelves in the caverns built into the rock under the police headquarters. If Baiba was wrong and Karlis hadn't in fact hidden his testimony close to the file bearing her own name, they were lost.

Mikelis drew a map for Wallander, who would have to negotiate three locked doors on his way to the archives. Mikelis would give him the keys. On the bottom floor, the basement archive, there would be a guard posted on the final door. Mikelis would lure him away with a telephone call at precisely 10:30 p.m. One hour later, at 11:30 p.m., Mikelis would go to the basement and take the guard away with him in order to help him with some task he would invent. That was when Wallander would have to leave the archive. After that, he was on his own. If he should come up against any duty officer in the corridors who became suspicious, Wallander would have to sort things out for himself.

Could he rely on Mikelis? Wallander asked himself that question, and decided the answer was irrelevant. He had no choice but to trust him. There was no alternative. He knew what he'd instructed Baiba to say to the young sergeant, but he had no idea what else she'd told him. He only knew it was then that Mikelis had been convinced he should help Wallander get into the archives. No matter what he did, he would have no control over what was happening around him.

After half an hour Mikelis left the interrogation room to arrange for a patrol car to be sent out with instructions to look out for any persons answering the description of the muggers who had

attacked Mr. Stevens, the English tourist. Mikelis had written out
some descriptions that could well have applied to most of the
citizens of Riga, and Wallander noticed that one of the descriptions could easily have been of Mikelis himself. The attack was
assumed to have taken place near the Esplanade, but Mr. Stevens
was still too upset to be able to go with the car and point out the
exact spot. When Mikelis returned, they went over the map of
the route to the archives once again. Wallander noticed he would
have to pass by the corridor where the colonels had their offices,
and where he himself had also had a room. The very thought
made him shudder. Even if one of them is in his office, he thought,
I can't know whether he was the one who ordered Sergeant Zids to
butcher Inese and her friends. Was it Putnis, or Murniers? Which
of them has sent out his dogs to hunt down the people who are
searching for the major's testimony?

When it was time for the night shift to take over, Wallander
noticed that all the tension had affected his stomach. He badly
needed to go to the bathroom, but knew there was no time for
that. Mikelis opened the door into the corridor, then gave
Wallander the order to go. He had memorized the map and knew
he couldn't afford to get lost—if he did, he would never reach the
last door in time for Mikelis's call that would distract the guard.

The building was deserted. He hastened along the lengthy corridors as quietly as he could, afraid that any moment a door would
be flung open and a gun pointed at him. He counted the staircases
as he passed them, heard the sound of footsteps echoing down
a distant corridor, and had the feeling of being in the middle of a
labyrinth where one could get lost all too easily. He started down
the stairs, wondering how far below street level the archives actually were. At last he got very close to the place where the guard
would be on duty, glanced at his watch and saw that Mikelis's

phone call was due in only a couple of minutes. He stood motion-less, listening. The silence unnerved him. Had he taken a wrong turn despite everything?

The shrill sound of the telephone ringing suddenly pierced the silence, and Wallander could start breathing again. He heard footsteps in the adjacent corridor, and when they died away he moved forward, came to the archive door and opened it with the two keys Mikelis had given him.

Wallander had been told where the light switches were, and groped his way along the wall until he came to them. Mikelis had assured him that the door fitted tightly and there would be no light seeping through the cracks to alert the guard.

The room was like a huge underground hangar. He had never imagined the archives would be as big as this. Just for a moment he paused, overwhelmed by the endless rows of cupboards and shelves crammed with files. The Evil Room, he thought. What was the major thinking when he came in here and planted the bomb he hoped would explode sooner or later?

He glanced at his watch and was annoyed at having allowed himself to waste time thinking such thoughts. He was also uncom-fortably aware that he couldn't wait much longer before emptying his bowels. There must be a bathroom somewhere in the archive, he thought desperately. But the question is, will I be able to find it?

He started walking in the direction Mikelis had indicated. He had warned Wallander how easy it was to get lost among the shelves and cupboards, which all looked the same. He cursed the fact that so much of his attention was being distracted by his rumbling stomach, and he was frightened by what would happen if he didn't find a bathroom soon.

He stopped and looked round. It was clear that he was off course—but had he gone too far or had he turned off somewhere

where he shouldn't, according to Mikelis's map? He retraced his steps. It struck him he was now completely disoriented, and he panicked. He looked at his watch and saw he had 42 minutes left, but he ought to have found the right section of the archive by now. He cursed to himself. Was Mikelis's map wrong? Why couldn't he find it? He decided he would have to start all over again and ran back between the rows of shelves to the entrance. In his haste he managed to kick over a metal wastebasket which bounced into a filing cabinet with a loud crash. The guard, he thought. This noise must have been audible from outside. He stood stock still, listening, but there was no rattling of keys in the locks. It was then that he was forced to accept he couldn't control his bowels a moment longer. He pulled down his trousers, crouched over the wastebasket and relieved himself. Feeling furious and disgusted at the same time, he reached for a file on the nearest shelf, ripped out some sheets of paper that were presumably the record of some interrogation or other, and wiped himself. Then he began all over again, knowing that this time he really had to find the correct spot or it would be too late. He made a silent plea to Rydberg, asking him to guide him, then started counting the racks and bays, and this time was sure he had gotten it right. It had taken far too long, though, and now he had only 30 minutes in which to find the testimony. He doubted that would be long enough. He started searching. Mikelis hadn't been able to tell him in detail how the various files were arranged, and Wallander was forced to feel his way forward. He could see immediately that the archive did not follow alphabetical order. There were sections and sub-sections, and perhaps even sub-sub-sections. These are all the disloyal citizens, he thought. Here are all the people who have been kept under observation and terrorized, all the people who have been reported or marked out as candidates for the title "enemy of the state." There are so many of them, I'll never be able to find Baiba's file.

He tried to identify the nerve center of the archive, to pinpoint the logical position for a file that had been inserted as a joker in the pack. Time went by, and still he was none the wiser. Frantically, he went back and started again, pulling out files that seemed to be different in color, trying hard all the time not to lose his cool.

There were only ten minutes to go, and still he hadn't found Baiba's file. He hadn't found anything at all, actually. He felt increasingly desperate at the thought of having come this far, but now being forced to admit defeat. There was no longer time for a systematic search. All he could do now was to make one last sweep along the shelves and hope that his instinct would lead him to the right place. But he was well aware that there wasn't a single archive in the world that was arranged according to intuition and instinct, and he was convinced he had failed. The major had been a wise man, much too clever for Kurt Wallander of the Ystad police.

Where, he thought. Where? What if this archive were a pack of cards? Where would the odd card be? At the side or in the middle?

He chose the middle, ran his hand over a row of files that all had brown covers, and suddenly noticed one that was blue. He pulled out the brown files from either side of the blue one—one was labelled Leonard Blooms, the other Baiba Kalns. Just for a moment, he couldn't think straight—and then it dawned on him that Baiba Liepa must have been called Kalns before she got married, and he took down the blue file, which he saw had no name at all, and no code number. He had no time to examine it, his time had run out already. He raced back to the entrance, put the light out and unlocked the door. There was no sign of the guard, but according to Mikelis's timetable he was due back any moment. Wallander hurried down the corridor, but then heard the echoing footsteps of the guard returning. He couldn't continue in that direction, and it was clear to Wallander he would have to ignore the map and try to find his way to the exit as best he could. He stood motionless as the guard went past along a parallel corridor. When the footsteps had died away, he decided the first thing he should do was to make his way up from the basement. He found a staircase and remembered how many flights he had walked down on his way there. When he came up to ground level, he had no idea where he was. He walked along the first empty corridor he came to.

The man who surprised him had been having a smoke. He must have heard Wallander's footsteps approaching, put out his cigarette with his boot, and wondered who on earth was on duty so late at night. When Wallander turned the corner, the man was only a few meters away. He seemed to be in his 40s, his tunic was unbuttoned, and the moment he saw Wallander with the blue file in his hand, he must have realized immediately that this man had no business to be in the building. He drew his pistol and shouted something in Latvian. Wallander didn't understand a word, but raised his hands over his head. The man had continued to shout as he approached, the pistol pointing at Wallander's chest. It occurred to Wallander that the police officer wanted him to kneel down, so he did so, his hands still raised in a pathetic gesture. There was no possibility of escape, he had been captured, and before long one of the colonels would appear and take possession of the blue file containing the major's testimony.

The man pointing his pistol at him was still shouting questions. Wallander was growing more and more terrified, realizing he was going to be shot here in the corridor, and could think of nothing better than to reply in English.

"It is a mistake," he said in a shrill voice. "It is a mistake. I am a police officer, too."

But it wasn't a mistake, of course. The officer ordered him to stand up with his hands over his head, then told him to start moving. He kept jabbing Wallander in the back with the barrel of his pistol.

It was when they came to an elevator that the opportunity presented itself. Wallander had given up hope, convinced he was well and truly caught. There was no point in resisting. The man wouldn't hesitate to shoot him. However, while they were waiting for the elevator his captor turned away slightly to light a cigarette, and in a split second Wallander realized that this was his only opportunity of getting away. He threw down the blue file at the man's feet, and simultaneously hit him in the back of the neck as hard as he could. He felt his knuckles crunching, and the pain was agonizing, but his captor fell headlong to the floor, the pistol sliding away over the stone flags. Wallander didn't know if the man was dead or just unconscious, but his hand was stiff with pain. He picked up the file, stuffed the pistol into his pocket, and decided the stupidest thing for him to do would be to use the elevator. He tried to work out where he was by looking out of a window facing the courtyard, and after a few seconds realized he must be on the opposite side from the colonels' corridor. The man on the floor started groaning, and Wallander knew he wouldn't be able to knock him out a second time. He hurried down the corridor to the left leading away from the elevator, and hoped he would come to an exit.

He was lucky. The corridor led to one of the canteens, and he managed to open a carelessly bolted door in the kitchen that was obviously a service entrance. He came out into the street. His hand was hurting badly and had started to swell.

The first rendezvous that he had agreed on with Baiba was at 12:30 a.m. Wallander stood in the shadows by the old church in

Esplanade Park that had been turned into a planetarium. All around him were tall, bare, motionless lime trees. There was no sign of her. The pain in his hand was now almost unbearable. When it reached 1:15 a.m., he was forced to accept that something must have happened. She wasn't going to come. He was extremely worried. Inese's blood-covered face hovered in his mind's eye, and he tried to work out what might have gone wrong. Had the dogs and their handlers realized that Wallander had managed to slip out of the university building unseen, despite their best efforts? In which case, what would they have done with Baiba? He did not dare to even think about that. He left the park, not knowing where to go next. What made him keep walking along the dark, deserted streets was really the pain in his hand. A military jeep with sirens blaring forced him to leap headfirst into a dark entrance, and not long afterwards a police car came racing down the street he was walking along, forcing him once more to withdraw into the shadows. He had put the file containing the major's testimony down the front of his shirt, and the edges were scratching against his ribs. He wondered where he was going to spend the night. The temperature had dropped, and he was trembling with cold. The alternative rendezvous he and Baiba had agreed on was the fourth floor of the central department store, but that wasn't until 11 a.m. the next morning, so he had nine hours to fill and couldn't possibly spend them walking the streets. He was convinced he had broken his hand, and knew he should go to a doctor, but he didn't dare go to an emergency room. Not now that he had the testimony with him. He wondered whether he ought to try and find shelter for the night at the Swedish embassy, assuming there was one, but he didn't like that option either. What if the law said that a Swedish police officer who had entered the country illegally should be sent home immediately under guard? He didn't dare take the risk.

Uneasily, he decided to go to the car that had served him well for two whole days now, but when he got to where he'd left it, it had gone. He thought for a moment that he was so disoriented by the pain in his hand that he had remembered wrongly. Was this really the place where he'd parked the car? Yes, it definitely was— no doubt the car had been dismantled and quartered like a farm animal by now. Whichever one of the colonels was pursuing him had doubtless made certain the major's testimony wasn't hidden somewhere in the car.

Where was he going to spend the night? He suddenly felt totally helpless, deep inside enemy territory, at the mercy of a pack of dogs managed by somebody who wouldn't hesitate to butcher him and sling him into the frozen harbor or bury him in a remote wood. His homesickness was primitive but tangible. The reason why he was now stranded in Latvia in the middle of the night—a life raft containing two dead men, washed up on the Swedish coast— seemed vague and distant, like it had never really happened.

For want of an alternative he made his way back through the empty streets to the hotel where he had earlier spent the night, but the door was locked and no lights went on upstairs when he rang the night bell. The pain in his hand was making him confused, and he was beginning to worry about whether he would lose his ability to think rationally altogether if he didn't get indoors soon and thaw out. He went on to the next hotel, but once again he was unable to get any response when he rang the night bell. At the third hotel, though, which was even more decrepit and unap- pealing than the others, the outer door was not locked and he went in to find a man asleep behind the reception desk, his head resting on a table, a half-empty bottle of vodka at his feet. Wallander shook the man to wake him up, flourished the passport he'd been given by Preuss, and was handed a room key. He pointed at the vodka bottle, put a Swedish hundred-krona note on the desk, and took it with him.

The room was small, with an acrid smell of musty furniture and nicotine-stained wallpaper. He flopped down on the edge of the bed, took a couple of long swigs from the bottle, and could feel his body warmth slowly starting to return. Then he took off his jacket, filled the sink with cold water, and immersed his swollen, throbbing hand. The pain began to ease, and he reconciled himself to having to sit like this all night. Occasionally he took another swig from the bottle, and wondered anxiously what could have happened to Baiba.

He took the blue file from inside his shirt and opened it with his free hand. It contained about 50 typewritten pages, plus some blurred photocopies, but no photographs, which was what he had hoped for. The major's text was in Latvian, and Wallander couldn't understand a word. He noted that from page nine onwards the names Murniers and Putnis kept recurring at regular intervals: sometimes they were together in the same sentence. He couldn't work out what that meant, whether both colonels were being accused or whether the major's accusing finger had been pointed at just one of them. He gave up the attempt to decipher the secret document, put the file down on the floor, refilled the sink with water, and leaned his head back against the edge of the table. It was 4 a.m., and he dozed off. When he woke up with a start, he found he'd been asleep for ten minutes. His hand had started hurting again, and the cold water was no longer easing the pain. He finished off what was left in the vodka bottle, wrapped a damp towel around his hand, and lay down on the bed.

Wallander had no idea what to do if Baiba failed to keep their rendezvous at the department store. He was beginning to have the feeling he had been defeated. He lay awake until dawn.

CHAPTER 18

He sensed danger the moment he woke. It was nearly 7 a.m. He lay quite still in the darkness, listening. Eventually, he realized the danger was not a threat outside the door or somewhere in the room, but inside himself. It was a warning that he still hadn't turned over every stone to discover what was lying underneath it.

The pain in his hand seemed to have eased a little. Carefully, he tried to move his fingers, although he still couldn't bear to look at his hand. The pain returned immediately. He wouldn't be able to last many hours more before seeing a doctor.

Wallander was exhausted. Before he'd dozed off, some hours earlier, he had felt defeated. The colonels' power was too great, and his own ability to handle the situation had been continually curtailed. Now, he could see that he was also being defeated by exhaustion. He didn't trust his own judgment, and he knew this was due to a lack of sleep over a long period.

He tried to analyze the nagging feeling he had experienced on waking. What had he overlooked? Where, in all his thoughts and his constant efforts to establish connections, had he drawn the wrong conclusions, or perhaps not thought things through properly? What had he still not managed to see? He couldn't ignore his instinct. Just now, in his dazed condition, it was his only chance of getting his bearings.

What had he still not managed to see? He sat up in bed carefully, still not having answered the question. He looked in disgust at his swollen hand for the first time, and filled the sink with cold water. He first dipped his face into it, then his injured hand. After a few minutes he went over to the window and opened the blind. There was a very strong smell of coal. Misty dawn was just breaking over the church towers of the city. He stayed at the window and watched all the people hurrying along the sidewalk, but he was still unable to answer his own question: what had he failed to see?

Then he left the room, paid, and allowed himself to be swallowed up by the city. It was as he walked through one of the city's many parks—he couldn't remember what it was called—that he noticed how many dogs there were in Riga. It wasn't just the invisible pack that was pursuing him. There were lots of other dogs, real ones, the kind people play with and take for walks. He paused to watch a pair of dogs involved in a violent fight. One was an Alsatian, the other a mutt. The two owners were shouting at their dogs as they tried to separate them, and then began to shout at each other as well. The owner of the Alsatian was an elderly man, but the mutt belonged to a woman in her 30s. Wallander had the feeling that what he was witnessing was symbolic of the opposing forces in Latvia. The dogs were fighting and the people as well, and there were no outcomes that could be predicted in advance.

He arrived at the central department store just as they were opening at 10 a.m. The blue folder was burning hot inside his shirt: his instinct told him he ought to get rid of it, to find a temporary hiding place.

While he'd been wandering around the streets that morning, he had monitored every movement behind and in front of him, and he was now certain that the colonels had encircled him again. There were more shadows than ever now, and the grim thought that a storm was brewing struck him. He stopped just inside the entrance and pretended to read an information board, but in fact he was observing a coat check where customers could leave bags and parcels. The counter was L-shaped. He had remembered it all correctly. He went over to the *bureau de change*, handed over a Swedish note and received a bundle of Latvian notes in exchange. Then he went up to the floor where they sold records. He picked out two LPs of Verdi, and noted that the records were just about the same size as the file. When he paid and had the records put in a shopping bag, he saw the closest of the shadows pretending to study a shelf with jazz records. He then went back to the coat check and waited for a few seconds until there were several people waiting to be served. He walked quickly to the farthest corner of the counter, pulled out the file and placed it between the records. He acted quickly, even though he could only use one hand properly. He handed in the shopping bag, was given a tag with a number, and walked away. The various shadows were dotted around near the entrance doors, but even so he felt pretty sure they hadn't noticed him putting the file into the bag. Of course, there was a risk that they would search the bag, but he thought it was unlikely since they had watched him buy the two records.

He looked at his watch: only ten minutes to go until Baiba was due at their meeting place. He was still uneasy, but he felt more secure now for having gotten rid of the file. He went upstairs to the furniture department. Although it was still early, there were lots of customers gazing dreamily or in resignation at suites and bedroom furniture. Wallander strolled slowly towards the area displaying kitchen equipment. He didn't want to arrive too soon, but wanted to get to the meeting place at the exact time they had planned, and so he filled the time by wandering around and looking at various light fixtures. They had agreed to meet among the ovens and refrigerators, all of which were made in the Soviet Union.

He saw her right away. She was examining a stove, and he noticed that it only had three hotplates. He could tell immediately that something was wrong. Something had happened to Baiba, something he had suspected the moment he woke up that morning. His uneasiness bristled and sharpened all his senses.

She noticed him at the same moment. She smiled, but he could see the fear in her eyes. Wallander walked towards her, not bothering to establish what positions the shadows had taken up. Just for the moment his whole attention was concentrated on finding out what had happened. He stood beside her, and they both stared at a dazzling white refrigerator.

"What's happened?" he asked. "Just tell me the important parts, we haven't much time."

"Nothing's happened," she said. "It was just that I couldn't leave the university since they had it under observation."

Why is she lying, he wondered frantically. Why is she trying to lie so convincingly that I won't notice?

"Did you get the file?" she asked.

He hesitated over whether he ought to tell the truth, but then he decided he was fed up with all the lies.

"Yes, I got the file," he said. "Mikelis was reliable."

She gave him a quick look.

"Give it to me," she said. "I know where we can hide it."

It was clear to Wallander that this was not Baiba speaking. It was her fear that was asking for the file, the threat she was exposed to.

"What's happened?" he asked again, this time more firmly, and perhaps with a note of anger.

"Nothing," she insisted.

"Don't lie," he said, unable to prevent his voice from rising. "I'll give you the file. What will happen if you don't get it?"

He could see she was at the end of her tether. Don't collapse just yet, he thought in desperation. We're still one step ahead of them as long as they are not sure whether or not I've got the major's testimony.

"Upitis will die," she whispered.

"Who has threatened you with that?"

She shook her head dismissively.

"I have to know," he said. "It won't have any effect on Upitis if you tell me."

She looked at him in horror. He took hold of her arm and shook her.

"Who?" he said. "Who was it?"

"Sergeant Zids."

He let her go. Her reply had made him furious. Would he never get to know which of the colonels was at the core of the conspiracy?

He noticed the shadows closing in on them. They now seemed to have decided that he had the major's testimony. Without pausing to think he grabbed hold of Baiba and dragged her with him in a race for the stairs. Upitis won't be the first to die, he thought. It'll be us, unless we can get away.

Their sudden flight had confused the pack of dogs. Even though he doubted whether they could get away, he knew they would have to try. He pulled Baiba after him down the stairs, elbowed aside a man who hadn't managed to get out of their way, and suddenly they found themselves in the clothing department. Sales assistants and customers stared at them in astonishment as they charged past. Wallander stumbled and fell into a rack of suits. As he pulled and grabbed at the suits, the rack overturned. When he fell, he'd landed on his injured hand and the pain shot through his arm like a knife. A security guard came running up and took hold of his arm, but Wallander had no inhibitions any longer. He punched the man in the face with his good hand, then pulled Baiba after him towards where he hoped there might be a back staircase or an emergency exit. The shadows were catching up, and making no attempt to conceal themselves now. Wallander was pushing and pulling at doors that refused to budge, but eventually came to one standing ajar. They emerged onto a back staircase, but he could hear footsteps coming towards them from below: there was no choice but to head for the upper floor.

He flung open a fire door and they came out onto a roof covered with gravel. He looked round for an escape route, but they were trapped. The only way down from the roof was the long leap into eternity. He noticed he was holding Baiba's hand. There was nothing to do but wait. He knew that the colonel who would soon step out onto the roof would be the man who had murdered the major. The gray fire door would reveal the answer at last, and he realized bitterly that it no longer mattered whether he'd guessed right or not.

When the door opened and Colonel Putnis stepped out accompanied by a group of armed men, however, he was surprised even so to see that he had been wrong. Despite everything, he had come to the conclusion that Murniers was the monster who had been lurking for so long in the shadows.

Putnis came towards them with a very serious expression on his face. Wallander could feel Baiba's nails digging into his hand. He can't very well order his men to shoot us here, Wallander thought desperately. Or maybe he can? He recalled the execution of Inese and her friends, and suddenly he could feel himself trembling, overcome by fear.

Then Putnis's face broke into a smile, and Wallander realized to his bewilderment that it wasn't an animal of prey standing before him and smiling, but a man displaying great friendliness.

"You don't need to look so perplexed, Mr. Wallander. You seem to think I'm the one behind this business. But I must say, you're a very difficult person to protect."

For one brief moment Wallander's mind stood still. Then he realized he'd been right after all, that it wasn't Putnis but Murniers who was the devil's henchman he'd been hunting for so long. He'd also been right in suspecting there was a third possibility, that the enemy also had an enemy. Everything fell into place. His judgment hadn't let him down, and he stretched out his left hand in order to greet Putnis.

"A somewhat unusual meeting place," Putnis said, "but you are obviously a man of surprises. I must admit that I wonder how you managed to get into the country without our border guards noticing."

"I hardly know myself," Wallander said. "It's a very long story."

Putnis seemed concerned about his injured hand. "You ought to get that treated as soon as possible," he said.

Wallander nodded, and smiled at Baiba. She was still tense and didn't seem to understand what was going on.

"Murniers," Wallander said. "So he was the one?"

Putnis nodded. "Major Liepa's suspicions were well founded."

"There's a lot I don't understand," Wallander said.

"Colonel Murniers is a very intelligent person," Putnis said. "Certainly, he's an evil man, but I'm afraid that only shows that sharp minds often have a tendency to be located in heads belonging to brutal people."

"Is that certain?" Baiba said suddenly. "That he was the one who killed my husband?"

"He wasn't the one who smashed his skull," Putnis said. "That is more likely to have been his faithful sergeant."

"My driver," Wallander said. "Sergeant Zids. The one who killed Inese and the others in the warehouse."

Putnis nodded. "Colonel Murniers has never liked the Latvian nation," he said. "Even though he played the part of a police officer who held the political world at a distance, as do all professionals, in his heart and soul he is a fanatical supporter of the old regime. As far as he's concerned, God will always be in the Kremlin. That was the guarantee for his being able to form an unholy alliance with various criminals without interference. When Major Liepa began to see through him, he set false trails implicating me. I have to admit it was a long time before I began to suspect what was happening. Then I decided I might as well continue pretending not to know what was going on."

"I still don't understand, though," Wallander said. "There must have been more to it than that. Major Liepa talked about a conspiracy, something that would make the whole of Europe realize what was happening in this country."

Putnis nodded sagely. "Of course there was more to it than that," he said. "Something much bigger than a high-ranking police officer being corrupt and protecting his privileges with as much brutality as was necessary. It was a devilish plot, and Major Liepa had realized that."

Wallander felt cold. He was still holding Baiba's hand. Putnis's armed men had withdrawn and were standing by the fire door.

"It was all very cleverly worked out," Putnis said. "Murniers had an idea and succeeded in selling it to the Kremlin and the leading Russian circles in Latvia. He had seen the possibility of killing two birds with one stone."

"By using the new Europe, where the border controls no longer existed, in order to earn money from the organized smuggling of drugs," Wallander said. "Including Sweden. But at the same time, he also used the drug smuggling to discredit the Latvian national movements. Am I right?"

Putnis nodded. "I could see from the start that you were a good police officer, Inspector Wallander. Very analytical, very patient. That's exactly how Murniers had worked it out. The blame for the drug trafficking would be attached to the freedom movements here in Latvia, and in Sweden public opinion would be radically altered. Who would want to support a political freedom movement that thanked you for the support it was receiving by flooding your country with drugs? It can't be denied that Murniers had created a weapon that was both dangerous and cleverly devised, a weapon that could have smashed the freedom movement in this country once and for all."

Wallander thought about what Putnis had said.

"Do you understand?" he asked Baiba.

She nodded slowly.

"Where is Sergeant Zids?" he asked.

"As soon as I have the necessary proof, Murniers and Sergeant Zids will be arrested," said Putnis. "I have no doubt Murniers is feeling very worried just now. He probably hasn't realized that all the time we've been keeping watch on those of his men who've been keeping watch on you. Of course, you could criticize me for exposing you to unnecessary danger, but I assumed it was probably the only way of finding the papers Major Liepa must have left behind."

"When I left the university yesterday, Zids was lying in wait for me," said Baiba. "He told me that if I didn't hand over the papers, Upitis would die."

"Upitis is innocent, of course," Putnis said. "Murniers had taken

his sister's two small children hostage, and told him they'd be
killed unless Upitis confessed to being Major Liepa's murderer.
There really is no limit to what Murniers is capable of doing. It will
come as a relief to the whole country once he's been exposed for
what he is, and condemned to death and executed, as will Sergeant
Zids. The major's evidence will be published. The plot will be
revealed, not just in the courts, but it will be circulated to the
whole nation. I've no doubt it will also be of interest to people
beyond our borders."

Wallander could feel relief seeping through his body. It was all
over.

Putnis smiled.

"All that remains is for me to read Major Liepa's documents,"
he said. "And now you can go back home for real, Inspector
Wallander. We are deeply grateful for the help you have given us."

Wallander took the numbered tag out of his pocket.

"The file is blue," he said. "It's in a shopping bag at the coat
check. Along with two records that I would like to have back."

Putnis laughed. "You really are very clever, Mr. Wallander. You
don't put a foot wrong unless you're forced to."

Was it something in Putnis's tone of voice that gave him away?
Wallander never managed to work out precisely why he was suddenly struck by the awful thought—but just as Putnis was putting
the tag into his pocket, it became crystal clear to Wallander that
he had just made the biggest mistake of his life. He simply knew
without knowing why he knew. He could no longer distinguish
between intuition and rational thought, and his mouth was as
dry as a desert.

Putnis continued to smile as he took his pistol from out of his
pocket. His men closed in, spreading themselves all over the
roof and pointing their machine guns at Baiba and Wallander.

She didn't seem to grasp what was happening, and Wallander was struck dumb with fear and humiliation. At that very moment the fire door opened, and Sergeant Zids stepped out onto the roof. It occurred to Wallander's confused mind that Zids must have been there behind the door all the time, waiting to make his entrance. The show was over now, and he didn't need to wait in the wings anymore.

"Your only mistake," Putnis said, his voice expressionless. "Everything I've just told you is absolutely true, of course. The only thing that distances my words from reality is my good self. Everything I said about Murniers applies to me. You were right and wrong at the same time, Inspector Wallander. If you had been a Marxist, like me, you would have realized that one must occasionally stand the world on its head in order to put it on its feet."

Putnis took a step backwards. "I trust you will realize that it is not possible for you to return to Sweden," he said. "After all, you'll be quite close to heaven when you die, up here on the roof."

"Not Baiba," Wallander pleaded. "Not Baiba."

"I'm so sorry," Putnis said.

He raised his gun, and Wallander realized he was going to shoot Baiba first. There was nothing he could do; he would die here on the roof in the center of Riga. At that very moment the fire door burst open. Putnis gave a start and turned to see what had caused the unexpected noise. At the head of a large number of armed police officers pouring out onto the roof was Colonel Murniers. When he saw Colonel Putnis standing there with his gun in his hand, he did not hesitate. His own pistol was already drawn, and he shot Putnis through the chest, three bullets in rapid succession. Wallander threw himself over Baiba in order to shield her. A violent gun battle raged all over the roof. Murniers's and Putnis's men tried to hide behind chimneys and ventilators. Wallander saw

he was in the firing line, and tried to pull Baiba with him behind
Putnis's corpse. He suddenly noticed Sergeant Zids crouching
behind one of the chimneys. Their eyes met, then Zids noticed
Baiba, and it was immediately clear to Wallander that Zids was
going to try to take both of them hostage in order to secure a safe
passage for himself. Murniers's men outnumbered the others, and
several of Putnis's henchmen had already been killed. Wallander
could see Putnis's pistol lying beside his body, but before he
could reach it Zids had flung himself at him. Wallander thrust his
injured hand into Zids's face, and cried out in agony. Zids reeled
from the force of the blow, his mouth started bleeding, but he
had not been seriously hurt by Wallander's desperate reaction.
There was hatred in his eyes as he raised his gun to shoot the
Swedish police officer who had caused him and his superior so
much trouble. But when the shot rang out and Wallander realized
he was still alive, he opened his eyes and registered that Baiba was
kneeling beside him. She had Putnis's pistol in her hands, and
had shot Sergeant Zids between the eyes. She was crying, but he
knew it was due to a mixture of fury and relief rather than the
fear and misery she had been subjected to for so long.

The gunfire on the roof ceased just as suddenly as it had begun.
Two of Putnis's men were wounded, the rest were dead. Murniers
looked grim as he examined one of his own men who had received
a number of gunshots to the chest, then he walked over to Baiba
and Wallander.

"I'm sorry it had to turn out like this," he said apologetically,
"but I had to know what Putnis said."

"You'll no doubt be able to read the full story in the major's
papers," Wallander said.

"How could I have been sure they existed? And still less that
you had found them?"

"By asking," Wallander said.

Murniers shook his head. "If I'd contacted either of you, I'd have entered into open warfare with Putnis, he'd have fled the country and we'd never have been able to catch him. I had no option but to keep watch over you by constantly following on the heels of Putnis's shadows."

Wallander suddenly felt far too weary to listen anymore. His hand was throbbing and the pain was agonizing. He took Baiba's hand and pulled himself up.

Then he passed out. When he came around he was on a table in a hospital, his hand was in a cast and the pain had gone at last. Colonel Murniers was standing in the doorway, cigarette in hand, watching him and smiling.

"Do you feel better now?" he asked. "Our doctors are very good. Your hand was not a pretty sight. You can have the X-rays to take home with you."

"What happened?" Wallander asked.

"You fainted. I'm sure I would have too, if I'd been in your situation."

Wallander looked around the examination room. "Where's Baiba?"

"She's at home in her apartment. She was very calm when I left her there a few hours ago."

Wallander's mouth was dry. He sat up gingerly on the edge of the treatment table.

"Coffee," he said. "Can you get a cup of coffee here?"

Murniers burst out laughing.

"I've never known a man to drink as much coffee as you do," he said. "Of course you can have some coffee. If you are feeling up to it, I suggest you come to my office so that we can wind up the whole business. Then I expect you and Baiba Liepa will have plenty to talk about. A police surgeon will give you an injection of painkillers if your hand starts hurting again. The doctor who put it in a cast said that could well happen."

They drove across the city. It was already quite late in the day, and it was starting to get dark. When they drove through the arch into the courtyard of the police headquarters, it seemed to Wallander that this must surely be for the last time. On the way up to his office, Murniers paused to unlock a safe and take out the blue file. An armed guard was sitting beside the imposing safe.

"I suppose it's a good idea to keep it locked up," Wallander said.

Murniers looked at him in surprise. "A good idea?" he echoed. "It's necessary, Inspector Wallander. Even if Putnis is now out of the way, it doesn't mean that all our problems are solved. We are still living in the same world as before. We are living in a country torn apart by conflicting forces, and we won't get rid of those simply by putting three bullets into the chest of a police colonel."

Wallander reflected on Murniers's words as they continued to his office. A man with a coffee tray was standing to attention outside the door. Wallander recalled his first visit to that dingy room. It seemed like a distant memory. Would he ever be able to grasp everything that had happened in between?

Murniers took a bottle out of a desk drawer and filled two glasses.

"It's not pleasant to drink a celebratory toast when so many people have died," he said, "but nevertheless, I think we deserve it. Especially you, Inspector Wallander."

"I've done practically nothing except make mistakes," Wallander said. "I've been on the wrong track, and didn't catch on to how various things fitted together until it was too late."

"On the contrary," Murniers said. "I am very impressed by what you've done, and not least by your courage."

Wallander shook his head. "I'm not a brave man," he said. "I'm amazed that I'm still alive."

They emptied their glasses and sat down at the table with the major's testimony between them.

"I suppose I really only have one question," Wallander said. "Upitis?"

Murniers nodded thoughtfully. "There was no limit to Putnis's cunning and brutality. He needed a scapegoat, a plausible murderer. And he also needed an excuse to send you home. I could see right from the start that he was uneasy about your competence, and scared. He had his men kidnap two small children, Inspector Wallander. Two small children whose mother is Upitis's sister. If Upitis didn't confess to the murder of Major Liepa, those children would die. Upitis didn't really have any choice. I often wonder what I would have done in the same situation. He's been released now, of course. Baiba Liepa already knows he was not a traitor. We've also found the children who were being held hostage."

"It all started with a life raft being washed ashore on the Swedish coast," Wallander said, after a few moments' thought.

"Colonel Putnis and his fellow conspirators had just commenced the large-scale operation involving the smuggling of drugs into various countries, including Sweden," Murniers said. "Putnis had placed a number of agents in Sweden. They had tracked down various groups of Latvian émigrés and were about to start distributing the drugs that would lead to the discrediting of the Latvian freedom organization. But something happened on one of the vessels smuggling the drugs from Ventspils. It seems that some of the colonel's men had improvised a sort of palace revolution and intended to commandeer a large amount of amphetamines for their own profit. They were found out, shot, and set adrift in a life raft. In the confusion nobody remembered the drugs stashed away inside the raft. As I understand it they spent a whole day searching for the raft, but failed to find it. We can now consider ourselves lucky that it was washed ashore in Sweden—if it hadn't been, it is very likely that Colonel Putnis would have succeeded in his intentions. It was also Putnis's agents who were cunning enough to retrieve the drugs from your police station once they had realized nobody had discovered what was hidden in the life raft."

"Something else must have happened," Wallander said thought-fully. "Why did Putnis decide to kill Major Liepa the moment he got back home?"

"Putnis lost his nerve. He didn't know what Major Liepa was up to in Sweden, and he couldn't risk letting him stay alive without being able to check what he was doing all the time. As long as Major Liepa was in Latvia, it was possible to keep an eye on him, or at least to be aware of the people he met. Colonel Putnis simply got nervous. Sergeant Zids was given the order to kill Major Liepa. And he did."

They sank into a long silence. Wallander could see Murniers was tired and worried.

"What happens now?" asked Wallander at last.

"I shall study Major Liepa's papers thoroughly, of course," Murniers replied. "Then we shall see."

The reply made Wallander uneasy. "They must be published, of course," he said.

Murniers didn't respond, and Wallander suddenly realized that was not definite so far as Murniers was concerned. His interests were not necessarily the same as those of Baiba Liepa and her friends. For him it could well be enough to have unmasked Putnis. Murniers might have an entirely different view of the appropriate-ness of giving the story wider circulation. Wallander was upset at the thought that Major Liepa's testimony might be swept under the carpet.

"I'd like a copy of the major's report," he said.

Murniers saw through his request immediately. "I didn't know you could read Latvian," he said.

"One can't know everything," Wallander replied.

Murniers stared at him for a long time, without speaking. Wallander looked him in the eye, and knew he must not give way. This was the last time he would be involved with Murniers in a trial of strength, and it was absolutely essential that he was not defeated. He owed that to the nearsighted little major.

All at once, Murniers made up his mind. He pressed the button fixed to the underside of the table, and a man appeared to fetch the blue folder. A little later Wallander received a copy, the existence of which would never be recorded. Murniers would disclaim any responsibility for it. A copy the Swedish police officer Inspector Wallander had appropriated for himself, without permission and against all the laws and regulations governing practices between friendly nations, and which he had then passed onto people who had no right to these secret documents. By doing this the Swedish police officer Kurt Wallander had displayed exceptionally poor judgment and should be condemned out of hand.

That is what would happen, that is what would pass for the truth. If anybody should ever ask, which was unlikely. Wallander would never know why Murniers allowed it to happen. Was it for the major's sake? For the country's? Or did he just think Wallander deserved an appropriate farewell present?

That was the end of the conversation. There was nothing more to say.

"The passport you are currently holding is of very doubtful validity," Murniers said, "but I'll make sure you get back home to Sweden without any problems. When are you thinking of going?"

"Maybe not tomorrow," Wallander said, "but the day after, perhaps."

Colonel Murniers accompanied him down to the car that was waiting in the yard. Wallander suddenly remembered his Peugeot that was parked in a barn somewhere in Germany, not far from the Polish border.

"I wonder how on earth I'm going to get my car back home," he said.

Murniers stared at him in bewilderment. Wallander realized he would never discover how close Murniers was to the people who considered themselves to be a guarantee for a better future in Latvia. He had only scraped the surface of what he had been allowed to come into contact with. That was a stone he would never overturn. Murniers simply had no idea how Wallander had got into Latvia.

"It doesn't matter," Wallander said.

That damned Lippman, he thought angrily. I wonder if the Latvian organizations in exile have funds with which to compensate Swedish police officers for lost cars.

He felt hard used, without being fully able to explain why. Perhaps he was still hampered by his overwhelming exhaustion. His judgment would continue to be unreliable until he'd had an opportunity to rest properly.

They bade each other farewell when they got to the car waiting to take Wallander to Baiba Liepa.

"I'll go to the airport with you," Murniers said. "You'll receive two tickets, one for the flight to Helsinki, and one for Helsinki to Stockholm. As there are no passport controls within the Nordic countries, no one will ever know you have been in Riga."

The car drove out of the courtyard. A glass panel separated

the backseat from the driver. Wallander sat in the dark, thinking about what Murniers had said. Nobody would ever know he had been in Riga. It dawned on him that he would never be able to talk to anybody about it, not even to his father. One very good reason for it remaining a secret was that it had all been so improbable, so incredible. Who would ever believe him?

He leaned back in his seat and closed his eyes. The important thing now was his meeting with Baiba Liepa. What would happen when he got back to Sweden was something he could think about when it happened.

He spent two nights and a day in Baiba Liepa's apartment. All the time he was waiting for what, not being able to think of anything better, he called "the right moment," but it never occurred. He didn't utter a word about the conflicting feelings he had for her. The closest he came to her was when they sat next to each other on the sofa the second evening, looking at photographs. When he got out of the car that had taken him from Murniers to her house, her greeting had been muted, as if he had become a stranger to her again. He was put out, without even being sure what it was he was put out about. What had he expected, after all? She cooked a meal for him, a casserole with some tough chicken as the main ingredient, and he got the impression that Baiba wasn't exactly an inspired cook. I mustn't forget that she's an intellectual, he thought. She's the kind of person who is probably better qualified to dream about a better society than to cook a meal. Both types are needed, even if presumably they can't always live happily alongside each other.

Wallander was weighed down by feelings of melancholy that, luckily, he had no trouble keeping to himself. He no doubt belonged to the good cooks of this world. He wasn't one of the dreamers. A police officer could hardly be preoccupied with dreams; he had to stick his nose in the dirt rather than point it heavenwards. But he knew that he had begun to fall in love with her, and that was the real cause of his melancholy. He would be forced to retain this sadness in his heart as he concluded the strangest and most dangerous mission he had ever undertaken. It hurt him deeply. When she told him his car would be waiting for him in Stockholm when he got back there, he barely reacted. He had started feeling sorry for himself.

She made a bed up for him on the sofa. He could hear her calm breathing from the bedroom. He couldn't sleep, despite his exhaustion. He kept getting up, walking across the cold floorboards and looking down onto the deserted street where the major had been murdered. The shadows were no longer there, they had been buried alongside Putnis. All that was left was the gaping void, repulsive and painful.

The day before he left they went to visit the unmarked grave where Colonel Putnis had buried Inese and her friends. They wept openly. Wallander sobbed like an abandoned child, and he felt as if he had seen for the first time what an awful world he lived in. Baiba had taken some flowers, some frail-looking roses, frozen stiff, and she laid them on the heap of soil.

Wallander had given her the copy of the major's testimony, but she didn't read it while he was still there.

The morning he flew home it was snowing in Riga.

Murniers came to fetch him himself. Baiba embraced Wallander in the doorway, they clung to each other as if they had just survived a shipwreck, and then he left.

Wallander walked up the steps to the airplane.

"Have a good journey," Murniers shouted after him.

He's also glad to see the last of me, Wallander thought. He's not going to miss me.

The plane made a wide turn to the left over Riga, then the pilot headed over the Gulf of Finland. Wallander was asleep before they even reached cruising level, his head resting on his chest.

That same evening he landed in Stockholm. A voice on the public address system asked him to report to the information desk. He was handed an envelope containing his passport and car keys. The car was parked next to the taxi stand, and to his surprise Wallander noted that it had been cleaned. It was warm inside. Somebody had been sitting there, waiting for him. He drove home to Ystad that same night and was back in his apartment in Mariagatan just before dawn.

EPILOGUE

Early one morning at the beginning of May, Wallander was in his office, carefully but unenthusiastically filling in his soccer pool, when Martinsson knocked on the door and came in. It was still chilly—spring hadn't yet reached Skåne—but even so Wallander had his window open, as if he needed to give his brain a thorough airing. He had been absentmindedly weighing the chances of the various teams beating each other while listening to a chaffinch singing away in a tree. When Martinsson appeared in the doorway, Wallander put the form away, got up from his chair and closed the window. He knew Martinsson was always worrying about catching a cold.

"Am I disturbing you?" Martinsson asked.

Since his return from Riga Wallander had been offhand and brusque with his colleagues. Some of them had wondered, strictly between themselves, how he could have grown so out of sorts just because he'd broken his hand skiing in the Alps. Nobody wanted to ask him about it straight out, however, and they all thought his bad mood would gradually die away of its own accord.

Wallander was aware that he was behaving badly towards his colleagues. He had no business making their work more difficult, but he didn't know how he should go about becoming the Wallander of old again, the firm but good-humored officer of the Ystad police. It was as if that person no longer existed. Nor did he know whether he really missed him. There was very little he did know about himself. The supposed trip to the Alps had exposed how little genuine truth there was in his life. He knew that he was not the kind of man who consciously surrounded himself with lies, but he had begun to ask himself whether his ignorance of what the world really looked like was in itself a sort of lie, even though it was founded in naïvete rather than a conscious effort to cut himself off.

Every time someone came into his office, he felt a twinge of guilt, but he could think of nothing better to do than to pretend that there was nothing wrong.

"No, you're not disturbing me," he said, trying hard to sound friendly. "Sit down."

Martinsson sat down in the visitor's chair that sagged and was most uncomfortable. "I thought I'd tell you a strange story," he said. "Or rather, I've two stories to tell you. It looks as if we've been visited by ghosts from the past."

Wallander didn't like Martinsson's way of expressing things. The grim reality they had to deal with as police officers always seemed to him unsuitable for dressing up in poetic terms. But he said nothing and waited.

"Do you remember that man who phoned to tell us that a life raft was going to be washed up near here," Martinsson continued, "the guy we never caught up with, and who never identified himself?"

"There were two men," Wallander interrupted.

Martinsson nodded. "Let's start with the first one," he said. "A few weeks ago Anette Brolin was wondering whether to charge a man accused of a particularly nasty assault and battery, but since he had a clean record, she let him go."

Wallander's ears had pricked up.

"His name's Holmgren," said Martinsson. "I just happened to see the papers about that assault and battery case lying on Svedberg's desk. I noticed he was down as the owner of a fishing boat called *Byron*, and bells started ringing in my head. It became even more interesting when I saw that this Holmgren had beaten up one of his closest friends, a fellow called Jakobson, who used to work as a crewman on the boat."

Wallander recalled that night in Brantevik harbor. Martinsson was right. They had been visited by ghosts from the past. He realized how keen he was to hear what was coming next.

"The funny thing was that Jakobson hadn't reported the incident, even though it was very brutal and seemed to have been unprovoked," Martinsson said.

"Who did report it, then?"

"Holmgren attacked Jakobson with a crank handle out at Brantevik harbor, and someone saw him and phoned the police. Jakobson was in the hospital for three weeks. He was pretty badly beaten, but he didn't want to report Holmgren. Svedberg never did manage to find out what was behind the violence, but I started to wonder if it might have something to do with that life raft. Remember how neither of them wanted the other one to know that they'd both contacted us? Or at least, that's what we thought."

"I remember," Wallander said.

"I thought I'd have a word with Mr. Holmgren," Martinsson continued. "He used to live in the same street as you, by the way, Mariagatan."

"Used to live?"

"Exactly. When I went to see him, he'd moved. A long way away, as well. He'd gone off to Portugal. He'd sent in various documents that classified him as an immigrant, and given his new address as somewhere in the Azores. He'd sold *Byron* to some Danish fisherman or other for a real bargain basement price."

Martinsson paused, and Wallander watched him thoughtfully.

"You have to agree that it's a pretty strange story," Martinsson said. "Do you think we ought to pass this information on to the police in Riga?"

"No," Wallander said. "I don't think that's necessary. But thanks for telling me."

"I haven't finished yet," Martinsson said. "Here comes part two of the story. Did you read the papers yesterday?"

Wallander had stopped buying newspapers ages ago, unless he was involved in a case the press was displaying more than routine interest in. He shook his head, and Martinsson continued.

"You should have. There were reports on how the customs in Göteborg fished up a life raft that later proved to have come from a Russian trawler. They'd found it drifting off Vinga, which seemed odd because there was no wind at all that day. The skipper of the trawler maintained they'd had to dock for some repairs to a damaged propeller. They'd been fishing at Dogger Bank, and he claimed they'd lost the life raft without noticing. By pure coincidence a sniffer dog happened to pass the life raft, and it got very interested. They found a few kilos of top-grade amphetamine hidden inside the life raft, and traced it to some laboratories in Poland. That could well give us the explanation we were looking for—the raft that was stolen from our basement probably had something hidden in it that we ought to have found."

It seemed to Wallander that this was a reference to his fatal mistake. Martinsson was right, of course. It had been inexcusable carelessness. All the same, he felt tempted to confide in Martinsson, to tell somebody what had really happened instead of that holiday in the Alps that had only been an excuse. But he said nothing. He didn't think he had the strength.

"I expect you're right," he said. "But I don't suppose we'll ever find out why those men were murdered."

"Don't say that," Martinsson said, getting to his feet. "You never know what tomorrow might have in store to astonish us. In spite of everything, it looks as though we might have gotten a little bit closer to winding up that particular story, don't you think?"

Wallander nodded. But he didn't say anything.

Martinsson paused in the doorway and turned round.

"Do you know what I think?" he asked. "It's only my own opinion, of course, but I figure Holmgren and Jakobson were involved in some kind of smuggling, and they just happened to see that life raft. They had a pretty good reason for not getting too closely involved with the police, though."

"That doesn't explain the assault and battery," Wallander said.

"Maybe they'd agreed not to contact us? Maybe Holmgren thought Jakobson had been telling tales out of school?"

"You could be right. But we'll never know."

Martinsson left. Wallander opened the window again, then went back to his soccer pool. He thought of the letter he had found on his return from Riga, thanking him for his application and inviting him to an interview at the Trelleborg Rubber Company. He had told them he was not able to consider the job for the time being, but he kept the letter in his drawer.

Later that day he drove out to a new café close to the harbor. He ordered a cup of coffee and started to write a letter to Baiba Liepa. Half an hour later he read through what he'd written and tore it up. He left the café and went out onto the pier. He scattered the pieces of paper over the water like breadcrumbs. He still didn't know what to write to her. But his longing was very strong.

AFTERWORD

The revolutionary events that took place in the Baltic countries during the last year were the basis of this novel. Writing a book with a setting and plot located in an environment unfamiliar to the author is, of course, a complicated business. It is even more problematic when one tries to steer a course through a social and political landscape that is still fluid. Apart from straightforward practical difficulties—Is a particular statue still standing on its pedestal on a given day, or has it already been pulled down and taken away? Does a particular street still have the same name as it did on a certain day in February 1991?—there are other more fundamental problems. Not least among them is the fact that we now have at least a provisional answer to the direction developments in the Baltic countries will take, but that knowledge had to be put aside in writing this book.

Reconstructing thoughts and emotions is, of course, the job of an author, but some assistance may well be necessary. In connection with this novel, I am greatly indebted to many people: I would like to thank two in particular, one by name and the other anonymously. Guntis Bergklavs put himself completely at my disposal to explain, remember, and make suggestions. He also taught me a lot about the secrets of Riga. I would also like to express my gratitude to the detective in the Riga "homicide squad" who so patiently taught me how he and his colleagues went about their business.

We should bear in mind all the time what it was like then.

Everything was so very different, even more vague than it is now. The fate of the Baltic countries is not yet decided, not by any means. There are still large numbers of Russian troops on Latvian territory. The future will be an intense struggle between the old and the new, between the familiar and the unfamiliar.

Just a few months after this book was finished, in the spring of 1991, the coup took place in the Soviet Union—the key incident that accelerated declarations of independence in the Baltic countries. Obviously, that coup (or the possibility that such a coup could happen) was at the very core of this novel, but like everybody else, I couldn't possibly foresee that it really would happen, or how it would turn out.

This is a novel. That means it is possible that not everything actually happened or looks exactly the same as I have described it in the book. But it could have happened, exactly as described. Poetic license gives the author the freedom to create a coat check in a department store where there is no such thing in fact. Or to invent a furniture department out of thin air. If necessary. And it sometimes is.

HENNING MANKELL, APRIL 1992